THE WORD IS MURDER

Also by Anthony Horowitz

The House of Silk
Moriarty
Trigger Mortis
Magpie Murders

THE WORD IS MURDER

A NOVEL

anthony horowitz

HARPER

An Imprint of HarperCollins*Publishers*

THE WORD IS MURDER. Copyright © 2018 by Anthony Horowitz. All rights reserved. Printed in the United States of America. No part of this book may be used or reproduced in any manner whatsoever without written permission except in the case of brief quotations embodied in critical articles and reviews. For information, address HarperCollins Publishers, 195 Broadway, New York, NY 10007.

HarperCollins books may be purchased for educational, business, or sales promotional use. For information, please email the Special Markets Department at SPsales@harpercollins.com.

Originally published in Great Britain in 2017 by Penguin Random House UK.

FIRST U.S. EDITION

Library of Congress Cataloging-in-Publication Data has been applied for.

ISBN 978-0-06-267678-8

18 19 20 21 22   OFF/LSC   10 9 8 7 6 5 4 3 2 1

THE WORD IS MURDER

One
Funeral Plans

Just after eleven o'clock on a bright spring morning, the sort of day when the sunshine is almost white and promises a warmth that it doesn't quite deliver, Diana Cowper crossed the Fulham Road and went into a funeral parlour.

She was a short, very business-like woman: there was a sense of determination in her eyes, her sharply cut hair, the very way she walked. If you saw her coming, your first instinct would be to step aside and let her pass. And yet there was nothing unkind about her. She was in her sixties with a pleasant, round face. She was expensively dressed, her pale raincoat hanging open to reveal a pink jersey and grey skirt. She wore a heavy bead-and-stone necklace which might or might not have been expensive and a number of diamond rings that most certainly were. There were plenty of women like her in the streets of Fulham and South Kensington. She might have been on her way to lunch or to an art gallery.

The funeral parlour was called Cornwallis and Sons. It stood at the end of a terrace, with the name painted in a classical font both on the front of the building and down the side so that you would notice it from whichever direction you were coming. The two inscriptions were prevented from meeting in the middle by a Victorian clock which was mounted above the front door and which had come to a stop, perhaps appropriately, at 11.59. One minute to midnight. Beneath the name, again printed twice, was the legend: *Independent Funeral Directors: A Family Business since 1820.* There were three windows looking out over the street, two of them curtained, the third empty but for an open book made of marble, engraved with a quotation: *When sorrows come, they come not single spies, but in battalions.* All the wood – the window frames, the frontage, the main door – was painted a dark blue, nudging black.

As Mrs Cowper opened the door, a bell on an old-fashioned spring mechanism sounded loudly, once. She found herself in a small reception area with two sofas, a low table and a few shelves with books that had that peculiar sense of sadness that comes with being unread. A staircase led up to the other floors. A narrow corridor stretched ahead.

Almost at once, a woman appeared, stout, with thick legs and heavy, black leather shoes, coming down the stairs. She was smiling pleasantly, politely. The smile acknowledged that this was a delicate, painful business but that it would be expedited with calm and efficiency. Her name was Irene Laws. She was the personal assistant to Robert Cornwallis, the funeral director, and also acted as his receptionist.

'Good morning. Can I help you?' she asked.

'Yes. I would like to arrange a funeral.'

'Are you here on behalf of someone who has died recently?' The word 'died' was instructive. Not 'passed away'. Not 'deceased'. She had made it her business practice to speak plainly, recognising that, at the end of the day, it was less painful for all concerned.

'No,' Mrs Cowper replied. 'It's for myself.'

'I see.' Irene Laws didn't blink – and why should she? It was not at all uncommon for people to arrange their own funerals. 'Do you have an appointment?' she asked.

'No. I didn't know I'd need one.'

'I'll see if Mr Cornwallis is free. Please take a seat. Would you like a cup of tea or coffee?'

'No, thank you.'

Diana Cowper sat down. Irene Laws disappeared down the corridor, reappearing a few minutes later behind a man who so exactly suited the image of the funeral director that he could have been playing the part. There was, of course, the obligatory dark suit and sombre tie. But the very way he stood seemed to suggest that he was apologising for having to be there. His hands were clasped together in a gesture of profound regret. His face was crumpled, mournful, not helped by hair that had thinned to the edge of baldness and a beard that had the look of a failed experiment. He wore tinted spectacles that were sinking into the bridge of his nose, not just framing his eyes but masking them. He was about forty years old. He too was smiling.

'Good morning,' he said. 'My name is Robert Cornwallis. I understand you wish to discuss a funeral plan with us.'

'Yes.'

'You've been offered coffee or tea? Please come this way.'

The new client was taken down the corridor to a room at the end. This was as understated as the reception area – with one difference. Instead of books there were folders and brochures which, if opened, would show images of coffins, hearses (traditional or horse-drawn) and price lists. A number of urns had been arranged on two shelves should the discussion veer towards cremation. Two armchairs faced each other, one beside a small desk. Cornwallis sat here. He took out a pen, a silver Mont Blanc, and rested it on a notepad.

'The funeral is your own,' he began.

'Yes.' Suddenly Mrs Cowper was brisk, wanting to get straight to the point. 'I have already given some consideration to the details. I take it you have no problem with that.'

'On the contrary. Individual requirements are important to us. These days, pre-planned funerals and what you might call bespoke or themed funerals are very much the mainstay of our business. It is our privilege to provide exactly what our clients demand. After our discussion here, and assuming our terms are acceptable to you, we will provide you with a full invoice and breakdown of what has been agreed. Your relatives and friends will have nothing to do except, of course, to attend. And from our experience I can assure you that it will give them great comfort to know that everything has been done exactly in accordance with your wishes.'

Mrs Cowper nodded. 'Excellent. Well, let's get down to it, shall we?' She took a breath, then dived straight in. 'I want to be buried in a cardboard coffin.'

Cornwallis was about to make his first note. He paused,

the nib hovering over the page. 'If you are considering an eco-funeral, might I suggest recycled wood or even twisted willow branches rather than cardboard? There are occasions when cardboard can be . . . not entirely effective.' He chose his words carefully, allowing all sorts of possibilities to hang in the air. 'Willow is hardly more expensive and a great deal more attractive.'

'All right. I want to be buried in Brompton Cemetery, next to my husband.'

'You lost him recently?'

'Twelve years ago. We already have the plot, so there'll be no problems there. And this is what I want in the service . . .' She opened her handbag and took out a sheet of paper, which she laid on the desk.

The funeral director glanced down. 'I see that you have already put a great deal of thought into the matter,' he said. 'And this is a very well-considered service, if I may say so. Partly religious, partly humanist.'

'Well, there's a psalm – and there's the Beatles. A poem, a bit of classical music and a couple of addresses. I don't want the thing going on too long.'

'We can work out the timings exactly . . .'

Diana Cowper had planned her funeral and she was going to need it. She was murdered about six hours later that same day.

At the time of her death, I had never heard of her and I knew almost nothing about how she was killed. I may have noticed the headline in the newspapers – ACTOR'S MOTHER MURDERED – but the photographs and the bulk of the story were all focused on the more famous son, who had just been cast as the lead in a new American television series. The conversation that I have described is only a rough approximation because, of course, I wasn't there. But I did visit Cornwallis and Sons and spoke at length to both Robert Cornwallis and his assistant (she was also his cousin), Irene Laws. If you were to walk down the Fulham Road you would have no trouble identifying the funeral parlour. The rooms are exactly as I describe them. Most of the other details are taken from witness statements and police reports.

We know when Mrs Cowper entered the funeral parlour because her movements were recorded on CCTV both in the street and on the bus that took her from her home that morning. It was one of her eccentricities that she always used public transport. She could easily have afforded a chauffeur.

She left the funeral parlour at a quarter to twelve, walked up to South Kensington tube station and took the Piccadilly line to Green Park. She had an early lunch with a friend at the Café Murano, an expensive restaurant on St James's Street, near Fortnum & Mason. From there, she took a taxi to the Globe Theatre on the South Bank. She wasn't seeing a play. She was on the board and there was a meeting on the first floor of the building that lasted from two o'clock until a little before five. She got home at five past six. It had just begun to rain but she had an umbrella with her and left it in a faux-Victorian stand beside the front door.

Thirty minutes later, somebody strangled her.

She lived in a smart, terraced house in Britannia Road just beyond the area of Chelsea that is known – appropriately, in her case – as World's End. There were no CCTV cameras in the street, so there was no way of knowing who went in or left around the time of the murder. The neighbouring houses were empty. One was owned by a consortium based in Dubai and was usually rented out, though not at this particular time. The other belonged to a retired lawyer and his wife but they were away in the South of France. So nobody heard anything.

She was not found for two days. Andrea Kluvánek, the Slovakian cleaner who worked for her twice a week, made the discovery when she came in on Wednesday morning. Diana Cowper was lying face down on the living-room floor. A length of red cord, normally used to tie back the curtains, was around her throat. The forensic report, written in the matter-of-fact, almost disinterested manner of all such documents, described in detail the blunt-force injuries of the neck, the fractured hyoid bone and conjunctiva of the eyes. Andrea saw something a great deal worse. She had been working at the house for two years and had come to like her employer, who had always treated her kindly, often stopping to have a coffee with her. On the Wednesday, as she opened the door, she was confronted with a dead body and one that had been lying there for some time. The face, what she could see of it, had gone mauve. The eyes were empty and staring, the tongue hanging out grotesquely, twice its normal length. One arm was outstretched, a finger with a diamond ring pointing at her as if in accusation. The central heating had been on. The body was already beginning to smell.

According to her testimony, Andrea did not scream. She was not sick. She quietly backed out of the house and called the police on her mobile phone. She did not go in again until they arrived.

To begin with, the police assumed that Diana Cowper had been the victim of a burglary. Certain items, including jewellery and a laptop computer, had been taken from the house. Many of the rooms had been searched, the contents scattered. However, there had been no break-in. Mrs Cowper had clearly opened the door to her attacker, although it was unclear if she had known the person or not. She had been surprised and strangled from behind. She had barely put up a fight. There were no fingerprints, no DNA, no clues of any sort, suggesting that the perpetrator must have planned this with a great deal of care. He had distracted her and plucked the red cord off the hook beside the velvet curtain in the living room. He had crept up behind her, slipped it over her head and pulled. It would have taken only a minute or so for her to die.

But then the police found out about her visit to Cornwallis and Sons and realised that they had a real puzzle on their hands. Think about it. Nobody arranges their own funeral and then gets killed on the same day. This was no coincidence. The two events had to be connected. Had she somehow known she was going to die? Had someone seen her going in or coming out of the funeral parlour and been prompted, for some reason, to take action? Who actually knew she had been there?

It was definitely a mystery and one that required a specialist approach. At the same time, it had absolutely nothing to do with me.

That was about to change.

Two

Hawthorne

It's easy for me to remember the evening that Diana Cowper was killed. I was celebrating with my wife: dinner at Moro in Exmouth Market and quite a lot to drink. That afternoon I had pressed the Send button on my computer, emailing my new novel to the publishers, putting eight months' work behind me.

The House of Silk was a Sherlock Holmes sequel that I had never expected to write. I had been approached, quite out of the blue, by the Conan Doyle estate, who had decided, for the first time, to lend their name and their authority to a new adventure. I leapt at the opportunity. I had first read the Sherlock Holmes stories when I was seventeen and they had stayed with me all my life. It wasn't just the character I loved, although Holmes is unquestionably the father of all modern detectives. Nor was it the mysteries, as memorable as they are. Mainly I was drawn to the world that Holmes and Watson inhabited: the Thames, the growlers rattling over the cobblestones, the gas lamps, the swirling London fog. It was as if I'd been invited to move into 221b Baker Street and become a quiet witness to the greatest friendship in literature. How could I refuse?

It struck me from the very start that my job was to be invisible. I tried to hide myself in Doyle's shadow, to imitate his literary tropes and mannerisms, but never, as it were, to intrude. I wrote nothing that he might not have written himself. I mention this only because it worries me to be so very prominent in these pages. But this time round I have no choice. I'm writing exactly what happened.

For once, I wasn't working on any television. *Foyle's War*, my wartime detective series, was no longer in production and there was a question mark over its return. I'd written more than twenty two-hour episodes over a sixteen-year period, almost three times longer than the war itself. I was tired. Worse still, having finally reached 15 August 1945, VJ Day, I had run out of war. I wasn't quite sure what to do next. One of the actors had suggested 'Foyle's Peace'. I didn't think it would work.

I was also between novels. At this time I was known mainly as a children's author although I secretly hoped that *The House of Silk* would change that. In 2000, I'd published the first in a series of adventures about a teenaged spy called Alex Rider which had sold all over the world. I loved writing children's books but I was worried that with every year that passed I was getting further and further away from my audience. I had just turned fifty-five. It was time to move on. As it happened, I was about to travel to the Hay-on-Wye literary festival to talk about *Scorpia Rising*, the tenth and supposedly last book in the series.

Perhaps the most exciting project on my desk was the first draft of a film screenplay: 'Tintin 2'. To my amazement, I had been hired by Steven Spielberg, who was currently reading it. The film was going to be directed by Peter Jackson. It was quite hard to get my head around the fact that suddenly I was working with the two biggest directors in the world; I wasn't sure how it had happened. I'll admit that I was nervous. I had read the script perhaps a dozen times and was doing my best to convince myself it was moving in the right direction. Were the characters working? Were the action sequences strong enough? Jackson and Spielberg happened to be in London together in a week's time and I was going to meet them and get their notes.

So when my mobile rang and I didn't recognise the number, I wondered if it might be one of them – not, of course, that they would call me personally. An assistant would check it was me and then pass me across. It was about ten o'clock in the morning and I was sitting in my office on the top floor of my flat, reading *The Meaning of Treason*, by Rebecca West, a classic study of life in Britain after the Second World War. I was beginning to think that this might be the right direction for Foyle. Cold War. I would throw him into the world of spies, traitors, communists, atomic scientists. I closed the book and picked up my mobile.

'Tony?' a voice asked.

It certainly wasn't Spielberg. Very few people call me Tony. To be honest, I don't like it. I've always been Anthony or, to some of my friends, Ant.

'Yes?' I said.

'How are you doing, mate? This is Hawthorne.'

In fact, I'd known who he was before he'd spoken his name. There could be no mistaking those flat vowels, that strangely misplaced accent, part cockney, part northern. Or the word 'mate'.

'Mr Hawthorne,' I said. He had been introduced to me as Daniel but from the very first I had felt uncomfortable using his first name. He never used it himself . . . in fact I never heard anyone else use it either. 'It's nice to hear from you.'

'Yeah. Yeah.' He sounded impatient. 'Look – you got a minute?'

'I'm sorry? What's this about?'

'I was wondering if we could meet. What are you doing this afternoon?'

That, incidentally, was typical of him. He had a sort of myopia whereby the world would arrange itself to his vision of how things should be. He wasn't asking if I could meet him tomorrow or next week. It had to be immediately, according to his needs. As I've explained, I wasn't doing anything very much that afternoon but I wasn't going to tell him that. 'Well, I'm not sure . . .' I began.

'How about three o'clock at that café where we used to go?'

'J&A?'

'That's the one. There's something I need to ask you. I really would appreciate it.'

J&A was in Clerkenwell, a ten-minute walk from where I lived. If he had wanted me to cross London I might have hesitated, but the truth is I was intrigued. 'OK,' I said. 'Three o'clock.'

'That's great, mate. I'll see you there.'

He rang off. The Tintin script was still on the computer screen in front of me. I closed it down and thought about Hawthorne.

I'd first met him the year before when I was working on a five-part television series which was due to be screened in a few months' time. It was called *Injustice*, a legal drama, starring James Purefoy.

Injustice was inspired by one of those perennial questions screenwriters sometimes ask themselves when they're casting around for a new idea. How can a barrister defend someone when they know they're guilty? The short answer, incidentally, is that they can't. If the client confesses to the crime before the trial, the barrister will refuse to represent him . . . there has to be at least a presumption of innocence. So I came up with a story about an animal rights activist who gleefully confesses to the murder of a child shortly after his barrister – William Travers (Purefoy) – has managed to get him acquitted. As a result, Travers suffers a nervous breakdown and moves to Suffolk. Then, one day, waiting for a train at Ipswich station he happens to see the activist again. A few days later, the activist is himself killed and the question is: was Travers responsible?

The story boiled down to a duel between the barrister and the detective inspector who was investigating him. Travers was a dark character, damaged and quite possibly dangerous, but he was still the hero and the audience had to root for him. So I deliberately set out to create a detective who would be as unpleasant as possible. The audience would find him menacing, borderline racist, chippy and aggressive. I based him on Hawthorne.

To be fair, Hawthorne was none of those things. Well, he wasn't racist, anyway. He was, however, extremely annoying to the extent that I used to dread my meetings with him. He and I were complete opposites. I just couldn't make out where he was coming from.

He had been found for me by the production supervisor working on the series. I was told that he'd been a detective inspector with the Metropolitan Police Service in London, working out of the sub-command in Putney. He was a murder specialist with ten years on the force which had come to an abrupt end when he had been kicked out for reasons that weren't made clear. There are a surprising number of ex-policemen helping production companies make police dramas. They provide the little details that make the story ring true and, to be fair, Hawthorne was very good at the job. He had an instinctive understanding of what I needed and what would work on-screen. I remember one example. In an early scene, when my (fictitious) detective is examining a week-old corpse, the crime scene examiner hands him a tub of Vicks VapoRub to smear under his nose. The Mentholatum covers the smell. It was Hawthorne who told me that, and if you watch the scene you'll see how that moment somehow makes it come alive.

The first time I saw him was at the production office of Eleventh Hour Films, which was the company making the series. Once we got started, I'd be able to contact him at any time of the day to throw questions at him and would then weave the answers into the script. All of this could be done over the telephone. This meeting was really just a formality, to introduce us. When I arrived he was already sitting in the reception area with one leg crossed over the other and his coat folded over his lap. I knew at once that he was the person I had come to meet.

He wasn't a large man. He didn't look particularly threatening. But even that single movement, the way he got to his feet, gave me pause for thought. He had the same silken quality as a panther or a leopard, and there was a strange malevolence in his eyes – they were a soft brown – that seemed to challenge, even to threaten, me. He was about forty years old with hair of an indeterminate colour that was cut very short around the ears and was just beginning to turn grey. He was clean-shaven. His skin was pale. I got the feeling that he might have been very handsome as a child but something had happened to him at some time in his life so that, although he still wasn't ugly, he was curiously unattractive. It was as if he had become a bad photograph of himself. He was smartly dressed in a suit, white shirt and tie, the raincoat now held over his arm. He looked at me with almost exaggerated interest, as if I had somehow surprised him. Even as I came in, I got the feeling that he was emptying me out.

'Hello, Anthony,' he said. 'Nice to meet you.'

How did he even know who I was? There were lots of people coming in and out of the office and nobody had announced me. Nor had I told him my name.

'I'm a great admirer of your work,' he said, in a way that

17

told me he'd never read anything I'd written and that actually he didn't care if I knew it.

'Thank you,' I said.

'I've been hearing about this programme you want to make. It sounds really interesting.' Was he deliberately being sarcastic? He managed to look bored even as he spoke the words.

I smiled. 'I'm looking forward to working with you.'

'It'll be fun,' he said.

But it never was.

We spoke on the phone quite often but we also had about half a dozen meetings, mainly at the office or in the courtyard outside J&A (he smoked all the time, sometimes roll-ups but if not, cheap brands like Lambert & Butler or Richmond). I had heard that Hawthorne lived in Essex but I had no idea where. He never talked about himself or his time in the police force and certainly not how it had ended. The production supervisor who had contacted him in the first place told me that he had worked on a number of high-profile murder investigations and had quite a reputation but I couldn't find anything about him on Google. He clearly had a remarkable mind. Although he made it clear that he was no writer himself and showed no interest at all in the series that I was trying to create, he always came up with exactly the right scenarios before I even asked for them. There's another example of his work in the opening scenes. William Travers is defending a black kid who has been framed by the police for the theft of a medal which, they claim, they found in the boy's jacket. But the medal had recently been cleaned and, when the boy's pockets are examined, there are no traces of sulphamic acid or ammonia – the most common ingredients in silver polish – proving that it couldn't have been there. All of that was his idea.

I can't deny that he helped me, and yet I slightly dreaded meeting him. He always got straight down to business with almost no small talk. You'd have thought he would have an opinion about something – the weather, the government, the earthquake in Fukushima, the marriage of Prince William. But he never talked about anything except the matter in hand. He drank coffee (black, two sugars) and he smoked but never ate when he was with me, not so much as a biscuit. And he always wore exactly the same clothes. Quite honestly, I could have been looking at the same photograph of him every time he came in. He was as unchanging as that.

And yet here's the funny thing. He seemed to know an awful lot about me. I'd been out drinking the night before. My assistant was ill. I'd spent the whole weekend writing. I didn't need to tell him these things. He told me! I used to wonder if he'd been talking to someone in the office but the information he came up with was completely random and seemed spontaneous. I never quite worked him out.

The biggest mistake I made was to show him the second draft of the script. I usually write about a dozen drafts before an episode is filmed. I get notes from the producer, from the broadcaster (ITV in this case), from my agent – and later on from the director and the star. It's a collaborative process although one that can sometimes leave me overwhelmed. Won't the bloody thing ever be right? But it works so long as I feel that the project is moving forward, that each draft is better than the one before. There has to be a certain amount of give and take and there's some comfort in the fact that, at the end of the day, everyone involved is trying to make the script more effective.

Hawthorne didn't understand this. He was like a brick wall and once he'd decided that something was wrong, nothing was going to get past him. There was a scene I'd written where my detective meets his senior officer, a chief superintendent. This is shortly after the dead body of the animal rights activist has been found in a remote farmhouse. The CS invites him to sit down and the detective replies, 'I'll stand if you don't mind, sir.' It was a tiny point. I was just trying to show that my character was a man who had problems with authority, but Hawthorne wouldn't have any of it.

'That wouldn't happen,' he said, flatly. We were sitting outside a Starbucks – I forget exactly where – with the script on a table between us. As usual, he was wearing a suit and tie. He was smoking his last cigarette, using the empty packet as an ashtray.

'Why not?'

'Because if your governor tells you to sit down, you sit down.'

'He does sit down.'

'Yeah. But he argues about it first. What's the fucking point? He just makes himself look stupid.'

Hawthorne swore all the time, by the way. If I was going to replicate his language exactly, I'd be writing the f-word every other line.

I tried to explain. 'The actors will understand what I'm trying to get at,' I said. 'It's just a detail. It introduces the scene but it's a key to how the two men relate to each other.'

'But it's not true, Tony. It's a load of cobblers.'

I tried to explain to him that there are many different sorts of truth and that television truth might have very little connection with real life. I argued that our understanding of policemen, doctors, nurses . . . even criminals is largely inspired by what we see on the screen, not the other way round. But Hawthorne had made up his mind. He had helped me with the script but now that he was reading it he didn't believe it and so he didn't like it. We argued about everything, every scene which involved the police. All he saw was the paperwork, the uniforms, the anglepoise lamps. He couldn't find his way to the story.

I was quite relieved when all five scripts were written and handed in and I no longer had to deal with him. When there were further queries I got the production office to email him. We shot the series in Suffolk and in London. The part of the detective was played by a brilliant actor, Charlie Creed-Miles, and the funny thing was that, physically, he was remarkably similar to Hawthorne. But it didn't end there. Hawthorne had got under my skin and, quite deliberately, I'd put a lot of his darker side into the character. I'd also given him a very similar name. From Daniel to Mark: one biblical character to another. And Wenborn instead of Hawthorne. This is something I often do. When I killed him off at the end of Episode Four, it made me smile.

I was curious to know what he wanted but at the same

time I had a vague sense of misgiving as I strolled down to the café that afternoon. Hawthorne did not belong to my world and frankly I had no need for him just then. On the other hand, I hadn't had lunch and, as it happens, J&A serve the best cakes in London. They're in a little alleyway, just off the Clerkenwell Road, and because they're tucked away they're usually not too busy. Hawthorne was waiting for me outside, sitting at a table with a coffee and a cigarette. He was wearing exactly the same clothes as the last time I'd seen him: the same suit, tie and raincoat. He looked up as I arrived, and nodded – which was about all I was going to get by way of a greeting.

'How's the programme?' he asked.

'You should have come to the cast and crew screening,' I said. We'd taken over a hotel in London and shown the first two episodes. Hawthorne had been invited.

'I was busy,' he replied.

A waitress came out and I ordered tea and a slice of Victoria sponge. I know I shouldn't eat stuff like that but you try spending eight hours a day on your own. I used to smoke between chapters but gave up thirty years ago. Cake's probably just as bad.

'How are you?' I asked.

He shrugged. 'Can't complain.' He glanced at me. 'You been in the country?'

As it happened, I'd got back from Suffolk that very morning. My wife and I had just been there for a couple of days. 'Yes,' I said, warily.

'And you got a new puppy!'

I looked at him curiously. This was absolutely typical of him. I hadn't told anyone that I'd been out of London. I certainly hadn't tweeted about it. As for the puppy, it belonged to our neighbours. We'd been looking after it while they were away. 'How do you know all that?' I asked.

'It was just an educated guess.' He waved my question aside. 'I was hoping you could help me.'

'How?'

'I want you to write about me.'

Every time I met him, Hawthorne had a way of surprising me. You know where you are with most people. You form a relationship, you get to know them, and after that the rules are more or less set. But it was never like that with him. He had this strange, mercurial quality. Just when I thought I knew where we were going, he would somehow prove me wrong.

'What do you mean?' I asked.

'I want you to write a book about me.'

'Why would I want to do that?'

'For money.'

'You want to pay me?'

'No. I thought we'd go fifty-fifty.'

A couple of people came and sat down at the table next to us. I used the moment, as they made their way past, to work out what to say. I was nervous about turning Hawthorne down. That said, I already knew – I'd known instantly – that was exactly what I was going to do.

'I don't understand,' I said. 'What sort of book are you talking about?'

Hawthorne gazed at me with those muddy, choirboy eyes. 'Let me explain it to you,' he said, as if it were perfectly obvious. 'You know I do a bit of work here and there for TV, that sort of stuff. You probably heard that I got kicked out of the Met. Well, that's their loss – and I don't want to go into all that. The thing is, I do a bit of consultancy too. For the police. It's unofficial. They use me when something unusual happens. Most cases are pretty straightforward but sometimes they aren't. When something's outside their everyday experience, that's when they come to me.'

'Seriously?' I found it hard to believe.

'That's how it is with the modern police these days. They've made so many cutbacks, there's no-one left to do the job. You've heard of Group 4 and Serco? They're a bunch of tossers but they're in and out all the time. They've sent in investigators that couldn't find their way out of a paper bag. And that's not all. We used to have a big laboratory down at Lambeth – we'd send down blood samples and stuff like that – but they sold it off and now they use private companies. Takes twice as long and costs twice as much but that doesn't seem to bother them. Same with me. I'm an external resource.'

He paused as if to be sure that I was following him. I nodded. He lit a cigarette and went on.

'I do well enough out of it. I get a daily rate plus expenses and all that. But the thing is, you see – and to be honest, I don't like to mention this – I'm a bit short. There just aren't enough people getting murdered. And when I met you on that TV show of yours and heard that you write books, I had this idea that actually we could help each other. Fifty-fifty. I get sent some really interesting stuff. You can write about me.'

'But I hardly know you,' I said.

'You'll get to know me. I've got a case on at the moment, as a matter of fact. It's early days but I think it could be right up your street.'

The waitress arrived with my cake and tea but now I wished I hadn't ordered them. I just wanted to get home.

'Why do you think anyone would want to read about you?' I asked.

'I'm a detective. People like reading about detectives.'

'But you're not a proper detective. You got fired. Why did you get fired, by the way?'

'I don't want to talk about that.'

'Well, if I was going to write about you, you'd have to tell me. I'd have to know where you live, whether you're married or not, what you have for breakfast, what you do on your day off. That's why people read murder stories.'

'Is that what you think?'

'Yes!'

He shook his head. 'I don't agree. The word is murder. That's what matters.'

'Look – I'm really sorry.' I tried to break it gently. 'It's a good idea and I'm sure you've got a really interesting case but I'm afraid I'm far too busy. Anyway, it's not what I do. I write about fictional detectives. I've just finished a story about Sherlock Holmes. I used to do *Poirot* and *Midsomer Murders*. I'm a fiction writer. You need someone who writes true crime.'

'What's the difference?'

'All the difference in the world. I'm in control of my stories. I like to know what I'm writing about. Creating the crimes and the clues and all the rest of it is half the fun. If I were to follow you around, just writing down what you saw and what you said, what would that make me? I'm sorry. I'm not interested.'

He glanced at me over the tip of his cigarette. He didn't look surprised or offended, as if he'd known that was what I was going to say. 'I reckon you could sell a ton of copies,' he remarked. 'And it would be easy for you. I'd tell you every-thing you need to know. Don't you want to hear what I'm working on?' I didn't – but he went on before I could stop him. 'A woman walks into a funeral parlour, just the other side of London, in South Kensington. She's arranged her own funeral, right down to the last detail. And that same day, six hours later, someone murders her . . . goes into her house and strangles her. That's a bit unusual, wouldn't you say?'

'Who was she?' I asked.

'Her name doesn't matter just for now. But she was rich. She's got a famous son. And here's another thing. As far as we can see, she didn't have an enemy in the world. Everybody liked her. That's why I got called in. None of it makes any sense.'

For a brief moment, I was tempted.

The hardest part of writing murder stories is thinking up the plots and at that particular moment I didn't have any more in my head. After all, there are only so many reasons why anyone wants to kill someone else. You do it because you want something from them: their money, their wife, their job. You do it because you're afraid of them. They know something about you and perhaps they're threatening you. You kill them out of revenge because of something they knowingly or unknowingly did to you. Or, I suppose, you kill them by accident. After twenty-two episodes of *Foyle's War*, I'd pretty much covered every variation.

And then there was the question of research. If I decide that the killer is going to be, say, a hotel chef, then I have to create his world. I have to visit the hotel. I have to understand the catering business. Making him believable means a lot of hard work and he's only the first of twenty or thirty characters I have to invent, all of them lurking somewhere inside my head. I have to understand police procedure: fingerprints, forensic science, DNA . . . all the rest of it. It can be months before I write the first word. I was tired. I wasn't sure I had the stamina to begin another book so soon after finishing *The House of Silk*.

Effectively, Hawthorne was offering me a short cut. He was giving me the whole thing on a plate. And he was right. The case did sound interesting. A woman walks into a funeral parlour. It was actually quite a good opening. I could already see the first chapter. Spring sunshine. A smart area of town. A woman crosses the road . . .

It was still unthinkable.

'How did you know?' I asked suddenly.

'What?'

'Just now. You told me I'd been in the country and you said I'd got a puppy. Who told you that?'

'Nobody told me.'

'Then how did you know?'

He scowled – as if he didn't want to tell me. But at the same time he was trying to get something out of me and so, briefly, I had the upper hand. 'There's sand stuck in the tread of your shoes,' he said. 'I saw it when you crossed your leg. So either you've walked across a building site or you've been on the coast. I heard you got a place in Orford, so I suppose you must have been there.'

'And the puppy?'

'There's a paw-print on your jeans. Just below the knee.'

I examined the material. Sure enough, it was there, so faint that I wouldn't have noticed it. But he had.

'Wait a minute,' I said. 'How did you know it was a puppy? It could have been a breed of small dog. And for that matter, how do you know I didn't just meet it in the street?'

He looked at me sadly. 'Someone's sat down and chewed your left shoelace,' he said. 'I don't suppose that was you.'

I didn't look. I have to admit I was impressed. But at the same time I was annoyed that I hadn't worked it out for myself. 'I'm sorry,' I said. 'It's certainly an interesting case from the sound of what you say and I'm sure you could find a writer who would do it for you. But it's like I said. You need to ask a journalist or someone like that. Even if I wanted to do it, I can't. I'm working on other things.'

I wondered how he would respond. Again, he wrong-footed me. He just shrugged. 'Yeah. All right. It was just a thought.' He got to his feet, his hand reaching towards his trouser pocket. 'Do you want me to get that?'

He meant the tea and cake. 'No. It's all right. I'll pay,' I said.

'I had a coffee.'

'I'll get that too.'

'Well, if you change your mind, you know where to reach me.'

'Yes. Of course. I can talk to my literary agent, if you like. She might be able to recommend someone who can help.'

'No. Don't worry. I'll find someone.' He turned round and walked away.

I ate the cake. It was a shame to waste it. Then I went back home and spent the rest of the afternoon reading. I tried not to think about Hawthorne but I couldn't get him out of my mind.

When you're a full-time writer, one of the hardest things to do is to turn down work. You're slamming a door which may not open again and there's always the fear of what you may have missed on the other side. Years ago, a producer rang me to ask if I might be interested in working on a musical based on the songs of a Swedish pop group. I turned her down – which is why I'm not on the posters (and have enjoyed none of the royalties) of *Mamma Mia!* I don't have any regrets, incidentally. There's no saying the show would have been such a success if I had ended up writing it. But it just shows the level of insecurity that most writers live with day by day. A bizarre crime that happened to be true. A woman walks into a funeral parlour. Hawthorne, an odd, complicated but genuinely brilliant detective, gets called in as some sort of consultant. Had I made another mistake, refusing his offer? I picked up my book and went back to work.

Two days later, I was in Hay-on-Wye.

It's funny how many literary festivals there are all over the world. There are some writers I know who never actually write any more; they simply spend their time travelling from one shindig to the next. I've often wondered how I would have managed if I'd been born with a stammer or chronic shyness. The modern writer has to be able to perform, often to a huge audience. It's almost like being a stand-up comedian except that the questions never change and you always end up telling the same jokes.

Whether it's crime in Harrogate, children's books in Bath, science fiction in Glasgow or poetry in Aldeburgh, it feels as if there's a literary festival in every city in the UK, and yet Hay, which takes place in a disturbingly muddy field on the edge of a tiny market town, has become one of the most pre-eminent. People come from miles around and over the years speakers have included two US presidents, several Great Train Robbers and J. K. Rowling. I was excited to be there, talking to about five hundred children in a large tent. As usual, there was a scattering of adults too. People who know my television writing will often come to my events and will happily sit through forty minutes of Alex Rider in order to talk about *Foyle's War*.

The session had gone well. The children had been lively and had asked some good questions. I'd managed to get in some stuff about *Foyle*. I was almost exactly sixty minutes in and had received a signal to close things down when something rather strange happened.

There was a woman sitting in the front row. At first, I'd taken her for a teacher or perhaps a librarian. She was very ordinary-looking, about forty, round-faced with long, fair hair and glasses dangling from a chain around her neck. I'd noticed her because she seemed to be on her own and also because she didn't seem particularly interested in anything I had to say. She hadn't laughed at any of my jokes. I was afraid she might be a journalist. Newspapers often send reporters to author talks these days and any joke you make, any unguarded comment, may be quoted out of context and used against you. So I was on my guard when she put up her hand and one of the attendants handed her the roving mike.

'I was wondering,' she said. 'Why is it that you always write fantasy? Why don't you write anything real?'

Most of the questions that I've been asked at literary festivals, I've been asked many times before. Where do my ideas come from? Which are my favourite characters? How long does it take to write a book? Nobody had ever asked me this and I was a little put out. Her tone wasn't offensive but there was still something in what she'd asked that rankled.

'*Foyle's War* is real,' I replied. 'Every episode is based on true stories.'

I was about to go on to explain how much research I did, that I had spent the whole of the last week reading about

Alan Nunn May, who had shared atomic secrets with the Soviets and who might be the inspiration for my next episode if a new series of *Foyle* went ahead. But she interrupted me. 'I'm sure you do use true stories, but what I'm trying to say is, the crimes aren't real. And your other television shows – *Poirot* and *Midsomer Murders* – they're all completely fantastical. You write stories about a fourteen-year-old spy and I know a lot of children enjoy them, but that's the same. I don't mean to be rude, but I wonder why you're not more interested in the real world.'

'What is the real world?' I countered.

'I just mean real people.'

Some of the children were getting restless. It was time to move on. 'I like writing fiction,' I said. 'That's what I do.'

'Aren't you worried that your books might be considered irrelevant?'

'I don't think they have to be real to be relevant.'

'I'm sorry. I do like your work. But I disagree.'

It was an odd coincidence, given the proposal Hawthorne had put to me just a couple of days before. I looked for the woman again before I left but I didn't see her and she didn't come to get a book signed. On the train back to London, I couldn't help thinking about what she had said. Was she right? Was my work too focused on fantasy? I was about to launch myself as an adult writer but my first outing, *The House of Silk*, was about as far from the modern world as it was possible to be. Some of my television work – *Injustice*, for example – was set in a recognisable, twenty-first-century London but perhaps it was true that I had spent too long living in my own imagination and that if I wasn't careful, I would lose touch. Maybe I already had. Maybe a crash course in reality would do me good.

It's a long, long way from Hay-on-Wye to Paddington station. By the time I got home, I had made up my mind. As soon as I got in, I picked up the phone.

'Hawthorne?'

'Tony!'

'All right. Fifty-fifty. I'm in.'

Three

Chapter One

Hawthorne did not like my first chapter.

I'm jumping ahead here because I didn't actually show it to him until a while later and even then it was only with reluctance. I remembered all too well what had happened with *Injustice* and would have preferred to keep it under wraps – but he insisted and since this was meant to be an equal partnership, how could I refuse? But I think it's important to explain how the book was written; the rules of engagement, so to speak. These are my words but they were his actions and the truth is that, to begin with, the two didn't quite fit.

The two of us were sitting in one of the many Starbucks that seemed to punctuate our investigation. I had emailed him the pages and I knew I was in trouble when he took them out of his case and I saw that he had printed them, covering them with red crosses and circles. I am very protective of my writing. It's fair to say that I think about every single word I write. (Do I need 'single'? Would 'true' be better than 'fair'?) When I had agreed to work with Hawthorne, I had assumed that although he was in charge of the case, he would take a back seat when it came to the actual narrative. He quickly disabused me.

'It's all wrong, Tony,' Hawthorne began. 'You're leading people up the garden path.'

'What do you mean?'

'The very first sentence. It's wrong.'

I read what I had written.

Just after eleven o'clock on a bright spring morning, the sort of day when the sunshine is almost white and promises a warmth that it doesn't quite deliver, Diana Cowper crossed the Fulham Road and went into a funeral parlour.

'I don't see what's wrong with that,' I said. 'It was about eleven o'clock. She went into a funeral parlour.'

'But not the way you say.'

'She took the bus!'

'She caught it at the top of her street. We know that because we've got her on CCTV. The driver also remembered her and gave the police a statement. But here's the problem, mate. Why do you say she crossed the road?'

'Why shouldn't I?'

'Because she didn't. We're talking about the number fourteen bus, which she picked up at Chelsea Village. That's the stop marked "U" exactly opposite Britannia Road. It took her to Chelsea Football Club, Hortensia Road, Edith Grove,

Chelsea & Westminster Hospital, Beaufort Street and finally Old Church Street, stop HJ, where she got off.'

'You have a terrific knowledge of London bus routes,' I said. 'But I don't quite get the point.'

'She didn't have to cross the road. When she left the bus, she was already on the right side.'

'Does it really make any difference?'

'Well, yes, it might. If you say she crossed the road, it means she must have gone somewhere else before she went into the undertaker's — and that might be important. She could have gone to the bank and taken out a load of money. She could have had a row with someone that very morning and that could have been the reason she was killed. That same person could have followed her across the road and seen where she was going. She could have stopped in front of someone who was driving a car and that could have led to an altercation. Don't look at me like that! Road rage murders are more common than you think. But the facts of the matter are that she got up in her house, alone. She had breakfast, then she got on a bus. It was the first thing she did.'

'So what would you want me to write?'

He had already scribbled something on a sheet of paper. He handed it to me. I read:

At exactly seventeen minutes past eleven, Diana Jane Cowper exited from the number 14 bus at the Old Church Street (HJ) stop and retraced her steps twenty-five metres along the pavement. She then entered Cornwallis and Sons funeral parlour.

'I'm not writing that,' I said. 'It reads like a police report.'
'At least it's accurate. And what's the bell doing there?'
'What bell?'

'In the fourth paragraph. Right here. You say there's a bell on a spring mechanism leading into the funeral parlour. Well, I didn't notice any bell. And that's because it's not there.'

I tried to stay calm. That was something I would soon learn about Hawthorne. When he put his mind to it, he could annoy me more easily than anyone I'd ever met.

'I put the bell in for atmosphere,' I explained. 'You've got to allow me some sort of dramatic licence. I wanted to show how traditional and old-fashioned the business was — Cornwallis and Sons — and that was a simple, effective way.'

'Maybe. But it makes a big difference. Suppose someone followed her in there. Suppose someone overheard what she said.'

'You're talking about the man she had the altercation with?' I asked, sarcastically. 'Or maybe someone she met at the bank? Is that what you think?'

Hawthorne shrugged. 'You're the one saying that there was a link between Mrs Cowper arranging her funeral and her getting murdered the same day. At least, that's what you're suggesting to your readers.' He lingered on the first syllable of 'readers', making it sound like a dirty word. 'But you have to consider the alternatives. Maybe the timing of the funeral and the murder was just a coincidence — although I'll be honest with you. I don't like coincidences. I've been working in crime for twenty years and I've always found everything has its place. Or maybe Mrs Cowper knew she was going to die. She'd been threatened and she arranged the funeral because she knew there was no way out. That's possible, but it doesn't make a lot of sense because why didn't she just go to the police? And a third possibility: somebody found out what she was doing. It could have been anyone. They could have followed her in off the street and listened to her making all the arrangements because there's no sodding bell on the door. Anyone could come in or go out without being heard. But not in your version.'

'OK,' I said. 'I'll take out the bell.'

'And the Mont Blanc pen.'

'Why?' I stopped him before he could answer. 'All right. It doesn't matter. I'll lose that too.'

He pushed and prodded the pages as if trying to find a single sentence that he liked. 'You're being a bit selective with the information,' he said, at length.

'And what do you mean by that?'

'Well, you say that Mrs Cowper only used public transport but you don't explain why.'

'I say she was eccentric!'

'I think you'll find there was rather more to it than that, mate. And then there's the question of the funeral itself. You know exactly what she requested for her service but you haven't written down what it was.'

'A psalm! The Beatles!'

'But which psalm? Which Beatles track? Don't you think it might be important?' He took out a notebook and opened it. 'Psalm 34. *I will bless the Lord at all times: his praise shall continually be in my mouth*. The song was "Eleanor Rigby".

39

The poem was by someone called Sylvia Plath. Maybe you can help me with that one, Tony, because I read it and it didn't make a word of bleeding sense. The classical music was the Trumpet Voluntary by Jeremiah Clarke. She wanted her son to give the main address . . . what do you call it?'

'The eulogy.'

'Whatever. And maybe you should have mentioned who she had lunch with at the Café Murano. His name is Raymond Clunes. He's a theatrical producer.'

'Is he a suspect?'

'Well, she'd just lost fifty grand in a musical he'd produced. From my experience, money and murder have a way of going hand in hand.'

'Did I miss anything else?'

'You don't think it's significant that Mrs Cowper resigned from the board of the Globe Theatre that very same day? She's been doing it for six years and the day she dies, she decides to give it all up. Then there's Andrea Kluvánek – the cleaner. Where did you get that stuff about her tiptoeing out into the street and calling the emergency services?'

'It came from her interview with the police.'

'I read it too. But what makes you think she wasn't lying?'

'Why would she be?'

'I don't know, mate. But she's got a criminal record so maybe she's not all sweetness and light.'

'How do you know that?'

'I checked. And finally, there's Damian Cowper, the son. It might have been worth pointing out that he's just inherited two and a half million quid from his old mum, which is going to come in handy as I'm told he has money problems out there in L.A.'

I fell silent. There was a sinking feeling in my stomach. 'What money problems?' I asked.

'From what I understand, most of them have gone up his nose. But there's the house in Hollywood Hills, the pool, the Porsche 911. He's got an English girlfriend who lives with him but she can't be too fond of him either because there's a load of other women knocking around . . . knocking being the operative word.'

'Is there anything in the chapter that was any good?' I asked.

Hawthorne thought for a moment. 'I liked that gag about World's End,' he said.

I looked at the pages scattered in front of me. 'Maybe this is a bad idea,' I said.

Hawthorne smiled at me for the first time. When he smiled, that was when I saw the child he had once been. It was as if there was something inside him always struggling to be released but it had got trapped inside the suit, the tie, the pale features, the malevolent gaze. 'Early days, mate. It's only a first chapter. You can tear it up and start again. The thing is, we've got to find a way of working together, a . . .' He searched for the right phrase.

'A *modus operandi*,' I suggested.

He pointed a finger. 'You don't want to use posh words like that. You'll just get people's backs up. No. You've just got to write what happens. We'll talk to the suspects. I'll make sure you have all the information. All you have to do is put it in the right order.'

'And what happens if you don't solve it?' I said. 'Maybe the police will find out who killed Diana Cowper before you do.'

He looked offended. 'The Met are a load of tossers,' he said. 'If they had a clue, they wouldn't have hired me. That's what I explained to you. A lot of murders are solved in the first forty-eight hours. Why? Because most murderers don't know what they're doing. They get angry. They lash out. It's spontaneous. And by the time they start thinking about blood splatter, car number plates, CCTV – it's too late. Some of them will try to cover their tracks but with modern forensics they haven't got a hope in hell.

'But then there are the tiny amount of murders – maybe only two per cent – that are premeditated. They're planned. They might be a contract killing. Or some nutter who's doing it for fun. The police always know. They know when they've got a sticker . . . that's what they call this type of murder. And that's when they reach out to someone like me. They know they need help. So what I'm saying is, you have to trust me. If you want to add extra details, ask me first. Otherwise, just write down what you see. This isn't Tintin. OK?'

'Wait a minute!' Once again, Hawthorne had managed to throw me off balance. 'I never told you I was writing Tintin.'

'You told me you were working for Spielberg. And that's what he's directing.'

'He's producing.'

'Anyway, what was it that made you change your mind about writing this? Was it your wife? I bet she told you what was good for you.'

'Stop right there,' I said. 'If we're going to have rules, the main rule is that you never ask me about my private life: not my books, not my TV, not my family, not my friends.'

'I'm interested you put them in that order . . .'

'I'll write about you. I'll write about this case. And when you solve it – *if* you solve it – I'll see if I can get my publisher interested. But I'm not going to be bullied by you. This is still my book and I'm going to be the one who decides what goes into it.'

His eyes widened. 'Calm down, Tony. I'm just trying to help.'

This is the agreement that we made. I wouldn't show Hawthorne any more of the book, certainly not while I was writing it and probably not even after it was finished. I would write what I wanted to write and if that meant criticising him or adding thoughts of my own I would simply go ahead. But when it came to the scene of the crime, the interrogations or whatever, I would stick to the facts. I wouldn't imagine, extrapolate or embroider the text with potentially misleading descriptions.

As for Chapter One, forget the bell and the Mont Blanc pen. Diana Cowper had lunch with Raymond Clunes. And Andrea Kluvánek may not have been telling the truth. But be assured that the rest of it, including a clue which would indicate, quite clearly, the identity of the killer, is spot on.

Four
Scene of the Crime

There was a uniformed policeman standing outside Diana Cowper's home on the Monday morning when I presented myself there. A strip of that blue and white plastic tape — POLICE LINE DO NOT CROSS — hung across the front door but someone must have told him I was coming because he let me in without even asking me my name. It was a week after the murder. Hawthorne had sent across copies of the police files and early interviews, which I had read over the weekend. He had attached a brief note telling me to meet him here at nine. I stepped round a puddle in the short path that led to the front door and went in.

Normally, when I visit a crime scene, it's one that I have myself manufactured. I don't need to describe it: the director, the locations manager, the designer and the props department will have done most of the work for me, choosing everything from the furniture to the colour of the walls. I always look for the most important details — the cracked mirror, the bloody fingerprint on the windowsill, anything that's important to the story – but they may not be there yet. It depends which way the camera is pointing. I often worry that the room will seem far too big for the victim who supposedly lived there – but then ten or twenty people have to be able to fit inside during filming and the viewers never notice. In fact, the room will be so jammed with actors, technicians, lights, cables, tracks, dollies and all the rest of it that it's quite difficult to work out how it will look on the screen.

Being the writer on a set is a strange experience. It's hard to describe the sense of excitement, walking into something that owes its existence entirely to what happened inside my head. It's true that I'm completely useless and that no matter where I stand I'm almost certain to be in the way, but the crew is unfailingly polite and pleasant to me even if the truth is that we have nothing to say. My work finished weeks ago; theirs is just beginning. So I'll sit down in a folding chair which never has my name on the back. I'll watch from the side. I'll chat to the actors. Maybe a runner will bring me a cup of tea in a styrofoam cup. And as I sit there, I'll take comfort in the knowledge that this is all mine. I am part of it and it is part of me.

Mrs Cowper's living room couldn't have been more different. As I stepped onto the thick-pile carpet with its floral pattern etched out in pink and grey and took in the crystal chandelier, the comfortable, faux-antique furniture, the *Country Life* and *Vanity Fair* magazines spread out on the coffee table, the books (modern fiction, hardback, nothing by me) on the built-in shelves, I felt like an intruder. I was on my own, wandering through what might as well have been a museum exhibit as a place where someone had recently lived.

The police investigators had left those yellow numbers on plastic tags that mark out crime scenes but there weren't very many of them, suggesting that there hadn't been much to find. A full glass of what looked like water (12) had been left on an antique sideboard and next to it I noticed a credit card (14) with Diana Cowper's name. Were they clues? It was hard to say, just seeing them there. The room had three windows, each of them with a pair of velvet curtains hanging all the way to the floor. Five of the curtains were tied back with knotted red cords and tassels. The curtain nearest the door (6) was hanging loose and it reminded me that not so long ago, a middle-aged woman had been strangled right where I was standing. It was all too easy to see her in front of me, her eyes staring, her fists pummelling the air. I looked down and noticed a stain on the carpet, marked by two more police numbers. Her bowels had loosened just before she died, the sort of detail I would normally have spared an ITV audience.

Hawthorne came into the room, dressed in the same suit as usual – and that's one sentence I definitely don't need to write again. He was eating a sandwich and it took me a moment to realise that he must have made it for himself, in Mrs Cowper's kitchen, using her food. I stared at him.

'What is it?' he asked, with his mouth full.

'Nothing,' I said.

'Have you had breakfast?'

'I'm fine, thanks.'

He must have heard the tone in my voice. 'Shame to waste it,' he said. 'And she don't need it any more.' He waved the sandwich around the room. 'So what do you think?'

I wasn't sure how to respond. The room was very neat. Apart from the flat-screen television – on a stand rather than mounted on the wall – everything in the room belonged to a former age. Diana Cowper had lived an orderly life with the magazines placed just so and the ornaments – glass vases and china figurines – regularly dusted. She had even died tidily. There had been no last-minute struggle, no upturned furniture. The assailant had left just one mark: a muddy half-footprint on the carpet near the door. I could imagine her frowning if she had seen it. She had not been brutally beaten or raped. In many ways this murder had been sedate.

'She knew the killer,' Hawthorne said. 'But he wasn't a friend. He was a man, at least six feet tall, well built, with poor eyesight. He came here with the specific intention of killing her and he wasn't here very long. She left him alone for a while and went into the kitchen. She hoped he was going to leave – but that was when he killed her. After he had finished, he searched the house and took a few things but that wasn't the reason he was here. This was personal.'

'How can you possibly know all that?' Even as I spoke the words I was annoyed with myself. I knew it was exactly what he wanted me to ask. I had fallen right into the trap.

'It was getting dark when he arrived,' Hawthorne said. 'There have been quite a few burglaries in the area. A middle-aged woman, living alone in an expensive part of town, wouldn't open her door to a complete stranger. He was almost certainly a man. I've heard of women strangling women but – take it from me – it's unusual. Diana Cowper was five foot three and it would have been helpful if he'd been taller than her. He fractured her hyoid bone when he killed her, which tells me he was strong, although I admit she was a bit of an old biddy so it might have snapped anyway.

'How do I know he came here to kill her? Three reasons. He didn't leave any fingerprints. It was a warm evening but he made sure he was wearing gloves. He didn't stay here very long. He was only in this room and as you can see there are no coffee cups, no empty glasses of G and T. If he'd been a friend, six o'clock, they'd probably have had a drink together.'

'He might have been in a hurry,' I said.

'Look at the cushions, Tony. He didn't even sit down.'

I went over to the glass I'd seen and resisted the temptation to pick it up. The police and forensics must have been here and I was more than a little surprised that they'd left it behind. Wouldn't they have taken it away for immediate analysis? I said as much to Hawthorne.

'They've brought it back,' he said.

'Why?'

'For me.' He smiled that bleak little smile of his, then finished the rest of the sandwich.

'So someone did have a drink,' I said.

'It's only water.' He chewed and swallowed. 'My guess is that he asked her for a glass of water before he left. That got her out of the room long enough for him to unhook the curtain and steal the tie. He couldn't have done that with her watching.'

'But he didn't drink it.'

'He didn't want to leave his DNA.'

'What about the credit card?' I read the name, printed across it: MRS DIANA J. COWPER. It had been issued by Barclays bank. Its expiry date was November. Six months after hers.

'That's an interesting one. Why isn't it in her purse with all the others? Did she take it out to pay for something and is that why she opened the door? There are no fingerprints on it except her own. So you've got a possible scenario. Someone asks her for payment. She takes out the credit card and while she's fiddling around with it, he slips behind her and strangles her. But then, why isn't it on the floor?' He shook his head. 'On the other hand, it may have nothing to do with what happened. We'll see.'

'You said the killer had poor eyesight,' I said.

'Yes—'

'That was because he missed the diamond ring on her finger.' I'd cut in before Hawthorne could explain everything down to the last detail. 'It must be worth a fortune.'

'No, no, mate. You've got that all wrong. He obviously wasn't interested in the ring. Whoever did this nicked a few pieces of jewellery and a laptop to make it look like a burglary, but he either forgot the ring or he couldn't get it off her finger and decided not to bother with a pair of secateurs. There was no way he could have missed it. He was right up close when he was strangling her.'

'Then how do you know his eyesight was bad?'

'Because he stepped in the puddle outside the door, which

is how he left a mark on the carpet. It looks like a man's shoe, by the way. In every other respect he was careful. That was the one thing he missed. Aren't you going to write all this down?'

'I can remember most of it.' I took out my iPhone. 'But I'll take some pictures if that's OK.'

'You go ahead.' He pointed at a black-and-white photograph of a man in his forties, also on the sideboard. 'Make sure you get a shot of him.'

'Who is he?'

'Her husband, at a guess. Lawrence Cowper.'

'Divorced?'

He looked at me sadly. 'If they were divorced, she wouldn't keep his picture, would she! He died twelve years ago. Cancer.'

I took the picture.

After that, I followed Hawthorne around the house as he went from room to room, photographing everything that he pointed out to me. We started in the kitchen, which had the look of a showroom: expensively stocked but underused. Diana Cowper had enough equipment to cook a Michelin-starred meal for ten but probably went to bed with a boiled egg and two pieces of toast. The fridge was covered with magnets: classical art and famous Shakespearean quotes. A metal tin, merchandise from the Narnia film *Prince Caspian*, stood on the fridge. Using a cloth to keep his hands from coming into contact with the metal, Hawthorne opened it and looked inside. It was empty apart from a couple of coins.

Everything was in exactly the right place. There were

recipe books – Jamie Oliver and Ottolenghi – on the window-sill, notebooks and recent letters in a rack beside the toaster, a blackboard with notes for the week's shopping. Hawthorne glanced through the letters then returned them. A wooden fish had been mounted on the wall above the counter with five hooks which Diana used to hang keys and he seemed particularly interested in these – there were four sets, each one of them labelled, and I duly took a picture, noting that according to the tags they opened the front door, the back door, the cellar and a second property called Stonor House.

'What's this?' I asked.

'She used to live there before she moved to London. It's in Walmer, Kent.'

'A bit odd that she should keep the key . . .'

We found a household drawer full of older letters and bills, which Hawthorne glanced through. There was also a brochure for a musical called *Moroccan Nights*. The front cover showed a picture of a Kalashnikov machine gun with its shoulder strap lying in the shape of a heart. One of the producers, listed on the first page, was Raymond Clunes.

From the kitchen, we went upstairs to the bedroom, passing wallpaper with faint stripes and old theatre programmes in frames: *Hamlet*, *The Tempest*, *Henry V*, *The Importance of Being Earnest*, *The Birthday Party*. Damian Cowper had appeared in all of them. Hawthorne bulldozed ahead but I entered the bedroom with a sense of unease that surprised me. Once again I felt as if I was intruding. Only a week ago, a middle-aged woman would have undressed here, standing in front of the full-length mirror, sliding into the queen-sized bed with the copy of Stieg Larsson's *The Girl Who Played with Fire* that was lying on the bedside table. Well, at least Mrs Cowper had been spared the slightly disappointing ending. There were two sets of pillows. I could see the indentation on one of them, made by her head. I could imagine her waking up, warm, perhaps smelling of lavender. Not any more. Death for me had always been little more than a necessity, something that moved the plot on. But standing in the bedroom of a woman who had so recently died, I could feel it right there beside me.

Hawthorne rifled through the drawers, wardrobes and bedside cabinets. He glanced briefly at a framed photograph of Damian Cowper, propped up on her make-up table. I vaguely recognised him, although to be honest I'm not good with faces and most of these young, handsome English actors blend into one another . . . particularly once they've made the move to Hollywood. He discovered a safe behind Mrs Cowper's shoe rack, scowled when he found it was still locked but then forgot it. I was fascinated by the way he searched for clues. He didn't speak to me. He barely noticed I was there. He reminded me a little of a sniffer dog at an airport. There is never any reason to suppose that there will be drugs or bombs in any of the suitcases but the dog will examine every one of them and will be sure to find anything that's there. Hawthorne had the same vagueness, the same certainty.

From the bedroom, he moved into the bathroom. There were about twenty little bottles gathered around the bath:

she'd had the habit of taking the shampoo and bath gel from hotels. He opened a cabinet above the basin and took out three packets of temazepam – sleeping pills. He showed them to me.

'Interesting,' he said. It was the first word he had spoken for a while.

'She was worried about something,' I said. 'She couldn't sleep.'

I followed Hawthorne as he continued around the house. There were two guest rooms on the upper floor but they clearly hadn't been used for a while. They were almost too clean with a chill in the air, the central heating turned down to save on bills. He took a brief look around, then went back out into the corridor.

'What do you think happened to the cat?' he muttered.

'What cat?' I asked.

'The old lady's cat. A Persian grey. One of those horrible bloody things that look like a medicine ball with fur.'

'I didn't see a photograph of a cat.'

'Nor did I.'

He didn't add anything and I was suddenly irritated. 'If I'm going to write about you, you're going to have to tell me how you work. It's all very well making these pronouncements but you can't just leave them hanging in the air.'

He frowned as if he was trying to make sense of what I had just said, then nodded. 'It's pretty bloody obvious, Tony. There was a feeding bowl down in the kitchen. And the pillow. Didn't you notice?'

'The indentation? I thought that was her head.'

'I doubt it, mate. Not unless she had short, silky hair and smelled of fish. She slept on the left side of the bed. That was where the book was. The cat slept with her on the other side. It was obviously heavy, quite big. I'd guess a Persian grey. It's just the sort of pet a woman like her would have – but it's not here.'

'Maybe the police took it.'

'Maybe they did.'

We went back downstairs and as we re-entered the living room, I saw that we were no longer alone. A man in a cheap suit was sitting on the sofa with his legs apart and a file spread out across his lap. His tie was crooked and two of the buttons on his shirt were undone. I had a feeling he was a smoker. Everything about him was unhealthy: the colour of his skin, his thinning hair, broken nose, stomach pressing against the waistband of his trousers. He was about the same age as Hawthorne but bigger, flabbier. He could have retired from the boxing ring but I guessed he must be a police officer. I had seen his sort often enough on television – not in dramas but on the news, standing outside courtrooms, awkwardly reading a prepared statement to the camera.

'Hawthorne,' he said, without any enthusiasm.

'Detective Inspector Meadows!' Hawthorne had used the formal title ironically, as if it somehow wasn't deserved. 'Hello, Jack,' he added.

'I couldn't believe it when they told me they'd brought you in on this one. It seems straightforward enough to me.' He noticed me for the first time. 'Who are you?'

I wasn't quite sure how to introduce myself.

'He's a writer,' Hawthorne said, stepping in. 'He's with me.'

'What? Writing about you?'

'Writing about the case.'

'I hope you've got that authorised.' He paused. 'I left everything for you, like I was told. Brought stuff back. Laid it all out just like we found it. Complete waste of time if you ask me.'

'I don't, Jack. No-one ever does.'

He took that on the chin. 'You had a chance to look round, then? Have you finished?'

'I was just leaving.' But Hawthorne stayed where he was. 'You say it's straightforward. So what are your thoughts?'

'I'm not going to share my thoughts with you, if you don't mind.' He got lazily to his feet. He was a bigger man than I had thought. He towered over both of us. He had gathered up the pages and, almost as an afterthought, he handed them over. 'They told me to give you these.'

The file contained photographs, forensic reports, witness statements and records of all the telephone calls made to and from both the house and Diana Cowper's mobile phone in the past two weeks. Hawthorne glanced at the top page. 'She sent a text message at six thirty-one.'

'That's right. Just before she was strangled. My killer was Aaaaagh . . .' He smiled at his own joke. 'I've read the text. It doesn't make a lot of sense so I'll leave you to work it out.' He went over to the glass of water that I had noticed on the sideboard, next to the credit card. 'I'll take this now, if you don't mind.'

'Be my guest.'

56

For the first time I noticed that Meadows was wearing gloves. He had some sort of plastic cap which he used to seal the glass, then lifted it to take it with him.

'The only fingerprints on it are hers,' Hawthorne said. 'And there's no DNA. Nobody drank out of it.'

'You've seen the report?' Meadows seemed puzzled.

'No need to see anything, mate. It's bloody obvious.' He smiled. 'You look at that tin in the kitchen? *Prince Caspian*?'

'A few coins. No fingerprints. Nothing.'

'No surprise there either.' Hawthorne glanced at the sideboard. 'How about the credit card?'

'What about it?'

'When was it last used?'

'You'll find all her financial details in there.' Meadows nodded at the file. 'Fifteen thousand quid in her private account. Another two hundred thou' in savings. She was doing all right.' He remembered what Hawthorne had asked. 'The last time she used the card was a week ago. Harrods. That's where she bought her groceries.'

'Smoked salmon and cream cheese.'

'How did you know that?'

'It was in the kitchen. I had it for breakfast.'

'That's evidence!'

'Not any more.'

Meadows scowled. 'Anything else you want to know?'

'Yes. Did you find the cat?'

'What cat?'

'That answers the question.'

'Then I'll leave you to it.' Meadows was holding the glass

as if he were a magician about to make a goldfish appear. He nodded at me. 'Nice to meet you,' he said. 'But I'd watch out for yourself when you're around this one. Particularly if you go near any stairs.'

He was pleased with that. He took one last look around the room and then, still holding the glass in front of him, he left.

Five

The Lacerated Man

'What did he mean . . . that crack about the stairs?'

'Charlie Meadows is a pillock. He didn't mean anything.'

'Charlie? You called him Jack.'

'Everyone does.'

We were sitting outside a café close to Fulham Broadway station – fortunately the sun was shining – so Hawthorne could smoke. He had gone through the documents that Meadows had given him, sharing them with me too. There were photographs of Diana Cowper before and after she had died and I was shocked by the difference. The corpse that Andrea Kluvánek had discovered bore almost no resemblance to the smart, active socialite who had invested in theatre and eaten lunch in expensive restaurants in Mayfair.

I come in at eleven o'clock. Is the start of my work time. I see her and I know at once that something very bad has happen.

Andrea's statement was attached, reproduced word for word in her broken English. There was a photograph of her: a slim, round-faced woman, quite boyish, with short, spiky hair, staring defensively at the camera. Hawthorne had told me she had a criminal record but I found it difficult to imagine her murdering Diana Cowper. She was too small.

There was plenty of other material too. In fact it occurred to me that it might be possible for Hawthorne to solve the murder right here at this table over his coffee and cigarette. I hoped not. If that happened, it would be a very short book. Perhaps it was with that thought in mind that I wanted to talk about other things first.

'How do you know him?' I asked.

'Who?'

'Meadows!'

'We worked in the same sub-command in Putney. He had the office next to mine and although I always held my nose, there were a few times I had to walk down the dark side.'

'I don't know what that means.'

'It's when you have to ask another team for help. When we were doing house-to-house . . . that sort of thing.' Hawthorne seemed anxious to move on. 'Do you want to talk about Diana Cowper?'

'No,' I said. 'I want to talk about you.'

He gazed at the paperwork spread out on the table. He didn't need to say anything. This was all that mattered to him. But for once, I was on my home ground and I was determined. 'The only way this is going to work is if you allow me into your life,' I said. 'I've got to know about you.'

'Nobody's interested in me.'

'If that were true, I wouldn't be here. If it's true, the book won't sell.' I watched as Hawthorne lit another cigarette. For the first time in thirty years, I was tempted to ask for one myself. 'Listen to me,' I went on, carefully. 'They're not called murder victim stories. They're not called criminal stories. They're called detective stories. There's a reason for that. I'm taking a big risk here. If you solve this crime right now, I won't have anything to write about. Worse than that, if you don't solve it at all, it'll be a complete waste of time. So getting to know you matters. If I know you, if I can find something that makes you more . . . human, at least that's a start. So you can't just brush aside every question I ask you. You can't hide behind this wall.'

Hawthorne shrank away. It was funny how, with his pale skin and those troubled, almost childlike eyes, he could make himself seem vulnerable. 'I don't want to talk about Jack Meadows. He didn't like me. And when the shit hit the fan, he was happy to see me go.'

'What shit? What fan?'

'When I left.'

That was all he was going to say, so I made a mental note to follow it up later. Obviously, now wasn't the right time. I opened the notebook which I had brought with me and took out a pen. 'All right. While we're sitting here, I want to ask you a few questions about yourself. I don't even know where you live.'

He hesitated. This really was going to be blood out of a stone. 'I've got a place in Gants Hill,' he said at length. I'd often driven through Gants Hill, a suburb in north-east London, on the way to Suffolk.

'Are you married?'

'Yes.' I could see that there was more to come but it took a while to arrive. 'We're not together any more. Don't ask me about that.'

'Do you support a football team?'

'Arsenal.' He said it without much enthusiasm and I suspected that if he was a football fan, he was a fairly casual one.

'Do you go to the cinema?'

'Sometimes.' He was getting impatient.

'What about music?'

'What about it?'

'Classical? Jazz?'

'I don't listen to music much.'

I'd been thinking of Morse and his love of opera but that had just gone out of the window too. 'Do you have children?'

He swiped the cigarette out of his lips, holding it like a poison dart, and I saw that I'd pushed too hard, too soon. 'This isn't going to work,' he snapped, and at that moment I could easily imagine him in a police station, in an interrogation room. He was looking at me with something close to contempt. 'You can write what you like about me. You can make it all up if you want to. What difference does it make? But I'm not going to play fucking *University Challenge* with you now or at any time. I've got a dead woman and somebody strangled her in her own front room and that's all that matters to me right at this moment.' He snatched up one of the pages. 'Do you want to look at this or not?'

I could have gone home right then. I could have forgotten the whole thing – and, given what happened later on, it might have been better if I had. But I had just left the murder scene. It was almost as if I knew Diana Cowper and for some reason – maybe it was the photographs I had seen, the violence of her death – I felt I owed her something.

I wanted to know more.

'All right,' I said. I put down my pen. 'Show me.'

The page contained a screenshot of the text that Diana Cowper had sent to her son just before she died.

I have seen the boy who was lacerated and I'm afraid

'What do you make of that?' he asked.

'She was interrupted before she finished,' I said. 'There's no full stop. She didn't have time to say what she was afraid of.'

'Or maybe she was just afraid. Maybe she was too afraid to worry about the full stop at the end of the sentence.'

'Meadows was right. It doesn't make any sense.'

'Then maybe this will help.' Hawthorne pulled out three more pages, copies of newspaper articles written ten years before.

DAILY MAIL — FRIDAY, 8 JUNE 2001

TWIN BOY KILLED IN HIT-AND-RUN HORROR
His brother is in critical condition but doctors say he
will recover.

An eight-year-old boy was fighting for his life and his
twin brother was killed by a short-sighted motorist who
ploughed into both children before driving off.

Jeremy Godwin was left with injuries which include
a fractured skull and a severe laceration of the brain.
His brother, Timothy, died instantly.

The accident took place at half past four on Thursday
afternoon on The Marine in the coastal resort of Deal,
Kent.

The two boys, who have been described as 'insepar-
able', were returning to their hotel with their nanny,
25-year-old Mary O'Brien. She told the police: 'The car
came round the corner. The driver didn't even try to
slow down. She hit the children and drove straight off.
I've been with the family for three years and I'm devastated. I couldn't believe she didn't stop.'

Police have arrested a 52-year-old woman.

THE TELEGRAPH — SATURDAY, 9 JUNE 2001

POLICE ARREST SHORT-SIGHTED DRIVER WHO KILLED TWIN

The woman who killed eight-year-old twin Timothy Godwin, and inflicted life-threatening injuries on his brother, has been named as Diana Cowper. Mrs Cowper, 52, is a long-term resident of Walmer, Kent, and was returning from the Royal Cinq Ports Golf Club when the accident took place.

Mrs Cowper, who had been drinking at the clubhouse with friends, was not over the limit and witnesses have confirmed that she was not speeding. However, she was driving without her spectacles and in a test conducted by the police she was unable to read a registration plate 25 feet away.

Her lawyers have made the following statement. 'Our client had spent the afternoon playing golf and was on her way home when the incident took place. She had unfortunately mislaid her glasses but thought she would be able to drive the relatively short distance without them. She admits that she panicked following the accident and drove straight home. However, she was fully aware of the seriousness of what she had done and contacted the police within two hours that same evening.'

Police have charged Mrs Cowper under Sections 1 and 170 (2) and (4) of the Road Traffic Act of 1988.

She faces charges of causing death by dangerous driving and failing to stop at the scene of an accident.

Mrs Cowper gave her address as Liverpool Road, Walmer. She had recently lost her husband after a long illness. Her 23-year-old son, Damian Cowper, is an actor who has performed with the Royal Shakespeare Company and who was last seen in *The Birthday Party* on the West End stage.

THE TIMES — TUESDAY, 6 NOVEMBER 2001

FAMILY CALLS FOR CHANGE IN LAW AS HIT-AND-RUN DRIVER WALKS FREE

The mother of an eight-year-old boy killed as he was crossing the road in the seaside town of Deal, Kent, spoke out today as the driver walked free.

Timothy Godwin died instantly and his twin brother, Jeremy, received severe lacerations to the brain after Diana Cowper, 52, failed to see them. It turned out that Mrs Cowper had left her spectacles at the golf club where she had been playing and was unable to see beyond twenty feet.

Canterbury Crown Court had heard that she had not broken the law by not wearing her glasses. Judge Nigel Weston QC said: 'It was not a wise idea to drive without your spectacles but they were not a legal requirement as the law stands and there can be no doubting your

remorse. In the light of this, I have decided that a custodial sentence would not be appropriate.'

Mrs Cowper was disqualified from driving for a year,
had nine penalty points added to her licence and was
ordered to pay £900 costs. The judge also suggested
three months of restorative justice but the family of the
two boys have refused to meet her.

Speaking outside the court, Judith Godwin said:
'Nobody should be allowed to get behind the wheel of
a car if they can't see. If that's not against the law then
the law should be changed. My son is dead. My other
son has been crippled. And she just gets a slap on the
wrist. That can't be right.'

A spokesperson for Brake, the road safety charity,
said: 'Nobody should drive if they are not fully in control of their car.'

I looked at the dates above the three articles and made the
connection. 'This all happened exactly ten years ago,' I
exclaimed.

'Nine years and eleven months,' Hawthorne corrected me.
'The accident was at the start of June.'

'It's still pretty much the anniversary.' I handed back the
third article. 'And the boy who survived . . . he had brain
lacerations.' I picked up Diana Cowper's text. '. . . *the boy
who was lacerated*'.

'You think there's a connection?'

I assumed he was being sarcastic but I didn't rise to the
bait. 'Do you know where she lives?' I asked. 'Judith Godwin?'

Hawthorne searched through the other pages. 'There's an address in Harrow-on-the-Hill.'

'Not Kent?'

'They might have been on holiday. The first week in June . . . that's summer half-term.'

So perhaps Hawthorne had children after all. How else would he have known? But I didn't dare raise that subject again. Instead, I asked: 'Are we going to see her?'

'No need to hurry. And we've got a meeting with Mr Cornwallis just down the road.' My mind had gone blank for a moment. I had no idea who he was referring to. 'The undertaker,' he reminded me. He began to gather up the documents, drawing them towards him like a croupier with a pack of cards. It was interesting that as much as Detective Inspector Meadows had disliked him, someone higher up in the Met was taking him seriously. The crime scene had been left untouched for his examination. He was being kept fully in the loop.

Hawthorne stubbed out his cigarette. 'Let's go,' he said.

Once again, I noticed, I'd paid for the coffees.

We took the number 14 back down the Fulham Road, the same bus used by Diana Cowper on the day she died. We exited, as Hawthorne would have put it, at twelve twenty-six and retraced our steps to the funeral parlour.

I hadn't been to a funeral parlour since my father died – and that was a long time ago. I had been twenty-one years old. Although he had suffered a protracted illness, the end had come very suddenly and the whole family was poleaxed.

For reasons that still aren't clear to me, an uncle stepped in and took control of the burial arrangements . . . after years of agnosticism, my father had expressed a desire to have an orthodox funeral. I'm sure my uncle thought he was doing us a favour but unfortunately, he was a loud, opinionated man and I can't say I'd ever been very fond of him. Even so, I found myself accompanying him to a funeral parlour in north London. In Jewish families, the burial happens very quickly and I hadn't yet had time to accept what was happening; I was still in shock. I have vague memories of a large room that was more like a lost property office in a railway station than an undertaker's. Everything was very dark, in different shades of brown. There was a short, bearded man standing behind a counter, wearing an ill-fitting suit and a yarmulke: the funeral director or perhaps one of his assistants. As if in a nightmare, I see a crowd of people surrounding me. Were they other customers or staff? I seem to remember that there was no privacy.

My uncle was negotiating the price of the funeral, which was to take place the following day. He didn't ask me what I thought. He was discussing the various coffins and different options with the counter man and, as I stood there listening to them, their voices became more and more heated until I realised that the two of them were actually engaged in a full-blooded argument. My uncle accused the funeral director of cheating us and that was what finally did it. The other man exploded in rage. He had gone quite red in the face and now he was jabbing a finger at us, shouting, with saliva flecking at his lips.

'You want mahogany, you pay for mahogany!'

I have no idea whether my father was buried in mahogany or plywood and frankly I don't care. The fury of the undertaker and the words he spoke have echoed in my memory for almost forty years. They have made me determined that my own funeral will be short, cheap and non-denominational. And they were still with me as I followed Hawthorne into Cornwallis and Sons, closing the door (silently) behind me.

The funeral parlour was very much as I have described it, smaller and less threatening than the office I remembered from my past – but this time, of course, there was no personal connection for me. Hawthorne introduced himself to Irene Laws, who took us directly to Robert Cornwallis's office at the end of the corridor, the same room where Diana Cowper had made the arrangements that she would now be requiring. This time, Irene stayed, planting herself firmly in a chair as if Diana Cowper's untimely death had been her fault and she expected to be interrogated along with her cousin. Again, I found myself wondering what it must be like to work there, sitting in a room with those miniature urns, a constant reminder that everything you were and everything you'd achieved would one day fit inside. Hawthorne hadn't introduced me, by the way. He never did. They must have assumed I was his assistant.

'I have already spoken to the police,' Cornwallis began.

'Yes, sir.' It was interesting that Hawthorne called him 'sir'. I saw at once that he was quite different when he was dealing with witnesses or suspects or anyone who might help him with his investigation. He came across as ordinary, even obsequious. The more I got to know him, the more I saw that he did this quite deliberately. People lowered their guard when they were talking to him. They had no idea what sort of man he was, that he was only waiting for the right moment to dissect them. For him, politeness was a surgical mask, something he slipped on before he took out his scalpel. 'Because of the unusual nature of the crime, I've been asked to provide independent support to the investigation. I'm very sorry to take up your time . . .' He gave the funeral director a crocodile smile. 'Do you mind if I smoke?'

'Well, actually . . .'

It was too late. The cigarette was already between his lips, the lighter sparking. Mrs Laws frowned and slid a pewter saucer onto the desk for him to use as an ashtray. I noticed an engraving around the side: *Awarded to Robert Daniel Cornwallis, Undertaker of the Year 2008.*

'Would you mind going over your meeting with Mrs Cowper once again, starting from the beginning?'

Robert Cornwallis did exactly that, speaking in the same measured tone that he must have used many times in his years spent dealing with the bereaved. Hawthorne may have criticised some of the embellishments which I added in my first chapter but what he told us corresponded more or less exactly to what I had written. Mrs Cowper had been reasonable, business-like and precise. She had arrived without an appointment and she had left once everything had been agreed.

In retrospect, I may have been a little unfair to Robert Cornwallis. I described him as crumpled and mournful but it may be that I was confusing the man with his profession, and this time I was struck by how very ordinary he was. Take away the corpses, the embalming fluids, the interments and the tears and I'm sure he'd be perfectly pleasant, someone you'd be happy to chat to if you met him at a party. It would just be better not to ask him what he did.

'How long was Mrs Cowper with you?' Hawthorne asked.

It was as if Irene Laws had been waiting for the question. 'She was here for just over fifty minutes,' she replied with the clipped exactitude of a speaking clock.

'I was going to say an hour,' Cornwallis agreed. 'We went over all the arrangements very carefully. And the prices.'

'How much was she going to pay you?'

'Irene can provide you with a complete breakdown. She already had a plot in Brompton Cemetery, which saved a considerable amount of money. The price of a resting place in London has increased greatly over the years, in the same way as property. The final figure, including the Church of England burial fee and the gravedigger, was three thousand pounds.'

'Three thousand, one hundred and seventy,' Miss Laws corrected him.

'Did she pay with a credit card?'

'Yes. She paid in full although I assured her that there was a ten-day cooling-off period should she have second thoughts. In that respect, we're rather similar to double-glazing salesmen.' This was his little joke. He smiled. Irene Laws frowned.

'What do you do with that money?' I asked. 'I mean, if she hadn't died . . .'

'We would have placed it in escrow. We belong to a trust known as the Golden Charter which takes care of payments and also, of course, calculates for inflation.' Somewhere in the back of my mind it had occurred to me that the funeral parlour might have welcomed Mrs Cowper's death because they would be the first to profit from it, providing the funeral. But if she had already paid, the very reverse was true. I was glad I hadn't mentioned it.

Even so, Hawthorne threw an angry glance at me, letting me know that my contribution had annoyed him. 'What sort of mood would you say she was in?' he asked, changing the subject completely.

'The same mood as anyone who comes here,' Cornwallis replied. 'She was a little uncomfortable, at least to begin with. We have a great reticence, talking about death, in this country. I always say it's a shame we don't adopt the prac-tice of the Swiss, who invented what they call the Café Mortel, an opportunity to discuss one's mortality over tea and cake.'

'I wouldn't say no to a cup of tea if you've got one,' Hawthorne said.

Cornwallis glanced at Miss Laws, who got up and stomped out of the room.

'You say she'd already worked out everything she wanted for the funeral.'

'Yes. She'd written it down.'

'Do you still have that document?'

'No. She took it with her. I made a copy, which I included in the summary that I sent her.'

'Would you say there was any urgency on her part? Did she tell you why she'd chosen that particular day to come in?'

'She didn't appear to consider herself to be in danger, if that's what you mean.' Cornwallis shook his head. 'It's not unusual for people to plan their funerals, Mr Hawthorne. She wasn't ill. She wasn't nervous or afraid. I already said this to the police. I also told them that both I and Miss Laws were shocked when we heard the news.'

'Why did you telephone her?'

'I'm sorry?'

'I have her phone records. You telephoned her at five past two. She had just arrived for a board meeting at the Globe Theatre. You spoke to her for about a minute and a half.'

'You're quite right. I needed the plot number of her husband's grave.' Cornwallis smiled. 'I had to contact the Royal Parks Chapel Office to register the interment. It was the one piece of information she hadn't given me. There's something I should perhaps mention. She was having some sort of argument when I spoke to her. I heard voices in the background. She said she'd call back but of course she never did.'

Irene Laws returned with Hawthorne's tea. The cup rattled against the saucer as she set it down.

'Is there anything else I can help you with, Mr Hawthorne?' Cornwallis asked.

'I'd be interested to know . . . did you both speak to her?'

'Irene showed her into this office—'

'I spoke to her briefly in the reception area but I didn't stay for the meeting,' Miss Laws interrupted, as she took her place.

'Was she ever in here on her own?'

Cornwallis frowned. 'What a very odd question. Why do you want to know?'

'I'm just interested.'

'No. I was with her the whole time.'

'Just before she left, she used the cloakroom,' Miss Laws said.

'You mean the toilet.'

'That's what I said. That was the only time she was on her own. I took her to the room, which is just along the corridor, and then came back with her while she collected her things. I'd also like to say that she was in a perfectly pleasant state of mind when she left. If anything, she was relieved – but that's often the way when people come here. In fact, it's part of our service.'

Hawthorne downed his tea in three large gulps. We stood up to leave. Then one thought occurred to me. 'She didn't say anything about someone called Timothy Godwin, did she?' I asked.

'Timothy Godwin?' Cornwallis shook his head. 'Who is he?'

'He was a boy she accidentally killed in a car accident,' I said. 'He had a brother, Jeremy Godwin . . .'

'What a terrible thing to happen.' Cornwallis turned to his cousin. 'Did she mention either of those names to you, Irene?'

'No.'

'I doubt they're relevant.' Hawthorne had cut off the discussion before it could go any further. He stretched out a hand. 'Thank you for your time, Mr Cornwallis.'

Outside, in the street, he turned on me.

'Do me a favour, mate. Never ask questions when you're with me. Never ask anything. All right?'

'You just expect me to sit there and say nothing?'

'That's right.'

'I'm not stupid,' I said. 'I may be able to help.'

'Well, you're wrong on at least one of those counts. But the point is, you're not here to help. You said this was a detective story. I'm the detective. It's as simple as that.'

'Then tell me what you've learned,' I said. 'You've been to the crime scene. You've seen the phone records. You've talked to the undertaker. Do you know anything yet?'

Hawthorne considered what I'd said. He had a blank look in his eyes and, for a moment, I thought he was going to dismiss me out of hand. Then he took pity on me.

'Diana Cowper knew she was going to die,' he said.

I waited for him to add something more but he simply turned and stormed off down the pavement. I considered my options, then followed, in every sense struggling to catch up.

Six

Witness Statements

I didn't know very much about Diana Cowper but it was already clear to me that there couldn't have been whole crowds of people queuing up to murder her. She was a middle-aged woman, a widow, living on her own. She was well-off without being super-rich, on the board of a theatre and the mother of a famous son. She had difficulty sleeping and she had a cat. True, she'd lost money to a theatrical producer and she'd employed a cleaner with a criminal record but what reason would either of them have had to strangle her?

The one thing that stood out was the fact that she had killed a little boy and badly injured his brother. The accident had been caused by her own carelessness – she hadn't been wearing her spectacles – and, worse still, she had driven away without stopping. Despite all this, she had walked free. If I had been Timothy and Jeremy Godwin's father, if I had been related to them in any way, I might have been tempted to kill her myself. And all of this had happened exactly ten years ago: well, nine years and eleven months. Close enough.

It was an obvious motive for murder. If the Godwin family was living in north London, in Harrow-on-the-Hill, I couldn't understand why we weren't heading there straight away and I said as much to Hawthorne.

'One step at a time,' he replied. 'There are other people I want to talk to first.'

'The cleaner?' We were actually sitting in a taxi that was taking us around Shepherd's Bush roundabout on our way to Acton, which was where Andrea Kluvánek lived. Hawthorne had also telephoned Raymond Clunes and we were seeing him later. 'You don't suspect her, do you?'

'I suspect her of lying to the police, yes.'

'And Clunes? What's he got to do with this?'

'He knew Mrs Cowper. Seventy-eight per cent of female victims are killed by someone they know,' he went on before I could interrupt.

'Really?'

'I thought you'd have known that, you being a TV writer.' Ignoring the no-smoking sign, he pressed the button to lower the window of the cab and lit a cigarette. 'Husband, stepfather, lover . . . speaking statistically, they're the most likely killers.'

'Raymond Clunes wasn't any of those things.'

'He could have been her lover.'

'She saw the boy with the lacerations, Jeremy Godwin! She said she was afraid. I don't know why you're wasting your time.'

'There's no smoking!' the driver complained over the intercom.

'Fuck off. I'm a police officer,' Hawthorne replied, equanimously. 'What were those words you used? *Modus operandi.* This is mine.' He blew smoke out of the window but the wind just whipped it back into the cab. 'Start with the people who were closest to her and work outwards from there. It's like doing a house-to-house. You start with the neighbours. You don't start at the end of the street.' He turned his eyes on me, once again interrogating. 'You got a problem with that?'

'It just seems a bit crazy to be haring around London. And at my expense,' I added quietly.

Hawthorne said nothing more.

After what seemed like a very long drive, the taxi pulled up on the edge of the South Acton Estate, a sprawling collection of slab blocks and high-rise towers that had sprung up over the decades, starting at the end of the war. There was some landscaping – lawns, trees and pedestrian walkways – but the overall effect was dispiriting if only because there were so many homes packed together. We walked beside a skateboard park that looked as if it hadn't been used for years and then down into an underpass, the walls covered with crude graffiti images, bleeding garishly into one another. No Banksies here.

A huddle of twenty-somethings in hoodies and sweatshirts were sitting in the shadows, watching us with sullen, suspicious eyes. Fortunately, Hawthorne seemed to know where he was going and I stayed close to him, thinking back to what the woman at Hay-on-Wye had said to me. Perhaps this was the dose of reality she had prescribed.

Andrea Kluvánek lived on the second floor of one of the towers. Hawthorne had telephoned ahead and she was expecting us. I knew from the police files that she had two children, but it was one thirty in the afternoon and I guessed they were both at school. Her flat was clean but it was very small, with no more furniture than was needed: three chairs at the kitchen table, a single sofa in front of the TV. Even the most optimistic estate agent wouldn't have called the living room open-plan. The kitchen simply blended into it with no way of saying where one ended and the other began. This was a one-bedroom flat and I have no idea how they managed at night. Maybe the children had the bedroom and she slept on the sofa.

We sat down, facing her across the table. There were pots and pans hanging on hooks, inches behind our heads. Andrea did not offer us tea or coffee. She gazed at us suspiciously across the Formica surface of her kitchen table, a small, dark woman who looked even tougher in real life than she had in the photograph I had seen. She was wearing a T-shirt and jeans that had been torn in a way that wasn't a fashion statement. Hawthorne had lit a cigarette and she had taken one off him too, so I was sitting there surrounded by smoke, wondering if I would actually manage to finish the book before I died of some secondary-smoking-related disease.

To begin with, Hawthorne was quite pleasant with her. His tone was conversational as he took her through the statement she had given to the police and which I have already described. She had come into the house, seen the dead woman, gone straight outside and called the police. She had waited until they arrived.

'You must have got very wet,' Hawthorne said.

'What?' She looked at him suspiciously.

'It was raining that morning, when you discovered the body. If I'd been you, I'd have waited in the kitchen. Nice and warm and there's a phone in there too. No need to use your mobile.'

'I go outside. I already say all this. The police ask me what happen and I tell them.' Her English wasn't very good and it got worse, the angrier she became.

'I know, Andrea,' Hawthorne said. 'I read what you told the police. But I've come all the way across London to talk to you face-to-face because I want you to tell me the truth.'

There was a long silence.

'I speak the truth.' She didn't sound convincing.

'No, you don't.' Hawthorne sighed gently, as if this wasn't something he really wanted to do. 'How long have you been in this country?' he asked.

At once she was defensive. 'Five year.'

'Two years with Diana Cowper.'

'Yes.'

'How many days a week did you work for her?'

'Two days. Wednesday and Friday.'

'Did you ever tell her about that little trouble you had?'

'I have no trouble.'

Hawthorne shook his head sadly. 'You have a lot of trouble. In Huddersfield — that's where you were living. Shoplifting. A hundred-and-fifty-quid fine plus costs.'

'You no understand!' Andrea glowered at him. I was wishing the room was bigger. I felt out of place and uncomfortable being so close to her. 'I have nothing to eat. No husband. My children, four-year-old and six-year-old, have nothing ɔ eat.'

'So you nicked stuff from a charity shop. Well, it was Save the Children. I suppose you were taking it literally.'

'Is not . . .'

'And it was a second offence,' Hawthorne went on before she could deny it. 'You were already on a conditional discharge. I'd say you were lucky the judge was in a good mood.'

Andrea was still defiant. 'I work for Mrs Cowper for two year. She look after me so I no need to steal nothing. I am honest person. I look after my family.'

'Well, you won't be able to look after your family when you're in jail.' Hawthorne allowed this to sink in. 'You lie to me and that's where you'll end up. Your children will be in care – or maybe they'll be sent back to Slovakia. I want to know how much money you took.'

'What money?'

'The housekeeping money that your employer kept in a *Prince Caspian* tin. You know who Prince Caspian is? He's a character in Narnia. Her son, Damian Cowper, was in the film. She kept the tin in the kitchen. I looked in it and I found a couple of coins.'

'That's where she keep money, yes. But I don't take it. The thief take it.'

'No.' Hawthorne was angry. His eyes had darkened and the hand holding his cigarette had curled into a fist. 'A thief went through the house, it's true. He poked around a bit here and there. It was like he wanted us to know where he'd been. But this was different. The tin was put back in its right place. The lid was screwed back on. It was wiped clean of fingerprints by someone who'd been watching too many crime shows on TV. I don't think you get it. There had to be some fingerprints on the surface. Yours. Your boss's. My guess is you pulled out a wodge of notes and didn't notice the coins. How much was there?'

Andrea stared at him sullenly. I wondered how much she had understood. 'I take money,' she said, at last.

'How much?'

'Fifty pound.'

Hawthorne looked pained. 'How much?'

'One hundred and sixty.'

He nodded. 'That's better. And you didn't wait outside either. Why would you when it was pissing down? What I want to know is, what else did you do? What else did you take?'

I saw Andrea struggling with the decision that she had to make. Did she admit to further wrongdoing and possibly get herself into more trouble? Or did she try to deceive Hawthorne and risk angering him again? In the end, she bowed to her better sense. She got up and took a folded piece of paper out of a kitchen drawer. She handed it to him. He unfolded it and read:

Mrs Cowper,

You think you can just get rid of me but I will not leave you alone. What I said is just the beginning, I promise you. I have been watching you and I know the things that are dear to you. You are going to pay. Believe me.

It was a handwritten letter, unsigned, with no date or address. Hawthorne looked from it to Andrea, enquiry in his eyes.

'A man come to the house,' she explained. 'Three week ago. He go with Mrs Cowper in the living room. I was upstair in the bedroom but I hear them talking. He was very angry . . . shouting at her.'

'What time was this?'

'It was Wednesday. About one o'clock.'

'Did you see him?'

'I look out of the window when he leave. But it was raining and he have umbrella. I see nothing.'

'You're sure it was a man?'

Andrea considered. 'I think so, yes.'

'And what about this?' Hawthorne held up the sheet of paper.

'Is in her bedroom table.' Andrea actually managed to look ashamed although I think she was just afraid of what Hawthorne might do to her. 'I take a look in the house after she die and I find it.' She paused. 'I think this man kill Mr Tibbs.'

'Who's Mr Tibbs?'

'Mrs Cowper have a cat. Is a big grey cat.' She held out her hands, showing us its size. 'She call me on Thursday. She tell me not to come in. She very upset and she say that Mr Tibbs has gone.'

'Why did you take the letter?' I asked.

Andrea looked at Hawthorne as if asking his permission to ignore me.

Hawthorne nodded. He folded the letter back up and slipped it into his pocket. The two of us left.

'She took the letter because she thought she could make money out of it,' Hawthorne said. 'Maybe she knows the man who visited Diana Cowper, the man with the umbrella. Or maybe she thought she could find him. But she's an opportunist. She knew there was going to be a murder investigation and this was something she thought she could use.'

We were sitting together in another taxi, on our way back into town. We had one meeting left – with Raymond Clunes, the theatre producer who'd had lunch with Diana Cowper on the day she'd died. I was even more convinced now that this was a waste of time. Surely Hawthorne had the identity of the killer in his pocket. *You are going to pay.* What could have been clearer than that? But he said nothing more about the interview with Andrea Kluvánek. He was deep in thought. In fact it was more than that. He was totally absorbed. This was something I would learn about Hawthorne. He was some-one who was only fully alive when he was working on a case. He needed there to have been a murder or some other violent crime. It was his entire *raison d'être* – another posh phrase which I am sure he would have hated.

Clunes lived in rather different circumstances to Andrea Kluvánek. His home was behind Marble Arch, close to Connaught Square, and I wasn't at all surprised that this was the home of a theatre producer. The building itself was like a stage set, made of red brick and almost improbably two-dimensional with an imposing front door and brightly painted windows set in perfect symmetry. Everything was pristine, even the dustbins standing in a neat line on the other side of the metal railings. A flight of steps led down to a basement with its own separate entrance. There were four more floors rising above. I guessed I was looking at around five bedrooms and at least thirty million pounds' worth of central London property.

Hawthorne wasn't impressed. He jabbed at the doorbell as if he had some personal animosity against it. There was nobody else in the street and I got the feeling that most of the houses here would be empty, owned by foreign business-men. Didn't Tony Blair live somewhere close by? As central as it was, I'd never actually been to this particular area. It didn't feel like London at all.

The door was opened by that standby of every whodun-nit, something I had never expected to encounter in the twenty-first century. Clunes had a butler, the real thing, in pinstriped suit, waistcoat and gloves. He was a man of about my age with swept-back dark hair and a look of dignity that he must have nailed into place each day.

'Good afternoon, sir. Please come in.' He didn't need to ask our names. We were expected.

We went into a large hallway between two reception rooms, the floors fabulously carpeted, the ceilings triple height. It didn't look at all like someone's home. It was more like a hotel, though one without paying guests. As we climbed the stairs, I noticed a Hockney pool painting with a boy just disappearing beneath the surface, followed by a Francis Bacon triptych. We reached a landing with a huge Robert Mapplethorpe nude although it showed only a part of the subject's anatomy. It was a black-and-white photograph: the background white, the buttocks and erect penis black. Just to one side stood a classical sculpture of a naked shepherd boy. Hawthorne looked uncomfortable as we walked past this blatant homoerotic art. Not just his lips but his entire body curled in distaste.

A cavernous archway led into the upper living room, which ran the full length of the house, with furniture, lamps, mirrors and further artwork dotted around as far as the eye could see. Everything was expensive but I was more struck by how impersonal it was. It was all brand new, in perfect taste. I looked in vain for a discarded newspaper or a pair of muddy shoes that might suggest somebody actually lived there. It was somehow too silent for the centre of London. The whole place reminded me of a sarcophagus, as if the owner had deliberately filled it with the riches of a life he had left behind.

And yet, when Raymond Clunes finally appeared, he was

surprisingly ordinary. He was about fifty years old, dressed in a blue velvet jacket with a roll-neck jersey, poised with his legs crossed, so exactly in the centre of an oversized sofa that I wondered if the butler had taken out a tape measure before we arrived and marked out where he should sit. He was well built, with a shock of silver hair and humorous, pale blue eyes. He seemed pleased to see us.

'Do sit down.' He made a theatrical gesture, directing us to the seat opposite. 'Will you have some coffee?' He didn't wait for an answer. 'Bruce, let's have some coffee for our guests. And bring up those truffles.'

'Yes, sir.' The butler backed away.

We sat down.

'You're here about poor Diana.' He hadn't waited for Hawthorne to ask a question. 'I can't tell you how shocked I am by what's happened. I knew her through the Globe. That was where we first met. And of course I've worked with her son, Damian, a very, very talented young boy. He was in my production of *The Importance of Being Earnest* at the Haymarket. It was a huge success. I always knew he'd go far. When the police told me what had happened, I couldn't believe it. Nobody in the world would have wanted to hurt Diana. She was one of those people who only brought goodness and kindness to everyone she met.'

'You had lunch with her the day she died,' Hawthorne said.

'At the Café Murano. Yes. I saw her as she came out of the station. She waved to me across the road and I thought it was all going to be fine – but once we sat down, I could tell at once that she wasn't herself, poor thing. She was worried about her pussy cat, Mr Tibbs. Isn't that a hilarious name for a cat? He'd gone missing. I said to her not to worry. He's probably gone off chasing mice or whatever it is cats do. But I could see there was a lot on her mind. She couldn't stay long. She had a board meeting that afternoon.'

'You say you were old friends but, as I understand it, you'd fallen out.'

'Fallen out?' Clunes sounded surprised.

'She lost money in a show of yours.'

'Oh, for heaven's sake!' Clunes dismissed the accusation with a flick of his fingers. 'You're talking about *Moroccan Nights*. We didn't fall out. She was disappointed. Of course she was disappointed. We both were! I lost a great deal more money in that show than she did, I can assure you. But that's the business. I mean, right now I've got money in *Spider Man*, which is a complete, total disaster between you and me, but at the same time I turned down *The Book of Mormon*. Sometimes, you just get it wrong. She knew that.'

'What was *Moroccan Nights*?' I asked.

'A love story. Set in the Kasbah. Two boys: a soldier and a terrorist. It had a wonderful score and it was based on a very successful novel – but the audiences just didn't take to it. Maybe it was too violent. I don't know. Did you see it?'

'No,' I admitted.

'That's the trouble. Nor did anyone else.'

Bruce came back carrying a tray with three tiny cups of coffee and a plate with four white chocolate truffles arranged in a pyramid.

'Has anything you've ever done been successful?' Hawthorne asked.

Clunes was offended. 'Look around you, Detective Inspector. Do you think I'd have a house like this if I hadn't backed a few winners in my time? I was one of the first investors in *Cats*, if you really want to know, and I've invested in every one of Andrew's musicals since then. *Billy Elliot*, *Shrek*, Daniel Radcliffe in *Equus* . . . I think I can say I've had more than my fair share of success. *Moroccan Nights* should have worked but you can never tell. That's what being in musical theatre is all about. I can assure you of one thing, though, and that is – Diana Cowper had no bad feelings towards me when we had to put up the notices. She knew what she was getting into and at the end of the day the money she invested was hardly substantial.'

'Fifty grand?'

'That may be a great deal to you, Mr Hawthorne. It would be to a lot of people. But Diana could afford it. Otherwise, she wouldn't have gone ahead.'

There was a brief silence and I saw Hawthorne examining the other man with those bright, unforgiving eyes. I was expecting him to say something offensive but in fact his voice was measured as he asked: 'Did she tell you where she'd been that morning?'

'Before lunch?' Clunes blinked. 'No.'

'She went to an undertaker's in South Kensington. She arranged her own funeral.'

Clunes had picked up one of the coffee cups and was

holding it delicately in front of his face. He set it back down again. 'Really? You do surprise me.'

'She didn't mention it at the Café Murano?' Hawthorne asked.

'Of course she didn't mention it. If she'd mentioned it, I would have told you straight away. It's not something you'd forget, something like that.'

'You say she had a lot on her mind. Did she talk to you about anything that was worrying her?'

'Well, yes. There was one thing she mentioned.' Clunes thought back for a moment. 'We were talking about money and she mentioned that there was someone pestering her. It was all to do with that accident she had when she was living in Kent. That was just after we met.'

'She ran over two children,' I said.

'That's right.' Clunes nodded at me. He picked up the coffee cup again and took a single sip, emptying it. 'It was ten years ago. She was living on her own after she had lost her husband to cancer . . . terribly sad. He was a dentist. He had a great many celebrity clients and they had a lovely house, right on the sea. She was living down there and as it happened Damian was with her when the accident took place. As I recall, he was between tours or maybe he was doing that thing for the BBC. I really can't remember.

'Anyway, it absolutely wasn't her fault. There were two children. They were with their nanny but they ran across the road to get an ice-cream just as she was coming round the corner. She couldn't stop in time – but that didn't stop the family blaming her. I actually had a long chat with the judge and he was quite clear that Diana wasn't in any way responsible. Of course she was terribly upset by the whole thing. She moved back to London shortly after that – and as far as I know she never got behind the wheel of a car again. Well, you can't blame her, can you? The whole thing was a horrible experience.'

'Did she tell you who had been pestering her?' Hawthorne asked.

'Yes, she did. It was Alan Godwin, the father of the two boys. He'd been round to see her, making all sorts of demands.'

'What did he want?'

'He was asking her for money. I told her not to get involved. It had all happened a long time ago and it had nothing to do with her any more.'

'Did she mention that he'd written to her?' I asked.

'Had he?' Clunes looked into the mid-distance. 'No. I don't think so. She just said he'd been to see her and she didn't know what to do.'

'Wait a minute,' Hawthorne cut in. 'You say you spoke to the judge. How did that happen?'

'Oh – I know him. Nigel Weston is a friend of mine. He's also an investor. He put money into the musical version of *La Cage aux Folles*. He did very well out of it.'

'So what you're saying to me, Mr Clunes, is that Diana Cowper ran over and killed a child. She was an investor in your shows. And she was acquitted by a judge who was also an investor. Out of interest, had the two of them met?'

'I don't know.' Clunes seemed defensive. 'I don't think

so. I hope you're not suggesting there was some sort of impropriety, Detective Inspector.'

'Well, if there was, we'll find out. Is Mr Weston married?'

'I have no idea. Why do you ask?'

'No reason.'

But Hawthorne was bristling as we went back down the stairs and this time he didn't try to hide his disgust as we passed the Mapplethorpe. We left the house, walked around the corner, and he lit a cigarette. I watched him as he smoked furiously, refusing to look me in the eye.

'What's the matter?' I asked, eventually.

He didn't answer.

'Hawthorne . . . ?'

He turned on me, his eyes vengeful. 'You think it's all right, do you? That bloody queer, sitting there, surrounded by all that porn.'

'What?' I was genuinely shocked – not by what he thought. I'd already guessed that. But by the way he'd expressed it. He pronounced queer 'quee-ah', making it sound like something alien as well as unpleasant.

'First of all, that wasn't porn,' I said. 'Do you have any idea how much some of that stuff is worth? And secondly, you can't call him that.'

'What?'

'That word you used.'

'Queer?' He sneered at me. 'You don't think he was straight, do you?'

'I don't think his sexuality is relevant,' I said.

93

'Well, it might be, Tony. If him and his judge friend colluded to get Diana Cowper off the hook.'

'Is that why you asked if Weston was married? You think he's gay too?'

'It wouldn't surprise me. That sort look after their own.'

I was having to measure my words carefully. I was aware that suddenly, without warning, everything had changed. 'What are you talking about? What do you mean by "that sort"? You can't talk like that. Nobody talks like that any more.'

'Well, maybe I do.' He glared at me. 'I'm sure you've got lots of homosexual friends, you being a writer and working in TV. But speaking for myself, I don't like them. I think they're a load of pervs and if I walk into someone's house and I see a great big cock on the wall and find out they've got a pervy friend who put money into a pervy musical and who may have been persuaded to pervert the course of justice, then I'm going to speak my mind. Do you have a problem with that?'

'Yes. I do have a problem with that, actually. A very big problem.'

I couldn't believe what I was hearing. When I had first met him, Hawthorne had made one or two snide comments about the actors who would be performing in *Injustice* but for some reason it had never crossed my mind that he might be homophobic. And if that was what he was, there was no way I was going to write about him. He had said one thing that was true. I do have many close friends who are gay and if I made a hero out of Hawthorne, if I gave any space to his opinions, they probably wouldn't stay friends for long. I realised that I could be in terrible trouble. What about the critics? They would tear the book apart. Suddenly I saw my entire career disappearing down the plughole.

I walked away.

'Tony? Where are you going?' he called after me. He sounded genuinely surprised.

'I'm getting the tube home,' I said. 'I'll call you tomorrow.'

When I got to the end of the street, I glanced round. He was still standing there, watching me. He looked like an abandoned child.

Seven
Harrow-on-the-Hill

That night, I went to the National Theatre with my wife. I'd managed to get tickets for Danny Boyle's production of *Frankenstein* but I'm afraid I couldn't enjoy it. I wondered what Hawthorne would make of the actor, Jonny Lee Miller, who spent the first twenty minutes running around the stage, completely naked. We got home at about eleven thirty and my wife went straight to bed but I sat up late into the night, worrying about the book. I hadn't talked to her about it. I knew what she would say.

If I had sat down to write an original murder mystery story, I wouldn't have chosen anyone like Hawthorne as its main protagonist. I think the world has had quite enough of white, middle-aged, grumpy detectives and I'd have tried to think up something more unusual. A blind detective, a drunk detective, an OCD detective, a psychic detective . . . they'd all been done but how about a detective who was all four of those things? Actually, I'd have preferred a female detective, someone like Sarah Lund in *The Killing*. I'd have been much happier with someone who was younger, feistier, more independent, with or without the chunky jerseys. I'd also have given her a sense of humour.

Hawthorne was undoubtedly clever. I'd been impressed by the way his mind worked when we were together at the house in Britannia Road, and he'd quickly been proved right about the cleaner and the stolen money. And, for that matter, the disappearing cat. Detective Inspector Meadows might not have been pleased to see him but I had got the sense that there was a grudging respect and someone high up in the Metropolitan Police clearly had a high opinion of him too. *You got a new puppy!* I remembered how quickly he had pinned me down – where I'd been, what I was doing. He was clever all right. He might even be brilliant.

The trouble was, I didn't like him very much and that made the book almost impossible to write. The relationship between an author and his main protagonist is a very peculiar one. Take Alex Rider, for example. I'd been writing about him for over ten years and although I sometimes envied him (he never aged, everyone liked him, he had saved the world a dozen times) I was always fond of him and eager to get back to my desk to follow his adventures. Of course, he was my creation. I controlled him and made sure that I pressed all the right buttons for a young audience. He didn't smoke. He didn't swear. He didn't have a gun. And he certainly wasn't homophobic.

That was what was preying on my mind: Hawthorne's reaction to Raymond Clunes. I really had been shocked by what he had said outside the house. I didn't even understand why he'd opened up to me in that way when he was so secretive about everything else.

There are some people who argue that we are too sensitive these days, that because we're so afraid of causing offence, we no longer engage in any serious sort of argument at all. But that's how it is. It's why political chat-shows on television have become so very boring. There are narrow lines between which all public conversations have to take place and even a single poorly chosen word can bring all sorts of trouble down on your head.

I remember once that I was asked about gay marriage on a radio programme. This was at a time when a Christian husband and wife with a hotel in Cornwall had refused to give a room to a gay couple. I was careful. To begin with, I made it clear that I was one hundred per cent in favour of gay marriage and that I didn't agree with the hotel owners at all. However, having established that, I went on to say that we should try to understand their point of view, which was at least based on some sort of religious conviction (even if I didn't share it), and that perhaps they didn't deserve the hate mail and the death threats they had received. We need to tolerate intolerance. I thought that was a neat encapsulation of what I believed.

It didn't prevent a torrent of abuse hitting my Twitter feed. A couple of teachers wrote to me to say that my books would never appear in their schools again. Someone else thought all my books should be burned. These days, the world sees things in black and white, so although it may be all right for a twenty-first-century novelist to create a character who is homophobic, it will be much more sensible if that character is palpably vile, the villain of the piece.

Sitting in my office, gazing out of the window at the red lights twinkling on the cranes that had sprung up all over Farringdon during the construction of Crossrail, I asked myself if I could continue working with Hawthorne. What had drawn me into this in the first place and what possible benefit could I get from pursuing it any further? It would be much better to drop him now, before I was fully committed, and get on with other things. It was past midnight now and I was getting tired. *The Meaning of Treason* by Rebecca West, the book I was supposed to be reading, lay face down next to my computer. I reached out and dragged it towards me. That was where I should be spending my time. The 1940s were so much safer.

And that was when my phone pinged. I looked down at the screen. It was a text from Hawthorne.

Unico Cafe
Harrow on the Hill
9.30am. Breakfast.

Harrow-on-the-Hill was where the Godwins lived. He was telling me that that was where he was going next.

I really wanted to know who had killed Diana Cowper. That was the truth of it. Like it or not, I was involved. I had stood in her living room and I had got a sense of how she had lived . . . and died. I had seen the stain on the carpet. I wanted to know who had sent her that letter and if it was the same person who had taken her cat. Hawthorne had told me that she knew she was going to die. How was that possible and if it was the case, why hadn't she gone to the police? Most of all, I wanted to meet the Godwin family and Jeremy Godwin in particular – 'the boy who was lacerated'. One day I might come upon the solution to the mystery in a newspaper article. Hawthorne might even get someone else to write the book for him. But that wasn't good enough.

I wanted to be there myself.

It occurred to me that I could make up my own rules. Who had said that I had to write down everything exactly as it happened? There was absolutely no need to mention what Hawthorne had said about Raymond Clunes. For that matter, I could remove any reference to the black-and-white photograph and the other artwork that had sparked the whole thing off. In fact, I could describe him in any way I wanted. There was nothing to stop me making him younger, wittier, softer, more charming. It was my book! He wouldn't read it until it was published and by then it would be too late. He wouldn't care anyway, so long as it sold.

At the same time, I knew I couldn't do it. Hawthorne had approached me and he was what he was. If I changed him, it would be the first ripple in the pond, the start of a process that would shift everything back into the world of fiction. I could see myself reinventing all the people he spoke to and all the different places he went. That bloody Robert Mapplethorpe would be the first to go. What, then, would be the point? I might just as well go back to what I always did and make up the whole thing.

9.30 a.m. Harrow-on-the-Hill.

I was still holding my phone and I realised that there was only one way forward – although it would mean fundamentally changing the way I approached the book and, for that matter, my role in it. I didn't have to lie about Hawthorne. Nor did I need to protect him. He could look after himself. But I would challenge some of his attitudes . . . in fact it was my duty to do so. Otherwise, I'd be open to exactly the sort of criticism I feared.

I had just learned that he had a problem with gay men. Well, without in any way condoning it, I would explore why he felt that way and if as a result I came to understand him a little better, then surely nobody would complain. The book would be worthwhile.

It might be that he was gay himself. After all, when high-ranking politicians or clergymen have publicly spoken out against homosexuality, they've often turned out to be deep inside their own closets. I didn't want to expose him. Despite everything, I had no desire at all to hurt him. But suddenly I saw that I might have a purpose after all.

I would investigate the investigator.

I picked up my telephone and thumbed in three words:

See you there.

Then I went to bed.

The Unico café was just down the road from Harrow-on-the-Hill station, at the end of a dilapidated shopping parade,

near the railway line. Hawthorne had already ordered breakfast: eggs, bacon, toast and tea. It struck me that this was
the first time I'd ever seen him sitting down with a proper
meal. He ate warily, as if he was suspicious of what was in
front of him, cutting with a fast motion and then forking
the food into his mouth as quickly as possible to get rid of
it. He didn't seem to take any pleasure in what he ate. I
thought he might apologise for the way our last meeting had
ended but he just smiled at me. He wasn't at all surprised
that I'd turned up. I don't suppose it had occurred to him
that I wouldn't.

I slid behind the table opposite him and ordered a bacon
sandwich.

'How are you?' he asked.

'I'm all right.'

If I sounded distant, he didn't notice. 'I've been doing a
bit of work on the Godwin family,' he said. He talked while
he ate but somehow the food didn't get in the way of the
words. There was a notepad on the table next to him. 'The
father is Alan Godwin,' he went on. 'He's got his own business. He's an events organiser. His wife is Judith Godwin.
Works part-time for a kids' charity. They've only got the
one son. Jeremy Godwin is eighteen now. Brain damage.
According to the doctors, he needs full-time care – but that
could mean anything.'

'Can't you even feel slightly sorry for them?' I asked.

He looked up from his plate, puzzled. 'What makes you
think I don't?'

'Just the way you're rattling off the facts. "They've only

got the one son." Of course they have! The other one was killed. And as for the one who's still alive, you're already suggesting that he might be faking it or something.'

'I can see you got out of bed the wrong side.' He drank some tea. 'I don't know anything about Jeremy Godwin apart from what I've been told. But unless Diana Cowper made a mistake, it seems he may well have got out of his bed or out of his wheelchair and hiked down to Britannia Road on the night she died. And let's not forget that only yesterday, you were the one who was in a hurry to get up here. You'd got them all bang to rights: Alan Godwin, Judith Godwin and – if he was up to it – Jeremy Godwin. Correct me if I'm wrong.'

My bacon sandwich arrived. I didn't really feel like eating it. 'I'm just saying you could be a bit more sensitive about people.'

'Is that why you're here? Because you want to put your arms around the suspects and hold them close?'

'No. But—'

'You're here for the same reason as me. You want to know who killed Diana Cowper. If it was one of them, they'll be arrested. If it wasn't, we'll walk away and we'll never see them again. Either way, what we think about them, what we *feel* about them, doesn't make a sod of difference.'

He flicked over one of the pages. He had made the notes in handwriting that was very neat and precise, so small that I couldn't read it without my glasses. 'I've made a summary of the accident. If it won't upset you too much . . . an eight-year-old kid getting killed!'

'Go on,' I said.

'It's pretty much like Raymond Clunes told us. They were staying at the Royal Hotel in Deal . . . just the two brothers and a nanny, Mary O'Brien. They'd been on the beach all day and they were on their way back when the kids ran across the road to get ice-creams. The nanny got a bit of stick for that in court but she swore the road was clear. She was wrong. They were halfway across when a car came round the corner and slammed into them. It missed the nanny by inches, killed one kid, hurt the other, then drove off. There was quite a crowd, plenty of witnesses. If Diana Cowper hadn't turned herself in a couple of hours later, she'd have been in serious shit.'

'Do you think it was right she was acquitted?'

Hawthorne shrugged. 'You'd have to ask a brief.'

'She knew the judge.'

'She knew someone who knew the judge. Not the same thing.' He seemed to have forgotten that he had been suggesting a gay conspiracy only the day before. 'Judges know lots of people,' he added. 'It doesn't necessarily mean there was something nasty going on.'

We finished the breakfast in a moody silence. The waitress brought the bill. Hawthorne didn't look at it. He was expecting me to pay.

'That's another thing,' I said. 'So far, I notice that I've paid for every coffee and every taxi fare. If we're in this fifty-fifty, maybe we should split the expenses the same way.'

'All right!' He sounded genuinely surprised.

I was already regretting what I'd said. It was more a

reaction to what had happened the day before than a genuine desire to share costs. I watched as he took out his wallet and produced a ten-pound note so limp and crumpled that but for the colour I would have been unsure of its denomination. He laid it on the table like an autumn leaf that's been fished out of the gutter. There were no other notes in his wallet and even if my point had been justified, all I'd managed to do was to make myself seem petty and mean. That was just about the last time Hawthorne ever paid for anything, by the way. I never complained again.

We walked together from the café. I actually know Harrow-on-the-Hill quite well. We filmed quite a few scenes of *Foyle's War* there, with the old-fashioned high street doubling as Hastings'. It's amazing what a few seagulls added to the soundtrack can achieve. My first boarding school was nearby and it struck me how little the area had changed in fifty years. It was still a slightly improbable enclave, very green and unworldly, rising above the other north London suburbs that sprawled around.

'So what did you get up to last night?' I asked Hawthorne, as we continued on our way.

'What?'

'I just wondered what you did. Did you go out for dinner? Did you work on the case?' He didn't answer, so I added, 'It's for the book.'

'I had dinner. I made some notes. I went to bed.'

But what did he eat? Who did he go to bed with? Did he watch TV? Did he even own a TV?

He wasn't going to tell me and there wasn't time to ask.

We had arrived at a Victorian house on Roxborough Avenue, three storeys high, built out of those dark red bricks that always make me think of Charles Dickens. It was set back from the main road with a gravel path and a double garage and from the very first sight it struck me that I had never seen a building that exuded a greater sense of misery – from the scrawny, half-wild garden to the peeling paintwork, the window boxes with dead flowers, the blank, unlit windows.

This was the home of the Godwins . . . or, at least, the three members of the family who had survived.

Eight
Damaged Goods

One of my favourite screenwriters is Nigel Kneale, the inventor of the eccentric Professor Quatermass. He wrote a chilling television play, *The Stone Tape*, which suggested that the very fabric of a house, the bricks and mortar, might be able to absorb and 'play back' the various emotions, including the horrors, that it had witnessed. I was reminded of it as I entered the Godwins' home on Roxborough Avenue. It was an expensive house. Any property of this size in Harrow-on-the-Hill would have been worth a couple of million pounds. And yet the hall was cold – colder perhaps than it was outside – and poorly lit. It was crying out for redecoration. The carpets were a little threadbare with too many stains. There was a sense of something in the air that might have been damp or dry rot but was actually just misery, recorded and re-recorded until the memory bank was full.

The door had been opened by a woman in her fifties. She would have been about ten or fifteen years younger than Diana Cowper at the time of her death. She looked at us suspiciously, as if we had come to sell her something; in fact her entire body language was defensive. This was Judith Godwin. I could easily imagine her working for a charity. She had a brittle quality, as if she needed charity herself, but knew that she would never get it. The tragedy that had changed her life was still with her. When she asked you for help or for money it would always be personal.

'You're Hawthorne?' she asked.

'It's very good to meet you.' Hawthorne actually sounded as if he meant it and I saw that he had undergone another of his transformations. He had been hard with Andrea Kluvánek, coldly matter-of-fact with Raymond Clunes, but now it was a polite and accommodating Hawthorne who presented himself to Judith Godwin. 'Thank you for seeing us.'

'Would you like to come into the kitchen? I'll make us some coffee.'

Hawthorne hadn't explained who I was and nor did she seem interested. We followed her into a room on the other side of the stairs. The kitchen was warmer but it was also drab and dated. It's funny how much white goods tell you about a house and its owners. The fridge would have been expensive when it was installed but that was too long ago. The panels had a yellowy sheen, pockmarked with magnets and old Post-it notes containing recipes, telephone numbers, emergency addresses. The oven was greasy and the dishwasher worn out with overuse. There was a washing machine, grinding slowly round, murky water lapping at the window. The room was clean and tidy but it needed money spent on it. A

Weimaraner with mangy fur and a grey muzzle lay half-asleep in the corner but thumped its tail as we came in.

Hawthorne and I sat down at an uncomfortably large pine table while Judith Godwin plucked a percolator out of the sink, washed it under the tap and set about making coffee. She talked to us as she worked. I could see she was the sort of woman who never did just one thing at a time. 'You wanted to talk to me about Diana Cowper.'

'I assume you've spoken to the police.'

'Very briefly.' She went to the fridge and took out a plastic carton of milk, sniffed it, dumped it on the counter. 'They telephoned me. They asked me if I had seen her.'

'And had you?'

She turned round, her eyes defiant. 'Not in ten years.' Again, she busied herself, now putting biscuits on a plate. 'Why would I want to see her? Why would I want to go anywhere near her?'

Hawthorne shrugged. 'I wouldn't have thought you'd have been too sorry to hear she had died.'

Judith Godwin stopped what she was doing. 'Mr Hawthorne. Who exactly did you say you were?'

'I'm helping the police. This is a very delicate matter and obviously there are all sorts of ramifications. So they called me in.'

'You're a private detective?'

'A consultant.'

'And your friend?'

'I'm working with him,' I said. It was simple and true and begged no further questions.

'Are you suggesting I killed her?'

'Not at all.'

'You're asking if I saw her. You're suggesting I'm glad she's dead.' The kettle had boiled. She hurried over to flick it off. 'Well, on that second point, I am. She destroyed my life. She destroyed my family's life. One second behind the wheel of a car she shouldn't have been driving and she killed my child and took everything away from me. I'm a Christian. I go to church. I've tried to forgive her. But I'd be lying to you if I said that I wasn't glad when I heard someone had murdered her. It may be a sin and it may be wrong of me but it's nothing less than she deserved.'

I watched her make the coffee in silence. She attacked the percolator, the mugs and the milk jug as if she was taking out her anger on them. She carried a tray over to the table and sat down opposite us. 'What else do you want to know?' she demanded.

'I want to know everything you can tell us,' Hawthorne said. 'Why don't you start with the accident?'

'The accident? You're talking about what happened to my two sons in Deal.' She smiled briefly, bitterly. 'It's such a simple word, isn't it. An accident. It's like when you spill the milk or bump into another car. I was in town when they rang me and that's what they said. "I'm afraid there's been an accident." And even then I thought that maybe something had happened at the house or at work. I didn't think that my Timmy was lying in the morgue and that my other boy was never going to have a normal life.'

'Why weren't you with them?'

'I was at a conference. I was working for Shelter at the time and there was a two-day event in Westminster. My husband was in Manchester on a business trip.' She paused. 'We're not together any more. You can blame that on the accident too. It was half-term and we decided to send the boys on a trip with their nanny. She took them to the coast, to Deal. The hotel had a special offer. That's the only reason we chose it. The boys couldn't have been more excited. Castles and beaches and the tunnels up at Ramsgate. Timmy had a wonderful imagination. Everything in his life was an adventure.'

She poured three cups of coffee. She left us to add the sugar and the milk.

'Mary, the nanny, had been with us for just over a year and she was absolutely wonderful. We trusted her completely – and although we went over and over what had happened, we never thought for a minute that it was her fault. The police and all the witnesses agreed. She's still with us now.'

'She looks after Jeremy?'

'Yes.' Judith let the word hang in the air. 'She felt responsible,' she went on. 'When Jeremy finally came out of hospital, she found she couldn't leave him. And so she stayed.' Another pause. She had to make an effort to revisit the past. 'The three of them had been on the beach. They'd been paddling. It was a nice day but it wasn't warm enough to swim. The road runs right next to the beach. There's just a low sea wall and a promenade. The children saw an ice-cream shop and although Mary shouted out to them, they ran across. I've never understood why they did that. They were only eight years old but they usually had more sense.

'Even so, Mrs Cowper should have been able to stop. She had plenty of time. But she wasn't wearing her glasses and she just ploughed right into them. As we discovered later, she could barely see from one side of the road to the other. She shouldn't have been driving. And as a result, Timmy was killed immediately. Jeremy was flung into the air. He had terrible head injuries but he survived.'

'Mary wasn't hurt?'

'She was very lucky. She had run forward to grab hold of the boys. The car missed her by inches. This all came out in the trial, Mr Hawthorne. Mrs Cowper didn't stop. Later on, she told the police that she had panicked, but you have to ask yourself what sort of woman does that, leaving two children in the road!'

'She went home to her son.'

'That's right. Damian Cowper. He's quite a well-known actor now and he was staying with her at the time. The Crown lawyers said that she was trying to protect him as much as herself. He was still at drama school and she didn't want his name dragged into the press. If that's true, then the two of them are as bad as each other. Anyway, she turned herself in later that same day – but only because she had no choice. There were lots of witnesses and she knew that her number plate had been seen. You'd have thought the judge would have taken that into consideration when it came to sentencing but it didn't seem to make any difference. She walked free.'

She picked up the plate of biscuits and offered me one. 'No, thank you,' I said, at the same time thinking how bizarre it was that she should manage to do something so homely, so banal, in the middle of such a conversation. But I guessed that was how she was. She had lived the last ten years in the shadow of what had happened in Deal until, for her, it had become the new normality. It was as if she had been locked up in a lunatic asylum for so long that she had forgotten she was actually mad.

'I know this is painful for you, Mrs Godwin,' Hawthorne said. 'But when exactly did you and your husband split up?'

'It's not painful, Mr Hawthorne. It's actually the opposite. I'm not sure I've felt anything since I answered the telephone that day. I think that's what this sort of thing does to you. You go to work. Or you go to visit friends. Or maybe you're having a lovely holiday and everything seems to be completely perfect and then something like this happens and a sort of disbelief kicks in. I never actually believed it. Even when I was at Timmy's funeral, I kept on waiting for someone to tap me on the shoulder and tell me to wake up. You see, I had two gorgeous twins. The boys were just perfect in every way. I was happily married. Alan's business was going well. We'd just bought this house . . . the year before. You never realise how fragile everything is until it breaks. And that day it was all smashed.

'Alan and I blamed ourselves for not being there, for letting the boys go in the first place. He was on business in Manchester. I think I told you that. There had been a certain amount of strain between us. Any marriage is difficult,

115

particularly when you're bringing up twins, but our marriage was never the same after we lost Timmy and although we got counselling, although we did everything we could, we had to face up to the truth, which was that it wasn't working any more. He moved out over a month ago, as a matter of fact. I don't think it's fair to say we split up though. We just couldn't bear to be together.'

'Can you tell me where I can find him? It might be useful to have a word.'

She scribbled on a sheet of paper and handed it to Hawthorne. 'This is his mobile number. You can call him if you want to. He's living in a flat in Victoria until we sell here.' She stopped. She might not have meant to give us this information. 'Alan's business hasn't gone very well recently,' she explained. 'We can't keep this house up so we're putting it on the market. We only stayed here because of Jeremy. It's his home. Because of his injuries, we thought it was better for him to be somewhere he knew.'

Hawthorne nodded. I always knew when he was about to go on the attack. It was as if someone had waved a knife in front of his face and I had seen it reflected, for an instant, in his eyes. 'You say you haven't seen Diana Cowper. Do you know if your husband approached her?'

'He didn't tell me that he had. I can't imagine why he would.'

'And you weren't anywhere near her home on Monday of last week? The day she died?'

'I've already told you. No.'

Hawthorne rocked his head briefly from side to side. 'But you were in South Kensington.'

'I'm sorry?'

'You came out of South Kensington station at half past four in the afternoon.'

'How do you know?'

'I've been looking at the CCTV footage, Mrs Godwin. Are you going to deny it?'

'Of course I'm not going to deny it. Are you telling me that's where Diana Cowper lived?' Hawthorne didn't answer. 'I had no idea. I thought she was still living in Kent. I went shopping on the King's Road. The estate agent wants me to buy a few things for the house, to cheer it up. I went to some of the furniture shops.'

It didn't sound very likely to me. The house was run-down and it was obvious that Judith Godwin had no money. It was the reason she was selling. Did she really think a few expensive items of furniture would make any difference?

'Did your husband mention that he'd written to Mrs Cowper?'

'He wrote to her? I don't know anything about that. You'll have to ask him.'

'What about Jeremy?' She stiffened when Hawthorne spoke his name, and he went on, quickly. 'You said that he lives with you.'

'Yes.'

'Could he have approached her?'

She thought for a moment and I wondered if she was going to ask us to leave. But once again she was calm, matter-of-fact. 'I'm sure you know that my son received severe injuries when he was eight years old, Mr Hawthorne. The lacerations occurred in the temporal and occipital lobes of the brain which control, respectively, memory, language and emotions and vision. He's eighteen now, but he will never be able to have a normal life. He has a number of issues, which include short-term and working memory loss, aphasia and limited concentration. He requires and receives full-time care.'

She paused.

'He does leave the house – but never on his own. Any suggestion that he might approach Mrs Cowper to speak to her or to do her harm is as ridiculous as it is offensive.'

'Nonetheless,' Hawthorne said, 'just before she was murdered, Mrs Cowper sent a rather strange text message. If I understand her correctly, she claims to have seen your son.'

'Then perhaps you haven't understood her correctly.'

'She was fairly specific. Do you know where he was last Monday?'

'Yes, of course I know where he was. He was upstairs. He's upstairs now. He doesn't often leave his room and certainly never on his own.'

The door opened behind us and a young woman came into the kitchen, dressed in jeans and a loose-fitting jersey. I knew at once that this was Mary O'Brien. She somehow had the look and the manner of a nanny, with a sort of seriousness about her, thick arms crossed over her chest, a plump face, very straight black hair. She was about thirty-five, so would have been in her mid-twenties when the accident occurred.

'I'm sorry, Judith,' she said. Her Irish accent was immediately distinctive. 'I didn't know you had company.'

'That's all right, Mary. This is Mr Hawthorne and . . .'

'Anthony,' I said.

'They're asking questions about Diana Cowper.'

'Oh.' Mary's face fell. Her eyes flicked back to the door. Perhaps she was wondering if she could leave. Perhaps she was wishing that she had never come in.

'They may want to talk to you about what happened in Deal.'

Mary nodded. 'I'll tell you whatever it is you want to know,' she said. 'Although, heaven knows, I've gone over it a thousand times.' She sat down at the table. She had lived here so long that she was on equal terms with Judith. She treated the house as her own. At the same time, though, Judith got up and moved to the other side of the room and I wondered if, after all, there might be some tension between them.

'So how can I help you?' Mary asked.

'You can tell us what happened that day,' Hawthorne said. 'I know you've said it all before but it may help us, hearing it from you.'

'All right.' Mary composed herself. Judith watched from the side. 'We'd come off the beach. I'd promised the boys they could have an ice-cream before we went back to the hotel. We were staying at the Royal Hotel, which was just a short distance away. The boys had been told never to cross the road without holding my hand and normally they never would have – but they were overtired. They weren't thinking straight. They saw the ice-cream shop and they got excited and before I knew what had happened, they were running across.

'I ran after them, trying to grab them. At the same time, I saw the car coming – a blue Volkswagen. I was sure it would stop. But it didn't. Before I could reach them, the car had hit them. I saw Timothy knocked to one side and Jeremy flying through the air. I was convinced he would be the worst hurt of the two.' She glanced at her employer. 'I hate going over this in front of you, Judith.'

'It's all right, Mary. They need to know.'

'The car came screeching to a halt. It would have been about twenty yards further up the road. I was sure the driver was going to get out but she didn't. Instead, she suddenly accelerated and drove off down the road.'

'Did you actually see Mrs Cowper behind the wheel?'

'No. I only saw the back of her head and even that didn't really register with me. I was in shock.'

'Go on.'

'There's not very much more to tell. A whole crowd of people seemed to appear from nowhere very quickly. There was a chemist's next to the ice-cream shop and the owner was the first to arrive. His name was Traverton. He was very helpful.'

'How about the people from the ice-cream shop?' Hawthorne asked.

'It was closed,' Judith said and there was a bitter quality to her voice.

'It somehow makes it even worse that the boys hadn't noticed,' Mary agreed. 'The shop was closed anyway. But there was just a small sign in the door and they hadn't seen it.'

'What happened next?'

'The police arrived. An ambulance came. They took us to hospital . . . all three of us. All I wanted to do was ask about the boys but I wasn't their mother and they wouldn't tell me. I got them to call Judith . . . and Alan. It was only when they finally got there that I found out.'

'How long did it take the police to find Diana Cowper?'

'Her son drove her to the police station in Deal two hours later. She would never have got away with it. One of the witnesses had seen her registration number so they knew who the car belonged to.'

'Did you see her again?'

Mary nodded. 'I saw her at the trial. I didn't speak to her.'

'And you haven't seen her since?'

'No. Why would I want to? She's the last person in the world I'd want to see.'

'Someone murdered her last week.'

'Are you implying I did it? That's ridiculous. I didn't even know where she lived.'

I didn't believe her. It's easy enough to find anyone's address these days. And she was certainly hiding something. Looking at her more closely, I realised Mary O'Brien was more attractive than I had first thought. There was a freshness about her, a lack of sophistication, that made her very appealing. At the same time, though, I didn't trust her. I got the feeling that she wasn't telling us the whole truth.

'Mr Hawthorne thinks that Jeremy might have visited that woman on his own,' Judith Godwin said.

'That's completely impossible. He never goes anywhere on his own.'

Hawthorne wasn't even slightly fazed. 'That may be the case. But you might as well know that, just before she was murdered, Mrs Cowper sent a rather strange text message which suggested she had seen him.' He rounded on the nanny. 'Were the two of you here on Monday the ninth?'

Mary didn't hesitate. 'Yes.'

'You didn't accompany Mrs Godwin on her shopping trip to South Kensington?'

'Jeremy hates shops. It's a nightmare buying him clothes.'

'Why don't you talk to him?' Judith suggested. Mary looked surprised. 'It's the easiest way to show them.' Judith turned back to Hawthorne. 'You can ask him some questions if you want to, although I would ask you to be a little more sensitive. He gets upset very easily.'

I was as surprised as the nanny but I suppose it was the easiest way to get rid of us. Hawthorne nodded and Judith took us up. The stairs creaked underneath our feet. The further up we went, the older and dowdier the house seemed to be. We reached the first floor and crossed a landing into what might once have been the master bedroom, with views out onto Roxborough Avenue. It had been given over to Jeremy, who had his bed-sitting room here. Judith knocked on the door and took us in without waiting for an answer.

'Jeremy?' she said. 'There are two people who want to see you.'

'Who are they?' The boy had his back to us.

'They're just friends of mine. They want to talk to you.'

Jeremy Godwin had been sitting in front of a computer when we came in. He was playing a game – Mortal Kombat,

I think. Hearing him speak, it was immediately obvious that something was wrong. His words were half formed, coming as if from the other side of a wall. He was overweight, with long black hair that he hadn't brushed, and wore baggy jeans and a thick, shapeless sweater. The bedroom was decorated with Everton football posters and an Everton quilt on the bed, which was a double. Everything was well looked after but still seemed shabby, as if it had somehow been left behind. Jeremy came to the end of a level in his game and hit the Pause button. As he turned to face us, I saw a round face, thick lips, a wispy beard around his cheeks. The brain damage was painfully evident in brown eyes which showed no curiosity and simply didn't connect with us. I knew he was eighteen but he looked older.

'Who are you?' he asked.

'I'm Hawthorne. I'm a friend of your mum's.'

'My mum doesn't have many friends.'

'I'm sure that's not true.' Hawthorne looked around him. 'You've got a nice room, Jeremy.'

'It's not my room any more. We're selling it.'

'We'll find somewhere just as nice for you,' Mary said. She had brushed past us and sat down on the bed.

'I wish we didn't have to go.'

'Do you want to ask him anything?' Judith was standing by the door, anxious for us to be on our way.

'Do you go out a lot, Jeremy?' Hawthorne asked.

I couldn't see any point in the question. This young man would never be able to take himself off into the centre of London. Nor did he seem to have a shred of aggression

123

about him. The accident had taken that from him, along with the rest of his life.

'I go out sometimes,' Jeremy replied.

'But not on your own,' Mary added.

'Sometimes,' he contradicted her. 'I went to see my dad.'

'We put you in a taxi and he met you at the other end.'

'Have you ever been to South Kensington?' Hawthorne asked.

'I've been there lots of times.'

'He doesn't know where it is,' his mother said, quietly.

I couldn't stay here any more and quietly backed away, for once taking the initiative. Hawthorne followed me out. Judith Godwin took the two of us downstairs.

'It's a credit to the nanny that she stayed with you,' Hawthorne said. He sounded impressed but I knew he was digging for more information.

'Mary was devoted to the boys and after the accident she refused to leave. I've been glad to have her here. It's very important for Jeremy to have continuity.' There was a coldness in her voice and I was aware of something being unsaid.

'Will she stay with you when you move?'

'We haven't discussed it.'

We reached the front door. She opened it. 'I'd prefer it if you didn't come back,' she said. 'Jeremy hates disruption and he finds strangers very difficult. I wanted you to see him so you'd understand how he is. But we have nothing to do with what happened to Diana Cowper. The police clearly don't believe we're involved. We really have nothing more to say.'

'Thank you,' Hawthorne said. 'You've been very helpful.'
We left. The door closed behind us.

The moment we were outside, Hawthorne took out a packet of cigarettes and lit one. I knew how he felt. I was glad to be out in the open air.

'Why didn't you show her the letter?' I asked.

'What?' He shook the match, extinguishing it.

'I was surprised that you didn't show her the letter that Diana Cowper received. The one you got from Andrea Kluvánek. Maybe Judith wrote it. Or her husband. She might have recognised the writing.'

He shrugged. His thoughts were elsewhere. 'That poor little sod,' he muttered.

'It's a horrible thing to have happened,' I said. And I meant it. My two sons insist on cycling in London. They often forget to put on their helmets and I shout at them – but what can I do? They're in their late twenties. For me, Jeremy Godwin was the embodiment of a nightmare I tried not to have.

'I've got a son,' Hawthorne said, abruptly, answering the question I'd put to him about twenty-four hours before.

'How old is he?'

'Eleven.' Hawthorne was upset, his thoughts elsewhere. But before I could ask anything more, he suddenly turned on me. 'And he doesn't read your fucking books.'

Pinching the cigarette between his fingers, he raised it to his lips, then walked away. I followed.

As we went, something strange happened. Maybe it was some instinct or maybe a movement caught my eye but I realised that we were being watched. I turned round and looked at the house we had just left. Someone had been standing in the window of Jeremy Godwin's room, staring down at us, but before I could see who it was, they had backed away.

Nine

Star Power

As we walked back to the tube station together, Hawthorne received a call on his mobile phone. He answered it but didn't give his name. He just listened for about half a minute and then rang off.

'We're going to Brick Lane,' he said.

'Why?'

'The prodigal son has returned. Damian Cowper is back in London. It must have been difficult for him, fitting it into his busy diary. His mum's been dead for over a week.'

I thought about what he had just said. 'Who was that?' I asked.

'What?'

'On the phone.'

'What does it matter?'

'I'd just be interested to know where you're getting your information.' Hawthorne didn't answer, so I went on. 'You knew that Judith Godwin was at South Kensington station. Someone gave you access to the CCTV footage. You also knew about Andrea Kluvánek's criminal record. For an ex-policeman, you seem to be remarkably well informed.'

He gave me the look that he did so well, as if I'd surprised and offended him at the same time. 'It's not important,' he said.

'It is important. If I'm writing this book about you, I can't just have information being pulled out of thin air. Tell me you meet someone in a garage and we'll call him Deep Throat if you like. No. Forget that. I need the truth. You've obviously got someone helping you. Who is it?'

We were walking through the village and passed a group of Harrow schoolboys wearing their uniforms: blue jackets, ties, straw boaters. 'I wonder if they realise they look like complete wankers,' Hawthorne said.

'They look fine. And don't change the subject.'

'All right.' He frowned. 'It was my old DCI. I'm not going to give you his name. He wasn't too happy about what happened, the way I got blamed for what wasn't my fault. In fact, he knew it was a load of bollocks and anyway he needed me. I mean, you've met Meadows. If you added up the IQ of half the officers in the murder squad, you still wouldn't reach three figures. He brought me in as a consultant and he's been using me ever since.'

'How many of you are there, working for the police?'

'There's only me,' Hawthorne said. 'There are other consultants but they don't get results. A total waste of time.' He spoke without malice.

'Brick Lane . . .' I said.

'Damian Cowper flew in yesterday, business class from

L.A. His girlfriend is with him. Her name's Grace Lovell. They've got a kid.'

'You didn't mention he had a child.'

'I mentioned he had a cocaine habit. From what I'm told, that matters to him more. He's also got a flat in Brick Lane, which is where we're heading now.'

We had passed Harrow School and headed back down the hill towards the station. I was beginning to worry about my role in all this. I was simply following Hawthorne around London, which reminded me that I wasn't feeling comfortable with the shape of the book. From Britannia Road to the funeral parlour, then South Acton, Marble Arch, Harrow-on-the-Hill and, next up, Brick Lane . . . it felt more like an A to Z of London than a murder mystery.

I was annoyed that we seemed to have drawn a complete blank with Jeremy Godwin. Diana Cowper had texted that she had seen him but there was no way he could have crossed the city on his own, certainly not to commit a violent and well-planned murder. But if he hadn't strangled her, who had? If I were in control of events I would have introduced the killer by now but I wasn't at all certain that we had met anyone yet who fitted the bill.

There was something else preying on my mind. I hadn't mentioned any of this to my literary agent, who was confidently expecting me to turn up with an idea for the next book after *The House of Silk*. I knew I was going to have to confront her sooner or later and I had a feeling she wouldn't be pleased.

We took the tube to Brick Lane. We had to cross London

all the way from west to east and it would have taken for ever in a taxi. The carriage was almost empty as we sat down facing each other, and just as the doors slid shut, Hawthorne leaned forward and asked: 'Have you got a title yet?'

'A title?'

'For the book!' So he'd been thinking about it too.

'It's much too early,' I told him. 'First of all, you've got to solve the crime. Then I'll have a better idea what I'm writing about.'

'Don't you think of the title first?'

'Not really. No.'

I've never found it easy coming up with titles. Almost two hundred thousand books are published in the UK every year and although some of them will have the advantage of a well-known author attached, the vast majority have just two or three words on a surface measuring no more than six by nine inches to sell themselves. Titles have to be short, smart and meaningful, easy to read, easy to remember and original. That's asking a lot.

Many of the best titles are simply borrowed from else-where. *Brave New World*, *The Grapes of Wrath*, *Of Mice and Men*, *Vanity Fair* . . . all of these were drawn from other works. Agatha Christie used the Bible, Shakespeare, Tennyson and even *The Rubaiyat of Omar Khayyam* for many of her eighty-two titles. For my money, nobody has beaten Ian Fleming: *From Russia, with Love*; *You Only Live Twice*; *Live and Let Die*. His titles have passed into the English language although even he didn't find it easy. *Live and Let Die* was almost published as 'The Undertaker's Wind'. *Moonraker* was 'The Moonraker Secret', 'The Moonraker Plot', 'The Moonraker Plan' and even, for a short time, 'Mondays Are Hell', while *Goldfinger* began life as 'The Richest Man in the World'.

I didn't have a title for my new book. I wasn't even sure I had a book.

Hawthorne and I didn't speak for a long while. I let my thoughts wander as I watched the various stations rush past: Wembley Park, West Hampstead and then Baker Street, its tiled walls picking out the silhouette of Sherlock Holmes. Now there was another master of the title, although Conan Doyle often had second thoughts too. Would *A Study in Scarlet* have struck such a chord if it had remained as 'A Tangled Skein'?

'I was thinking of "Hawthorne Investigates",' Hawthorne said, suddenly.

'I'm sorry?'

'For the book.' The carriage had got more crowded. He crossed over and sat next to me. 'The first one anyway. I think all of them should have my name on the cover.'

It had never occurred to me that he was thinking of a series. I have to say, my blood ran cold.

'I don't like it,' I said.

'Why not?'

I searched for a reason. 'It's a bit old-fashioned.'

'Is it?'

'*Parker Pyne Investigates*. That's Agatha Christie. *Hetty Wainthropp Investigates*. It's been done before.'

'Yeah. Well.' He nodded. 'I'll come up with something.'

'No, you won't,' I said. 'It's my book. I'll think of the title.'

'It's got to be a good one,' he said. 'To be honest with you, I don't much like *The House of Silk.*'

I'd forgotten I'd even mentioned it to him. '*The House of Silk* is a great title,' I exclaimed. 'It's a perfect title. It sounds like a Sherlock Holmes story and it's what the whole plot is about. The publisher likes it so much, he's even going to put a white ribbon in the book.' I'd been shouting above the roar of the train but I suddenly realised we'd stopped. We were sitting in Euston Square. The other passengers were looking at me.

'No need to be touchy, mate. I'm just trying to help.'

The doors slid shut and we were carried once again into the darkness.

In fact, I already knew quite a bit about Damian Cowper. I'd googled him the night before. Generally, I avoid Wikipedia. It's very helpful if you know what you're looking for but it contains so much misinformation that a writer, trying to appear authoritative, can all too easily fall flat on his face. More than that, I could imagine a successful actor doctoring his own entry, so preferred to look elsewhere. Fortunately, Damian had been the subject of quite a few newspaper articles, allowing me to stitch together his history.

He left the Royal Academy of Dramatic Art – RADA – in 1999 and had been snapped up by Hamilton Hodell, one of the major talent agencies, whose clients include Tilda Swinton, Mark Rylance, and Stephen Fry. For the next two years, he played a series of parts with the Royal Shakespeare Company: Ariel in *The Tempest*, Malcolm in *Macbeth*, the title role in *Henry V*. After that he moved into television, starting with the BBC conspiracy thriller *State of Play*, which aired in 2003. He won his first BAFTA nomination for his role in *Bleak House*, another BBC drama, and in the same year picked up the Emerging Talent Award at the Evening Standard Theatre Awards for his performance as Algernon in *The Importance of Being Earnest*. It was rumoured that he turned down the opportunity to play Doctor Who (David Tennant was cast instead) but by now his career was taking off in films. He had been directed by Woody Allen in *Match Point* and followed this with *Prince Caspian*, two of the Harry Potter films, *The Social Network* and, in 2009, the reboot of *Star Trek*. He moved to Hollywood that year and was cast in two seasons of *Mad Men*. There was also a pilot that wasn't picked up. Finally he'd been given the lead role in a new series, *Homeland*, with Claire Danes and Mandy Patinkin, which had been about to start shooting when his mother died.

I'm not sure at what stage he'd been able to afford a two-bedroom flat on Brick Lane but this was where he lived when he was in London. It was on the second floor of a warehouse that had been carefully converted to show off its original features: stripped wooden floors, exposed beams, old-fashioned radiators and lots of brickwork. My first impressions of the vast, double-height living room was that it looked almost fake, like a television set. There were different living areas with an industrial-style kitchen stage left, then a seating area with vintage leather sofas and armchairs around a coffee table, and finally a raised platform with glass doors leading out to a roof terrace: I could see lots of terra-cotta pots and a gas barbecue on the other side. A Wurlitzer jukebox stood against the far wall. It had been beautifully renovated, with polished aluminium and neon lights. A spiral staircase led up to the next floor.

Damian Cowper was waiting for us when we arrived, perched on a bar stool beside the kitchen counter. There was something that wasn't quite real about him too: the languid pose, the shirt with its wide collar open at the neck, the gold chain resting against the chest hair, the tan. He could have been posing for the front cover of a fashion magazine. He was remarkably handsome – and probably knew it – with jet-black hair swept back, intense blue eyes and exactly the right amount of designer stubble. He looked tired, which might have been jet-lag, but I was aware he had spent much of the day being interviewed by the police. There was also a funeral to arrange – or, at least, to attend. The arrange-ments, of course, had all been made for him.

He had opened the door for us using an intercom and he was talking on his mobile as he waved us in. 'Yeah, yeah. Look. I'll get back to you. I have people here. Look after yourself, babe. I'll see you.'

He rang off.

'Hi. I'm sorry about that. I only got back yesterday and, as you can imagine, it's a bit crazy around here.' He had just enough of a transatlantic accent to be annoying. I remem-bered what Hawthorne had told me about money problems, girlfriends, drugs, and I decided at once that I believed him. Everything about Damian Cowper made my hackles rise.

We shook hands.

'You want a coffee?' Damian asked. He pointed at the sofa, inviting us to sit down.

'Thank you.'

He had one of those machines that take capsules and spin the milk round in a metal cylinder to froth it up. 'I can't tell you what a nightmare this whole thing has been. My poor mum! I spoke to the police for a long time yesterday afternoon – and again this morning. When they told me the news, I couldn't believe it . . . not at first.' He stopped himself. 'I'll tell you anything you want to know. Anything I can do to help you catch the bastard who did this . . .'

'When did you last see your mother?' Hawthorne asked.

'It was the last time I was over, in December.' Damian opened the fridge and took out some milk. 'She wanted to spend time with the baby – she has a granddaughter – and it's easier for us to come here. I had some stuff to do anyway so we spent Christmas together. She and Grace get on really well. I'm glad they were able to get to know each other a bit better.'

'You and your mum were close.' Even as Hawthorne spoke there was a glint of something in his eye that suggested he thought otherwise.

'Yeah. Of course we were. I mean, it wasn't easy for her when I moved to America but she was a hundred per cent behind my work. She was proud of what I was doing and, you know, with Dad dying a long time ago and her never remarrying, I think my success meant a lot to her.' He had made two coffees, drawing a pattern across the foam even as he reminisced about his dead father. He glanced down at his work, then handed the cups over, adding: 'I can't tell you how gutted I was when I heard about it.'

'She died over a week ago,' Hawthorne remarked, without any particular rancour.

'I had things to deal with. We're rehearsing a new show. I had to shut down the house and get the dog looked after.'

'You've got a dog. That's nice.'

'It's a labradoodle.'

It was that last remark that made me wonder if the concerned, caring, recently bereaved Damian Cowper might not be quite as sincere as he seemed. It wasn't just that his new show had come first in his list of priorities. He wanted us to know the breed of his dog – as if it might somehow help the investigation into his mother's brutal murder.

'How often did the two of you speak?' Hawthorne asked.

'Once a week.' He paused. 'Well, once a fortnight, anyway. She used to come in here and check the place out for me, water the plants on the terrace and all the rest of it. She forwarded my mail.' He shrugged. 'We didn't always speak. She was busy and the time difference didn't help. We did lots of texts and emails.'

'She texted you the day she died,' I said.

'Yes. I told the police about that. She said she was afraid.'

'Do you know what she meant by that?'

'She was referring to that kid, the one who got hurt in Deal—'

'He was more than hurt,' Hawthorne cut in. He had taken the corner of the sofa and was sitting there quite languidly with his legs crossed . . . more like a doctor than a detective. 'He's got serious brain damage. He needs twenty-four-hour care.'

'It was an accident.' Suddenly Damian seemed agitated. He searched in his pockets and, guessing that he wanted a cigarette, Hawthorne offered him one of his own. Damian took it. They both lit up. 'Are you suggesting he's got something to do with what happened? Because I spent half the afternoon talking to the police and they didn't mention him. They think my mum died because of a burglary that went wrong.'

'That may be one theory, Mr Cowper. But it's my job to look at the whole picture. I'd be interested to know what you can tell me about Deal. After all, you were there.'

'I wasn't in the car. Christ!' He ran a hand through his immaculate hair. This was a man who wasn't used to being questioned – not unless it was for a glossy magazine. For once, there wasn't a publicist in the room, guiding the interview. 'Look, it was a long time ago,' he said. 'Mum was living in Walmer, which is the village next to Deal. We'd always lived there. It's where I was born. And after Dad died, she wanted to stay. The house meant a lot to her – the house and the garden. It was her birthday and I went down to see her for a few days. I was in my second year at RADA and everything was going well for me. Mum always said I was going to be a star. She was sure of it. Anyway, the accident happened on a Thursday. She'd gone to play golf.

We were meant to be going out to dinner that night but when she came in she was in a terrible state. She said she'd forgotten her glasses and she'd just hit someone in her car. She knew they were hurt but she had no idea that she'd actually killed one of them.'

'So why didn't she stop?'

'I don't mind telling you the truth, Mr Hawthorne. After all, you can't prosecute her now. The fact of the matter is that she was worried about me. My career was taking off. I'd just had fantastic reviews for *Henry V* and they were even talking about taking it to Broadway. She thought that the bad publicity might hurt me and – I'm not saying she wouldn't have turned herself in to the police. That was never in her mind. She just wanted to talk to me first.'

'She'd killed a child.' Suddenly Hawthorne was leaning forward, accusingly. It was another of those instant trans-formations I was getting used to: from witness to prosecutor, from friend to dangerous enemy.

'I've already told you, she didn't know.' He paused. 'Anyway, for what it's worth, there were plenty of things about that accident that never added up.'

'Such as?'

'Well, the nanny said that the two children ran across the road to get to an ice-cream shop. But the ice-cream shop was closed so that doesn't make any sense. And then there was the question of the witness who disappeared.'

'What witness was that?'

'A man who was first on the scene. He tried to help. But

when the police and the ambulance arrived, he suddenly took off and nobody ever found out who he was or what he'd seen; not at the inquest, not in court.'

'Are you suggesting your mother wasn't responsible?'

'No.' Damian drew on his cigarette. He held it like a black-and-white film star, in the O formed by his thumb and index finger. 'Mum should have been wearing her glasses and she knew that. You have no idea how much it all upset her. She never drove again. And although it broke her heart, she realised she couldn't stay living in Walmer. A few months later, she sold up and moved to London.'

Outside, in another room, we heard a telephone ring a few times before it was picked up.

'So she never had any further communication with the family,' Hawthorne asked.

'The Godwins?' Damian shrugged. 'She did have "further communication" with them. Very much so. They never forgave her and they never accepted the court's verdict. In fact the father, Alan Godwin, was hassling her just a couple of weeks before she died.'

'How do you know?'

'She told me. He actually came to the house in Britannia Road. Can you believe that? He was asking her for money to support his failed business. And when she told him to leave, he wrote to her. If you ask me, that's harassment. I told her to go to the police.'

Alan Godwin had lost a child. His other child had been crippled. It was hard to think of Diana Cowper as the victim in all this. But before Hawthorne could say as much, a young, very attractive black woman came down the spiral stairs, leading a little girl by the hand and holding a mobile phone.

'Dame, it's Jason,' she said. She sounded nervous. 'He says it's important.'

'Sure.' He took the phone from her and began to walk towards the terrace. 'I'm sorry. It's my manager. I've got to take this.' He stopped at the window and frowned. 'I thought you were putting Ashleigh down for a nap.'

'She's jet-lagged. She doesn't know if it's night or day.'

He went outside, leaving us with the woman and her child. This had to be Grace Lovell. There could be no doubt that she was – or had been – a model or an actress. She had the physique and the confidence that go with the job, a sort of look-at-me quality that demanded to be put on the screen. She was in her early thirties, quite tall, with very high cheek-bones; a long neck; and delicate, rounded shoulders. She was wearing the skinniest of jeans and an expensive loose-knit jersey that floated off her. The toddler couldn't have been more than three. She was staring at us with saucer eyes. I imagined she'd had to get used to being trundled around the world.

'I'm Grace,' she said. 'And this is Ashleigh. Are you going to say hello, Ashleigh?' The child said nothing. 'Has Damian offered you coffee?'

'We're OK, thank you.'

'Are you here about Diana?'

'I'm afraid so.'

'He's totally destroyed by this although you probably

won't have seen it. Damian is very good at hiding his feelings.'

I wondered why she felt the need to defend him.

'He was devastated when he heard the news,' she went on. 'He adored his mum.'

'He mentioned you were with her last Christmas.'

'Yes. We did spend some time together although she was more interested in Ashleigh than me.' She took a carton of juice out of the fridge, poured some into a plastic cup and handed it to the child. 'I suppose that's understandable. The first-grandchild thing.'

'Are you an actor too?' I asked.

'Yes. Well, I was. That's how we met. We were at RADA together. He played Hamlet. It was a fantastic production. They still talk about it years later. Everyone knew he was going to be a star. I was Ophelia.'

'You've been together for a while, then.'

'No. After RADA, he got picked up by the RSC and went off to Stratford-upon-Avon. I did a whole load of TV . . . *Holby City*, *Jonathan Creek*, *Queer as Folk* . . . that sort of thing. We actually met up again a few years ago. It was a first-night party at the National. We got together – and then Ashleigh came along.'

'It must be difficult for you,' I said. 'Having to stay at home.'

'Not really. It's my choice.'

I didn't believe her. There was a nervousness in her eyes. I'd seen it when she held out the telephone for Damian. She'd been afraid he was going to snatch it from her. In fact, she was probably afraid of Damian. I had no doubt that success had made him a very different man from the one she had met at drama school.

Damian had finished the call and came back into the room. 'Sorry about that,' he said. 'They're all going crazy out there. We start shooting next week.'

'What did he want?' Grace asked.

'He wants to know when I'm coming back. Jesus! He's such an arsehole. I've only just arrived.' He looked at his watch, a great chunk of steel with several dials. 'It's five o'clock in the morning in L.A. and he's already on his treadmill. I could hear it as he talked.'

'When will you go back?' Hawthorne asked.

'The funeral's Friday. We'll go back the day after.'

'Oh.' Grace's face fell. 'I hoped we could stay longer.'

'I'm meant to be rehearsing. You know that.'

'I wanted to spend a bit of time with Mum and Dad.'

'You've already had a week with them, babe.'

That word – 'babe' – sounded both patronising and faintly menacing. 'Is there anything else you need?' he asked us, his mind clearly elsewhere. 'I don't see how I can really help you. I told everything I know to the police and, to be honest with you, their investigation seems to be moving in a completely different direction. Losing Mum is bad enough but having to go over what happened in Deal really sucks.'

Hawthorne grimaced, as if it genuinely upset him to continue with this line of enquiry. It didn't stop him though. 'Did you know your mother had planned her funeral?' he demanded.

'No. She didn't tell me.'

'Do you have any idea why she might have decided to do that?'

'Not really. She was someone who was very organised. That was part of her character. The funeral, the will, all of that . . .'

'You know about the will?'

When Damian was angry, two little pinpricks of red, almost like light bulbs, appeared in his cheeks. 'I've always known about the will,' he said. 'But I'm not going to discuss it with you.'

'I imagine she left everything to you.'

'As I said, that's private.'

Hawthorne stood up. 'I'll see you at the funeral. I understand you're going to be performing.'

'Actually, that's not what I'd call it. Mum left instructions for me to say a few words. And Grace is going to read a poem.'

'Sylvia Plath,' Grace said.

'I didn't know she liked Plath. But I had a call from the undertaker, a woman called Irene Laws. Apparently, everything was written down.'

'You don't think it's a bit strange that she made all these arrangements the same day she died?'

The question seemed to annoy him. 'I think it was a coincidence.'

'A funny coincidence.'

'I don't see anything funny in it at all.' Damian walked over to the front door and opened it for us. 'It's been nice meeting you,' he said.

He hadn't even tried to make that sound sincere. We left and went down the single flight of stairs and out into the busy street.

Once we got there, Hawthorne stopped. He looked back, deep in thought. 'I missed something,' he said.

'What?'

'I don't know what. It was when you asked him about the text that Diana Cowper sent. After what I told you, why couldn't you keep your mouth shut?'

'The hell with you, Hawthorne!' Right then, I'd really had enough. 'Don't you ever talk to me like that. I'm listening to you. I'm taking notes. But if you think I'm going to follow you around London like some kind of pet dog, you can forget it. I'm not stupid. What was wrong with asking him about the text? It's obviously relevant.'

Hawthorne glared at me. 'You think!'

'Well, isn't it?'

'I don't know! Maybe it is, maybe it isn't. But there was something he'd just told me that was important. You broke my train of thought and I haven't picked up on it. That's all I'm saying.'

'You can ask him at the funeral.' I walked away. 'Let me know what he says.'

'It's eleven o'clock on Friday!' he called after me. 'Brompton Cemetery.'

I stopped and turned round. 'I can't come. I'm busy.'

He stalked after me. 'You've got to be there. It's a big deal. That's what this is all about, remember? She wanted a funeral.'

'And I've got an important meeting. I'm sorry. You'll just have to take notes and tell me about it afterwards. I'm sure you'll be more accurate than me anyway.'

I saw a taxi and flagged it down. This time, Hawthorne didn't try to stop me. I was careful not to turn round but I saw him reflected in the mirror – standing there, lighting another cigarette as we accelerated round a corner.

Ten

Script Conference

There was a reason why I couldn't attend the funeral. The day before, I'd finally had a phone call from Steven Spielberg's office. Both he and Peter Jackson had arrived in London and wanted to meet me to discuss the first draft of the Tintin script at the Soho Hotel in Richmond Mews, just off Dean Street.

I know the hotel well. Although it's hard to believe, it was once an NCP car park (the low ceilings and the lack of windows are the only clues) but has now become something of a focal point for the British film industry. It's surrounded by production houses and post-production facilities and has two screening rooms of its own. Once or twice I've had lunch in its busy, ground-floor restaurant, Refuel. It's almost impossible not to spot someone you know and the very fact that you're meeting there can make you feel that, somehow, you've arrived. In this respect, it's London's own little corner of Los Angeles.

I forgot all about Damian Cowper and his mother for the

next couple of days. Instead, I immersed myself in the script, going through it line by line, trying to remember the thought processes that had got me this far. I was convinced that there were lots of good things in it but I still had to be prepared to fight my corner if need be. I wasn't sure how either Jackson as director or Spielberg as producer was going to respond to my work.

This was the problem.

Tintin is a European phenomenon and one that has never been particularly popular across the Atlantic. Part of the reason for this may be historical. The 1932 album, *Tintin in America*, is a ruthless satire on the United States, showing Americans to be vicious, corrupt and insatiable: the very first panel shows a policeman saluting a masked bandit who is walking past with a smoking gun – and no sooner has Tintin arrived in New York and climbed into a taxi than he finds himself being kidnapped by the Mob. The entire history of Native Americans is brilliantly told in five panels. Oil is discovered on a reservation. Cigar-smoking businessmen move in. Soldiers drive the crying Native American children off their land. Builders and bankers arrive. Just one day later, a policeman tells Tintin to get out of the way of a major traffic intersection. 'Where do you think you are – the Wild West?'

There's a total cultural disconnect too. What would the Americans make of the bizarre relationships that seem quite normal in the world of Tintin? There are his friendships with the not entirely reformed drunk, Captain Haddock, and with the stone-deaf Professor Calculus (who was given no part in the first film). There is a talking dog. There are the idiotic, one-joke detectives, Thompson and Thomson, who can only be told apart by the shapes of their moustaches. But most of all there is the inconsequentiality of the adventures. Marvel and DC comics dealt with fantastical characters but at least they sent them on recognisable journeys, providing them with origin stories, personal tragedies (the villain Magneto was revealed to be a Holocaust survivor), love affairs, psychological issues, political awakenings and all the rest of it. Very few of the Tintin albums have anything that comes close to a proper narrative shape and one of them – *The Castafiore Emerald* – was deliberately designed to have no story at all.

Tintin has no girlfriend. Although he is supposedly a journalist, he is hardly ever seen to work. His age is indeterminate. He could actually be a child, a grown-up Boy Scout. His dress sense and hairstyle are ridiculous. Unlike all the other characters, who are carefully delineated, he is deliberately drawn as a cipher. His face is made up of three dots for his eyes and mouth and a small letter c which is his nose. Although presumably Belgian, he has no national characteristic that might make him a foreigner abroad. He has no parents, no real home (until he moves into Marlinspike Hall with Captain Haddock), no emotions beyond a desire to travel and have adventures. How could he possibly be the hero of a $135-million Hollywood film?

I had been drawn into the world of Tintin in a rather strange way. I'd originally been invited to work on the computer game that would go out with the first film, *The Secret of the Unicorn*, working with the French company who had just had a huge hit with Assassin's Creed. This isn't something I would normally consider. I don't play computer games. I don't particularly like them. And writing random dialogue for nameless pirates wandering around the deck of the *Unicorn* didn't particularly appeal to me even if – in an early draft – I had them all earnestly discussing my books. But the truth is that Spielberg is Spielberg and I wondered where the job might take me.

It took me to Wellington and the home of Peter Jackson. Somehow I found myself drawn into the sequel, just as the first film was nearing completion. Even more bizarrely, it turned out that *The Secret of the Unicorn* had problems and almost by accident I was asked to help with the shape and the narrative flow – even to add a few extra scenes. Some of these actually made the final cut. There's a tiny moment in the film when a man runs into a lamp-post. He falls to the floor and, in the style of a Hergé illustration, a little circle of tweety-birds flutter around his head. But there's a twist. The camera pulls back to reveal that the incident has taken place outside a pet shop and the birds are real: the owner is there with a net, trying to recapture them.

I mention this only because it was filmed by Steven Spielberg and in all the writing I have ever done over forty years, it's probably the scene of which I'm most proud. When he showed it to me in a Los Angeles screening room, I almost leapt off the sofa in excitement. This was the man who had shot *Jaws*, *E.T.*, *Indiana Jones*, *Schindler's List*. And now his filmography included forty seconds by me. In fact, when I look back at the entire Tintin experience, that's the moment I like to remember. Nothing else was ever quite as good again.

That said, I loved working with Peter Jackson. In fact I had liked him the moment I met him at the Weta studios in Wellington. He showed me a long corridor with a stationery cupboard about halfway down. This was actually the secret entrance to his office. He pressed a button and the back wall swung open on hidden hydraulics, revealing a huge space behind. A secret door! The Tintin books are full of them. I even have one (although it's much less elaborate) in my home in London. Jackson was such a pleasant, even-tempered, amicable man that it was easy to forget that, with *The Lord of the Rings*, he had written, produced and directed three of the most successful blockbusters in cinema history, making himself hundreds of millions of dollars in the process. Nothing about the way he dressed or the way he lived fitted the stereotype of the movie mogul. After that first meeting we usually worked at his house, which I remember as being messy, cosy, lived-in. When it was time for lunch, his assistant would phone one of the Wellington takeaways. The food was awful.

Together we had decided to adapt one of Hergé's double albums: *The Seven Crystal Balls* and *Prisoners of the Sun*. The story begins with a group of professors who stumble, Tutankhamun-style, on the tomb of the high priest Rascar Capac. They are searching for an ancient bracelet which has magical properties and which will in turn lead to the Inca's lost city of gold. Or something like that. By the time I finished the screenplay, about half the story was Hergé's and quite a bit of it was mine. I'd added one or two huge action sequences, including a chase on two steam trains that turned into a rollercoaster ride around the Andes, and a new climax that involved an entire golden mountain being melted by a primitive laser. We couldn't use the actual ending of the book – an eclipse – because it had appeared in another very successful film (Mel Gibson's *Apocalypto*) five years before.

So that was how things stood as I went into the meeting at the Soho Hotel. Peter Jackson had already told me he had notes but that was hardly surprising. A screenplay for a film of this size might pass through twenty or thirty drafts before it was ready for production, and I would almost certainly be fired somewhere along the way. I was quite prepared for that. I just hoped I wouldn't be dropped immediately. It would be nice if they let me have two or three attempts to get the script right. At this stage, incidentally, *The Secret of the Unicorn* hadn't been released. I had seen it and I thought it was extraordinary. Spielberg had used a technique called motion capture, which had magically transformed the actors Jamie Bell and Andy Serkis into Tintin and Haddock. Both of them were lined up for the sequel.

I arrived at the Soho Hotel at ten o'clock, as I had been instructed, and I was shown into a room on the first floor with a large conference table, three glasses and a bottle of Fiji mineral water. Peter Jackson arrived a few minutes later. He was as genial as ever, with the crumpled look of someone who had just flown across the world. He had lost a lot of weight and his clothes were hanging off him. We talked about London, the weather, recent movies . . . anything except the script. Then the door opened and Spielberg came in. He tended to wear more or less the same clothes: a leather jacket, jeans, trainers, a baseball cap. His glasses and beard made him instantly recognisable. As always, I had to remind myself that this was really happening, that I was sitting in the same room as him. He was someone I had wanted to meet pretty much all my life.

Spielberg got straight to the point. I have never come across anyone so focused on film-making and storytelling. In the short time that I had known him he'd never asked me a personal question and it often struck me that he had no interest in me outside what I had put on the page. I had been wondering where he would begin. Did he like my way into the narrative? Did the characters work? Were the action sequences in the right place? Were my jokes funny? I always dread the moment when a director opens a script of mine. The first words that come out of his – or her – mouth may change the next year of my life.

'You've chosen the wrong book,' he said.

It was impossible. Peter and I had discussed which books we were going to adapt when we were in Wellington. I had spent three months on this draft. It was the last thing I had expected him to say.

'I'm sorry?' I'm not sure those were the exact words I used.

'*The Seven Crystal Balls. Prisoners of the Sun*. Those are the wrong books . . .'

'Why?'

'I don't want to do them.'

I turned to Peter. He nodded. 'OK.'

And that, actually, was it. It didn't matter that Peter Jackson was directing and Spielberg was producing. They both had copies of my script but we weren't going to discuss it at all: not the plot, the characters, the action, the jokes. There was nothing to talk about.

'We can do *Prisoners of the Sun* as the third film,' Peter said, brushing it aside with a casual wave of his hand. 'Which book do you think Anthony should start working on for number two?'

Anthony! That was me. I wasn't going to be fired.

But before Spielberg could answer, the door opened again and, to my shock and utter dismay, Hawthorne walked in. As always he was in his suit and white shirt but this time he'd also put on a black tie.

For the funeral.

He didn't seem to have any idea what sort of meeting he'd just interrupted – or how important it was to me. He wandered in as if he had been invited and when he saw me, he smiled as if he hadn't expected me to be there. 'Tony,' he said. 'I've been looking for you.'

'I'm busy,' I said, feeling the blood rush to my face.

'I know. I can see that, mate. But you must have forgotten. The funeral!'

'I told you. I can't come to the funeral.'

'Who's died?' Peter Jackson asked.

I glanced at him. He looked genuinely concerned. On the other side of the table, Spielberg was sitting very straight, a little annoyed. I could imagine that he belonged to a world where nobody would walk in unless they were expected and only if they were being escorted by an assistant. Apart from anything else, there was his security to consider.

'It's nobody,' I said. I still couldn't quite believe Hawthorne had come here. Was he deliberately trying to embarrass me? 'I told you,' I said quietly. 'I really can't come.'

'But you have to. It's important.'

'Who are you?' Spielberg asked.

Hawthorne pretended to notice him for the first time. 'I'm Hawthorne,' he said. 'I'm with the police.'

'You're a police officer?'

'No. He's a consultant,' I cut in. 'He's helping the police with an investigation.'

'A murder,' Hawthorne explained, helpfully, once again sitting on that first vowel to make the word somehow more violent than it already was. He was looking at Spielberg, only now recognising him. 'Do I know you?' he asked.

'I'm Steven Spielberg.'

'Are you in films?'

I wanted to weep.

'That's right. I make films . . .'

'This is Steven Spielberg and this is Peter Jackson.' I don't know why I said that. Part of me was trying to take back control. Perhaps I was hoping I could overawe Hawthorne and get him out of the room.

'Peter Jackson!' Hawthorne's face brightened. 'You did those three films . . . *The Lord of the Rings*!'

155

'That's right.' Jackson was relaxed. 'Did you see them?'

'I watched them on DVD with my son. He thought they were great.'

'Thank you.'

'The first one, anyway. He wasn't too sure about the second. What was it called . . . ?'

'*The Two Towers*.' Peter was still smiling, even if it was a smile that had slightly frozen in place.

'We didn't much like those trees. The talking trees. We thought they were stupid.'

'You mean . . . the Ents.'

'Whatever. And Gandalf. I thought he was dead and I was a bit surprised when he turned up again.' Hawthorne thought for a moment and I waited with a sense of mounting dread for what was going to come next. 'The actor who played him, Ian McEwan, he was a bit over the top.'

'Sir Ian McKellen. He was nominated for an Oscar.'

'That may be the case. But did he win it?'

'Mr Hawthorne is a special consultant for Scotland Yard,' I cut in. 'I've been commissioned to write a book about his latest case . . .'

'It's called "Hawthorne Investigates",' Hawthorne said.

Spielberg considered. 'I like that title,' he said.

'It's good,' Jackson agreed.

Hawthorne glanced at his watch. 'We've got the funeral at eleven o'clock,' he explained.

'And I've already said, I can't be there.'

'You have to be there, Tony. I mean, everyone who ever knew Diana Cowper is going to attend. It's an opportunity to see them all interacting. You could say it's a bit like having a read-through before a film. You wouldn't want to miss that, would you!'

'I explained—'

'Diana Cowper,' Spielberg said. 'Isn't that Damian Cowper's mother?'

'That's her. She was strangled. In her own house.'

'I heard.' It had often struck me that Spielberg, the man who had shot the bloodiest opening in cinema history with *Saving Private Ryan* and who had re-created Nazi atrocities in *Schindler's List*, didn't actually like talking about violence. I could have sworn he'd gone a little pale once when I was outlining an idea I'd had for Tintin. Now he turned to Peter. 'I met Damian Cowper last month. He came in for a chat about *War Horse*.'

'Poor kid,' Peter Jackson said. 'That's a horrible thing to happen.'

'I agree.' Both Spielberg and Jackson were looking at me as if I had known Damian Cowper all my life and not attending his mother's funeral would be the meanest thing I could possibly do. Meanwhile, Hawthorne was sitting there like some passing angel who'd wafted in to appeal to my better conscience.

'I really think you should go, Anthony,' Spielberg said.

'But it's just a book,' I assured them. 'To be honest, I'm having second thoughts about writing it. This film is much more important to me.'

'Well, we don't really have much to talk about where the second movie is concerned,' Peter said. 'Maybe we all need to take a rain check and rethink where we are in a couple of weeks.'

'We can do a conference call,' Spielberg said.

We'd been talking about Tintin for less than two minutes. My script had been thrown out in its entirety. And before I could start coming up with ideas for *The Calculus Affair* or *Destination Moon* or even *Flight 714 to Sydney* (spaceships . . . Spielberg liked spaceships, didn't he?) I was being thrown out. It wasn't fair. I was in a meeting with the two greatest film-makers in the world. I was meant to be writing a film for them. And yet I was being dragged out to the funeral of someone I hadn't even met.

Hawthorne got to his feet. It tells you something about my state of mind that I hadn't even noticed when he'd sat down. 'Very nice to meet you,' he said.

'Sure,' Spielberg said. 'Do please pass on my condolences to Damian.'

'I'll do that.'

'And don't worry, Anthony. We'll give your agent a call.'

They never did call my agent. In fact I never saw either of them again and my only consolation as I sit here now is that so far there has been no new Tintin film. *The Secret of the Unicorn* got rave reviews and made $375 million worldwide but the response in America was less enthusiastic. Maybe that's dissuaded them from continuing with the sequel. Or maybe they're working on it now. Without me.

'They seemed very nice,' Hawthorne said, as he walked down the corridor.

'For Christ's sake!' I exploded. 'I told you I didn't want

to come to the funeral. Why did you come here? How did you even know where I was?'

'I rang your assistant.'

'And she told you?'

'Listen.' Hawthorne was trying to calm me down. 'You don't want to do Tintin. It's for children. I thought you were leaving all that stuff behind you.'

'It's being produced by Steven Spielberg!' I exclaimed.

'Well, maybe he'll make a film of your new book. A murder story! He knows Damian Cowper.' We pushed through the main doors of the hotel and went out into the street. 'Who do you think will play me?'

Eleven
The Funeral

I know Brompton Cemetery well. When I was in my twenties, I had a room in a flat just five minutes away and on a hot summer afternoon I'd wander in and write there. It was somewhere quiet, away from the dust and the traffic, a world of its own. In fact it's one of the most impressive cemeteries in London – a member of the so-called 'magnificent seven' – with a striking array of Gothic mausoleums and colonnades peopled by stone angels and saints, all of them constructed by the Victorians partly to celebrate death but also to keep it in its place. There's a main avenue that runs in a straight line all the way from one end to the other and walking there on a sunny day I could easily imagine myself in ancient Rome. I would find a bench and sit there with my notebooks, watching the squirrels and the occasional fox and, on a Saturday afternoon, listening to the distant clamour of the crowd at Stamford Bridge football club on the other side of the trees. It's strange how different locations around London have played such a large part in my work. The River

Thames is one of them. Brompton Cemetery is most certainly another.

It was ten to eleven when Hawthorne and I arrived and
made our way between the two red telephone boxes that
seemed to stand guard on either side of the main gate. We
followed a narrow, twisty path with bollards that could be
lowered to allow vehicles – presumably hearses – to come in.
A few mourners walked ahead of us. This part of the cemetery was shabbier and more depressing than I remembered. I
noticed a headless statue on a plinth. Another greeted us with
a severed arm. I took pictures of them with my iPhone. A
few pigeons pecked at the grass.

We turned a corner and the Brompton chapel appeared
ahead of us, a building that consisted of a perfect circle with
two wings. If viewed from above, it would have the same
shape as a London Underground sign . . . vaguely appropriate when you think about it. We had approached it from the
back and, sure enough, there was a hearse parked on a square
of concrete next to an open door. The willow casket that
Diana Cowper had requested was inside, as – I realised with
a jolt in my stomach – was she. Four men in black tailcoats
stood waiting to carry her in.

The path bent round and brought us to the main entrance:
a door with four pillars facing north. There was a small
crowd making its way inside. Nobody was speaking to each
other, instead keeping their heads down as if they were embarrassed to be there. It felt odd joining them when I had never
met Diana Cowper. I had never even heard of her until a
week ago. As a rule, I don't go to funerals. I find them too

horrible and upsetting and the older I get, of course, the more invitations I receive. As a favour to my friends, I'll make sure that none of them are told the date of mine.

I recognised quite a few of the people who had turned up to this one. Andrea Kluvánek had decided to come to say goodbye to her old employer and was just disappearing in through the door as we turned the corner. Raymond Clunes was also there, wearing a brand-new black cashmere coat that he might have bought specially for the occasion. He had brought a younger, bearded man with him, quite possibly his partner. I glanced nervously at Hawthorne, who was watching them with narrow, guarded eyes. Fortunately, at least for the time being, he was saying nothing.

Clunes was also being observed by a second, very elegant man, possibly Hong Kong Chinese, with long black hair curling down to his shoulders. He was immaculately dressed in a suit and white silk shirt fastened with one of those Dr. No collars, and black shoes that had been polished until they dazzled. Curiously, I had met him once before. His name was Bruno Wang and, like Clunes, he was a major theatre producer. He was also a well-known philanthropist, on first-name terms with various members of the royal family, and had given large sums to the arts. He often came to first nights at the Old Vic theatre – where I was on the board. From the way he was looking at Clunes, I could tell at once that the two men were definitely not friends.

We found ourselves next to him at the door and I greeted him. 'Did you know Diana Cowper?' I asked.

'She was a dear, dear friend,' Wang replied. He spoke

softly, always considering his next words, as if he was about to recite a poem. 'A woman of great kindness and spirituality. I was devastated to hear the news of her passing and it almost breaks my heart to be here today.'

'Was she one of your investors?' I asked.

'Sadly not. I had invited her many times. She had exceptional taste. Unfortunately, her judgement could sometimes be found wanting. If she had one fault, it was that she had too kind a heart. She was too trusting. I did speak to her. Only a few weeks ago, I tried to warn her . . .'

'What did you warn her about?' Hawthorne asked. He had effortlessly stepped into the forefront, pushing me aside.

Wang looked around. We were on our own. Everyone else had gone into the chapel ahead of us. 'I don't want to speak out of turn.'

'Why don't you give it a try?'

'I don't think we've met!' Wang had been put on the defensive and frankly I wasn't surprised. Hawthorne's brand of low-key menace – the pale skin, the haunted eyes – was off-putting at the best of times. In a cemetery it was positively sinister. If a vampire had decided to turn up for the funeral it might have been less unnerving.

'This is Daniel Hawthorne,' I said. 'He's a police investigator looking into what happened.'

'You know Raymond Clunes?' Hawthorne asked. He had also noticed Wang examining the other man just a few moments before.

'I can't say I know him. But we've met.'

'And . . . ?'

'I don't like to speak unkindly about another human being,' Wang said in his carefully measured way. 'And particularly not in a place such as this. In my view, there's already too much unkindness in the world. However . . .' He drew a breath. 'You will find, I think, that Raymond Clunes is being investigated by the authorities. He made certain claims with respect to his last production which turned out to be, to say the least, exaggerated.'

'Are you talking about *Moroccan Nights*?' I asked.

'I did tell dear Diana, just a few weeks before the tragedy that took her from us. She was fully intending to take action which, in my view, she had every right to do.'

'But then she got strangled,' Hawthorne said, flatly.

Wang stared at him, making the connection for the first time. 'I understood that it was a burglary.'

'I don't think it was a burglary.'

'In that case, I've probably said too much. I don't think Diana had invested a great deal of money. I certainly didn't mean to imply anything . . . untoward.' He spread his hands. 'Excuse me. I don't want to miss the service.' He hurried inside.

We were left alone.

'So that's interesting,' Hawthorne said, as much to himself as to me. 'She finds out Clunes has been stiffing her. She plans to have it out with him. And before you know it, she's a stiff herself.'

'That's a nice way of putting it.'

'That's my pleasure. You can use it.'

There were a couple of men loitering a short distance

away with cameras. I only noticed them when one of them snapped a photograph.

'Fucking journalists,' Hawthorne muttered.

It was true. They must have come here to catch a shot of Damian Cowper.

'What have you got against journalists?' I asked, thinking I might have to add them to the list.

Hawthorne threw down the cigarette he'd been smoking and ground it out beneath his foot. 'Nothing. We always used to get them sniffing around the crime scene. They never got anything right.'

We went into the chapel.

It was a circular space, white, with pillars holding up a domed roof and windows positioned too high up to allow a view of anything other than the sky. About forty chairs had been arranged to face the coffin, which was being carried in as we took our places. Looked at more closely, the coffin had a strange and unfortunate resemblance to an enormous picnic basket, the lid fastened with two leather straps. There was a yellow and white floral garland resting on the top. A recording of Jeremiah Clarke's Trumpet Voluntary was already playing on the speaker system. It was odd because, of course, that piece of music is more often associated with weddings. I wondered if it had accompanied Diana Cowper down the aisle when she got married.

The coffin was carefully laid down on two trestles and while that was happening I examined the rest of the crowd, a little surprised by how few people had turned out. There couldn't have been more than a couple of dozen in the room.

Bruno Wang and Raymond Clunes were both in the front row, some distance apart. Andrea, in a cheap, black leather jacket, was over to the side. Detective Inspector 'Jack' Meadows had turned up too. I saw him stifling a yawn, sitting uncomfortably on a chair that was slightly too small for him.

I suppose Damian Cowper had the star role in this production and he seemed to know it. He had dressed for the part in a beautifully tailored suit, grey shirt and black silk tie. Grace Lovell was next to him, in a black dress, but there was a space around them as if this was the VIP area of the chapel and the other mourners could notice them but, please, don't come too close. I'm not exaggerating: there were only two people sitting in the row behind him. Later I would discover that one of them had been sent by Damian's London agent and the other was his personal trainer, a very muscular black man who seemed to be acting as his bodyguard.

Otherwise, the congregation was made up of friends and colleagues of Diana Cowper, none of them under fifty. Looking around, it struck me that although there were a great many emotions on display in the chapel – boredom, curiosity, seriousness – nobody seemed particularly sad. The only person who showed any sense of loss was a tall man with straggly hair, sitting a few chairs away from me. As the vicar stood up and approached the coffin, he took out a white handkerchief and dabbed at his eyes.

The vicar was a woman, short, fleshy, with a downturned smile. I know this is a sad occasion, she seemed to be saying, but I'm very glad you're here. I could see that she was going to be modern rather than traditional in her approach. She waited until the music ended then stepped forward, rubbed her hands together and began her address.

'Hello, everybody. I'm so very glad to welcome you here to this very beautiful chapel, built in 1839 and inspired by St Peter's in Rome. I think it's a very special, very beautiful place to come together today to pay our respects to a lovely, lovely lady. Death is always difficult for those of us who are left behind. And as we say goodbye to Diana Cowper, who was snatched so very suddenly and violently from the path of life, it's particularly hard to see any reason for it and it's very difficult to come to terms with what has happened.'

I was already wishing she'd stop saying 'very' all the time. I wondered if Diana Cowper would have enjoyed being described as 'a lovely, lovely lady'. It made her sound like a special guest on a television game show.

'Diana was someone who always tried to help. She did a fantastic amount of work for charity. She was on the board of the Globe Theatre and of course she was the mother of a very famous son. Damian has flown all the way from America to be here today, and although we understand the sadness you must be feeling, Damian, we're very, very glad to see you.'

I turned round and noticed Robert Cornwallis, the under-taker, standing next to the door. He was whispering quietly to Irene Laws, both of them dressed formally for the funeral. She nodded and he slipped outside. I thought briefly of Steven Spielberg and Peter Jackson, who were probably still at the Soho Hotel. Maybe they'd popped down together for an early lunch at Refuel. And I should have been with them! I felt a surge of rage at having been dragged here.

'Diana Cowper was someone who was aware of her own mortality.' The vicar was still talking. 'She had arranged every aspect of today's service, including the music you have just heard. She wanted to keep it short, so that's enough from me! We are going to begin with Psalm 34. I hope that when Diana chose this, she understood that death is not always something to be feared. The righteous person may have many troubles, but the Lord delivers him from them all. Death can be a comfort too.'

The vicar read the psalm. Then Grace Lovell stood up, walked forward and recited 'Ariel' by Sylvia Plath.

> Stasis in darkness
> Then the substanceless blue
> Pour of tor and distances . . .

I was impressed that she had learned it off by heart – and she certainly put her heart into it. Damian watched her with a strange coolness in his handsome eyes. Next to me, Hawthorne yawned.

Finally, it was Damian's turn. He got up and walked slowly forward, then turned so that he was standing with his back to his mother's coffin. His words were brief and unemotional.

'I was just twenty-one when my dad died and now I've lost my mother too. It's harder to come to terms with what happened to her because Dad was ill but Mum was attacked in her own home and I was away in America when it happened. I'll always be sorry that I never got a chance to say goodbye but I know she was proud of what I was doing and I think she'd have enjoyed my new show, which starts shooting next week. It's called *Homeland* and it should be on Showtime later this year. Mum always supported me being an actor. She encouraged me and she had total belief that I'd become a star. She came to every one of my productions when I was at Stratford – Ariel in *The Tempest*, Henry V, and Mephistopheles in *Doctor Faustus*, which was her favourite. She always said I was her little devil.' This got a few murmurs of sympathetic laughter from the mourners. 'I think I'll always look for her in the audience when I'm onstage and I'm always going to see the empty seat. I hope they can resell the ticket . . .' They were less sure about that last remark. Was it actually a joke?

I had been recording everything he said on my iPhone but I stopped listening at this point. Damian Cowper's funeral address had confirmed my feelings about him. He talked for a few more minutes and then the sound system came back on with 'Eleanor Rigby', the doors were opened and we all trooped out into the cemetery. The man with the straggly hair was right in front of us. He dabbed at his eyes a second time.

We traipsed off to the western side of the cemetery, behind the colonnades. A grave had been dug in a long stretch of unkempt grass next to a low wall. There was a railway line on the other side. I couldn't see it but as we walked forward I heard a train go past. We came to a gravestone with the inscription *Lawrence Cowper, 3 April 1946 – 22 October 1999. After a long illness, borne with fortitude.* I remembered that he had lived and presumably died in Kent, and wondered how he had come to be buried here. The sun was shining but a couple of plane trees provided shade. It was a pleasant, warm afternoon. Damian Cowper, Grace Lovell and the vicar had stayed behind to accompany the body on its last journey and as we waited for them Detective Inspector Meadows lumbered over to us. He was wearing a suit that could have come out of a charity shop – or should have been on the way to one.

'So how's it going, Hawthorne?' he asked.

'Not too bad, Jack.'

'You getting anywhere with this?' Meadows sniffed. 'You don't want to solve it too soon, I'd have thought. Not if you're being paid by the day.'

'I'll wait for you to come up with an answer,' Hawthorne said. 'That way, I'll make a fortune.'

'Actually, I may have to disappoint you there. Looks like we're closing in . . .'

'Really?' I asked. If Meadows actually solved the case before Hawthorne, it would be catastrophic for the book.

'Yes. You'll read about it in the newspapers soon enough so I might as well tell you now. There have been three burglaries in the area around Britannia Road recently with an identical MO. The intruder dressed up as a dispatch rider, delivering a package. A motorbike helmet covered his face. He targeted single women living on their own.'

'And he murdered them all, did he?'

'No. He beat up the first two and locked them in a cupboard while he ransacked their houses. The third one was smart. She didn't let him in. She dialled 999 and he hiked it. But we know who we're looking for. We're looking at CCTV footage now. We should be able to track down the bike without too much trouble and that'll lead us to him.'

'And what's your theory for how Diana Cowper got herself strangled? Why didn't he just beat her up like the rest of them?'

Meadows shrugged his rugby player's shoulders. 'It just went wrong.'

There was a movement on the other side of the trees. Diana Cowper was being brought to her final resting place in a procession which included the four men from the funeral parlour – they were carrying the basket – along with the vicar, Damian Cowper and Grace Lovell. Finally, Irene Laws followed behind at a discreet distance, her hands clasped behind her back, making sure that everything was being done correctly. There was no sign of Robert Cornwallis.

'You know what? I think your theory is a lot of shit,' Hawthorne said. His language jarred with the setting – the sunlight, the cemetery and the approaching coffin with its garland of flowers. 'You always were complete crap at the job, mate. And when you finally track down your masked dispatch rider, you can give him best wishes from me because I bet you any money you like he never went anywhere near Britannia Road.'

'And you always were an insufferable bastard when you

were in the Met,' Meadows growled. 'You don't know how glad we were to see you go.'

'It's just a shame what happened to your targets,' Hawthorne responded, his eyes glittering. 'I hear they nose-dived after I went. And while we're on the subject, it's too bad about your divorce.'

'Who told you about that?' Meadows jerked back.

'It's written all over you, mate.'

It was true. Meadows looked neglected. His crumpled suit, the shirt that hadn't been ironed and was missing a button and his scuffed shoes all told one half of the story. He was still wearing a wedding ring though, so either his wife had died or she had left him. Either way, the comments had hit home. In fact I was almost expecting the two of them to come to blows – like Hamlet and Laertes on the side of the grave – but just then the coffin arrived and I watched as it was set down on the grass, the willow creaking. Two ropes ran underneath it and the four pall-bearers took a moment to run the ends through the handles, securing it, while Irene Laws looked on approvingly.

I glanced at Damian Cowper. He was staring into the mid-distance, unaware of anyone around him. Grace was standing beside him but there was no contact between them. She wasn't holding his arm. The photographers I had noticed earlier were some distance away but their cameras had zoom lenses and I imagined they could get everything they needed.

'It's time to lower the coffin,' the vicar intoned. 'Let us

all stand together and maybe you'd like to hold hands while we take these last few moments to think about the very special life that has now ended.'

The coffin was lifted and manoeuvred over the grave that waited to receive it. The small crowd stood around, watching as it was lowered. The man with the handkerchief touched his eyes. Raymond Clunes had found himself standing next to Bruno Wang and I noticed them exchange a few quiet words. The four pall-bearers began to lower the coffin into the dark slit that was waiting to receive it.

And then, quite suddenly, music began to play. It was a song. A children's song.

> *The wheels on the bus go round and round,*
> *Round and round*
> *Round and round*
> *The wheels on the bus go round and round*
> *All day long.*

The sound quality was thin and tinkly and my immediate thought was that it was somebody's mobile phone. The mourners were looking among themselves, wondering whose it was and who was going to be embarrassed. Irene Laws stepped forward, alarmed. Damian Cowper was standing closest to the grave. I saw him look over the edge with an expression that was somewhere between horror and fury. He pointed down and said something to Grace Lovell. That was when I understood.

The music was coming from inside the grave.

It was inside the coffin.

The second verse began.

The wipers on the bus go swish, swish, swish
Swish, swish, swish,
Swish, swish, swish . . .

The four pall-bearers had frozen, not knowing whether to drop the coffin the rest of the way and hope that the depth of the grave would muffle the sound or whether to pull it out again and somehow deal with it. Could they actually bury the dead woman with this hideously inappropriate song accompanying her? It was quite obvious now that the source of the music was some sort of digital recorder or radio inside the coffin. Had Diana Cowper chosen a more traditional material, mahogany for example, there's every chance that we would have been unable to hear it. The dead woman might have been left to rest in peace . . . at least, once the battery ran out. But the words were leaking out of the twisted willow branches. There was no escaping them.

The driver on the bus goes 'Move on back'

On the far side of the cemetery, the photographers raised their cameras and moved forward, sensing that something was wrong. At the same time, Damian Cowper lashed out at the vicar, not physically but ferociously. He needed someone to blame and she was close by. 'What's going on?' he snarled. 'Who did this?'

Irene Laws had reached the edge of the grave, moving as fast as her short, stubby legs would allow. 'Mr Cowper . . .' she began, breathlessly.

'Is this some sort of joke?' Damian looked ill. 'Why are they playing that song?'

'Raise the coffin.' Irene had taken charge. 'Lift it back out again.'

'Move on back, move on back . . .'

'I want you to know I'm going to sue your fucking company for every penny—'

'I'm most dreadfully sorry!' Irene was talking over him. 'I just don't understand . . .'

The four men pulled the coffin back out rather faster than they had lowered it. It came clear over the edge of the grave and bumped onto the grass, almost toppling onto its side. I could imagine Diana Cowper inside, being rocked to and fro. I examined the other mourners, wondering if one of them was responsible, for presumably this had been done deliberately. Was it a sick joke? Was it some sort of message?

Raymond Clunes was clutching on to his partner. Bruno Wang was staring, his hand over his mouth. Andrea Kluvánek – I could have been wrong but she seemed to be smiling. Next to her, the man with the handkerchief was gazing at the coffin with an expression I couldn't make out at all. He brought his hand to his mouth as if he was going either to throw up or to burst into laughter, then twisted round and backed away. I watched him as he hurried out of the cemetery, heading up the path that would lead him to the Brompton Road.

The driver on the bus goes 'Move on back'
All day long.

It wouldn't stop. That was the worst of it. The music was so trite, the voice full of that hideous cheerfulness that adults put on when they sing for children.

'I've had enough of this,' Damian announced. From the look of him, he was in total shock. It was the first real emotion he had shown since the funeral began.

'Damian . . .' Grace reached out to take his arm.

He shook her off. 'I'm going home. You go to the pub. I'll see you at the flat.'

I was aware of the photographers snapping with their cameras, their long-distance lenses protruding obscenely over the gravestones. The personal-trainer-cum-bodyguard was doing his best to stand in their way but the lenses swivelled to follow Damian as he stormed off.

The vicar turned to Irene, helpless. 'What should we do?' she asked.

'Let's take the coffin back to the chapel.' Irene was trying not to lose her composure. 'Quickly,' she snapped in an undertone.

The pall-bearers picked Diana Cowper up and carried her back across the grass, away from the grave, moving as quickly as they could without actually running, still trying to display some measure of decorum. They weren't succeeding. They looked ridiculous, I thought, moving out of sync, bumping into each other and almost tripping over in their haste to get away. The tinkling music faded into the distance.

The horn on the bus goes . . .

Hawthorne watched them disappear. I could almost see the different thoughts turning over in his head.

'*Beep, beep, beep*,' he muttered tunelessly, then set off at a brisk pace, following the coffin back towards the chapel.

Twelve
The Smell of Blood

We had left the other mourners standing in a confused circle around the empty grave as we set off after the coffin, which now reminded me of a tiny ship being tossed around in a stormy sea.

I had a suspicion that Hawthorne was amused by what had happened. It might be that the bleak, vindictive joke – if that's what it was – had appealed to the darker side of his nature. More likely, it was the knowledge that the theory Meadows had put forward had been completely blown apart. Just a few minutes ago, he had been talking about a burglary that had gone wrong. There was no question of that now. Everything that had happened had pushed the crime far outside normal police experience and gave Hawthorne all the more opportunity to call the investigation his own.

I looked back and saw Meadows lumbering after us but for the time being Hawthorne and I were alone as we headed towards the chapel, which lay a short way ahead.

'What do you think that was all about?' I asked.

'It was a message,' Hawthorne said.

'A message . . . who for?'

'Well, Damian Cowper, for one. You saw his face.'

'He was upset.'

'That's putting it mildly. He was white as a bloody sheet. I thought he was going to pass out!'

'This has got to be about Jeremy Godwin,' I said.

'He wasn't run over by a bus.'

'No. But maybe he was carrying a toy bus when he was hit. Maybe he liked travelling on buses . . .'

'You're right about one thing, mate. It was a kiddy's nursery rhyme so it's likely to have something to do with a dead kiddy.' Hawthorne stepped delicately over a grave. 'Damian's gone home,' he went on. 'But we'll catch up with him soon enough. I wonder what he's got to say.'

'It's been ten years since the accident in Deal.' I was thinking out loud. 'First Diana Cowper is killed. Then this. Someone's certainly trying to make a point.'

We had reached the chapel. The coffin had already gone in. We waited until Meadows caught up with us.

'I always knew things would go pear-shaped once you were involved,' he grunted. He was terribly out of shape. Even the short walk had left him breathless. If he didn't watch his diet, quit smoking and take exercise, he would soon be back in the cemetery for a more permanent visit.

'I'll be interested to hear how your burglar pulled this one off,' Hawthorne said. 'I can't say I noticed anyone dressed up as a dispatch rider.'

'What happened here may have nothing to do with the

murder and you know it,' Meadows replied. 'There's a Hollywood celebrity involved. It was a practical joke ... someone with a twisted mind. That's all.'

'You might be right.' Hawthorne's tone of voice made it clear he didn't believe a word of it.

We went into the chapel. By now the coffin was back on the trestles and Irene Laws was busily undoing the straps, watched by the vicar – wide-eyed with shock – and the four men from Cornwallis and Sons. She looked up as we came in.

'I've been in this business for twenty-seven years,' she said. 'And nothing like this – nothing – has ever happened before.'

At least the nursery-rhyme music had stopped. I heard only the creak of willow as Irene finished her work and lifted the lid. I flinched. I had no desire to see Diana Cowper a week after she had died. Fortunately, she was covered by a muslin shroud and although I could make out the shape of her body, I was spared the sight of the staring eyes or the sewn-together lips. Irene leaned in and removed what looked like a bright orange cricket ball which had been placed between Diana Cowper's hands. She handed it to Meadows.

He examined it with distaste. 'I don't know what this is,' he said.

'It's an alarm clock.' Hawthorne reached out and Meadows handed it to him, glad to be rid of it.

I saw that it was indeed a digital alarm clock, with the correct time displayed in a circular panel on one side. It had a number of perforations, like an old-fashioned radio, and two switches. Hawthorne flicked one of them up and it began again.

The wheels on the bus go round and round . . .

'Turn it off!' Irene Laws shuddered.

He did as she asked. 'It's an MP3 recording alarm clock,' he explained. 'There are plenty of them on the internet. The idea is, you can download your kids' favourite songs so it wakes them up in the morning. I got one for my boy except I put my own voice on it. "Wake up, you little bastard, and get a move on." He thinks it's hilarious.'

'How was it activated?' I asked.

Hawthorne turned it over in his hands. 'It was set for eleven thirty. Whoever put it there timed it to go off in the middle of the funeral. They couldn't have done a better job.' He rounded on Irene Laws. 'Have you got an explanation for how it got there?' he asked.

'No!' She was taken aback, as if he was accusing her.

'Was the coffin left on its own at any time?'

'You'd really have to ask Mr Cornwallis.'

Hawthorne paused. 'Where is Cornwallis?'

'He had to leave early. It's his son's school play this afternoon.' She was staring at the orange ball. 'Nobody in our company would have done something like this.'

'Then it must have been someone from outside, hence my question: was the coffin left on its own?'

'Yes.' Irene squirmed, hating to admit it. 'The deceased was laid out at our facility on the Fulham Palace Road. She was brought from there today. Unfortunately, we don't have enough space at our South Kensington office. We have a chapel close to Hammersmith roundabout, a place of bereavement. Members of the family and close friends would have been able to visit Mrs Cowper if they so wished.'

'And how many of them so wished?'

'I can't tell you now. But we have a visitors' book and nobody would have been allowed in without some form of identification.'

'How about here at the cemetery?' Hawthorne asked. Irene said nothing, so he went on: 'When we arrived, the coffin was inside the hearse, which was parked around the back. Was there someone there the whole time?'

Irene deflected the question to one of the pall-bearers, who shuffled his feet and looked down. 'We were there most of the time,' he muttered. 'But not all of it.'

'And who are you?'

'Alfred Laws. I'm a director of the company.' He took a breath. 'Irene is my wife.'

Hawthorne smiled mirthlessly. 'Keep it all in the family, don't you! So where were you?'

'When we first arrived, we parked the vehicle and came in here.'

'All of you?'

'Yes.'

'And was the hearse locked?'

'No.'

'In our experience, nobody has ever tried to remove a dead person,' Irene remarked, icily.

'Well, maybe that's something you should think about in the future.' Hawthorne closed in on her, almost menacing. 'I'll need to talk to Mr Cornwallis. Where can I find him?'

'I'll give you his address.' Irene held out a hand and her husband passed her a notebook and a pen. She scribbled a few lines on the first page, then tore it out and handed it to Hawthorne.

'Thank you.'

'Wait a minute!' Meadows had been standing to one side throughout all this and it was as if he had only just realised he hadn't said anything. At the same time – I saw it in his eyes – he knew he had nothing more to say. 'I'll take the alarm clock,' he muttered, asserting his authority. 'It shouldn't have been handled,' he added, forgetting that he had been the one who had taken it from Irene in the first place. 'Forensics aren't going to like that.'

'I doubt forensics will find very much,' Hawthorne said.

'Well, if it was bought on the internet, there's a good chance we'll be able to find the identity of the purchaser.'

Hawthorne handed it to him. Meadows made a point of gripping it very carefully, with his thumb and second finger on each side of the digital clock.

'Good luck,' Hawthorne said.

It was a dismissal.

The wake, if that was what it was, was being held at a gastro-pub on the corner of Finborough Road, a few minutes' walk from the cemetery. This was the place that Damian had mentioned before he had stormed off. He wasn't the only one who had gone straight home: half the mourners had decided to give it a miss too. That left Grace Lovell and about a dozen men and women hitting the Prosecco and miniature sausages, trying to console each other not just on the loss of an old friend but on the terrible farce that her funeral had become.

Hawthorne had said he wanted to talk to Damian Cowper and he had already called through to Robert Cornwallis, leaving a message on his mobile phone. But first of all he wanted to catch up with the other mourners. After all, if they hadn't known Diana Cowper well, they wouldn't have come to the funeral, and it was his one chance to catch them while they were all together. There was a definite spring in his step as we crossed the Fulham Road and went in. Any sort of mystery energised him – and the more bizarre the better.

We saw Grace straight away. Although she was wearing black, her dress was very short and she had a velvet tuxedo jacket with extravagantly padded shoulders. Leaning against the bar, she could just as easily have come from a film premiere as a funeral. She wasn't talking to anyone and smiled anxiously as we came over to her.

'Mr Hawthorne!' She was clearly glad to see him. 'I don't know what I'm doing here. I hardly know any of these people.'

'Who are they?' Hawthorne asked.

She looked around, then pointed. 'That's Raymond Clunes. He's a theatre producer. Damian was in one of his plays.'

'We've met.'

'And that's Diana's G P.' She nodded at a man, in his sixties, pigeon-shaped in a dark, three-piece suit. 'His name's Dr Butterworth, I think. The woman next to him is his wife. The man standing in the corner is Diana's lawyer, Charles Kenworthy. He's dealing with the will. But I don't know anyone else.'

'Damian went home.'

'He was very upset. That song was deliberately chosen to upset him. It was a horrible joke to play.'

'You know about the song?'

'Well, yes!' She hesitated, unsure if she could continue. 'It goes back to that horrible business with those two children,' she said. 'It was Timothy Godwin's favourite song. They played it when they buried him . . . in Harrow Weald.'

'How do you know that?' Hawthorne asked.

'Damian told me. He often talked about it.' For some reason she felt a need to defend him. 'He's not someone to show his feelings but it really mattered to him, what happened all those years ago.' She had a glass of Prosecco and drained it. 'God, what a horrible day. I knew it was going to be horrible when I woke up this morning but I never dreamed it would be anything like this!'

Hawthorne was examining her. 'I got the impression you didn't much like Damian's mother,' he said, suddenly.

Grace blushed, the straight lines at the very top of her cheekbones darkening. 'That's not true! Who told you that?'

'You said she ignored you.'

'I said nothing of the sort. She was just more interested in Ashleigh, that's all.'

'Where is Ashleigh?'

'In Hounslow, at my parents' place. I'm picking her up when I leave here.' She put her glass down on the bar and picked up another one from a passing waiter.

'So you were close to her, then,' Hawthorne said.

'I wouldn't say that.' She thought for a moment. 'Damian and I had only been together a short while before Ashleigh arrived and she was nervous that being a father would hold him back.' She stopped herself. 'I know how that sounds but you have to understand that she was quite a lonely person. After Lawrence died, she only had Damian and she doted on him. His success meant the world to her.'

'And the baby was in the way?'

'She wasn't planned, if that's what you mean. But Damian loves her now. He wouldn't have it any other way.'

'How about you, Miss Lovell? Ashleigh can't have helped your career.'

'You do say the most unpleasant things, Mr Hawthorne. I'm only thirty-three. I love Ashleigh to bits. And it doesn't make any difference to me if I don't work for a few years. I'm very happy with the way things are.'

She can't have been that good an actress, I thought. I certainly wasn't convinced by her now.

'Do you enjoy Los Angeles?' Hawthorne asked.

'It's taken me a while to get used to it. We have a house in the Hollywood Hills and when I wake up in the morning, I can't believe I'm there. It was always my dream when I was at drama school – to wake up and see the Hollywood sign.'

'I imagine you've got lots of new friends.'

'I don't need new friends. I've got Damian.' She looked over Hawthorne's shoulder. 'If you don't mind, I have to say hello to some of these people. I'm meant to be looking after everyone and I don't want to stay too long.'

She slipped away. Hawthorne followed her with his eyes. I could see his thoughts ticking over.

'What now?' I asked.

'The doctor,' he said.

'Why him?'

Hawthorne glanced at me tiredly. 'Because he knew Diana Cowper inside out. Because if she had any problems, she may have talked to him. Because he may have been the one who killed her. I don't know!'

Shaking his head, Hawthorne approached the man in the three-piece suit whom Grace had pointed out. 'Dr Butterworth,' he said.

'Buttimore.' The doctor shook hands. He was large, bearded, with gold-framed glasses, the sort of man who would happily describe himself as 'old school'. It had offended him, Hawthorne getting his name wrong, but he warmed up a little once Hawthorne had explained his connection to Scotland Yard. I often noticed this. People enjoy being drawn into a murder investigation. Part of them wants to help but there's something salacious about it too.

'So what was all that about, back in the cemetery?' Buttimore asked. 'I bet you've never seen anything like that,

Mr Hawthorne. Poor Diana! God knows what she would have made of it. Do you think it was done on purpose?'

'I wouldn't have thought anyone would have loaded an alarm clock into a coffin by accident, sir,' Hawthorne said.

I was grateful for the final 'sir'. Otherwise, he would have sounded too obviously contemptuous.

'That's absolutely true. I take it you're going to look into it.'

'Well, Mrs Cowper's murder is my first priority.'

'I thought the culprit had already been identified.'

'A burglar,' his wife said. She was half the size of her husband, in her fifties, severe.

'We have to explore every avenue,' Hawthorne explained. He turned back to the husband. 'I understand you were a close friend of Mrs Cowper, Dr Buttimore. It would be helpful to know when you last saw her.'

'About three weeks ago. She visited my surgery in Cavendish Square. She'd come in to see me quite a few times, as a matter of fact.'

'Recently?'

'Over the last few months. She was having trouble sleeping. It's quite common, actually, among women of a certain age – although she was also having anxiety issues.' He glanced left and right, nervous of sharing confidential information in a public place. He lowered his voice. 'She was worried about her son.'

'And why would that be?' Hawthorne asked.

'I'm speaking to you as her doctor as well as her friend, Mr Hawthorne. The truth is that she was worried about his lifestyle in Los Angeles. She had been opposed to his going in the first place and then she'd read all these vile things in the gossip columns – drugs and parties and all the rest of it. Of course, there wasn't an iota of truth in it. The newspapers will print rubbish and lies about anyone who's famous. That's what I told her. But she was clearly in a state so I prescribed sleeping pills. Ativan to begin with and, later on, when that wasn't strong enough, temazepam.' I remembered the pills that we had found in the dead woman's bathroom. 'They seemed to do the trick,' Buttimore went on. 'I last saw her, as I just mentioned, at the end of April. I gave her another prescription—'

'You weren't afraid of her getting addicted?'

Dr Buttimore smiled benignly. 'Forgive me, Mr Hawthorne, but if you knew anything about medicine, you'd know there's very little chance of addiction with temazepam. It's one of the reasons I prescribe it. The only danger is short-term memory loss but Mrs Cowper seemed generally in excellent health.'

'Did she talk to you about visiting a funeral parlour?'

'I'm sorry?'

'She went to a funeral parlour. She arranged her funeral the very same day she died.'

Dr Buttimore blinked. 'I'm absolutely astonished. I can't think of any reason why she would have done that. I can assure you that apart from the anxiety problem, she had no reason to believe her health was in decline. I can only assume the timing of her death was a coincidence.'

'It was a burglary,' his wife insisted.

'Exactly, dear. She couldn't possibly have known it was going to happen. It was a coincidence. Nothing more.'

Hawthorne nodded and the two of us moved away. 'Fucking prat,' he muttered, as soon as we were out of earshot.

'Why do you say that?'

'Because he didn't have a clue what he was talking about.'

I looked puzzled.

'You heard what he said. It didn't make any sense,' Hawthorne said.

'It made sense to me.'

'He's a prat. Just make sure you write that down.'

'A fucking prat? I assume you'd like the expletive.'

Hawthorne said nothing.

'I'll just make sure it's clear it was you who said it,' I added. 'That way, he can sue you instead of me.'

'He can't sue anyone if it's the truth.'

We moved on to Charles Kenworthy, the lawyer. He was still in the corner, talking to a woman I assumed to be his wife. He was short and round with curling, silver hair. She was a similar shape but heavier. The two of them could have come down to London from the country as they both had a horsey quality, with ruddy cheeks from all that fresh air. He was drinking Prosecco. She had a fruit juice.

'How do you do? Yes, yes. I'm Charles Kenworthy. This is Frieda.'

He could hardly have been more affable. As soon as Hawthorne had introduced himself, Kenworthy made it his business to tell us as much about himself as he could. He had known the dead woman for more than thirty years and had been a close friend of Lawrence Cowper ('Pancreatic cancer. Absolutely shocking. He was a remarkable man . . . a first-rate dentist'). He still lived in Kent – in Faversham. He had helped Diana sell the house after that 'dreadful business' and move to London.

'Did you advise her at the time of the trial?' Hawthorne asked.

'Absolutely.' Kenworthy couldn't help himself. He didn't just talk. He gushed. 'There was no case against her. The judge was absolutely right.'

'Did you know him?'

'Weston? We'd met once or twice. A fair-minded chap. I told her she had nothing to worry about, no matter what the newspapers said. Still, it was a difficult time for her. She was very upset.'

'When did you last see her?'

'Last week . . . the day she died. At a board meeting. We were both on the board of the Globe Theatre. As you may know, the theatre is an educational charity. We rely very heavily on donations to be able to continue.'

'What sort of plays do you put on?'

'Well . . . Shakespeare obviously.'

I wasn't sure if Hawthorne really was unaware that the Globe was a reconstruction of a theatre that had stood on the south bank of the Thames four hundred years ago and that it specialised in authentic performances of mainly Elizabethan plays. There was nothing about him that suggested he had any interest in drama – or, for that matter, literature, music or art. At the same time, though, he was remarkably well informed about a great many things and it was quite possible that he was simply trying to get under the lawyer's skin.

'I understand that you had a bit of an argument that day.'

'I wouldn't say so. Who told you that?'

Hawthorne didn't answer. It was actually Robert Cornwallis who had heard raised voices when he had called Diana Cowper to ask about plot numbers in Brompton Cemetery. 'She resigned from the board,' he said.

'Yes. But that wasn't because of any particular disagreement.'

'So why did she resign?'

'I have no idea. She simply said that she'd been thinking about it for some time and that she would leave with immediate effect. Her announcement took us all by surprise. She had been a passionate supporter of the theatre and a driving force in our fundraising and educational programmes.'

'Was she unhappy about something?'

'Not at all. If anything, I would have said she was quite relieved. She had been on the board for six years. Maybe she thought it was enough.'

Next to him, his wife was becoming uneasy. 'Charles — maybe we ought to be on our way.'

'All right, dear.' Kenworthy turned to Hawthorne. 'I can't really tell you anything more about the board. It's confidential.'

'Can you tell me about Mrs Cowper's will?'

'Well, yes. I'm sure that will become public knowledge soon enough. It's quite simple. She left everything to Damian.'

'From what I understand, that's quite a bit.'

'It's not for me to go into details. It's been very nice meeting you, Mr Hawthorne.' Charles Kenworthy put down his glass. He fished in his pocket and handed a car key to his wife. 'Off we go then, dear. You'd better drive.'

'Righty-ho.'

'The keys . . .' Hawthorne was speaking to himself. His eyes were fixed on Charles and Frieda Kenworthy as they walked away but at the same time he was no longer interested in them. His thoughts were elsewhere. Frieda was still holding the car key. I saw it in her hand as she went through the door, and realised that it had thrown some sort of switch, reminding Hawthorne of something he had missed.

And then he worked it out. I actually saw the moment when it happened. It was almost shocking, as if he had been physically hit. I wouldn't say that the colour drained from his face, as there had never been much colour to begin with. But it was there in his eyes: the terrible realisation that he had got something wrong. 'We're going,' he said.

'Where?'

'There's no time. Just move.'

He was already on his way, pushing past a waiter, making for the door. We overtook the Kenworthys, who were saying goodbye to someone they knew, and burst out onto the street. We arrived at a corner and Hawthorne came to a halt, seething with fury.

'Why are there no bloody taxis?'

He was right. Despite the heavy traffic, there wasn't a taxi in sight – but as we stood there, I saw one pull in on the other side of the road. It had been hailed by a woman carrying shopping bags. Hawthorne shouted – a single exclamation. At the same time, he ran across the road, blind to the traffic. Taking a little more care – I was remembering that the cemetery was just around the corner – I followed. There was the screech of tyres, the blast of a horn, but somehow I made it to the other side. Hawthorne had already interposed himself between the woman and the driver – who had clicked on the meter, turning off his yellow light.

'Excuse me . . .' I heard the woman say, her voice rising with indignation.

'Police,' Hawthorne snapped. 'It's an emergency.'

She didn't ask him for ID. Hawthorne had been in the police force long enough to have assumed its authority. Or maybe it was just that he looked too dangerous, somebody you wouldn't want to argue with.

'Where do you want to go?' the driver asked as we both bundled in.

'Brick Lane,' Hawthorne said.

Damian Cowper's home.

I will never forget that taxi journey. It was a few minutes past midday and there wasn't actually that much traffic but every snarl-up, every red traffic light, was torture for Hawthorne, who sat hunched up next to me, almost writhing. There were all sorts of questions I wanted to ask him. What was it about a set of car keys that had alerted him? Why had they put him in mind of Damian Cowper? Was

Damian in some sort of danger? But I was sensible enough to keep silent. I didn't want Hawthorne's anger to be turned on me and – I don't know why – but somewhere in the back of my mind a voice was whispering that whatever was happening, it might somehow be my fault.

It's a long way from Fulham to Brick Lane. We had to cross the whole of London, west to east, and it might have been faster to take the tube. We actually went past several stations – South Kensington, Knightsbridge, Hyde Park Corner – and each time I saw Hawthorne making the calculation, trying to work out the amount of traffic ahead. As we headed down towards Piccadilly, he took out some of his frustration on the driver.

'Why are you going this way? You should have gone past the bloody palace.'

The driver ignored him. It was true that the traffic crawled as we came down towards Piccadilly Circus but when you're in a hurry in London, every route will be the wrong one. I looked at my watch. It had so far taken us twenty-five minutes to get here. It felt a lot longer. Next to me, Hawthorne was muttering under his breath. I sat back and closed my eyes. He still hadn't told me what was actually going on.

Eventually, we reached Damian Cowper's flat. Hawthorne leapt out, leaving me to pay. I handed the driver £50 and, without waiting for change, followed Hawthorne through the narrow doorway and staircase that led up between two shops. We reached the entrance on the first floor. Ominously, the door was ajar.

We went in.

It was the smell of blood that hit me first. I'd written about dozens of murders for books and television but I had never imagined anything like this.

Damian Cowper had been mutilated. He was lying on his side in a puddle of dark brown blood that had spread all around him, seeping into the floorboards. One of his hands was stretched out and the first thing I noticed was that two of his fingers had been half severed as he had flailed out, trying to protect himself from the knife that had cut him half a dozen times and which had finally been left sticking out of his chest. One of the blows had slashed him across the face and this injury was more horrible than any of the others because when we meet someone it's the first thing we look at. Lose an arm or a leg and you are still you. Lose your face and almost everything we know about you is taken away.

Damian had a deep cut that had taken out one eye and folded back a great flap of skin all the way down to his mouth. His clothes might hide the worst of his other injuries but here there was no disguising the madness of what had been done to him. One of his cheeks was pressed against the floor and his whole head had taken on the melting quality of a punctured football. He no longer looked anything like himself. I had really only recognised him by his clothes and the tangled black hair.

The smell of his blood filled my nostrils. It was rich, deep, like freshly dug earth. I had never known that blood smelled like that but then there was so much of it and the flat was warm, the windows closed, the walls bending . . .

*   *   *

197

'Tony? Come on! For Christ's sake!'

For some reason, I was looking at the ceiling. The back of my head was hurting. Hawthorne was leaning over me. I opened my mouth to speak, then stopped myself. I couldn't have fainted. That was impossible. It was ridiculous. It was embarrassing.

But I had.

Thirteen
Dead Man's Shoes

'Tony? Are you all right?'

Hawthorne was leaning over me, filling my vision. He didn't look concerned. If anything, he was puzzled, as if it was a strange thing to do, to faint after seeing a hideously mutilated and still-bleeding corpse.

I wasn't all right. I'd hit my head on Damian Cowper's warehouse-style floor and I felt sick. The smell of blood was still in my nostrils and I was afraid that I might have tumbled into it. Grimacing, I felt around me. The floorboards were dry.

'Can you help me up?' I said.

'Sure.' He hesitated, then reached down and seized my arm, pulling me to my feet. Why the hesitation? Here was a moment of insight. In all the time I had known him, during this investigation and while he had helped me with my research, there had never been any physical contact between us. We had never so much as shaken hands. In fact, now that I thought about it, I had never seen him come into physical contact with anyone. Was he a germophobe? Or was he simply antisocial? It was another mystery for me to solve.

I sat down in one of the leather armchairs, away from the body and the blood.

'Do you want some water?' he asked.

'No. I'm OK.'

'You're not going to throw up, are you? It's just that we have to protect the crime area.'

'I'm not going to throw up.'

He nodded. 'It's not very nice, seeing a dead body. And I can tell you this is about as bad as it gets.' He shook his head. 'I've seen decapitations, people with their eyes gouged out—'

'Thanks!' I could feel the nausea rising. I took a breath.

'Someone certainly didn't like Damian Cowper,' he said.

'I don't get it,' I said. I thought of what Grace had told us after the funeral. 'This was planned, wasn't it? Someone put the music player in the coffin because they knew it would get to Damian. They wanted to drive him away so he'd be on his own. But why him? If this is all about the accident in Deal, he can hardly take the blame. He wasn't even in the car.'

'You've got a point.'

I tried to think it through. A woman drives a car recklessly and kills a child. Ten years later, she is punished. But why extend that to her son? Could there be some biblical reason: an eye for an eye? That made no sense. Diana Cowper was already dead. If someone had wanted to use her son to hurt her, they would have killed him first.

'His mother didn't go to the police at first, because she was trying to protect him,' I mused. 'That was the reason why she drove away. Maybe it was enough to make him responsible.'

Hawthorne thought for a moment in silence – but not about what I'd said. 'I've got to leave you for a minute,' he said. 'I've already called 999. But I've got to check the flat.'

'Go ahead.'

Funnily enough, it was something I remembered from our time working on *Injustice*. We had been talking about one of the scenes in Episode One, when the animal rights activist is found dead in a farmhouse. Hawthorne had told me then that when a body is discovered, the first priority for any policeman or detective will be their own self-preservation. Are they under threat? Is the assailant still in the building? They'll make sure they're safe. Then they'll look for possible witnesses . . . classically, the child hiding in the wardrobe or under the bed. Hawthorne would have dialled 999 while I was lying on the floor. I suppose it was nice of him to notice me at all.

He left the room, disappearing up the spiral staircase. I sat in the armchair trying to ignore the body, trying not even to think of the dreadful injuries. It wasn't easy. If I closed my eyes, I became more aware of the smell. If I opened them, I found myself glimpsing the blood, the sprawled-out limbs. I had to turn my head away to keep Damian Cowper out of my line of vision.

And then he groaned.

I twisted round, thinking I'd imagined it. But there it was again, a quite gruesome, rattling sound. Damian's head was facing away from me but I was quite certain it was coming from him.

'Hawthorne!' I shouted. At the same time, I felt the bile rising in my throat. 'Hawthorne!'

He came hurrying back down the stairs. 'What is it?'

'It's Damian. He's alive.'

He looked at me doubtfully, then went over to the body. 'No, he isn't,' he said, tersely.

'I just heard him.'

Damian moaned again, louder this time. I hadn't imagined it. He was trying to speak.

But Hawthorne just sniffed. 'Stay where you are, Tony, and forget about it, all right? His muscles are stiffening and that includes the muscles around his vocal cords. And there are gases in his stomach which are trying to escape. That's all you're hearing. It happens all the time.'

'Oh.' I profoundly wished that I wasn't here. Not for the first time, I wished that I'd never agreed to write this bloody book.

Hawthorne lit a cigarette.

'Did you find anything upstairs?' I asked.

'There's no-one else here,' he said.

'You knew he was going to be killed.'

'I knew it was a possibility.'

'How?'

He cupped his hand and tapped ash into his palm. I could see that he was reluctant to tell me. 'I was stupid,' he said, at last. 'But when the two of us were here the first time, you distracted me.'

'So it was my fault?'

'I told you, when I'm talking to someone, I need to focus and when you interrupt, it sort of breaks what I'm thinking, my train of thought.' He softened. 'It was my fault. I'll hold my hands up. I was the one who missed it.'

'Missed what?'

'Damian said that his mum came in and watered the plants on the terrace. He said she forwarded his mail. I should have remembered. When we were at Diana Cowper's place, there were five hooks in the kitchen. Do you remember?'

'They were on a wooden fish.'

'That's right. And there were four sets of keys. If Diana Cowper was coming in here while he was in L.A., it followed that she had his keys but I didn't see one with that label.'

'There was an empty hook.'

'That's right. Someone kills her. They search the place. They notice the keys. And they take the opportunity to snatch them.' He stopped and I saw him playing back what he had just said. 'That's one possibility anyway.'

I heard the stamp of feet on the stairs leading up to the front door and a moment later, two uniformed police constables arrived. They looked from the body to the two of us, trying to work out what was going on.

'Stay right where you are,' the first one said. 'Who made the call?'

'I did,' Hawthorne said. 'And you took your time getting here.'

'Who are you, sir?'

'Ex-Detective Inspector Hawthorne, formerly with MIT.

I've already contacted DI Meadows. I've reason to believe that this murder may be connected to a current investigation. You'd better get in the local DI and the murder squad.'

The British police have a particular way of addressing each other, a formal and slightly tortuous turn-of-phrase, as in 'I have reason to believe' and 'contacted' instead of 'called'. It's one reason why I've always found them so difficult to dramatise on television. It's hard to care about a character who talks in clichés. They also look so much less interesting than their American counterparts, with their white shirts, stab vests and those hopeless blue helmets. No guns. No sunglasses. These two policemen were young and earnest. One was Asian, the other white. They hardly spoke to us again.

One of them took out his radio and called in the situation while Hawthorne set about examining the room for himself. I watched him as he went over to the door that led out to the terrace. He was careful not to touch the handle, using a handkerchief which he pulled out of his pocket. The door was unlocked. He disappeared outside and although I was still feeling dreadful, I hauled myself out of the chair and followed. The policemen had made their calls. They didn't seem to have anything else to do. They glanced uncertainly in my direction as I left. They hadn't even asked who I was.

I felt better immediately, being out in the afternoon air. Like the interior of the flat, the terrace – with its deckchairs, potted plants and gas barbecue – reminded me of a studio set. It resembled the balcony where Joey and Chandler and the rest of them used to hang out in *Friends*, looking out towards the back of the building with a metal fire escape leading to an alleyway. Hawthorne was standing at the edge, gazing down. I noticed he had taken off his shoes, presumably to avoid leaving footprints. He was smoking again. He consumed a suicidal number of cigarettes a day, at least twenty, maybe more. He turned round as I approached.

'He was waiting out here,' he said. 'By the time Damian Cowper got back from the funeral, he'd already let himself into the flat, using the keys he'd taken from Britannia Road. Then he came out here and he waited. He also left this way when it was over.'

'Wait a minute. How do you know all that? How do you even know it was a he?'

'Diana Cowper was strangled with a curtain cord. Her son was chopped to pieces. The killer was either a man or a really, really angry woman.'

'What about the rest of it? How can you be sure that's how the murder happened?'

Hawthorne just shrugged.

'If you want me to write about it, you're going to have to tell me. Otherwise, I'll have to make it up.' It was a threat I'd made before.

'All right.' He flicked the cigarette over the side of the building. I watched it spin in the air before it disappeared. 'Start by putting yourself in the killer's place. Think about what's going on in his mind.

'You know Damian's going to be coming back here from the funeral. That crap with the MP3 player and "The wheels on the bus" was done deliberately to drive him here. Or it could be that you were in the cemetery – in the crowd or hiding behind one of the gravestones. You heard him tell his girlfriend: *I'm going home*. That's when you made your plan.

'The only trouble is, you can't be certain he's going to be alone. Maybe Grace will come along after all. Maybe he'll bring the vicar. So you have to wait somewhere you can see him and if the opportunity doesn't present itself, you can piss off again.' He jerked a thumb. 'There's a staircase down to ground level.'

'Perhaps he came up that way?'

'He can't have. The door into the living room is locked and bolted on the inside.' Hawthorne shook his head. 'He had the key. He let himself in the front door. He looked for somewhere to hide and came out here. It was perfect. He could look in through the window and see if Damian had someone with him. But as things turned out, Damian was alone, which was what he wanted. The killer went back into the living room and . . .' He left the rest of the sentence hanging.

'You said he left this way too,' I reminded him.

'There's a footprint.' Hawthorne pointed and I saw a red quarter moon next to the fire escape, made by the sole of someone's shoe after they'd stepped in Damian's blood. It reminded me of the footprint we'd found at Diana Cowper's house, presumably left behind by the same foot.

'Anyway, he couldn't use the front door,' Hawthorne went on. 'You've seen the stab wounds. There'd have been a lot of blood. He'd have been covered in it. You think he could stroll down Brick Lane without being noticed? My guess is he put on a coat or something, climbed down here and disappeared down the alleyway.'

'Do you know how the alarm clock got into the coffin?'

'Not yet. We're going to have to talk to Cornwallis.' He rolled the cigarette between his fingers. 'But we're not going to be able to leave here for a while. You may have to give a statement to Meadows when he finally turns up. Don't say too much. Just play dumb.' He glanced at me. 'It shouldn't be too difficult.'

Over the next couple of hours, Damian Cowper's flat became more and more crowded while the two of us sat there with nothing to do. The police constables who had first arrived on the scene had summoned their detective inspector, who had in turn called in the Murder Investigation Team. There were about half a dozen of them, wearing those plasticised paper suits with hoods, masks and gloves that made them almost indistinguishable from each other. Every few seconds, the room seemed to freeze as a police photographer captured some section of it with a dazzling flash. A man and a woman, both part of the forensic team, were crouching over Damian's body, delicately swabbing his hands and neck with cotton buds. I knew what they were looking for. If there had been any bodily contact between Damian and his attacker during the knife attack, they might be able to pick up DNA. Both of his hands had been bagged, the opaque plastic securely taped. It was extraordinary how quickly he had been dehumanised – and worse was to come. When they were finally ready to remove him, two men knelt down and wrapped him in polythene which they sealed with gaffer tape. The process turned him into something that reminded me of both ancient Egypt and Federal Express.

They'd used blue and white tape to create a cordon which began at the front door and blocked off the stairs. I wasn't sure how they would deal with the neighbours on the upper and lower floors. As for me, although I hadn't been questioned, a woman in a plastic suit had asked me to remove my shoes and taken them away. That puzzled me. 'What do they need them for?' I asked Hawthorne.

'Latent footprints,' he replied. 'They need to eliminate you from the enquiry.'

'I know. But they haven't taken yours.'

'I've been more careful, mate.'

He glanced at his feet. He was still in his socks. He must have slipped his shoes off the moment he saw Damian's body.

'When will I get them back?' I asked.

Hawthorne shrugged.

'How long are we going to be here for?'

Again, he didn't answer. He wanted another cigarette but he wasn't allowed to smoke inside and it was making him irritable.

After a while, Meadows arrived, signing himself in with the log officer at the door. He had taken charge – the murder of Damian Cowper was being folded into his current investigation – and this time I saw a different side of him. He was cool and authoritative, checking with the crime scene manager, talking to the forensic team, taking notes. When he finally came over to us, he got straight to the point.

'What were you doing here?'

'We came over to offer our condolences.'

'Piss off, Hawthorne. This is serious. Did he call you? Did you know he might be in danger?'

Meadows wasn't as stupid as Hawthorne had suggested. He was right. Hawthorne had known. But would he admit it?

'No,' he said. 'He didn't call me.'

'So why did you come here?'

'Why do you think? That business at the funeral – there's obviously something sick going on and if you hadn't been so busy chasing your non-existent burglar, you'd have seen it too. I wanted to ask him about what had happened. I just got here too late.'

No mention of the keys. Hawthorne would never admit he'd made a mistake. He'd forgotten that one day Meadows would read it in my book.

'He was already dead when you got here.'

'Yes.'

'You didn't see anyone leaving?'

'There's a bloody footprint out on the terrace, if you care to take a look. It might give you a shoe size. I'd say the killer left down the fire escape into the alley, so perhaps you'll catch him on CCTV. But we didn't see anything. We got here too late.'

'All right, then. You can get lost. And take Agatha Christie here with you.'

He meant me. Agatha Christie is something of a hero of mine but I was still offended.

Hawthorne got up and I followed him to the front door, both of us padding across the wooden floor in our socks. I was about to point this out when he swept a pair of black leather shoes off the art deco sideboard and handed them to me. I hadn't noticed when he'd put them there. 'These are for you,' he said.

'Where did you get them?'

'I nicked them out of the cupboard when I went upstairs. They belonged to him.' He nodded in the direction of Damian Cowper. 'They should be about your size.'

I looked uncertain, so he added: 'He won't be needing them.'

I slipped them on. They were Italian, expensive. They fitted perfectly.

He put on his own shoes and we walked out, past more uniformed policemen and down into Brick Lane. There were three police cars parked outside and, next to them, a vehicle with the words 'Private Ambulance' printed on the side. It wasn't anything of the sort. It was just a black van brought here to transport Damian Cowper to the mortuary. More policemen were at work, erecting a screen from the front of the house to the edge of the pavement so that nobody would see the body when it was carried out. A large crowd was being held back on the other side of the road. The traffic had been blocked. Not for the first time, I found myself thinking of all the television programmes I'd been involved with. We'd never have been able to afford so many extras and all these vehicles, let alone the central London location.

A taxi had pulled in just ahead of us and I nudged Hawthorne as Grace Lovell got out. She was dressed in the same clothes that she had worn to the funeral, with her handbag over her arm – but now she had Ashleigh with her, wearing a pink dress and clutching her hand. Grace stopped and looked around, shocked by all the activity. Then she saw us and hurried over.

'What's happened?' she asked. 'Why are the police here?'

'I'm afraid you can't go in there,' Hawthorne said. 'I've got some bad news.'

'Damian . . . ?'

'He's been killed.'

I thought he could have put it more gently. There was a three-year-old girl standing in front of him. What if she had heard and understood? Grace had had the same thought. She drew her daughter closer towards her, a protective arm around her shoulders. 'What do you mean?' she whispered.

'Someone attacked him after the funeral.'

'He's dead?'

'I'm afraid so.'

'No. That's not possible. He was upset. He said he was going home. It was that horrible joke.' She looked from Hawthorne to the door, then back again. She realised that the two of us had been on our way out. 'Where are you going?'

'There's a DI in the flat called Meadows. He's in charge of the investigation and he'll want to talk to you. But if you'll take my advice, you won't go inside. It's not very pleasant. Have you been with your parents?'

'Yes. I went to pick up Ashleigh.'

'Then get back in the taxi and go back to them. Meadows will find you soon enough.'

'Can I do that? They won't think . . . ?'

'They won't think you had anything to do with it. You were at the pub with us.'

'That's not what I meant.' She made up her mind, then nodded. 'You're right. I can't go inside. Not with Ashleigh.'

'Where's Daddy?' Ashleigh spoke for the first time. She seemed confused and scared by the police and all the activity around her.

'Daddy's not here,' Grace said. 'We're going back to Granny and Grandpa.'

'Do you want someone to travel with you?' I asked. 'I don't mind coming with you, if you like.'

'No. I don't need anyone.'

I didn't know what to make of Grace Lovell. I've never been very comfortable with actors, because I can never tell if they're being sincere or if they're simply . . . well, acting. This was how it was now. Grace looked upset. There were tears in her eyes. She could have been in shock. And yet there was a part of me that said it was all just a performance, that she had been rehearsing her lines from the moment the taxi drew in.

We watched as she got back into the car and closed the door. She leaned forward and gave instructions to the driver. A moment later, it pulled away.

'The grieving widow,' Hawthorne muttered.

'Do you think so?'

'No, Tony. I've seen more grief at a Turkish wedding. If you ask me, I'd say there's a lot of things she's not telling us.' The taxi passed through the traffic lights at the top of Brick Lane and disappeared. Hawthorne smiled. 'She didn't even ask how he died.'

Fourteen
Willesden Green

It was a 1950s semi-detached house, red brick on the first floor, then off-white stucco topped with a gabled roof. It was as if three architects had worked on it at the same time without ever being introduced to one another but they must have been pleased with their work because they'd replicated it on the house next door, which was an exact mirror of its neighbour, with a wooden fence dividing the drives and a single chimney shared between the two properties. Each one of them had a bay window which looked out over an area of crazy paving running down to a low wall, with the street, Sneyd Road, on the other side. I guessed it had about four bedrooms. A poster in the front window advertised a fun run for the North London Hospice. A garage stood open to one side, with a bright green Vauxhall Astra, a tricycle and a motorbike fighting for space.

The doorway was arched, the door fake-medieval with thick panels of frosted glass. There was a novelty welcome mat which read: 'Never mind the dog – beware of the owner!' When Hawthorne pressed the doorbell, it played the opening notes of the theme from *Star Wars*. Chopin's Funeral March might have been more appropriate. For this was where Robert Cornwallis lived.

The woman who opened the door was almost aggressively cheerful, as if she had been looking forward to our visit all week. *There you are, at last*, she seemed to say as she beamed out at us. *What took you so long?*

She was about forty years old and was hurtling into middle age with complete recklessness, actually embracing it with a baggy, out-of-shape jersey, ill-fitting jeans (with a flower embroidered on one knee), frizzy hair and cheap, chunky jewellery. She was overweight – an earth mother, she might call herself. She had a huge pile of laundry under one arm and a cordless telephone in her hand but didn't seem to notice either of them. I could imagine her balancing the laundry on her raised thigh with the phone squeezed between her ear and her shoulder as she struggled to open the door.

'Mr Hawthorne?' she asked, looking at me. She had a pleasant, well-educated voice.

'No,' I said. 'That's him.'

'I'm Barbara. Please come in. I'm afraid you're going to have to excuse the state of the house. It's six o'clock and we're just putting the children to bed. Robert's in the other room. I'm sure you'll understand, we've had a bit of a day! Irene told us what happened at the funeral. It's shocking. You're with the police. Is that right?'

'I'm helping the police with this enquiry.'

'This way! Mind the roller skate. I've told the children

not to leave them in the hall. One day someone's going to break their neck!' She glanced down, noticing the laundry for the first time. 'Look at me! I'm so sorry. I was just putting on the wash when the door rang. I don't know what you must think of me!'

We stepped over the loose roller skate and went into a hallway cluttered with coats, wellington boots and different-sized shoes. A motorbike helmet sat on a chair. Two children were racing around the house. We heard them before we saw them – screaming, high-pitched voices. A second later, they came charging out of a doorway, two little boys, both fair-haired, aged about five and seven. They took one look at us, then turned round and disappeared, still screaming.

'That's Toby and Sebastian,' Barbara said. 'They'll be going up for their bath in a minute and then maybe we'll get a bit of peace. Do you have children? Honestly, sometimes this place is like a battlefield.'

The children had taken over the house. There were clothes on radiators, toys everywhere . . . footballs, plastic swords, stuffed animals, old tennis rackets, scattered playing cards and pieces of Lego. It was difficult to see past the mess but as we were shown through an archway and into the living room I got the impression of a comfortable, old-fashioned home, with dried flowers in the fireplace, seagrass carpets, an upright piano that would almost certainly be out of tune, throws on the sofas and those round paper lampshades that never seem to have gone completely out of fashion. The pictures on the walls were abstract and colourful, the sort of art that might have come out of a department store.

'Do you work in your husband's business, Mrs Cornwallis?'
Hawthorne asked as we followed her towards the kitchen.

'God, no! And call me Barbara.' She dumped the laundry
on a chair. 'We see enough of each other as it is. I'm a
pharmacist . . . part-time, the local branch of Boots. I can't
say I love that either but we have to pay the bills. Watch
out! That's the other roller skate. Robert's in here . . .'

The kitchen was bright and cluttered, with a breakfast
bar and a white, rustic-style table. Dirty plates were piled up
in the sink with clean ones beside them. I wondered how
Barbara would be able to sort out which was which. French
windows looked out over a garden that was little more than
a green rectangle with a few shrubs growing down one side,
boxed in by fences. Even this had been colonised by the children, with a trampoline and a climbing frame occupying – and
killing – much of the lawn.

Robert Cornwallis, in the same suit that he had worn at
the Brompton chapel but without the tie, was sitting at the
table, going through some accounts. It was strange seeing
him here, a funeral director outside his parlour. At least, it
was strange because I knew he *was* a funeral director. I
wondered what it was like to come home to this cosy, domes-
tic normality after a day stitching up bodies in the morgue.
Did he or his wife feel in any way tainted by it? Did his
children know what their father did? I've never actually had
an undertaker as a character in any of my books and I was
rather hoping that Hawthorne would ask him more about
his work. I store all sorts of information like that. You never
know when it may be useful.

The kitchen had been invaded like the rest of the house. There were more plastic toys, crayons and paper on the table, brightly coloured scribbles sellotaped onto every wall. I remembered the house in Harrow-on-the-Hill and Judith Godwin's life, destroyed by the loss of a child. The Cornwallises' house was defined by children too but in a very different way.

'Here's Robert,' Barbara announced, then chided him. 'Are you still doing that? We've got the supper to cook and the children to put to bed and now we've got the police in the house!'

'I've just finished, dear.' Cornwallis closed his account books. He gestured at the empty seats in front of him. 'Mr Hawthorne. Please, sit down.'

'Would you like some tea?' Barbara asked. 'I can offer you English breakfast, Earl Grey or lapsang souchong.'

'Nothing, thank you.'

'How about something stronger, maybe? Robert – we've still got that wine in the fridge.'

I shook my head.

'I might have a glass, if you don't mind. After all, it's the weekend . . . almost. Will you have one, Robbie?'

'No, thank you, dear.'

Hawthorne and I sat down on the other side of the table. Hawthorne was about to start his interrogation when suddenly the two children came charging in, racing around the table, demanding a bedtime story. Robert Cornwallis raised his hands, trying to take control of the situation. 'All right, you two. That's enough!' The children ignored him. 'Why don't you go out in the garden? As a special treat you can have ten minutes on the trampoline before bed!'

The children yelled with delight. Their father got up and opened the French windows. They ran out and we watched as they climbed onto the trampoline.

'Lovely kids,' Hawthorne muttered, with all the malice in the world.

'They can be a bit of a handful at this time of day.' Cornwallis sat down again. 'Where's Andrew?' he called over to his wife, who was standing beside the fridge with a half-full bottle of white wine.

'Upstairs, doing his homework.'

'Or playing on his computer,' Cornwallis said. 'I can't get him off it – but then he's nine.'

'All his friends are the same,' Barbara agreed, pouring the wine. 'I don't know what it is with children these days. They're not interested in the real world.'

There was a pause. In this house, a moment of silence was something of a luxury.

'Irene told me about the funeral,' Cornwallis began, echoing what Barbara had said in the hall. 'I cannot tell you how dismayed I am. I have been ten years in this business. My father ran the company before me, and my grandfather before that. I can assure you that nothing like this has ever happened before.' Hawthorne was about to ask him something but he continued. 'I am particularly sorry that I wasn't there. I try to be present at every funeral but, as I'm sure Irene will have told you, it was my son's school play.'

'He spent weeks learning his lines,' Barbara exclaimed.

'Every night before bed. He took it very seriously.' She had filled a large glass with wine and came over and joined us. 'He would never have forgiven us if we hadn't been there. Acting runs in his blood . . . it's all he ever talks about. And he was absolutely brilliant. Well, I would say that, wouldn't I? But he was!'

'I shouldn't have gone. I knew it at the time. I had this gut feeling that something was going to go wrong.'

'Why was that, Mr Cornwallis?'

He thought back. 'Well, everything about Mrs Cowper's death had been unusual. It may surprise you, but I am no stranger to violent crime, Mr Hawthorne. We have another branch in south London and we have been summoned by the police on more than one occasion . . . knife crime, gang violence. But in this instance, for Mrs Cowper to have arranged her funeral the very day that it would be required . . .'

'You said to me you were worried about it,' Barbara agreed. 'Only this morning, when you were getting dressed, you were going on about it.' She ran her eyes over him. 'Why are you still in that suit? I thought you were going to get changed.'

Barbara Cornwallis was a pleasant, friendly woman but she never stopped talking and being married to her would have driven me insane. Her husband ignored her last question. 'That was why I asked Irene to be there,' he explained. 'I knew there would be police and journalists and of course Damian Cowper had a certain celebrity. I didn't trust Alfred to handle it on his own. Even so, I should have stayed.'

'You never even got to talk to Damian Cowper.' There

was a bowl of crisps on the table. Barbara slid them towards herself and took a handful. In the garden, the boys were bouncing up and down. We could hear their excited laughter on the other side of the double glazing. 'And he's one of your favourite actors too.'

'That's true.'

'We've seen everything he's done. What was the television programme he was in? The one about the journalists?'

'I can't remember, dear.'

'Of course you can remember. You bought the DVD. You've watched it lots of times.'

'*State of Play*.'

'That's the one. I couldn't follow it myself. But he was very good. And we saw him in the theatre, didn't we, in Oscar Wilde. *The Importance of Being Earnest*. I took Robert for our anniversary.' She turned to her husband. 'We both thought he was brilliant.'

'He was a very good actor,' Cornwallis agreed. 'But I would never have approached him at his mother's funeral, even if the opportunity had arisen. It wouldn't have been appropriate.' He allowed himself a little joke. 'I was hardly going to ask him for an autograph!'

'Well, I have some news that may surprise you,' Hawthorne said. He helped himself to a single crisp, holding it as if it were evidence. 'Damian Cowper is also dead.'

'What?' Cornwallis stared at him.

'He was murdered this afternoon. Just an hour or so after the funeral.'

'What are you talking about? That's impossible!' Cornwallis looked completely shocked. I would have thought the news had already been on TV or the internet but the two of them must have been too busy with their children to have seen it.

'How was he killed?' Barbara asked. She looked shocked too.

'He was stabbed. In his flat in Brick Lane.'

'Do you know who did it?'

'Not yet. I'm surprised Detective Inspector Meadows hasn't been in touch with you.'

'We haven't heard anything.' Cornwallis gazed at us, searching for words. 'What happened at the funeral . . . is there a connection? I mean, there must be! When Irene told me about it, I thought it was just an unpleasant joke . . .'

'Someone with a grudge. That's what you said,' Barbara reminded him.

'That seemed the obvious conclusion but, as I said, it was completely outside my experience. But if Damian's been killed, I would imagine that puts everything in a very different light.'

Hawthorne had had second thoughts about the crisp. He dropped it back in the bowl. 'Somebody put an MP3 recording alarm clock inside the coffin. It went off at half past eleven and played a nursery rhyme. I think it's a safe bet that there is a connection. So I want to know how it got there.'

'I have no idea.'

'Why don't you have a little think for a minute?' Hawthorne was on edge. I think the mess of the place, the children bouncing up and down, Barbara with her wine and her crisps, everything about Willesden Green was beginning to get on his nerves.

Cornwallis looked at his wife as if seeking her support. 'I can assure you that it wasn't placed there by anyone who works for me. Everyone at Cornwallis and Sons has been with the company for at least five years and many of them are part of the family. I'm sure Irene told you. Mrs Cowper was taken directly from the hospital to our central mortuary at Hammersmith. We washed her and closed her eyes. Mrs Cowper did not wish to be embalmed. Nobody asked to view the body – even if they had, there would have been no opportunity to do anything amiss.

'She was placed in the natural Willow Weave coffin which she had chosen. That would have been at around half past nine this morning. I wasn't there but all four pall-bearers would have been in the room. She was then carried to the hearse. We have a private courtyard with an electric gate, so no-one can come in off the street. From there, she was taken directly to Brompton Cemetery.'

'So she would have been in someone's sight all the time.'

'Yes. As far as I can see, there were perhaps three or four minutes when the coffin was left unattended: when it was in the car park behind the chapel – and, incidentally, I shall make sure that in future this never happens again.

'But that was when the alarm clock could have been put in the coffin.'

'Yes. I suppose so.'

'How easy would it have been to open it?'

Cornwallis considered. 'It would have been the work of just a few moments. If it had been a traditional coffin, made of solid wood, the lid would have been screwed down. But with a willow coffin there are just two straps.'

Barbara had finished her drink. 'Are you sure you won't have a glass of wine?' she asked us.

'No, thank you,' I said.

'Well, I'm going to have another. All this talk about murder and death! We never discuss Robert's work in the house, usually. The children hate it. At Andrew's school, they had to give a talk about their dad's business in front of the whole class and he made everything up. He said Robert was an accountant.' She gave a hoot of laughter. 'I don't know where he got his facts from. He doesn't know anything about accountancy.' She went to the fridge and poured herself a second glass of wine.

As she closed the fridge door, another boy came in, wearing tracksuit trousers and a T-shirt. He was taller than the other two, with darker hair that fell clumsily over his face. "Why are Tobes and Seb in the garden?' he asked. He noticed us. 'Who are you?'

'This is Andrew,' Barbara said. 'These men are policemen.'

'Why? What's happened?'

'It's nothing for you to worry about, Andrew. Have you finished your homework?' The boy nodded. 'Then you can watch television if you want to.' She smiled at him, showing him off. 'I was just telling these gentlemen about your school play. Mr Pinocchio!'

'He wasn't very good,' Cornwallis said. Then he mimed

his nose stretching. 'Wait a minute. That's a lie. He was brilliant!'

Andrew plumped himself out, pleased with himself. 'I'm going to be an actor when I grow up,' he announced.

'Let's not talk about that right now, Andrew,' Cornwallis interrupted him. 'If you want to help, you can go out and tell your brothers it's time for bed.'

Out in the garden, Toby and Sebastian had moved onto the climbing frame. They were shouting at each other, over-tired, sliding into that zone where they lost almost any resemblance to rational human beings. It was something I remembered well from my own children. Andrew nodded and did as he had been told.

'Can I ask you something?' I knew I was risking Hawthorne's anger but I was interested. 'It's not completely relevant but I'd like to know why you chose this line of work.'

'Being an undertaker?' Cornwallis didn't seem bothered by the question. 'In a way, it chose me. You saw the sign above the door of our South Kensington office. It's a family business. I think it was started by my great-great-grandfather and it's always been in the family. I have two cousins work-ing in it. You met Irene. My cousin George does the books. Maybe one of my boys will take it over one day.'

'Chance will be a fine thing!' Barbara scoffed.

'They may change their minds.'

'Like you did?'

'It's not very easy for young people these days. It'll be good for them to know there's a job for them if they want it.' He turned back to us. 'After I left college, I did other things. I travelled and in my own way I suppose I sowed a few wild oats. There was a part of me that resisted the idea of becoming a funeral director – but if I hadn't joined the firm, my life would have been very different.' He reached out and took hold of his wife's hand. 'It was how we met.'

'It was my uncle's funeral!'

'One of the very first where I was officiating.' Cornwallis smiled. 'It's probably not the most romantic way to meet your life partner, but it was the best thing that came out of that day.'

'I never much liked Uncle David anyway,' Barbara said.

It was getting dark outside and the two children were now arguing with their older brother, who was trying to bring them in. 'I'm afraid if you have no more questions, we're going to have to ask you to leave,' Cornwallis said. 'We have to get the boys into bed.'

Hawthorne got to his feet. 'You've been very helpful,' he said.

I wasn't sure if this was true.

'Can you let us know if you find anything?' Barbara asked. 'It's hard to believe that Damian Cowper has been killed. His mother first, then him. It makes you wonder who'll be next!'

She went outside to gather up her children while Cornwallis took us to the door. 'There was one other thing I thought I ought to mention to you,' he said as we stood on the crazy paving outside in the grey light. 'I'm just not sure if it's relevant or not . . .'

'Go on,' Hawthorne said.

'Well, two days ago, I got a telephone call. It was someone wanting to know where and when the funeral was going to take place. It was a man at the other end of the line. He said he was a friend of Diana Cowper and that he wanted to attend, but he refused to give me his name. In fact his entire manner was – how can I put it? – rather suspicious. I won't say he was deranged but he certainly sounded as if he was under a lot of strain. He was nervous. He wouldn't even tell me where he was calling from.'

'How did he know you were in charge of the funeral?'

'I wondered about that myself, Mr Hawthorne. I imagine he must have telephoned all the undertakers in west London, making the same enquiry, although we're one of the largest and best respected so he could have started with us first. Anyway, I didn't think very much of it at the time. I simply gave him the details that he wanted. But when Irene told me the awful things that had happened today, well, of course I was reminded of him.'

'I don't suppose you have his number?'

'Yes. I do. We keep a record of all our incoming calls and he rang me from a mobile, so his number showed up on our system.' Cornwallis took out a folded piece of paper and handed it to Hawthorne. 'I was in two minds whether to give this to you, to be honest. I don't want to get anyone into any trouble.'

'We'll look into it, Mr Cornwallis.'

'It's probably nothing. A waste of time.'

'I've got a lot of time.'

Cornwallis went back inside and closed the door. Hawthorne unfolded the paper and looked at it. He smiled. 'I know this number,' he said.

'How come?'

'It's the same number Judith Godwin gave me at her place in Harrow-on-the-Hill. It's for her husband, Alan Godwin.'

Hawthorne folded the piece of paper and slipped it into his pocket. He was smiling as if it had been something he had expected all along.

Fifteen
Lunch with Hilda

'You've bought new shoes,' my wife said as I left home the following Monday.

'No, I haven't,' I replied. I looked down and saw that I was wearing the shoes that Hawthorne had given me, the ones that had belonged to Damian Cowper. They were comfortable, Italian – but I had put them on without thinking. 'Oh, these!' I muttered.

My wife is a television producer. She has such an extraordinary eye for detail that she could easily be a detective or a spy. I stood there, awkwardly. I hadn't told her anything about Hawthorne.

'I've had them for some time,' I said. 'I just don't often wear them.' We don't lie to each other. Both statements were, broadly, true.

'Where are you going?' she asked.

'Lunch with Hilda,' I said.

Hilda Starke was my literary agent. I hadn't told her about Hawthorne either. I left as quickly as I could.

The relationship between writers and their agents is a peculiar one and I'm not even sure I fully understand it myself. Starting with the basics, writers need agents. Most writers are hopeless when it comes to contracts, deals, invoicing – in fact anything to do with business or common sense. Agents handle all of this in return for ten per cent of what you earn, a figure which is actually very reasonable until you start selling a lot of books – but when that happens, you no longer care. They don't do very much else. They won't really get you work. If they manage to raise your advance, it will be by quite a lot less than the amount they're taking for themselves.

An agent is not exactly your friend – or if they are, they're a particularly flirtatious one with dozens of other clients whom they're equally pleased to see. They may tentatively ask about your wife or children but actually it's the progress of your new book that most interests them. It could be said that they have a one-track mind and that it's perfectly in sync with Nielsen, the company that scans and tracks UK book sales. One week after I have a book published, Hilda will ring to tell me where it is in the charts even though she knows I hate it. 'Book sales aren't everything,' I will tell her. And that, in a nutshell, is the difference between us.

I remember meeting her at City Airport, shortly after she had taken me on. We were on our way to Edinburgh for a talk I was giving and I was already surprised that she had agreed to come. Didn't she have a home to go to, a family? I would never find out. She didn't invite me to her home and I've never met her family. When I saw her, on the other side of security, she was yelling at someone on her mobile and she signalled me not to interrupt. It took me about ten seconds to work out that it was a publisher at the other end and another ten seconds to realise that it was *my* publisher. She had put on her shoes, belt, jacket and marched into the airport branch of W. H. Smith where she had discovered that my new book wasn't stocked. She wanted to know why.

That was Hilda. Before I signed with her, I met her at book fairs in Dubai, Hong Kong, Cape Town, Edinburgh and Sydney. She knew everything about me: how well my latest book was doing, why my editor had just resigned, who was going to replace her. She really was the genie to my Aladdin, although as far as I could recall, I had never rubbed the magic lamp. It was inevitable that I would sign with her and in the end I did. I was far from her biggest author, by the way. Her talent was in making me believe that, actually, I was.

I always had to remind myself that, theoretically, she worked for me and not the other way round. Even so, I was always nervous when I was meeting her. She was a short, sharply dressed woman with tightly curled hair and very intense, searching eyes. Everything about her was tough: the way she jabbed her finger at you, the staccato phrases, the lack of emotion, the dress sense. She swore almost as much as Hawthorne. I liked her and feared her in equal measure.

I knew that I was going to have to tell her about the book I was writing. She would sell it. She would do the deal. I also knew that she would be annoyed that I had gone ahead without asking her first, which is why I held back for as long as I could, talking about anything else that mattered: marketing for *The House of Silk*, the possibility of a new Alex Rider (I had an idea for a book about Yassen Gregorovich, the assassin who had appeared in several of the adventures), ITV and the scheduling of *Injustice*, the next season of *Foyle's War* if there was actually going to be one. Hilda was unusually twitchy, even by her standards, and as the waiter cleared the plates, I asked her what was wrong.

'I wasn't going to mention it,' she said. 'But you'll probably read about it in the newspapers anyway. One of my clients has been arrested.'

'Who?'

'Raymond Clunes.'

'The theatre producer?'

She nodded. 'He raised money for a musical last year. *Moroccan Nights*. It didn't do as well as expected.' Hilda would never call anything a total flop, even if it had lost every penny. If a book was savaged by the critics, she would still find the single word that would allow her to claim it had had mixed reviews. 'Now some of the backers are alleging that he misled them. He's being investigated for fraud.'

So the story that Bruno Wang had told me before the funeral was true. I was surprised. I didn't even know that Hilda represented theatrical producers, and wondered if she had lost money herself. I didn't dare ask. But this was the opening I'd been looking for. I began by saying that I had recently met Clunes, that he'd been at Diana Cowper's funeral. This got me talking about Hawthorne and finally I described the book I had agreed to write.

She wasn't angry. Hilda never shouted at her clients. Incredulous would be a more accurate description. 'I really don't understand you,' she said. 'We've talked about moving you out of children's books and establishing you as an adult author . . .'

'This is an adult book.'

'It's true crime! You're not a true crime writer. And anyway, true crime doesn't sell.' She reached for her wine glass. 'I don't think this is a good idea. You've got *The House of Silk* coming out in a few months and you know how much I like that book. I thought the idea we agreed was that you were going to write a sequel.'

'I will!'

'You should be working on that now. That's what people are going to want to read. Why should anyone be interested in this . . . what's he called?'

'Hawthorne. Daniel Hawthorne but he doesn't use his first name.'

'They never do. He's a detective.'

'He used to be a detective.'

'So he's an unemployed detective! "The Unemployed Detective". Is that what you're going to call the book? Do you have a title yet?'

'No.'

She threw back the wine. 'I really don't understand what's attracted you to this. Do you like him?'

'Not terribly,' I admitted.

'Then why will anyone else?'

'He's very clever.' I knew how feeble that sounded.

235

'He hasn't solved the case.'

'Well, he's still working on it.'

The waiter arrived with the main courses and I told her about some of the interviews where I'd been present. The trouble was, apart from the notes I'd taken, I hadn't written anything down yet and, in the telling, it all sounded very vague and anecdotal . . . boring even. Imagine trying to describe, in detail, the plot of an Agatha Christie. That was how it was for me.

In the end she interrupted. 'Who is this man, Hawthorne?' she asked. 'What makes him fun? Does he drink single malt whisky? Does he drive a classic car? Does he like jazz or opera? Does he have a dog?'

'I don't know anything about him,' I said, miserably. 'He used to be married and he has an eleven-year-old son. He may have pushed someone down a flight of stairs at Scotland Yard. He doesn't like gay people . . . I don't know why.'

'Is he gay?'

'No. He hates talking about himself. He won't let me come close.'

'Then how can you write about him?'

'If he solves the case . . .'

'Some cases can take years to solve. Are you going to follow him around London for the rest of your life?' She had ordered veal escalope. She sliced into it as if it had caused her offence. 'You're going to have to change names,' she added. 'You can't just barge into people's houses and put them in a book.' She glared at me. 'You'd better change my name! I don't want to be in it.'

'Look, at the end of the day, this is an interesting case,' I insisted. 'And I think Hawthorne is an interesting man. I'm going to try and find out more about him.'

'How?'

'There's a detective I met. I'll start with him.' I was thinking about Charlie Meadows. Maybe he'd talk to me if I bought him a drink.

'Have you talked to Mr Hawthorne about money?' Hilda asked, chewing on her veal.

It was the question I had been dreading. 'I suggested fifty-fifty.'

'What?' She almost threw down her knife and fork. 'That's ridiculous,' she said. 'You've written forty novels. You're an established writer. He's an out-of-work detective. If anything, he should be paying you to write about him and certainly he shouldn't be getting more than twenty per cent.'

'It's his story!'

'But you're the one writing it.' She sighed. 'Do you really mean to go ahead with this?'

'It's a bit late to back out now,' I said. 'Anyway, I'm not sure I want to. I was there in the room, Hilda. I actually saw the dead body, cut to ribbons, covered in blood.' I glanced at my steak, then put down my knife and fork. 'I want to know who did it.'

'All right.' She gave me the sort of look that said that no good would come of this but it wasn't her fault. 'Give me his number. I'll talk to him. But I should warn you now, you're still under contract for two more books and at least one of them is meant to be set in the nineteenth century. I'm not sure your publishers are going to be interested in this.'

'Fifty-fifty,' I said.

'Over my dead body.'

After lunch, I headed off to Victoria, feeling like a schoolboy playing truant. Why was I suddenly hiding everything from everyone? I hadn't told my wife anything about Hawthorne and here I was, slipping off to meet him again without having mentioned it to Hilda. Hawthorne was worming his way into my life in a way that was definitely unhealthy. The worst of it was that I was actually looking forward to seeing him, to finding out what happened next. What I'd just said to Hilda was true. I was hooked.

I don't like Victoria and hardly ever go there. Why would I? It's a weird part of London on the wrong side of Buckingham Palace. As far as I know, it has no decent restaurants, no shops selling anything anyone could possibly want, no cinemas and just a couple of theatres that feel cut off and separated from their natural home in Shaftesbury Avenue. Victoria station is so old-fashioned you almost expect a steam train to pull in and the moment you step outside, you find yourself lost in a haphazard junction of shabby, seedy streets that all look the same. In recent years, they've introduced cheerful guides who stand on the forecourt of the station in bowler hats, giving tourists advice. The only advice I'd give them is to go somewhere else.

This was where Alan Godwin worked, running a company that organised conferences and social events for businesses.

His office was on the second floor of a 1960s building that had weathered badly, at the end of a narrow street crowded with unappetising cafés, close to the coach station. It was raining when I arrived – it had been cloudy all day – and with the puddles on the pavements and the coaches spraying water as they rumbled past, I could hardly imagine anywhere I would less like to be. The sign on the door read *Dearboy Events* and it took me a moment to work out where it had come from. It was a quotation from Harold Macmillan, who had once been asked what politicians should fear. His answer was: 'Events, dear boy, events.'

I was shown into a small, unevenly shaped reception room and I didn't need to be a detective to see the way this business was going. The furniture was expensive but it was getting tired and the trade magazines spread out on the table were out of date. The potted plants were wilting. The receptionist was bored and didn't make any attempt to disguise it. Her telephone wasn't ringing. There were a few awards on display on a shelf, handed out by organisations I'd never heard of.

Hawthorne was already there, sitting on a sofa with that sense of impatience I was beginning to know so well. It was as if he was addicted to crime and couldn't wait to begin his next interrogation. 'You're late,' he said.

I looked at my watch. It was five past three. 'How are you?' I asked. 'How was your weekend?'

'It was all right.'

'Did you do anything? Did you see a film?'

He looked at me curiously. 'What's the matter with you?'

'Nothing.' I was thinking about my lunch with Hilda. I sat down opposite him. 'Did you know that Raymond Clunes has been arrested?'

He nodded. 'I saw it in the papers. When he took that fifty grand off Diana Cowper, it looks like he was ripping her off.'

'Maybe she knew something about him. It could have given him a reason to kill her.'

Hawthorne considered my suggestion in a way that told me he had already dismissed it. 'Is that what you think?'

'It's possible.'

A young girl came into the reception area and told us, in a hopeless tone of voice, that Mr Godwin would see us. She led us down a short corridor past two offices – both of them empty, I noticed. There was a door at the end. She opened it. 'Here are your visitors, Mr Godwin.'

We went in.

I knew Alan Godwin at once. I had seen him at the funeral. He had been the tall man with the straggly hair and the white handkerchief. Now, he was sitting behind a desk with a window behind him and a view of the coach station over his shoulder. He was wearing a sports jacket and a round-necked jersey. He recognised us too as we came in. He knew that we had seen him at the cemetery. His face fell.

There were two seats opposite the desk. We sat down.

'You're a police officer?' He examined Hawthorne nervously.

'I'm working with the police, that's right.'

'I wonder if I could see some sort of identification.'

240

'I wonder if you could tell me what you were doing at Brompton Cemetery and for that matter what you did when you left.' Godwin didn't say anything, so Hawthorne went on. 'The police don't know you were there but I do and, if I tell them, I'm sure they'll be very interested to talk to you. Frankly, I think you'd find it a lot easier, talking to me.'

Godwin seemed to sink into his chair. Looked at more closely, he was a man weighed down by failure. It was hardly surprising. The accident that had taken one of his sons and cruelly injured the other had been the start of a general unravelling which had seen him lose his home, his marriage and his business. I knew he was going to answer Hawthorne's questions. He had almost no fight left in him.

'I didn't commit any crime going to the funeral,' he said.

'That may or may not be the case. You heard that music. "The wheels on the bus . . ." If memory serves, that one comes under the Burial Laws Amendment Act: riotous, violent or indecent behaviour at a funeral. But I suppose you could equally well put it down to breaking and entering. Someone broke into the coffin and inserted an MP3 player. Do you know anything about that?'

'No.'

'But you saw what happened.'

'Yes. Of course.'

'Did that song mean anything to you?'

Godwin paused and for a moment I saw two deep pits of despair opening in his eyes. 'We played it when we buried Timothy,' he rasped. 'It was his favourite song.'

Even Hawthorne faltered at that, but only briefly. Straight

away he was back on the attack. 'So why were you there?' he demanded. 'Why go to the funeral of a woman you had every reason to hate?'

'It was *because* I hated her!' Godwin's cheeks had reddened. He had heavy black eyebrows, which accentuated his anger. 'That woman with her stupidity and her carelessness killed my son, an eight-year-old boy, and turned his brother who was a livewire and who could make anybody laugh – turned him into pretty much a vegetable. She wasn't wearing her glasses and she destroyed my life. I went to the funeral because I was delighted she was dead and I wanted to see her put in the ground. I thought it would give me closure.'

'And did it?'

'No.'

'How about the death of Damian Cowper?' Hawthorne could have been a tennis player, slamming the ball back across the net. He had the same coiled-up energy, the same focus.

Godwin sneered. 'Do you think I killed him, Mr Hawthorne? Is that why you asked me what I did after the funeral? I went for a long walk, down the King's Road and then beside the River Thames. Yes, I know. That's very convenient, isn't it? No witnesses. Nobody to tell you where I was. But why would I have wished him any harm? He wasn't driving the car. He was at home.'

'His mother drove away, maybe to protect him.'

'That was her decision. It was cowardly and selfish but he had nothing to do with it.'

That chimed in with what I had been thinking. Alan

Godwin might have a good reason to kill Diana Cowper but I couldn't see how it could be extended to her son.

Both men had stopped as if they were in a boxing ring and had come to the end of a round. Then Hawthorne weighed in again. 'You went to see Mrs Cowper.'

Godwin hesitated. 'No.'

'Don't lie to me, Mr Godwin. I know you were there.'

'How do you know?'

'Mrs Cowper told her son. She was scared of you. According to him, you threatened her.'

'I did no such thing.' He stopped himself and took a breath. 'All right. I went to see her. I don't see why I should deny it. It was about three or four weeks ago.'

'Two weeks before she died.'

'I'll tell you when it was. It was two weeks after Judith asked me to leave the house, when we finally realised our marriage couldn't be saved. That's when I went to see her, because it occurred to me that maybe, just maybe, she might be able to help. I thought she might even want to.'

'Help you? In what way?'

'With money! What do you think?' He drew a breath. 'I might as well tell you what you want to know because – you know what? I don't really give a damn any more. There's nothing left. My company's down the pan. Businesses don't want to spend any more . . . not on corporate events. Gordon Brown ran this bloody country into the ground and the new lot don't have a clue. So everyone's tightening their belts and people like me are the first out the door.

'Judith and me – we're finished too. Twenty-four years

of marriage and you suddenly wake up and realise that you can't bear to be in the same room. That's what she said, anyway.' He pointed at the ceiling. 'There's a one-bedroom flat upstairs and that's where I'm living now. I'm fifty-five years old and I'm boiling eggs on a single gas ring or bringing in Big Macs in brown paper bags. That's what my life has come to.

'I can put up with all that. I don't care. But do you know what really hurts . . . why I went to see that bloody woman? We're losing my house, the house in Harrow-on-the-Hill. We can't keep up with the mortgage repayments. And even that wouldn't matter to me except it's *Jeremy's* house. It's his home. It's the one place he feels safe.' Anger sparked in his eyes. 'If I could find any way to protect him from that, I would do it. So that is why I swallowed my dignity and went to see Mrs Cowper. I thought she could help. She had a nice address in Chelsea and, from what I read in the newspapers, that son of hers was making a fortune out in Hollywood. I thought, maybe, if she had a shred of decency in her, she might like to make amends for what she'd done and actually help my family by reaching into her pocket.'

'And did she?'

'What do you think?' The sneer was back in place. 'She tried to slam the door in my face and when I forced my way in, she threatened to call the police.'

'You forced your way in? What exactly do you mean by that?' Hawthorne asked.

'I mean I persuaded her to let me speak to her. I didn't make any threats. I didn't use violence. I almost got down

on my bloody knees asking her for ten minutes of her time.'
He paused. 'All I wanted was a loan. Was it so much to ask?
I had a couple of pitches coming up. I might have been able
to turn a corner. I just needed a bit of breathing space. But
she wasn't having any of it. I don't know how any human
being can be so bloody cold, so removed. She told me to
leave her house and that's exactly what I did. I actually felt
sick with myself for having gone in the first place. It just
shows you how desperate I was.'

'Which room did this happen in, Mr Godwin?'

'The front room. The living room. Why?'

'What time?'

'It was lunchtime. Around midday.'

'So the curtains were tied back.'

'Yes.' He was puzzled by the question.

'How did you know she'd be in?'

'I didn't know. I went round on the off-chance.'

'And later on, you sent her a letter.'

Godwin hesitated very briefly. 'Yes.'

Hawthorne reached into his jacket pocket and took out
the letter which he had been given by Andrea Kluvánek. So
much had happened in the last few days that I'd almost forgotten about it. He unfolded it. '*I have been watching you and
I know the things that are dear to you,*' he read. 'You say you
didn't threaten her but that sounds pretty threatening to me.'

'I was angry. I didn't mean anything by it.'

'When did you send it?'

'I didn't. I hand-delivered it.'

'When?'

'It was about a week after I'd seen her. A Friday. I suppose it must have been the sixth or the seventh.'

'The weekend before she died!'

'I didn't go into the house. I just put it through the door.'

'Did she reply?'

'No. I never heard a word from her.'

Hawthorne glanced at the letter again. 'What do you mean – the things that are dear to you?'

'I didn't mean anything!' Godwin pounded his fist on the desk. 'It was just words. You put yourself in my position! It was stupid going to see her. It was stupid writing the letter. But when people are pushed into a corner, sometimes they do stupid things.'

'Mrs Cowper had a cat,' Hawthorne said. 'A Persian grey. I don't suppose you saw it.'

'No. I didn't see any fucking cat – and actually I've got nothing else to say to you. You haven't shown me any ID. I don't know who you are. I want you to leave.'

A telephone rang in the office next door. It was the only sound we'd heard since we'd entered the building. 'How much longer before you move out of here?' Hawthorne asked.

'I've got the lease for another three months.'

'Then we'll know where to find you.'

We walked through the almost empty office and back out into the rain. Hawthorne immediately lit a cigarette. 'I'm going to Canterbury tomorrow,' he suddenly announced. 'You up for that?'

'Why Canterbury?' I asked.

'I've tracked down Nigel Weston.' I'd forgotten who this

was. 'Nigel Weston QC,' Hawthorne reminded me. 'The judge who let Diana Cowper go free. And after that, I thought I'd wander over to Deal. You might like that, Tony. Get a bit of sea air.'

'All right,' I said, although I didn't really want to leave London. I was being dragged into unfamiliar territory in every sense and I didn't feel comfortable having Hawthorne as my guide.

'I'll see you then.'

We went our separate ways and it was only when I got to the end of the street that I remembered the one question I had been meaning to ask. Alan Godwin had said that he was glad she had been killed; in his own words, he was delighted. But when I had seen him at the funeral, he had been crying. His handkerchief had been constantly at his eyes. Why?

And there was something else.

'She wasn't wearing her glasses and she destroyed my life.'

That was what he had said just now, his voice half-strangled by anger. But there had been another witness, Raymond Clunes, talking about Diana Cowper, and he had said something quite different.

As soon as I got home, I looked through my notes and found what I was looking for. It was something that Hawthorne had missed – but it had been there all along, in front of our eyes, the reason why both the mother and the son had to die, and it told me precisely who had killed them. In fact it was obvious.

Suddenly I was looking forward to our train journey to Canterbury. For once, I had the upper hand.

Sixteen

Detective Inspector Meadows

With the end of the book in sight, I realised I needed more background. It was time to get in touch with Detective Inspector Charles Meadows.

In fact that turned out to be quite easy. I called the Metropolitan Police, gave his name and was immediately patched through – to his mobile, I think. I could hear a pneumatic drill in the background as we talked. At first, when I told him who I was and why I wanted to see him, he was suspicious. He started making excuses and would have hung up if I hadn't, frankly, bribed him. That is, I offered him £50 for an hour of his time and suggested we meet at a pub where I could buy him a drink. Warily, he agreed, although I had a feeling he didn't need much persuading. He didn't like Hawthorne and would surely take any opportunity to do him down.

We met that evening at the Groucho Club in Soho. He'd asked for a central London location and I thought he'd be impressed by a private club known for its celebrity clientele.

I also knew we could get a seat. He arrived ten minutes late, by which time I'd bagged a quiet corner upstairs. He ordered a vodka martini, which surprised me. The triangular glass looked ridiculous in his oversized hands and he took just three gulps before he needed – and asked for – another.

I had a lot of questions for him but first he wanted to know about me. How had I come across Hawthorne? Why was I writing a book about him? How much had he paid me? I told him how we had met and why I had agreed to do the job (without being paid) and made it clear that I had misgivings about Hawthorne too, that he wasn't my friend.

Meadows smiled at this. 'A man like Hawthorne doesn't have that many friends,' he said. 'I've nicked thieves and rapists who are more popular than him.'

So I told him about *Injustice*, how we had worked together and how he had approached me effectively to write about his most recent case. I didn't mention the encounter at Hay-on-Wye that had changed my mind. 'It just sounded interesting,' I said. 'I write a lot about murder but I've never met anyone quite like Hawthorne.'

He smiled a second time. 'There aren't many people like Hawthorne around, thank God.'

'Why exactly do you dislike him?'

'What makes you think I dislike him? I don't give a toss about him, to be perfectly honest. I just don't think it's right to employ people like him to do police work when he's not a policeman.'

'I'd like to know what happened. Why was he fired?'

'Did you tell him you were seeing me?'

'No, but he knows I'm writing about him. It's what he asked me to do. And I told him I'd find out everything I could about him.'

'Bit of a detective yourself, then.'

'That had occurred to me.'

I wondered what anyone would make of us if they glanced in our direction. Built like a rugby player, with his broken nose, lank hair and cheap suit, Meadows didn't look anything like the usual sort of person who drank at the Groucho. Like Hawthorne, there was something indefinably threatening about him. The waiter brought over a bowl of Twiglets and he plunged his hand into it. When he pulled it out again, the bowl was half empty.

'What did he tell you about the murder squad?' *Crunch, crunch, crunch.* The rest of our interview would be punctuated by those damned snacks being mechanically ground between his teeth.

'He didn't tell me anything. I know almost nothing about him. I'm not even sure where he lives.'

'River Court, Blackfriars.' That was only a mile or so from my own flat in Clerkenwell. 'It's quite a fancy place. Views out onto the Thames. I don't know what the arrangement is. He doesn't own it.'

'Do you know the number?'

He shook his head. 'No.'

'He told me he had a place in Gants Hill.'

'He lost that when he split up from his wife.'

'That's what I thought.' I paused. 'Did you ever meet her?'

'Once. She came to the office. About five foot eleven. Caucasian.' He was describing her as if she were a suspect in an investigation. 'She was quite pretty, fair hair, a few years younger than him. A bit nervous. She asked to see him and I took her to his desk.'

'What did they talk about?'

'I haven't got the faintest idea. No-one ever hung around with Hawthorne. I made myself scarce.'

'So what was he like to work with?'

'You couldn't work with him. That was his problem.' *Crunch, crunch, crunch.* He wasn't enjoying the Twiglets. He was just eating them. 'Can I have another of these?'

He raised his glass. I signalled at the waiter.

'Hawthorne came to us in 2005,' he said. 'He'd been in other sub-commands – in Sutton and Hendon – and they weren't having him and we soon found out why. They say there's a lot of competition working in murder. It's true that the teams can be at each other's throats. But at the same time, we rub along. We'll drink together after work. We try to help each other out.

'But he wasn't like that. He was a loner and if you want the truth, nobody likes a loner. I'm not saying people didn't respect him. He was bloody good at the job and he got results. We have something called the murder manual. You ever heard of that?'

'I can't say I have.'

'Well, there's no secret about it. You can download the whole thing on the internet if you want to look at it. It came out about twenty years ago and it's the definitive guide to homicide investigation. It says that on page one. Basically, it's the manual to everything from first response to crime scene strategy to house-to-house and post-mortem procedure and there are some investigating officers who carry it around with them like born-again Christians with their Bible. That's the thing about our job. Process is king. The trouble is, you can take it too far. There was one man I knew, he was investigating a skeleton that had been dug up in the crypt of a church, victim of a murder that had taken place back in the fifties. He was trying to work out a CCTV strategy because that's what it tells you to do in the manual – even though it was twenty-five years before CCTV was invented.

'Now the thing about Hawthorne was, he did things his own way. He'd just disappear without so much as a by-your-leave, because he had a hunch or maybe it was just a lucky guess or Christ knows really how he knew. But almost every single time he was right. That was what pissed people off. He had an arrest record that was second to none.'

'So what didn't they like?'

'Everything. On a day-to-day basis he was a pain in the arse. He was rude to the boss. He never clicked with anyone. And he didn't drink. I'm not holding that against him but it didn't help. Seven o'clock in the evening, he'd disappear. Maybe he went home to his wife although I heard whispers he was playing the field. It's no matter. If he'd made a few more friends, maybe there'd have been someone to stand by him when the shit hit the fan.'

'You told me not to go near any stairs.'

'I shouldn't have said that really. I couldn't resist having a dig at Hawthorne.' The third vodka martini arrived. He threw it back. 'There was a man called Derek Abbott, a sixty-two-year-old retired teacher, living in Brentford, who'd been arrested as part of Operation Spade. It was an international operation involving fifty countries, looking into the trafficking of child pornography by mail and internet. It had started in Canada and eventually there'd be more than three hundred arrests. Abbott was suspected of being the main distributor in the U K and so he'd been brought in for questioning. I'm not even sure what he was doing in Putney, but there he was.

'Anyway, he was in the custody office, which was on the second floor. He'd been booked in, pockets searched and all the rest of it, and someone had to take him to the interview room, which was in the basement. Normally, that would have been a civilian but there was nobody around and to this day I don't quite know what happened but Hawthorne volunteered. He took him down a corridor to the staircase — I forgot to mention he'd decided that Abbott needed to be handcuffed. There was no need for that. He was in his sixties. He had no history of violence. Well, you've probably guessed what happened next and a guess is all we have because the C C T V wasn't working in that part of the building. Abbott swore that Hawthorne tripped him. Hawthorne denied it. All I can tell you is that Abbott went head first down fourteen steps and because his hands were cuffed behind his back, there was nothing to break his fall.'

'How badly was he hurt?'

Meadows shrugged. 'Did his neck in, broke a few bones.

He could have been killed and if so, Hawthorne would probably be in jail. As it was, Abbott was in no position to make too much fuss and basically the whole thing was hushed up. That said, it couldn't all be brushed under the carpet. Too many people knew and, like I say, too many people had it in for him. So Hawthorne got the boot.'

There was nothing particularly surprising about this story. I had always been aware of a sort of smouldering violence in Hawthorne's make-up, a sense of outrage, even – ironically – injustice. If he was going to kick someone down a flight of stairs, of course it would be a paedophile. It reminded me of his behaviour when we had visited Raymond Clunes.

'Was he homophobic?' I asked.

'How would I know?'

'He must have said something. Even if he wasn't very sociable, he must have expressed an opinion – maybe if he'd read something in the newspaper or seen something on TV?'

'No.' Meadows looked in the Twiglet bowl. It was empty. 'People don't express opinions in the police force any more. You start mouthing off about gay people or black people, you're going to be out on your ear before you know it. We don't even use words like "manpower" any more. You've got to be aware of gender equality. Ten years ago, if you said something out of order you might get a clip on the ear. Not any more. These days, PC means more than police constable and you'd better know it.'

'What happened to Abbott?'

'I've no idea. He went to hospital and we never saw him again.'

'There's a detective chief inspector who's been helping Hawthorne.'

'That'd be Rutherford. He always had a soft spot for Hawthorne and he came up with this idea. It's almost like a parallel investigation. You were at the crime scene. You saw how we had to leave everything in place for Hawthorne to come along and make his deductions. He reports directly to Rutherford. By-passes the whole system ... ' Meadows stopped himself. He had said more than he intended. 'Rutherford won't talk to you,' he added, 'so I wouldn't waste your time.' He looked at his watch. 'Is there anything else?'

'I don't know. Is there anything else you can tell me?'

'No. But maybe there's something you can tell me. You've been following Hawthorne around. Has he spoken to a man called Alan Godwin?'

I felt a cold sinking in my stomach. I had never thought that Meadows might try to use me to help him get ahead of Hawthorne in his investigation. It only occurred to me now that this might have been the real reason why he had agreed to meet me. I knew at once that I couldn't tell him anything. If Meadows suddenly announced the identity of the killer, it would be a complete disaster. There would be no book!

At the same time, I was aware of a sense of loyalty to Hawthorne that must have developed over the past few days, because I'd certainly never noticed it before. We were a team. We – not Meadows or anyone else – were going to solve the crime. 'I haven't been to all the interviews,' I said, weakly.

'I'm not sure I believe that.'

'Look ... I'm sorry. I really can't talk to you about what Hawthorne is doing. We made an agreement. It's confidential.'

Meadows looked at me the way he might look at someone who has beaten up an old-age pensioner or killed a child. I had met him on three separate occasions and had considered him slow, inferior, even oafish. I suppose, in my mind's eye, I had been casting him as a Japp, a Lestrade, a Burden: the man who never solves the crime. Now I saw that I had underestimated him. He could be dangerous too.

'You don't seem to know a lot about anything, Anthony,' he said. 'But I take it you've heard of obstruction.'

'Yes.'

'Obstructing a police officer in the execution of their duty under the Police Act of 1991. You could be fined a thousand pounds or sent to jail.'

'That's ridiculous,' I said. And it was. This wasn't Scotland Yard – it was the Groucho Club. And I had invited him here!

'I'm asking you a simple question.'

'Ask him,' I said, holding his gaze. I had no idea what he was going to do. But then, quite suddenly, he relaxed. The cloud had passed. It was as if that little bit of nastiness had never happened.

'I forgot to mention,' he said. 'My son got very excited when he heard I was going to meet you.'

'Did he?' I'd been drinking gin and tonic. I took a sip.

'Yes. He's a big fan of Alex Rider.'

'I'm delighted to hear it.'

'As a matter of fact . . .' Suddenly Meadows was sheepish. He'd been carrying a leather briefcase and he reached into it. I knew what was going to happen next. Over the years, I've come to know the body language so well. Meadows pulled out a copy of *Skeleton Key*, the third Alex Rider novel. It was brand new. He must have stopped at a bookshop on the way to the club. 'Would you mind signing it?' he asked.

'It's a pleasure.' I took out a pen. 'What's his name?'

'Brian.'

I opened the book and wrote on the first page: *To Brian. I met your dad and he almost arrested me. All good wishes.*

I signed it and handed it back. 'It's been a pleasure meeting you,' I said. 'Thank you for your help.'

'I think you said you were going to pay me for my time.'

'Oh yes.' I reached for my wallet. 'Fifty pounds,' I said.

He looked at his watch. 'Actually, we've been here an hour and ten minutes.'

'As long as that?'

'And it took me thirty minutes to get here.'

He left with £100. I'd also paid for three cocktails and signed his book. And what had I got in return? I wasn't sure it had been much of a deal.

Seventeen
Canterbury

For once, I was looking forward to meeting Hawthorne and I saw that he was in a good mood when I joined him the next day at King's Cross St Pancras. He had already bought the tickets and he asked me to fork out only for mine.

We sat facing each other across a table as the train pulled out but before I could begin a conversation he suddenly produced a pad of paper, a pen and a paperback book. I looked at the cover upside-down. The book was *The Outsider*, by Albert Camus, translated from the French. It was a second-hand edition, a Penguin classic, with loose pages, falling apart at the spine. I was very surprised. It had never occurred to me that Hawthorne would read anything – except maybe a tabloid newspaper. He really didn't strike me as someone who had any interest in fiction and certainly not in the study of a young nobody plumbing the depths of existentialism in 1940s Algiers. If anyone had asked me, I would have imagined him settling back with a Dan Brown novel perhaps, or maybe something more violent: Harlan Coben or James

Patterson. Even that was a stretch. Hawthorne was clever and he was well educated but he didn't strike me as having any interior imaginative life at all.

I didn't want to interrupt but at the same time I was itching to tell him my theory, the solution to the murders of Diana Cowper and her son, and after fifteen minutes, sitting in silence with London slipping behind me, I couldn't resist it any more. He had read three pages in this time, by the way, turning them over with a decisiveness that suggested each one of them had been an effort and he was glad that he would never have to return to them again.

'Are you enjoying it?' I asked.

'What?'

'*L'Étranger*.' He looked blank, so I translated. '*The Outsider*.'

'It's all right.'

'So you like modern literature, then.'

He knew I was digging and he was briefly irritated. But for once he actually volunteered some information. 'I didn't choose it.'

'No?'

'It's my book group.'

Hawthorne in a book group! If he'd told me he was part of a knitting circle, it would be equally incongruous.

'I read it when I was eighteen,' I said. 'It had quite an effect on me. I identified with Meursault.'

Meursault is the title character. He drifts through the novel – 'Today my mother died. Or maybe yesterday . . .' – kills an Arab, goes to prison, dies. It was the bleakness of his outlook, his lack of connectivity, that appealed to me. As a teenager, there was a part of me that wished I could be more like him.

'Trust me, mate. You're nothing like Meursault,' Hawthorne replied. He closed the book. 'I meet people like him all the time. They're dead inside. They go out and they do stupid things and they think the world owes them a living. I wouldn't write about them. I wouldn't read about them either except it wasn't my choice.'

'So who's in the book group?' I asked.

'Just people.'

I waited for him to tell me more.

'They're from the library.'

'When do you meet?'

He said nothing. I looked out of the window at the rows of terraced houses backing onto the railway line, tiny gardens separating them from the endless rattle of the trains. There was litter everywhere. Everything was covered in grey dust.

'What other books have you read?' I asked.

'What are you on about?'

'I'd like to know.'

He thought back. I could see he was getting annoyed. 'Lionel Shriver. A book about a boy who kills his school mates. That was the last one.'

'*We Need to Talk About Kevin*. Did you like it?'

'She's clever. She makes you think.' He stopped himself. There was a danger that this was going to turn into a conversation. 'You should be thinking about the case,' he said.

'As a matter of fact, I am.' Hawthorne had given me exactly the opening I had been hoping for. I leapt in. 'I know who did it.'

He looked up at me with eyes that were both challenging and waiting for me to fail. 'So who was it?' he asked.

'Alan Godwin,' I said.

He nodded slowly, but not in agreement. 'He had a good reason to kill Diana Cowper,' he said. 'But he was at the funeral at the same time as us. You think he had time to cross London and get to Damian's flat?'

'He left the cemetery as soon as the music started playing – and who else would have put the MP3 player in the coffin if it wasn't him? You heard what he told us. It was his dead son's favourite song.' I went on before he could stop me. 'This has got to be about Timothy Godwin. It's the reason why we're on this train and the simple fact is that nobody else had any reason to kill Diana Cowper. Was it the cleaner because she was stealing money? Or Raymond Clunes with his stupid musical? Come on! I'm surprised we're even arguing about it.'

'I'm not arguing,' Hawthorne said, with equanimity. He weighed up what I had just said then shook his head, sadly. 'Damian Cowper was at home when the accident happened. He had nothing to do with it. So what was the motive for killing him?'

'I think I've worked that out,' I said. 'Suppose it wasn't Diana Cowper who was driving the car. Mary O'Brien didn't actually see her face and as far as we know she was only ever identified because of the registration number.'

'Mrs Cowper went to the police. She turned herself in.'

'She could have done that to protect Damian. He was the one behind the wheel!' The more I thought about it, the more it made sense. 'He was her son. She was certain he was going to be famous. Maybe he was drunk or on cocaine or something. She knew his career would be ruined before it even started if he was arrested, so she took the rap! And she made up that stuff about forgetting her glasses to get herself off the hook.'

'You have no evidence for that.'

'As a matter of fact I do.' I played my ace card. 'When you were talking to Raymond Clunes, he mentioned that when he had lunch with her, the day she was killed, he saw her as she came out of the tube station. *She waved to me across the road.* That's what he said. So if she could see him across the road, that means her eyesight was perfectly good. She made up the whole thing.'

Hawthorne treated me to a rare smile. It flickered across his face but was gone in an instant. 'I see you've been paying attention,' he said.

'I've been listening,' I said, warily.

'The trouble is, she might have been wearing her glasses when she came out of the station,' Hawthorne went on. He seemed genuinely sad, as if it pained him, demolishing my theory. 'Clunes didn't say anything about that. And if she wasn't the one who was driving, why did she never get behind the wheel of a car again? Why did she move house? She seems to have been pretty upset by something she didn't do.'

'She might have been just as upset that Damian had done

263

it. And she was an accessory. Somehow Alan Godwin found out the truth and that was why he killed both of them. They were in it together.'

The train had picked up speed. The buildings of east London were giving way to a little more greenery and some open spaces.

'I don't buy your theory,' Hawthorne said. 'The police would have checked her eyesight after the accident and, anyway, there's all sorts of things you're forgetting.'

'Like what?'

Hawthorne shrugged, as if he didn't want to continue the conversation. But then, perhaps, he took pity on me. 'What was Diana Cowper's frame of mind when she went to the undertaker?' he asked. 'And what was the first thing she saw when she went there?'

'You tell me.'

'I don't need to, mate. It was in that rubbish first chapter you showed me. But I think you'll find that's what matters most. Everything turns on it.'

What was the first thing that Diana Cowper saw when she went into the funeral parlour?

I tried to put myself in her shoes, stepping off the bus, walking down the pavement. Obviously, it was the name: Cornwallis and Sons, written not once but twice. Or maybe she saw the clock which had stopped at one minute to midnight. What could that possibly have to do with anything? There had been a book made out of marble in the window – the sort of thing you'd see in any undertaker's. And what of her frame of mind? Hawthorne had told me that Mrs

Cowper knew she was going to die. Somebody had threatened her but she hadn't gone to the police. Why not?

Suddenly I was angry.

'For God's sake, Hawthorne,' I said. 'You're dragging me halfway across England to the coast. You could at least tell me what we're meant to be doing.'

'I already told you. We're seeing the judge. Then we're going to the scene of the accident.'

'So you do think it's relevant.'

He smiled. I could see his face reflected in the glass with the countryside rushing past on the other side. 'When you're paid by the day, everything is relevant,' he said.

He went back to his book and didn't speak again.

Nigel Weston, the judge who had presided over the case of *The Crown* vs *Diana Cowper* but who had favoured the second of the two, lived in the very centre of Canterbury with a view of the cathedral on one side and St Augustine's College on the other. It was as if, having worked in law all his life, he had chosen to surround himself with history and religion: ancient walls, spires, missionaries on bicycles. His house was square, solid, with everything in proportion, looking out over a green. It was a comfortable place in a comfortable city with a man now enjoying a comfortable life.

Hawthorne had arranged to meet him at eleven o'clock and Weston was waiting for us at the door as I paid the taxi. He looked more like a musician than a retired barrister, a conductor perhaps: slender and fragile with long fingers, silver hair, inquisitive eyes. He was in his seventies, shrinking with age, disappearing into the heavy-knit cardigan and corduroys that he was wearing. He had slippers not shoes. His eyes were sunken, gazing out at us intently over rigid cheekbones like two clerks behind a bench.

'Do come in. I hope you had a good journey. Trains not playing up?'

I wondered why he was so genial. I assumed that Hawthorne hadn't told him why we were here.

We followed him into a hallway with thick carpets, antique furniture, expensive art. I recognised an Eric Gill drawing and a watercolour by Eric Ravilious – both originals. He showed us into a small living room with views over the green. There was a fire burning – it was real too. Coffee and biscuits had already been laid out on a table.

'I'm very pleased to meet you, Mr Hawthorne,' he began, after we had sat down. 'You have quite a reputation. That business with the Russian ambassador. The Bezrukov case. Excellent police work.'

'He was found not guilty,' Hawthorne reminded him.

'He had a brilliant defence and the jury, in my view, was misdirected. There was no question that he was guilty of the crimes. Will you have some coffee?'

I hadn't expected Hawthorne to be known to the judge, and wondered if the Bezrukov case had happened before or after he had left the force. The very name sounded unlikely. Would the Met have ever had dealings with the Russian embassy?

The judge poured for all three of us. I examined the

room, which was dominated by a miniature grand piano, a Blüthner, with half a dozen photographs in expensive frames arranged on the lid. Four of these showed Weston with another man. In one of them, they were dressed in Hawaiian shirts and shorts, arm in arm. I had no doubt that Hawthorne would have already noticed them too.

'So what brings you to Canterbury?' Weston asked.

'I'm investigating a double murder,' Hawthorne explained. 'Diana Cowper and her son.'

'Yes. I read about that. A horrible business. You're advising the Metropolitan police.'

'Yes, sir.'

'Very wise of them not to let you go! You believe that the traffic accident in Deal and the very unfortunate death of the young child connect in some way with the murders?'

'I'm ruling nothing out, sir.'

'Indeed. Well, emotions do run very high in these sorts of cases and I note that we are approaching the tenth anniversary of the actual event, so I would imagine it is a distinct possibility. That said, I'm sure you'll have had full access to the court reports, so I don't see quite how I can help you.'

He still spoke like a judge. No word left his lips before it had been carefully evaluated.

'It's always useful to speak to the actual people involved.'

'I agree. It's the difference between testimony and written evidence. Have you seen the family? The Godwins?'

'Yes, sir.'

'I feel very sorry for them. I felt sorry for them at the time and said so. They felt that justice had not been done

but – I'm sure I don't need to tell you this, Mr Hawthorne –
the views of the victim's family, particularly in a case such
as this, cannot be taken into consideration.'

'I understand.'

Just then the door opened and a second man looked in. I
recognised him from the photographs. He was short, quite
stocky and about ten years younger than Weston, holding a
supermarket bag-for-life.

'I'm just going out,' he said. 'Is there anything you want?'

'I left the list in the kitchen.'

'I've got it. I just wondered if there was anything you
forgot.'

'We need some more dishwasher tablets.'

'They're on the list.'

'I don't think there's anything else.'

'I'll see you.' The man disappeared again.

'That's Colin,' Weston said.

It was a great pity that Colin had chosen this moment to
introduce himself. I glanced at Hawthorne. Nothing in his
manner had changed but I was aware of a certain frisson in
the room that had not been there before and I'm sure that
the interruption influenced the interview and the direction it
now took.

'The newspapers weren't too happy with your verdict,'
Hawthorne said – and I saw a hint of malevolence dancing
in his eyes.

Weston gave him a thin smile. 'It was never my habit to
look at the newspapers,' he said. 'What made them happy
or unhappy had nothing to do with the facts.'

'The facts were that she killed an eight-year-old child, crippled his brother and walked away with a slap on the wrist.'

The smile became even thinner. 'It was the task of the prosecution to prove death by dangerous driving under Section 2a of the Road Traffic Act of 1988,' Weston said. 'This, they failed to do – and with good reason. Mrs Cowper did not ignore the rules of the road and did nothing that created a significant risk. There were no drugs or alcohol involved. Do I need to continue? She had no intention to kill anyone.'

'She wasn't wearing her glasses.' Hawthorne glanced at me, warning me not to interrupt.

'I agree, that was unfortunate – but you should be aware, Mr Hawthorne, that the incident took place in 2001. Since then, the law has been tightened on this particular point and I think that is entirely correct. But for what it's worth, if I were trying the case today, even given the new guidelines, I think I might well come to the same conclusion.'

'Why is that?'

'I refer you to the transcripts. As the defence successfully demonstrated, the responsibility did not lie exclusively with the accused. The two children ran into the road. They had seen an ice-cream shop on the other side. The nanny briefly lost control of them. She was in no way to blame but even if Mrs Cowper had been wearing her spectacles, it is quite possible she would still have been unable to stop in time.'

'Is that why you told the jury to let her off?'

Weston looked pained. He took a moment before answering. 'I did no such thing and, quite frankly, I find your use of language a little offensive. As a matter of fact, it would have been quite within my jurisprudence to advise the jury not to convict and they in turn could have ignored me. I will agree that my summing-up did lean generally in Mrs Cowper's favour but again you must consider the facts. We are talking about a very respectable person with no criminal record. She had committed no obvious offence given the law of the time. As tragic as it was for the family of the two children, a custodial sentence would have been completely inappropriate.'

Hawthorne leaned forward and once again I was reminded of the jungle animal, going in for the kill. 'You knew her.'

Three simple words and yet they were followed by a silence that was almost physical, that slammed shut like a mortuary door. It was the moment everything changed, when Nigel Weston knew there was danger in the room. I was aware of the crackling of the fire and felt the heat of it against my face.

'I'm sorry?' Weston said.

'I'm just interested that you knew her. I wonder if that had any bearing on the case.'

'You're mistaken. I didn't know her.'

Hawthorne looked puzzled. 'You were a close friend of Raymond Clunes,' he said.

'I don't think—'

'Raymond Clunes, the theatre producer. Not a name you'd forget, I'd have thought. Also, he made you a lot of money.'

Weston was keeping his composure with difficulty. 'I do

know Raymond Clunes, perfectly well. He is a social and a business connection.'

'You invested in a show.'

'I invested in two shows, as a matter of fact. *La Cage aux Folles* and *The Importance of Being Earnest.*'

'Damian Cowper starred in the second one of those. Did you meet him and his mother at the first-night party?'

'No.'

'But you discussed the case with Clunes.'

'Who told you that?'

'He did.'

Weston had had enough. 'How dare you sit here in my home and make these accusations,' he said. He hadn't raised his voice but he was furious. His hand had tightened around the end of his armchair. I could see the veins bulging out beneath the skin. 'I had a very distant, tangential connection with Mrs Cowper. Anyone with any intelligence would see that every judge in this country might find themselves in the same position and, according to your logic, would be forced to recuse themselves. I'm sure you've heard of six degrees of separation! Anyone in the court could join the dots between themselves and the accused. As it happens, I did go to a party following the first night of *The Importance of Being Earnest* but if Damian Cowper or his mother were there I did not see them and I did not speak to them.'

'And Mrs Cowper didn't ask Raymond Clunes to approach you at the time of the trial?'

'Why would she have done that?'

'To persuade you to see things from her point of view. You might have listened to him because you were both . . . what's the word I'm looking for?'

'You tell me.'

'Angels! You and Mrs Cowper were both investing in his plays.'

'I've had enough of this.' Weston got to his feet. 'I agreed to see you because I thought I could help and I also knew you by reputation. Instead, you come here with all sorts of unpleasant insinuations and I can see absolutely no point in continuing with this discussion.'

But Hawthorne hadn't quite finished. 'You know that Raymond Clunes is going to jail?'

'I've asked you to leave!' Weston thundered.

So we did.

Back out in the street and on our way to the station, I turned on him. 'What exactly did you hope to gain by that?' I asked.

Hawthorne didn't seem at all put out. He lit a cigarette. 'Just testing the water.'

'Do you really think there was some sort of gay conspiracy going on? That Raymond Clunes and Nigel Weston would have "got together", as you'd put it, because they happened to have the same sexual orientation? Because if that's what you think – I have to be honest with you – I think you've got a problem.'

'Maybe I've got lots of problems,' Hawthorne replied. He was walking more quickly, not looking at me. 'But I didn't mention anything about sex. I was talking about money.

Why have we come all this way? Because we want to know about the accident, the connection between Diana Cowper and the Godwins. Justice Nigel Weston was part of that connection and that was all I was exploring.'

'You think he had something to do with her murder?'

'Everyone we meet had something to do with her murder. That's how murder works. You can die in bed. You can die of cancer. You can die of old age. But when someone slashes you to pieces or strangles you, there's a pattern, a network – and that's what we're trying to work out.' He shook his head. 'I don't know! Maybe you're not right for this, Tony. It's a shame I couldn't go with one of the other writers.'

'What?' I was horrified. 'What are you talking about?'

'You heard me.'

'You spoke to other writers?'

'Of course, mate. They turned me down.'

Eighteen
Deal

I didn't speak to Hawthorne on the train to Deal. We sat across from each other, on opposite sides of the aisle, and there was more distance between us than there had ever been. Hawthorne read his book, resolutely turning the dog-eared pages. I stared morosely out of the window, thinking about what he had said. Perhaps I was wrong to be offended and I did wonder which other writers he'd approached, but by the time we arrived I'd managed to put the whole thing out of my head. It didn't matter how it had come to me. This was my book and it just made me all the more determined to make sure that I was the one in control.

I'd never visited Deal before but had always wanted to. I read all the Hornblower books when I was at school and this is where they began. It's the setting of the third James Bond novel, *Moonraker*: Hugo Drax plans to destroy London with a newfangled V2 rocket fired from his headquarters, nearby. And it's one of the settings in my very favourite novel, *Bleak House*. The hero, Richard Carstone, is garrisoned there.

In fact, I've always had a fondness for seaside towns, particularly out of season when the streets are empty and the sky is grey and drizzling. At the time when I was reading Hornblower, my parents would often go to the South of France but they would send me, my sister and my nanny to Instow in Devonshire and the whole language of the British seaside has stayed with me. I love the sand dunes, the slot machines, the piers, the seagulls, the peppermint rock with the name printed, impossibly, all the way through. I have a hankering for the cafés and the tea shops, old ladies pouring muddy tea out of pots, slabs of millionaire shortbread, shops that sell fishing nets, windbreaks and novelty hats. I suppose it's the age I am. These days, everyone leaps on a plane when they want a cheap holiday. But that's also part of the charm of all those little towns along the coast, the fact that they've been left behind.

Deal seemed to be surprisingly charmless as we came out of the station and walked down the main street with the seagulls screaming at us from the rooftops. It was May but the season had yet to kick off and the weather was utterly miserable. I wondered what it must be like to live here, trapped in the triangle formed by the massive Sainsbury's and the inevitable Poundland and Iceland supermarkets. A drink at the Sir Norman Wisdom pub, dinner at the Loon Hin Chinese restaurant and then on to the Ocean Rooms night club and bar ('Entrance next to the Co-op').

We came to the sea, as cold and uninviting as only the English Channel can be. Deal has a pier but it is one of the most depressing in the world, an empty stretch of concrete, brutalist in style, lacking any entertainments whatsoever: no penny arcades, no trampolines, no carousels. I wondered why the Godwins had sent their children here. Surely there must have been somewhere more fun?

But gradually the little town won me over. It had that peculiar defiance of all coastal resorts, that sense of being quite literally outside the mainstream, on the edge. Many of the houses and villas fronting the sea were brightly painted and had overflowing window boxes. The pebble beach, sloping down to the water, stretched into the distance, with a wide promenade and dozens of benches. There were flower beds, lawns and parkland, old fishing boats leaning on their side, dogs running, seagulls hovering. We came to a miniature castle and I began to see that in the sunshine Deal might provide a host of adventures. I was being too cynical. I needed to look at it with a child's eye.

We did not visit the accident site to begin with.

Hawthorne wanted to see where Diana Cowper had been living and so when we reached the sea, we turned right – towards the neighbouring village of Walmer. We still weren't talking to each other but as we continued along the seafront we passed an old antiques shop and Hawthorne suddenly stopped and looked in the window. There wasn't much there: a ship's compass, a globe, a sewing machine, some mouldering books and pictures. But as if to break the silence he pointed and said, 'That's a Focke-Wulf Fw 190.'

He was looking at a German fighter plane with three black crosses and the figure 1 on the fuselage, suspended on a thread. There was a tiny pilot just visible in the cockpit. It was from one of those plastic kits – Revell, Matchbox or Airfix – that children used to assemble although to be fair it had been so well made that I doubted that a child had been involved.

'It's a single-seat, single-engine fighter, developed in the thirties,' he went on. 'The Luftwaffe used it throughout the war. It was their favourite aircraft.'

It was quite a different Hawthorne who was speaking and I understood that he had given me this scrap of information as a peace offering, to make up for what he had told me on the train. It wasn't the history of the Focke-Wulf that interested me. It was the fact that Hawthorne had shown it to be one of his enthusiasms. He had actually revealed two things about himself in the space of one day. There was the reading group and there was this. It didn't add up to a character I particularly understood but it was a start and I was grateful.

We walked for another fifteen minutes and at some stage Deal turned into Walmer and we arrived at Stonor House, which was where Diana Cowper had lived until the accident that had forced her to move. It was sandwiched between two roads, Liverpool Road at the back and The Beach at the front, a private drive connecting them, with ornate metal gates at each end. From the little that I knew about Diana Cowper, I would have said the house had suited her very well. Certainly, I could imagine her living here. It was pale blue, solid, well maintained, with two floors, several chimneys and a garage. A pair of stone lions stood guard in front of the door. It was surrounded by topiary that had been precisely clipped and semi-tropical plants, equally disciplined, in narrow beds. The whole place was walled off so that it was both prominent and private. Of course, some of these particulars could have been installed by the new owners but I got the feeling that it was more likely they had inherited it the way it was.

'Are we going to ring the bell?' I asked. We were standing on the Liverpool Road side. As far as I could see, there was nobody at home.

'No. There's no need.' He took a key out of his pocket and I saw the name of the house on the tag dangling underneath it. For a moment, I was puzzled. Then I realised. He must have taken it from Diana Cowper's kitchen, although I wasn't sure when. I didn't think the police would have allowed him to remove evidence, so they were probably unaware it even existed.

The key was solid and chunky. Not a Yale. I saw now that it couldn't have fitted the front door. It was much more likely to open the gate. Hawthorne tried it a couple of times, then shook his head. 'Not this one.'

We walked around to the other side of the house and tried the gate that opened onto The Beach but the key didn't fit that one either. 'That's a pity,' Hawthorne muttered.

'Why did she hold on to the key?' I asked.

'That's what I wanted to find out.'

He looked around him and I thought we were going to walk back to Deal – but then he noticed a second gate on the other side of the road. Stonor House had a quite separate, private garden right next to the beach. Smiling to himself, he crossed the road and tried the key a third time. This time, it turned.

We entered a small square area, with bushes on all four sides. It wasn't exactly a garden; more a courtyard with miniature yew trees and rose beds surrounding a pretty marble fountain and two wooden benches that faced each other. The ground was paved with York stone. The effect was theatrical – like a scene from a children's story. Even as we walked up to the fountain, which was dry and hadn't been used for some time, I felt a sense of sadness and had a good idea what we were going to find.

And there it was, carved onto the stone shelf of the fountain: *Lawrence Cowper. 3 April 1946 – 22 October 1999. 'To sleep, perchance to dream.'*

'Her husband,' I said.

'Yes. He died of cancer and she built this place as a memorial to him. She couldn't stay in the house but she always knew she'd want to come back. So she kept a key.'

'She must have loved him very much,' I said.

He nodded. Just for once, we were equally uncomfortable, standing there. 'Let's get out of here,' he said.

The accident that had changed Diana Cowper's life had taken place close to the Royal Hotel in the centre of Deal. The Royal was the handsome Georgian building where Mary O'Brien had been staying with Jeremy and Timothy Godwin. The three of them had only been minutes from tea and bed when the car ran them down.

I remembered what Mary had told us. The children had come off the beach, which was behind us, with the pebbles sloping down. The pier was nearby. The road was wider here than at any other point in Deal and subsequently the cars travelled faster, sweeping down from King Street which formed a junction over to the right. There was a shop selling Deal rock and an entertainment arcade on the corner. This was the way Diana Cowper had come. In front of me, there were more shops in a short parade: a pub, a hotel, a chemist — it advertised itself as Pier Pharmacy. Finally, next to it, stood the ice-cream shop with a front made up entirely of plate-glass windows and a bright, striped canopy.

It was all too easy to see how it had happened: the car coming round the corner, moving quickly to avoid the cross traffic. The two children, choosing exactly that moment to slip away from their nanny, running across the pavement and then into the road in their hurry to reach the ice-cream shop in front of them. Nigel Weston might have been right. Even with glasses, Diana Cowper would have been hard-pressed to stop in time. The accident had taken place at exactly this time of the year, almost to the day. The promenade would have been just as empty, the afternoon light throwing long shadows across the street.

'Where do we start?' I asked.

Hawthorne nodded. 'The ice-cream shop.'

We could see it was open. We crossed the road and went in.

It was called Gail's Ice-Cream and it was a cheerful place with plastic chairs and a Formica floor. The ice-cream it sold was home-made, stored in a dozen different tubs in a freezer that had seen better days. The cones were stacked up against the window and looked as if they might have been there a while. Gail's also sold fizzy drinks, chocolate, crisps, and ready-mixed bags of sweets, another seaside staple. A menu on the wall advertised eggs, bacon, sausage, mushrooms and chips: *The Big Deal Fry-Up*. I'd wondered how long it would be before I saw the obvious pun based on the town's name.

Just two of the tables were occupied. An elderly couple sat at one. Two young mothers with pushchairs and babies were at the other. We went up to the counter where a large, smiling woman in her fifties, wearing a dress and an apron that matched the canopy, was waiting to serve.

'What can I get you?' she asked.

'I'm hoping you can help me,' Hawthorne said. 'I'm with the police.'

'Oh?'

'I'm making enquiries about the accident that happened here a while ago. The two children who were hit by the car.'

'But that was ten years ago!'

'Diana Cowper, the woman who was driving . . . she died. You didn't read about that?'

'I may have read something. But I don't see—'

'Fresh evidence may have come to light.' Hawthorne was keen to shut down the conversation.

'Oh!' She looked at us nervously, in a way that made me wonder if she had something to hide. 'I'm afraid I can't tell you very much about it,' she said.

'Were you here?'

'I'm Gail Harcourt. This is my shop. And I was here the day it happened. It makes me feel sick when I remember those poor little children. All they wanted was an ice-cream

282

and that was why they ran across the road. But they were wasting their time. We weren't open.'

'At the beginning of June? Why was that?'

She pointed at the ceiling. 'We had a burst pipe. It completely flooded the place, ruined the stock and put out the electrics. We weren't insured either, of course. Well, you should have seen the premium. It nearly ruined us.' She sighed. 'If only they'd stopped to look! They just ran across the road at the worst possible moment. I heard the accident. I didn't see it. I went out into the street and saw them both lying there. The nanny didn't know what to do. She was in shock – but then she was young herself. Only in her twenties. I turned my head and then I saw the car. It had stopped just the other side of the pier. It stayed there a minute and then it drove off.'

'Did you see the driver?' I asked. I got a dark look from Hawthorne but I didn't care.

'Only the back of her head.'

'So it could have been anyone?'

'It was that woman! They put her on trial!' She turned back to Hawthorne. 'I don't know how anyone could do that, drive away from the scene of the accident. And those two little children, lying there! What a bitch! She wasn't wearing her glasses, you know. But who gets behind the wheel of a car when they can't see? She should have been locked up for life and that judge, the one who let her walk free, he should have been sacked. It's disgusting. There's no justice any more.'

I was quite taken aback by her vehemence. For a moment, she seemed almost monstrous.

'I've never felt the same here since,' she continued. 'It's taken all the pleasure out of running this business but there's nothing else I can do.' Two more customers came in and she hitched up her apron strings, preparing for business. 'You should talk to Mr Traverton next door. He was there. He saw much more than me.' She brushed us aside and suddenly the plump, smiling lady was back, everyone's favourite aunt. 'Yes, dear. What would you like?'

'I remember it like it was yesterday. Quarter past four. It had been a beautiful day. Not like today. Perfect sunshine and warm enough to go paddling in the sea. I'd just been serving a customer – he was the one everyone was interested in later on. The mystery man. He left the shop about five seconds before it happened and it was thanks to him that I heard it so clearly. You see, he activated the entrance door. I actually heard the car hitting those two children. It was a horrible sound. You wouldn't have thought it would be so loud. I knew at once it was going to be bad. I grabbed my mobile phone and went straight out. There was nobody else in the shop, by the way, except Miss Presley, who used to work in natural remedies but she's married now and I don't think she lives in Deal. I made sure she stayed behind before I left. We have a lot of drugs and medicines here and we're not allowed to leave the premises unguarded, even in exceptional circumstances such as these.'

Pier Pharmacy was one of those strange, old-fashioned shops that seem very much at home in a British seaside resort. As we'd gone in, the door had folded open automatically to reveal a rack with a dozen varieties of hot water bottles. Nearby, a collection of brightly coloured scarves hung forlornly on a wire display. The shop seemed to sell a little bit of everything. Looking around, I saw stuffed toys, jam, chocolate bars, cereal, toilet paper and dog leads. It was like one of those crazy memory games I used to play with my children. There was a corner with stationery and terrible birthday cards, the sort you might find in a garage. A whole aisle was given over to herbal remedies. By far the biggest area was at the back of the shop, which contained the actual pharmacy. Deal might have more than its fair share of old-age pensioners but no matter what diseases their later years might bring, I was sure they would find a remedy here. The staff wore white coats. They had hundreds of different packets, foils and bottles within reach.

We were talking to one of them – Graham Traverton – the owner and manager, a man in his fifties, bald and ruddy-cheeked, with an off-putting gap between his two front teeth. He was keen to talk to us and I was astonished at his grasp of detail. He seemed to have a perfect memory of everything that had happened that day, to the extent that I wondered if he wasn't making some of it up. But then again, he had been interviewed before – by the police and by journalists. He'd had plenty of opportunities to rehearse his story. And I sup-pose, when something terrible happens, you do tend to hang on to the details that surround it.

'I went out through that door and almost bumped into the customer, who was standing on the pavement,' Traverton continued. 'I went straight up to him. "What happened?" I asked. He didn't tell me. He didn't say anything.

'I tell you, I can still see all of it. Every day when I go home, it's like a photograph engraved on my mind. The two children were in the road, both of them dressed in blue shorts and short-sleeve shirts. I knew that one of them had to be dead just from the way he was lying there with his arms and legs all wrong. His eyes were shut and he wasn't moving. The nanny – her name was Mary O'Brien – was kneeling beside the other little boy. She was obviously shocked – she was like a ghost. As I stood there, she looked up at me and for a min-ute she was staring right into my eyes. It was like she was pleading with me to help her but what could I do? I called the police. I think a lot of people must have done the same.

'There was a car, a blue Volkswagen, parked just a short way up the road. I noticed someone sitting in it and then, seconds later, it pulled out from the kerb and accelerated away. I swear it had smoke coming out of the exhaust and I heard the sound of the rubber tyres screaming against the tarmac. Of course, at the time I didn't know it belonged to the woman who was responsible for the accident but I took down her number and reported it to the police. That was when I noticed the man that I'd been serving. He suddenly turned round and walked away. He went round the corner into King Street and then he disappeared.'

'Did that strike you as strange?' Hawthorne asked.

'It most certainly did. He was behaving in a very peculiar way. I mean, what do you do when you see an accident like that? You either stay and you watch – that's human nature. Or you decide it's got nothing to do with you and you leave. But he hurried away like he didn't want to be

seen. And here's the point. He'd seen it. He must have. It
had happened right in front of him. But when the police
asked for witness statements, he never came forward.'

'What else can you tell us about him?'

'Not a lot – because that's the other thing. He was wearing
sunglasses. Now why would he do that? It was half past four
in the afternoon and as I recall it was fairly cloudy. There wasn't
a great deal of sun and he certainly didn't need glasses – unless
he was someone famous and he didn't want to be recognized.
I can't remember much else about him, to be honest. He was
also wearing a cap. But I can tell you what he bought.'

'And what was that?'

'A jar of honey and a packet of ginger tea. It was local
honey from a place in Finglesham. I recommended it.'

'So what happened next?'

Traverton sighed. 'There's not very much more to tell
you. The nanny was kneeling there. At least one of the
children was alive. I saw him open his eyes. He called out
for his father. "Daddy!" It was pitiful, really it was. Then
the police and the ambulance arrived. It hadn't taken them
very long to get there. I went back into the shop. Actually,
I went upstairs and had a cup of tea. I wasn't feeling at all
well and I don't feel that good now, remembering it all. I
understand the woman in the car has been killed. Is that why
you're here? That's a terrible thing, but I won't say she
deserved it. But driving away like that? All the harm she
caused! I think the judge let her off far too lightly and I'm
not at all surprised that someone else agreed.'

*　　*　　*

From the pharmacy, we walked the short distance to the Royal Hotel. Hawthorne said nothing. He had a son himself, of course, an eleven-year-old. He was just three years older than Timothy Godwin had been when he died, and it was possible that the story we had just heard had made an impression on Hawthorne. But I have to say that he didn't look particularly sad. If anything, he seemed to be in a hurry to be on his way.

We entered the sort of lounge you can only get in an English seaside hotel: low ceilings, wooden floors with scattered rugs and cosy leather furniture. It was surprisingly crowded, mainly with elderly couples tucking into sandwiches and beer. The room was almost unbearably warm, with radiators on full blast and a gas-effect fire to one side. We made our way through to the reception area. The friendly local girl who was working there said that she couldn't help us but telephoned the manager, who came up from the downstairs bar.

Her name was Mrs Rendell ('like the crime writer,' she said). She had been at the Royal Hotel for twelve years but hadn't been working on the day of the accident. She had, however, met Mary O'Brien and the two children.

'They were dear little things, very well behaved. They had the family room on the second floor. It has a king-sized bed and bunks. Would you like to see it?'

'Not really,' Hawthorne said.

'Oh.' He had offended her but she continued anyway. 'They came down on a Wednesday and the accident happened the next day. As a matter of fact, Miss O'Brien wasn't happy with the room. It doesn't have sea views. She'd requested a twin and a double with an adjoining door but we don't have such a thing in this hotel and we couldn't allow two small children to sleep on their own.' Mrs Rendell was a small, thin woman. She had the sort of face that finds it easy to express indignation. 'I can't say I terribly liked her,' she remarked. 'I didn't trust her and although I hate to have to say it, I was right. She should have been holding on to the two boys. Instead, she allowed them to run across the road and that was what killed them. I really don't think Mrs Cowper was to blame for the accident.'

'Did you know her?'

'Of course I knew her. She often came to the hotel for lunch or dinner. She was charming – and she had a son who was an actor. He's famous now. Deal is quite well known for its celebrities. Lord Nelson and Lady Hamilton are the best known but Norman Wisdom also came here. And Charles Hawtrey used to like sitting at the bar. He moved to Deal after he retired.'

Charles Hawtrey. I still remembered him: the skinny actor with dark wavy hair and round glasses. He was the gay, friendless, drunken star of the *Carry On* films, British humour at its most dysfunctional. I had watched him in black-and-white films when I was nine years old, at boarding school. They used to screen them in the gymnasium: *Carry on Nurse*, *Carry on Teacher*, *Carry on Constable*. It was the one big treat of the week, a break from the beatings, bad food and bullying that made up the rest of my time there. For some children, growing up begins the moment they discover that Santa Claus doesn't exist. For me, it was realising Charles Hawtrey wasn't and never had been funny. And he had sat here, in this hotel, sipping his gin and watching the boys go by.

Suddenly I didn't want to be here either. And I was glad when Hawthorne thanked the woman and said he had no more questions and the two of us left.

Nineteen
Mr Tibbs

I wasn't expecting to see Hawthorne the next day, so I was surprised to get a telephone call from him shortly after breakfast.

'Are you doing anything this evening?'

'I'm working,' I said.

'I need to come round.'

'Here?'

'Yes.'

'Why?'

Hawthorne had never been to my London flat before and I was happy to keep it that way. I was the one trying to insinuate myself into his life, not the other way round. And so far, he hadn't even told me his address. In fact, he had deliberately misled me. He had said his home was in Gants Hill when he actually had a flat in River Court, Blackfriars, on the other side of the river. I didn't like the idea of him casting his detective's eye over my home, my possessions, and perhaps coming to conclusions that he might later use against me.

He must have sensed the hesitation at the other end of the line. 'I need to set up a meeting,' he explained. 'I want it to be somewhere neutral.'

'What's wrong with your place?'

'That wouldn't be appropriate.' He paused. 'I've worked out what really happened in Deal,' he said. 'I think you'll agree that it's relevant to our investigation.'

'Who are you meeting?'

'You'll know who they both are when they get here.' He tried one last plea. 'It's important.'

As it happened, I was on my own that evening. And it occurred to me that if I allowed Hawthorne to see where I lived, perhaps I might be able to persuade him to do the same. I was still keen to find out how he could possibly afford a flat overlooking the river and although Meadows had said he didn't own it I was curious to see inside.

'What time?' I asked.

'Five o'clock.'

'All right,' I said, already regretting it. 'You can come here for an hour – but that's it.'

'That's great.' He rang off.

I spent the rest of the morning typing up my notes from the investigation so far: Britannia Road, Cornwallis and Sons, the South Acton Estate. I had made several hours' worth of recordings on my iPhone and I connected it to my computer, listening to Hawthorne's flat, wheedling voice through a set of headphones. I'd also taken dozens of photographs and I flicked through them, reminding myself of what I'd seen. I already had far more material than I needed and

I was sure that ninety per cent of it was irrelevant. For example, Andrea Kluvánek had talked at length about her childhood in the Banská Štiavnica district of Slovakia and how happy she had been until the death of her father in an agricultural accident. But even as she had gone on, I'd been doubtful that any of it would make the first draft.

I had never worked this way before. Normally, when I'm planning a novel or a TV script, I know exactly what I need and don't waste time with extraneous details. But without knowing what was going on inside Hawthorne's head, how could I tell what was relevant and what wasn't? It was exactly what he had warned me about when he'd read my first chapter. A spring bell mechanism on a door or its absence could make all the difference to the conclusion and leaving something out could be just as damaging as making it up. As a result, I was having to write down everything I saw in every room I visited – whether it was the Stieg Larsson in Diana Cowper's bedroom, the fish-shaped key hook in her kitchen or the Post-it notes in Judith Godwin's kitchen – and the rapidly growing pile of information was driving me mad.

I was still convinced that Alan Godwin was the killer. If it wasn't him, who else could it have been? That was the question I asked myself as I sat at my desk, surrounded by what felt like a devastation of white A4.

Well, there was Judith Godwin, for one. She had exactly the same motivation. I thought back to what Hawthorne had said about the killer when we were at the scene of the crime, then rifled through the pages until I found it. *He was almost*

*certainly a man. I've heard of women strangling women but —
take it from me — it's unusual.* Those were his exact words,
recorded and written down. As a result, I hadn't considered
any of the women I had met. But *almost certainly* was not
one hundred per cent definite and *unusual* was not impossible.
It could have been Judith. It could have been Mary O'Brien —
so devoted to the family that she had stayed working with
them for the whole ten years. And what about Jeremy
Godwin? It was always possible that he wasn't quite as helpless as everyone supposed.

And then there was Grace Lovell — the actress who had
moved in with Damian Cowper. Although she hadn't said
so in as many words, there was clearly no love lost between
her and Damian's mother, whose interest had extended no
further than her first grandchild, Ashleigh. The baby had
been the end of Grace's acting career and if the newspaper
stories were true, Damian had proved to be a far from ideal
partner. Drugs, parties, showgirls . . . it easily added up to
a motive for murder. On the other hand, she had been in
America when Diana was killed.

Or had she?

Once again, I scoured through my notes and found exactly
what I was looking for, a line spoken by Damian Cowper
that hadn't registered at the time but which, I now saw, was
hugely significant. Grace had complained that she didn't
want to go back to Los Angeles. She wanted to spend more
time with her parents. And Damian had said to her: *You've
already had a week with them, babe.* I felt a glow of satisfac-
tion. I really had missed nothing! It might even be that I was

ahead of Hawthorne on this one. A week might be an approximation. Grace could have arrived nine or ten days ahead of Damian. In which case she could easily have been in the country on the day that Diana was killed. That said, we had left her behind at the pub in the Fulham Road after the funeral and remembering how heavy the traffic was, I would have thought it impossible for her to have reached Brick Lane before us.

Who else was there? I had spent a lot of time with Robert Cornwallis – and, for that matter with his cousin, Irene Laws. Either of them could have slipped the music player into the coffin but why would they have? They only met Diana Cowper on the day she died. Neither of them had anything to gain from her death, or that of her son.

I spent the rest of the day working on my notes and hardly noticed the time when, at a quarter to five, the doorbell rang. I work on the fifth floor of the building, with an intercom that connects me to the street, although there are times when I don't feel connected at all, stuck in my ivory tower. I buzzed the door open, then went downstairs to meet my guest.

'Nice place,' Hawthorne said as he walked in. 'But I don't think we'll need the drinks.'

I'd laid out glasses with a choice of mineral water and orange juice as it seemed a polite thing to do. I noticed him examining the living room as I returned them to the fridge. The main floor of my flat is essentially one large space. It has bookshelves – I have about five hundred books in the house but I keep my favourite ones here – a kitchen area, a dining-room table and my mother's old piano which I try to play every day. There's a TV area and a couple of sofas around a coffee table. Hawthorne sat down here. He looked completely relaxed.

'So you know what really happened in Deal,' I said. 'Am I about to find out who killed Diana Cowper?'

Hawthorne shook his head. 'Not right now. But I think you'll find it interesting. I've got some good news, by the way,' he added.

'What's that?'

'Mr Tibbs has turned up.'

'Mr Tibbs?' It took me a few seconds to remember who he was. 'The cat?'

'Diana Cowper's Persian grey.'

'Where was he?'

'He'd got into the neighbour's house – through a skylight. Then he couldn't get out again. He was found by the owners when they got back from the South of France and they called me.'

'I suppose that is good news,' I said, wondering what Diana Cowper's cat had to do with anything. Then another thought struck me. 'Wait a minute. There was a lawyer living in the house next door.'

'Mr Grossman.'

'Why did he contact you? How did he even know who you were?'

'I put a note through his door. Actually, I put a note in all the houses in Britannia Road. I wanted to know if the cat had made an appearance.'

'Why?'

'Mr Tibbs is the reason everything happened, Tony. If it hadn't been for him, Mrs Cowper might never have been killed. And nor would her son.'

I was sure he was joking. But he was sitting there with that strange energy of his, that mix of malice and single-mindedness that made him so hard to read, and before I could challenge him the doorbell rang for a second time.

'Shall I answer it?' I asked.

Hawthorne waved a hand. 'It's your place.'

I went over to the intercom and picked up the telephone. 'Yes?'

'This is Alan Godwin.'

I felt a surge of excitement. So that was my first visitor. I told him to come up the three flights of stairs and buzzed him in.

He appeared a short while later, wearing a raincoat that looked a size too large for him, the same coat he had worn at the funeral. He came into the room like a man approaching the scaffold and I was quite certain that, despite what he had said to me on the way to Canterbury, Hawthorne had summoned him here to accuse him of the murders and that everything was about to be revealed to me. Then I remembered that there were two people coming. Could Godwin have had an accomplice?

'What is it you want?' he asked, heading straight for Hawthorne. 'You said there was something you had to tell me. Why couldn't you just do it over the phone?' He looked around him, noticing his surroundings for the first time. 'Do you live here?'

'No.' Hawthorne pointed in my direction. 'He does.'

Godwin realised that although we had met, he knew nothing about me. 'Who are you?' he demanded. 'You never told me your name.'

Fortunately, the doorbell rang again and I hurried over to answer it. This time there was silence from the street. 'Are you here to see Hawthorne?' I asked.

'Yes.' It was a woman's voice.

'I'll open the door. Just follow the stairs up to the flat.'

'Who is that?' Godwin demanded but from the fear in his voice I think he knew.

'Why don't you sit down, Mr Godwin,' Hawthorne said. 'Although you won't believe me, I'm actually trying to help you. Is there anything you want?'

'I've got juice,' I said.

'I'll have some water.' Godwin sat down on the other side of the table, facing Hawthorne but carefully avoiding his eye.

I went and got the water that Hawthorne had told me to put away. I'd just brought it over when I heard more footsteps and Mary O'Brien walked into the room. She was the last person I had expected to see but at the same time it suddenly seemed obvious that it should have been her. She took two steps towards us, then stopped dead. If she had been nervous and uncertain a moment before, she was now simply thunderstruck. She had noticed Alan Godwin and she was staring at him. He, equally shocked, stared back.

Hawthorne sprang to his feet. There was something almost devilish about him, a glee I had never seen before. 'I think you two know each other,' he said.

Alan Godwin was the first to recover. 'Of course we know each other. What do you mean by this?'

'I think you know exactly what's going on, Alan. Why don't you sit down, Mary? I think I can call you that. We're all friends here.'

'I don't understand!' Mary O'Brien was trying to keep her emotions in check but she was on the edge of tears. She looked at Godwin. 'Why are you here?'

'He told me to come.'

The two of them looked guilty, angry, afraid. Godwin stood up. 'I'm not staying here,' he said. 'I don't care what game you're playing, Mr Hawthorne. I'm not having any of it.'

'That's fine, Alan. But you walk out this room, the police are going to know everything. And so is your wife.'

Godwin froze. Mary also wasn't moving. Hawthorne was completely in charge.

'Sit down,' he said. 'You two have been colluding together and lying for ten years. But it's over. That's why you're here.'

Godwin sat down again. Mary joined him on the sofa, keeping a distance between them. As she took her place, I saw him mouth the words 'I'm sorry' – and right then I knew that the two of them were lovers and that Judith Godwin had suspected it too. That was the reason why there had been tension between the two women.

I sat down on the piano stool. Hawthorne was the only one in the room who was still on his feet.

'We need to get to the bottom of what happened in Deal,'

he began. 'Because I've heard this story half a dozen times and I've even been to the bloody place and it's never made any sense. That's not surprising. Everything you two have said has been a complete pack of lies. God knows what it must have been like for you but the trouble is, you had no choice. You were locked into this and there was no way out. I'd almost feel sorry for you. Except I don't.'

He took out a packet of cigarettes and lit one. I went into the kitchen, found an ashtray and put it on the table for him to use.

'When did you start your affair?' Hawthorne asked.

There was a long silence. Mary had begun to cry. Alan Godwin reached out to take her hand but she pulled it away.

Godwin must have known there was no point trying to pretend. 'It was very soon after Mary started with us,' he replied. 'I was the one who started it. I take full responsibility.'

'It's over now,' Mary said, quietly. 'It's been over for a long time.'

'To be honest with you, I don't care about your relationship,' Hawthorne said. 'I just want the facts, and the fact is that you were responsible for what happened in Deal – both of you. Diana Cowper may have forgotten her specs – but those two little kids got run over because of you and you know it. You've been living with it ever since.'

Mary nodded. The tears ran down her cheeks.

Hawthorne turned to me. 'I'll be honest with you, Tony. When you and I were in Deal, there was lots of stuff I didn't understand. Where do I even start? The kids run across the street to an ice-cream shop. Only it's closed. Not only that, it's flooded and all the electrics are bust. It's dark. I know they were only eight but they must have seen there was no chance they were going to get a Mr Whippy there. And then they get hit by the car and one of them is dead and the other's lying there and, according to Mr Traverton in the chemist shop, he's calling out for his daddy. But no child does that. When a child gets hurt, what he wants is his mummy. So what's going on there?'

He paused for a moment. Nobody spoke and it struck me that he was completely in control of the situation, that this might as well have been his flat as mine. Hawthorne certainly had a magnetic personality. Although, of course, magnets can repel as well as attract.

'Let's go back to the beginning,' he went on. 'Mary here takes the boys to Deal. Mum has a conference. Dad's on a business trip to Manchester. She books into the Royal Hotel but she doesn't want a family room. She wants a twin room for the kids and a double room next door. Why do you think that is?'

'The hotel said that the family room didn't have a sea view,' I said.

'It didn't have anything to do with the view. Why don't you tell him, Mary?'

Mary didn't look at me. When she spoke, her voice was almost robotic. 'We were meeting in Deal. We were going to be together.'

'That's right. The nanny and her boss. Having it off together. But you can't do it in Harrow-on-the-Hill, not in the family home. So you steal a weekend on the coast. The boys go to bed at six o'clock, which leaves the whole night for you to be together.'

'You're disgusting,' Godwin said. 'You make it sound so . . . sordid.'

'And it wasn't?' Hawthorne blew out smoke. 'You were the mysterious man in the chemist's shop. And what were you doing in there? It wasn't to get a pack of six. The reason you were in there was the same reason you were crying your eyes out at Diana Cowper's funeral.'

I had wondered why he had been so upset.

'It was hay fever!' Hawthorne explained. Once again, he addressed himself to me. 'When we were in Brompton Cemetery, did you notice the plane trees?'

'Yes,' I said. 'I made a note. They were right next to the grave.'

'Plane trees are the worst if you get hay fever. They've got a pollen grain that gets right up your nose. And shall I tell you two well-known cures for hay fever?'

'Honey,' I said. 'And ginger tea.'

'And that's exactly what Alan was buying in Pier Pharmacy.' He turned back to Godwin. 'It's also the reason why you were wearing sunglasses, even though it wasn't sunny. You'd gone down to Deal to meet your girlfriend. But then you got an attack of hay fever so you went into the chemist to get something to help. Traverton gave you some herbal stuff and you left the place seconds before the accident took place.

'And it was you who *caused* the accident. The two kids

were on the promenade next to the beach. They'd been told never to run across the road and anyway they could see perfectly well that the ice-cream shop was closed. But suddenly, in front of their eyes, their dad walked out of the chemist's shop next door and even with the cap and the sunglasses they recognised you, and because they were excited they ran towards you. That was the moment when Diana Cowper turned the corner and it happened right in front of your eyes. Both your children were hit.'

Godwin groaned and put his head in his hands. Beside him, Mary sobbed quietly.

'Timothy was killed. Jeremy was lying there and of course he called out for his dad because he'd seen him just a moment ago. I can't imagine what you must have been feeling right then, Alan. You'd just seen your two children knocked over by a car but you couldn't go to them because you were supposed to be in Manchester. How were you going to explain to your wife that you were actually in Deal?'

'I didn't realise they were so badly hurt,' Godwin rasped. 'There was nothing I could have done to help . . .'

'You know what? I think that's bollocks. I think you could have run into the road and cared for your children and to hell with your little subterfuge.' Hawthorne stubbed out his cigarette, the ash sparking red. 'But at the very moment, you and Mary came to some sort of an agreement. Traverton told us that Mary was staring into his eyes but he was wrong about that. You were staring at Alan, who was standing right next to him. You were telling him to get the hell out. Is that right?'

'There was nothing he could do.' Mary echoed the words that Alan had just spoken. She had a face like death, with tears glistening on both cheeks. She was staring into the mid-distance. Later on, I would be sickened that all this had happened in my home. I would wish that they had never come here.

'I sort of understand why you've stayed with the family all these years, Mary,' Hawthorne concluded. 'It's because you know you were responsible for what happened. Is that right? Or is it because you're still shagging Alan?'

'For God's sake!' Godwin was furious. 'We ended that years ago. Mary is there for Jeremy. Only for Jeremy!'

'Yeah. And Jeremy is there because of Mary. The two of you really are made for each other.'

'What do you want from us?' Godwin asked. 'Do you think we haven't been punished enough for what happened that day?' He closed his eyes for a moment, then continued. 'It was just bad luck. If I hadn't come out of the shop at that moment, if the boys hadn't seen me . . .' He was speaking very slowly, his tone almost matter-of-fact. 'All I've ever cared about is that Judith should never find out,' he said. 'It was bad enough losing Timothy. And Jeremy. But if she knew about Mary and me . . .' He stopped. 'Are you going to tell her?'

'I'm not going to tell her anything. It's none of my business.'

'Then why did you bring us here?'

'Because I needed to know I was right about the two of you. You want my advice? I'd tell your wife about what happened. She's already thrown you out. Your marriage is over. But this thing, this secret you've had between you, it's cancer. It's eating you up. I'd cut it out.'

Alan Godwin nodded slowly, then got to his feet. Mary O'Brien did the same. They moved towards the door but at the last moment Godwin turned back.

'You're a clever man, Mr Hawthorne,' he said. 'But you have no understanding at all about what we've been through. You have no feelings. We made a horrible mistake and we've had to live with it every day. But we're not monsters. We're not criminals. We were in love.'

But Hawthorne wasn't having any of it. It seemed to me that his face was paler and his eyes more vengeful than ever. 'You wanted sex. You were cheating on your wife. And because of that, a child died.'

Alan Godwin stared at him with something close to disgust. Mary had already passed through the door. He spun on his heel and followed her. We were left alone.

'Did you have to be so hard on them?' I asked, at length.

Hawthorne shrugged. 'You feel sorry for them?'

'I don't know. Yes. Maybe.' I tried to gather my thoughts. 'Alan Godwin didn't kill Diana Cowper.'

'That's right. He doesn't blame her for the accident in Deal. He blames himself. So he had no reason to kill her. She was just the instrument of what happened, not the cause.'

'And the driver of the car . . .'

'It doesn't matter who was driving the car. Damian, his mother, the lady next door. It's got nothing to do with it.'

Cigarette smoke hung in the air. I would have to explain

that to my wife later. I was still sitting on the piano stool. My number one theory about the murder had just crashed to the ground.

'So if the killer wasn't Alan Godwin, who was it?' I asked. 'Where do we go next?'

'Grace Lovell,' Hawthorne replied. 'We'll see her tomorrow.'

Twenty
An Actor's Life

Grace Lovell had not returned to the flat in Brick Lane and I can't say I blamed her. It would take a long time to wipe away all the blood that had been spilled and longer still to erase the memories of so much violence.

She and Ashleigh were staying at her parents' home in Hounslow, close to Heathrow Airport, where her father worked as a senior commercial manager. Martin Lovell had taken the day off. He was a large, intimidating man, wearing a polo shirt that was too small for him, with shoulders straining at the fabric and butcher's arms bursting out of the sleeves. He had shaved his head, which made it difficult to guess his age, but he must have been in his late fifties. Grace didn't look anything like him. He was holding Ashleigh and had to be careful to concentrate on what he was doing. I could easily imagine him accidentally smothering the little girl in his bear-like embrace. As usual, she was showing no interest in what was going on, absorbed in the pages of a rag book.

The house was clean and modern, part of an estate which must have been perfectly aligned with the main runway as we were deafened every few minutes by the roar of the planes taking off. Grace and her father didn't appear to notice the noise. Ashleigh positively enjoyed it, giggling with pleasure every time a plane went past. Grace had told us that Rosemary Lovell, her mother, was at work, teaching maths at a local secondary school. This left the five of us sitting awkwardly close to each other on sofas and armchairs that were rather too big for the room. Martin had offered us coffee, which we had refused. He sat quietly while Grace did most of the talking. From time to time I noticed him watching us with a strange, smouldering anger in his eyes.

Over the next twenty minutes, Grace described her life with Damian Cowper, how they had met, their relationship, their time in America. She was quite different from how she had been the last few times we had met her, as if Damian's death had released her from some sort of obligation. As she talked, I realised that she had fallen out of love with him a long time ago and I remembered Hawthorne sarcastically dismissing her as 'the grieving widow'. Well, he'd been right about that. She'd been the actress all along and this was her moment in the spotlight. I don't mean to be unkind. I liked her. She was young and charismatic and she had allowed her life to be stolen away from her. Although she never said as much, it was clear that Damian's death would give her a chance to start again.

This is what she said.

'I always wanted to be an actress, for as long as I can remember. I loved drama class when I was at school and I went to the theatre whenever I could afford it. I'd go to the National first thing in the morning and queue up for ten-pound seats or I'd get tickets right at the back of the top circle. I worked part-time in a hairdressing salon in the school holidays so I could afford it, and Mum and Dad were brilliant. They always supported me. When I told them I wanted to apply to RADA, they were a hundred per cent behind me.'

'I tried to talk you out of it!' Martin Lovell growled.

'You came into town with me, Daddy. When I had my first audition, you sat in that pub round the corner.' She turned back to us. 'I was eighteen years old and I'd just taken my A levels. Dad wanted me to go to university and apply when I finished but I couldn't wait. I had four auditions and they got more and more difficult. The last one was the worst. There were thirty of us and we were there for the whole day. We had to do a whole lot of classes and all the time we knew we were being watched by all these different people and that at least half of us wouldn't be coming back. I felt sick with nerves but of course if I'd shown it that would have been the end of me. And then a few days later I got a telephone call from the head of RADA – he actually rings everyone personally – to say that I'd been accepted and it was like "Oh my God! That's impossible!" It was all my dreams come true.

'Then, of course, I had to work out how to pay for it. Dad said he'd put up half the money, which was amazing . . .'

'I did it because I believed in you,' Martin muttered, contradicting what he had said a moment before.

'. . . but I still had to find the other half. There hadn't been local authority grants for five years and I couldn't borrow the money, so there was a time when I was really worried I wouldn't be able to go. In the end, RADA helped me out. There was a famous actor – they never told me his name – and he wanted to support someone who was just starting out. Maybe it helped that I was black. I heard they were keen to have a proper ethnic mix, so half my fees were taken care of and the following September I began.

'I loved being at RADA. I loved every minute of it. Sometimes I felt completely exposed. It was an incredibly tense atmosphere and they made us work really hard. There were only twenty-eight of us in the year and a couple of students – a Scottish boy and a girl from Hong Kong – dropped out, so it was very intimate but at the same time you had to make yourself vulnerable. That was part of the training. There were times when I thought I just couldn't do it and I'd go home and cry but then a teacher would encourage me or my friends would support me and somehow I'd get through it and I'd be stronger when I came out on the other side.

'You want to know about Damian. You have to understand that we were very close as a group. We all loved each other. We really did. And we weren't competitive at all – at least, not until the very end when we had to do our Tree and the agents were circling.'

'What's a tree?' I asked.

'Oh – it's a showcase. You have to perform short scenes and monologues and lots of agents come to see your work. It's named after the actor Beerbohm Tree.' She picked up her train of thought. 'At the beginning, of course, everyone got into different cliques. There were three girls from the north of England and we were all a bit scared of them. There were a couple of gay guys. Some of the students were older, in their late twenties, and they felt more comfortable with each other. To begin with, I was completely on my own. I remember sitting in a big circle on the first day, thinking to myself that these were the people I was going to spend the next three years of my life with and I didn't know any of them. I was terrified!

'But then, as I say, we got closer and almost from the very start if there was one person who stood out, it was Damian. Everyone knew him. Everyone admired him. He was the same age as me and he had hardly ever been in London – he lived in Kent – but he had this extraordinary confidence and the teachers were all over him. Nobody said he was a star; it didn't work like that. But Damian always got the best casting and the best feedback and everyone wanted to be his best friend. Somehow that ended up being me. We didn't sleep together, by the way. Well, we did . . . once. But it's like I told you, we only got together after we'd left, quite a few years later.

'Damian and me were very close but there was another girl he fancied – Amanda Leigh – although Damian always said that wasn't her real name. She was crazy about the actress Vivien Leigh, and people said she'd changed her name to be more like her. I'll tell you a bit more about her later. So there was Damian and Amanda and me and another boy, Dan Roberts, who was also a brilliant actor. A lot of people thought that Damian and Dan were into each other but that wasn't true. The four of us were best friends and we stayed that way for the whole time we were there. It was only after we left that we all went our separate ways but I suppose that's the business. My first job was with the Citizen's Theatre in Glasgow. Damian was with the RSC. Dan was in *Twelfth Night* in Bristol. And I can't remember what Amanda did but the main thing is we were apart.

'I could talk to you all day about RADA. What I remember most is just this sense of belonging, of being with the right people in exactly the right place. They made us work incredibly hard – movement classes, voice classes, singing classes – and you had a ton of homework too. Nobody ever had any money. That was the funny thing. We'd hang out in this disgusting café called Sid's and all the boys would be eating huge plates of chips and sausages and stuff like that because it was cheap. Some nights we'd go drinking at the Marlborough Arms. That was the pub where you waited for me, Daddy. But mainly everyone just went home and did their Lloyd or whatever else they had to do and then crashed out.'

I had no idea what doing a Lloyd meant. But this time I didn't interrupt.

'But if you're interested in Damian, then I have to tell you about the third-year production of *Hamlet*, because that was when everything sort of came to a head. It was a really,

really important production – first of all because it was *Hamlet* and whoever got that role was going to have a fantastic launch pad. Loads of agents would be there and it was going to be directed by Lindsay Posner, who'd done a whole load of great work at the Royal Court and we'd all seen his brilliant *American Buffalo* at the Young Vic. Everyone thought that Dan would get cast. He'd only had small parts in the last two productions and the rumour was that he'd been held back on purpose because he was going to be given this great chance to shine. Also, his Tree hadn't gone as well as expected – he'd fluffed some of his lines. So it was his turn.

'We were all excited, waiting for the list to go up. There was a tiny, cramped space near the pigeonholes where they'd put up the cast list and everyone would crowd around to see who was going to play what and which theatre was going to be used. By now, we were getting nervous too. We'd been there for three years and we were getting close to the end. The worst thing that could happen to you was to leave RADA without an agent. So these last productions really mattered.

'Anyway, the list went up, and sure enough, Dan was cast as Hamlet. I got Ophelia, which was fantastic. Amanda only got a tiny part, as Osric – they were going to do it cross-gender. She only turned up in Act 5 but she'd played Imogen in *Cymbeline* earlier in the year so that was fair enough. Damian was going to play Laertes and he was happy about that although a lot of people said he should have been Hamlet. He'd done the "rogue and peasant slave" soliloquy for his Tree and everyone said it was awesome. The production was going to be in modern dress and it was being staged in the GBS Theatre, which was down in the basement, and it was the coolest space in the building. Much cooler than the Vanbrugh.

'We had five weeks of rehearsals, which sounds a lot but it was incredibly demanding. And then, one week in, everything changed – and the reason I'm telling you about this is that you could say it's what changed my life. Dan got ill with glandular fever and couldn't come to rehearsals, so after a lot of discussion he changed parts with Damian, which meant that suddenly Damian and I were working together for hours and hours on all these incredibly intense scenes. When I look back on it, that's when I fell in love with him. When he was on the stage, he had this . . . magnetism. I mean, he was impressive when you met him in the street but when he was performing, it was like looking into a pool of water . . . or a well. He had a depth and a sort of clarity. Lindsay Posner loved working with him and that was how he got into the RSC. Lindsay was doing a whole lot of work at Stratford and the Barbican and he took Damian with him.

'People still talk about that production of *Hamlet*. Damian, Dan and I all got agents as a result of it and the artistic director told me it was one of the best he'd ever seen. We did it in the round with no set and very few props. We used a lot of masks – Lindsay had been very influenced by Noh theatre. And there was no doubt that Damian was brilliant. He stole the show. Dan was great too – you could feel the energy and the violence in the fight scene in Act 5 – it was done with fans, not with swords. We actually got a standing ovation and that's something that doesn't often happen at RADA, not with agents in the audience.

'But I remember it mainly because of Damian. You must know the play. Act 3, Scene 1. I was in tears at the end of it. *Oh, what a noble mind is here o'erthrown.* All the suffering and the madness in the scene stayed with me. At one moment, Damian grabbed me by the throat and his face was so close to mine I could feel his breath on my lips. When he let me go, he left bruises. After we'd got together, he said he didn't want to act with me again – but by then my acting career was on hold anyway, because of Ashleigh. I suppose what I'm trying to say is that what I loved most was the actor, more than the man. As a man, he could be . . .'

She couldn't find the word she was looking for so her father supplied it: 'A bastard.'

'Dad!'

'The way he treated you, the way he used you—'

'He wasn't always like that.'

'He and his mother were like that from the very start. Both of them, as bad as each other.'

Grace looked at him disapprovingly but she didn't argue with him. And then she was off again.

'I was signed up by Independent Talent and my first job was an appearance in a TV show, *Jonathan Creek*. I only had a few lines – I played a magician's assistant – but at least it was something on my CV. I got a few other jobs in TV: *Casualty*, *Holby City*, *The Bill*. And I did an advert for Stella Artois, which was amazing. I got to spend a week in Buenos

Aires! I also started getting a lot of theatre. My best job was the Jonathan Kent season at the Haymarket. I had good parts in *The Country Wife* and a play by Edward Bond, *The Sea*. I even got a mention in the reviews. Fiona Brown, my agent, was certain things were going to happen for me. I was getting some great auditions too.

'And then I met Damian again. He came to see *The Country Wife*. He hadn't even realised I was in it but he had a friend who was playing Mrs Fidget. We bumped into each other backstage and went out for a drink. It was terrible really. I mean, we'd known each other and we'd been so close, yet we hadn't seen each other for years and years.'

'That was him,' Martin Lovell said. Ashleigh had finished the rag book and fallen asleep in his arms. He laid her gently on the sofa. 'All he cared about was his career. He never had friends. He used you.'

'Don't say that, Daddy.' Grace still wasn't disagreeing with him. 'Damian was quite famous by now. I mean, people recognised his face even if they weren't queuing up for autographs. He'd been in a lot of big films and TV shows and he'd got an award from the *Evening Standard*. He was already working in Hollywood. He was about to start shooting *Star Trek*. I saw at once that he was different. He was harder than I remembered. He had a sort of steel edge to him that might have come with being so rich and so successful – he'd just bought the flat on Brick Lane – but actually I think a lot of it was a sort of defence. You've got to be hard in this business. I'd say it's part of an actor's life.

'We had a wonderful evening. Everyone loved the play

and there was a real buzz in the air. We had far too much to drink and we started talking about RADA and all the times we'd had together. Damian had worked with a couple of people from the school. He told me that Dan had dropped out of acting, which is a shame because he was super-talented but that's how it goes sometimes. You get offered tiny parts or understudies but the big auditions never quite click. Dan very nearly got the main part in *Pirates of the Caribbean* – in the end it went to Orlando Bloom. He also just missed out on *Doctor Zhivago* for ITV. Amanda had disappeared, of course. Damian talked a lot about himself. *Star Trek* was paying him enough to put a deposit on a house in Los Angeles and he was thinking about moving out there altogether.

'He was in England for three weeks, filming a mini-series, and we spent almost all that time together. I thought his flat in Brick Lane was amazing. I was sharing a tiny house in Clapham with two other actors and this was like another world. His phone never stopped ringing. It was his agent, his manager, his publicist, a newspaper, a radio station. I realised that this was the dream that I'd had in my head when I went to RADA except that for him it was real.'

'It'll be real for you too, Grace, now that he's gone.'

'That's not fair, Dad. Damian never stood in my way.'

'He got you pregnant just when your career was about to take off.'

'It was my choice.' She turned to us. 'When I told him the news, Damian said he wanted to have a baby with me. He was thrilled. He asked me to move in with him. He said he had more than enough money for both of us and the baby. He told me to get on the next flight to L.A.'

'Did the two of you get married?' Hawthorne asked. Unusually for him, he had been silent throughout Grace's testimony although he had been listening intently.

'No. We never did. Damian didn't think there was any point.'

'Damian was thinking of Damian,' her father insisted. 'He didn't want to be tied down. And his mother was just as bad. All she cared about was her precious son. She never gave you the time of day.'

'We both made the decision, Dad. You know that. And Diana wasn't that bad. She was just lonely and a bit sad and thought the world of him.' She went over to Ashleigh and brushed the hair out of her eyes. Then she continued: 'I did what he told me. He sent me the ticket . . .'

'Premium economy. He wouldn't even pay business class.'

'. . . and I moved in with him. His agents managed to get us a visa. I don't know how they did that but as things turned out Ashleigh was born in America and she even has American citizenship. Damian was already shooting *Star Trek* when I arrived, so I didn't see a lot of him, but I didn't mind. I helped him find the house that he bought. It only had two bedrooms but it was a lovely little place high up in the hills with wonderful views and a tiny pool. I loved it. He let me decorate it the way I wanted. I had a baby room decorated for Ashleigh and I went shopping in West Hollywood and Rodeo Drive. Damian came home late sometimes but we had weekends together and he introduced me to all his friends and I thought everything was going to be all right.'

She looked down and just for a moment I saw the sadness in her eyes.

'Only it wasn't. It was my fault, really. I didn't much like Los Angeles even though I tried to. The trouble is, it's not really a city at all. You have to get in the car to go anywhere but actually there isn't anywhere to go. I mean, it's shops and it's restaurants and it's the beach but somehow it all just feels a bit pointless. It was always too hot, particularly when I was pregnant. I found myself spending more and more time on my own in the house. I said that Damian introduced me to his friends, but he didn't actually have that many of them and they were always gossiping about the work they were doing so inevitably I felt left out. They were mainly Brits, mainly actors. It's funny out there. People seem to have their own little circles and they're not unfriendly but they don't want to let you in. And I was homesick! I missed Mum and Dad. I missed London. I missed my career.

'Damian and I didn't have fights but we weren't completely happy together. It seemed to me that he was quite different from the Damian I'd known at RADA. Maybe it was because he was getting so famous. He'd come home and he'd be glad to see me and sometimes we'd be close but I often thought it was all just an act. He was always telling me about the famous people he'd met – Chris Pine and Leonard Nimoy and J. J. Abrams – and of course I was just sitting at home and that made me resentful. I wanted to be a mother but I wanted to be more than that too. Ashleigh was born and that was magical and Damian had a big party and he was the proud dad. But after that I found that he was away more and more. He'd been cast in season four of *Mad Men* and his whole life seemed to be about parties, premieres, fast cars and models, while I was stuck at home with feeding bottles, prams and nappies . . . or diapers, I should call them. He was getting through the money like nobody's business. There was never enough for the gardeners and the grocery bills. It was like some cheap paperback version of Hollywood. All the clichés.'

'Tell them about the drugs,' her father said.

'He took cocaine and other stuff – but that wasn't anything special. All the Brits out there did the same. You couldn't go to a party without someone getting on their mobile and minutes later a motorbike dispatch rider would arrive with the little plastic bags. In the end, I stopped going to the parties. I've never taken drugs and I didn't feel comfortable.'

Ashleigh stirred on the sofa and Martin scooped her up again. The child lolled happily in his arms.

'I make it all sound awful,' Grace continued. 'But that's only because I'm telling it now that it's all over. You can't be completely unhappy in Los Angeles. Not when the sun is shining and the garden is full of bougainvillea. Damian never hurt me. He wasn't a bad man. He was just . . .'

'. . . selfish.' Martin Lovell finished the sentence.

'Successful,' Grace contradicted him. 'He was eaten up by success.'

'And now he's dead,' Hawthorne said. He glanced bleakly

in her direction. 'You might say that it couldn't have happened at a better time.'

'I don't know what you mean!' Grace was angry. 'I would never say that. He was Ashleigh's father. She's going to grow up without ever knowing him.'

'I understand he left a will.'

Grace faltered. 'Yes.'

'Do you know what's in it?'

'Yes. His lawyer, Charles Kenworthy, was at the funeral and I asked him then. I had to know we're going to be secure, if only for Ashleigh's sake. I don't have to worry. He left everything to us.'

'He had life insurance.'

'I don't know about that.'

'I do, Grace.' Sitting there in his suit with his legs crossed and his arms folded, Hawthorne was both at his most relaxed and at his most ruthless. His dark eyes were fixed on her, pinning her down. 'He took out a policy six months ago. From what I understand, you'll get almost a million quid. Not to mention the flat in Brick Lane, the house in Hollywood Hills, the Alfa Romeo Spider—'

'What are you saying, Mr Hawthorne?' her father demanded. 'Do you think my daughter killed Damian?'

'Why not? From the sound of it, you wouldn't have been too sorry and frankly, if I'd been stuck with him, I wouldn't have thought twice.' He turned back to Grace. 'I notice you arrived in England the day before Damian's mum died . . .'

I hadn't had a chance to tell Hawthorne what I had found,

looking through my notes. I was disappointed to hear he had got there without me.

'Did you see her?' he asked.

'I was going to visit Diana. But Ashleigh was exhausted after the flight.'

'I suppose you were flying premium economy again! So you didn't go round?'

'No!'

'Grace was here with me,' her father said. 'And I'll swear to that in a court of law if I have to. And when Damian was killed, she was still at the funeral.'

'And where were you during the funeral, Mr Lovell?'

'I was in Richmond Park with Ashleigh. I took her to see the deer.'

Hawthorne swung back to Grace. 'When you were telling us about RADA, you said there was something more that you wanted to tell us about the girl who called herself Amanda Leigh. What was that?'

'She was Damian's first girlfriend, but right at the end they split up. As a matter of fact, I think she left him for Dan Roberts. I saw them kissing just before we started rehearsing *Hamlet*. And I mean kissing! They were completely into each other.

'She played Osric in the production. I told you that. Afterwards, she did quite well. She did a couple of big musicals; that was her speciality. *The Lion King* and *Chitty Chitty Bang Bang*. But then she disappeared.'

'You mean she stopped working?' I asked.

'No. She disappeared. She went out for a walk one day

and she didn't come back. It was in all the newspapers. Nobody ever found out what happened to her.'

A quick Google search on my iPhone outside Martin Lovell's home produced the following newspaper report from eight years before:

SOUTH LONDON PRESS — 18 OCTOBER 2003

PARENTS APPEAL AS ACTRESS GOES MISSING

A woman, 26, has gone missing from her home in Streatham, sparking a police search operation.

Police officers are searching for Amanda Leigh, an actress who has appeared in several major West End musicals, including *The Lion King* and *Chicago*. She is described as slim, with long fair hair, hazel eyes and freckles.

Miss Leigh left her flat early Sunday evening. She was smartly dressed in a grey silk trouser suit and carrying a dark blue Hermès Kelly handbag. Police were informed when she failed to appear for the Tuesday evening performance at the Lyceum Theatre. It has now been six days since she was last seen.

Police have been talking to several internet dating agencies. The actress, who was single, was known to have met men online and could have been on her way to an assignation. Her parents have appealed for anyone who saw her that evening to come forward.

I showed it to Hawthorne, who nodded as if it was exactly what he had expected to read. 'So why are you interested in Amanda Leigh?' I asked.

He didn't answer. We were still standing in the middle of the estate, surrounded by identical houses and gardens, a few parked cars providing the only primary colours. Just then, another plane screamed overhead, its wheels lowered, its gigantic bulk blocking out the light. I waited for it to pass. 'Are you going to tell me that Amanda Leigh was also murdered? But she's got nothing to do with this. We never even heard of her before today.'

Hawthorne's phone rang. He held up a hand as he dug it out of his pocket and answered it. The conversation lasted about a minute although Hawthorne barely said anything – just 'yes' two or three times, then 'right' and 'OK.' Finally he rang off. His face was grim. 'That was Meadows,' he said.

'What's happened?'

'I've got to go back to Canterbury. He wants to talk to me.'

'Why?'

Hawthorne looked at me in a way that made me feel uneasy. 'Someone set fire to Nigel Weston's house last night,' he said. 'They poured petrol through the letter box and set it alight.'

'My God! Is he dead?'

'No. He and his boyfriend got out all right. Weston is in hospital. He has smoke inhalation injuries but nothing serious. He's going to be fine.' He looked at his watch. 'I'm going to get the train.'

'I'll come with you,' I said.

He shook his head. 'No. I don't think you should. I'll go there alone.'

'Why?' Another silence. I challenged him. 'You know who was responsible for the fire, don't you?' I said.

And there it was again, the bleakness in his eyes that I knew so well and which somehow told me that he saw the world in a completely different way from me and that we would never actually be close.

'Yes,' he said. 'You were.'

Twenty-one
RADA

I had no idea what Hawthorne meant, but the more I thought about it, the gloomier I became. How could I possibly have been responsible for an arson attack on Nigel Weston's home? I hadn't even known where he lived until I went there and I hadn't spoken a word while Hawthorne, with his customary lack of tact, had laid into the older man. Nor had I told anyone we were planning to see him – apart from my wife, my assistant and perhaps one of my sons. Was Hawthorne deliberately taking his anger out on me? It wouldn't have surprised me. Something had happened that he hadn't anticipated so he had lashed out at whoever happened to be closest.

I wondered where this left our enquiry. When he was at my flat, Hawthorne had more or less eliminated Alan Godwin from his investigation and I thought I'd heard the last of the former judge too. It was true that Weston's connection with Diana Cowper and the fact that he had allowed her to walk free were troubling but there was no proof that he had committed any crime. And yet now he had been attacked! Just when I was beginning to think that there was no connection between the murders and the car accident after all, the exact opposite had proved to be true.

Diana Cowper had been driving the car that had killed Timothy Godwin and injured his brother. She had fled from the scene to protect her son, Damian Cowper. Judge Weston had let her off with the very lightest slap on the wrist. All three of them had been attacked . . . two of them fatally. That couldn't be a coincidence.

But that raised another question. How did Amanda Leigh, the girl who had acted with Damian Cowper at RADA and who had mysteriously disappeared, fit into all this? It might be, of course, that she didn't. I had been the one who had looked her up on my iPhone after we left Grace Lovell's house and although Hawthorne had read the newspaper article he hadn't made any comment on it. So I couldn't be sure that it had any relevance at all.

I was suddenly disgusted with myself.

It was the middle of the afternoon and I was sitting on my own, in the cheap, garish café next to Hounslow East tube station which I had entered after I had parted company with Hawthorne. He had taken the tube. I was surrounded by mirrors, illuminated menus and a wide-screen TV showing some daytime antiques show. I had ordered two pieces of toast and a cup of tea which I didn't actually want. What had happened to me? When I had first met Hawthorne, I had been a successful writer. I was the creator of a television show that was seen in fifty countries and I also happened to be married to the producer. Hawthorne had worked for us. He had been paid ten or twenty pounds an hour to provide information which I had used in my scripts.

But in just a couple of weeks, everything had changed. I had allowed myself to become a silent partner, a minor character in my own book! Worse than that, I had somehow persuaded myself that I couldn't work out a single clue without asking him what was going on. Surely I was cleverer than that. For too long I had been following in his footsteps. Now, with Hawthorne away, there was an opportunity for me to take the lead.

There was an oily sheen on the surface of my tea. The toast had been covered in a spread that had melted into something that might have come out of a car. I pushed the plate away and took out my phone. Hawthorne was going to be away for the rest of the day, which gave me plenty of time to investigate this new suspect: Amanda Leigh. Oddly, there had been no photograph of her accompanying the article in the *South London Press*. I wondered what she looked like. There were no pictures that I could find on the net and only a couple of other references to her. She had disappeared and she had never been found. That was it. Her parents might still be grieving but public interest had evaporated.

I wanted to know more about her. If I really had been looking in the wrong direction all this time – which is to say, in the direction of Deal – then it was time to find out what I had been missing. What could possibly have happened at RADA that might link Amanda, Damian and Diana Cowper and how could it conceivably have led to murder?

Even as I considered the question, it occurred to me that I had a way in. Occasionally, RADA invites actors, directors and screenwriters to come in and meet the students and the year before I'd talked to a whole bunch of them about that curious love triangle: actor, writer, script. Over the course of an hour, I'd tried to explain to them how a good actor will always find things in a script that the writer doesn't know are there while a bad one will insert things that the writer would prefer they didn't. I'd talked to them about the way a character is created. Christopher Foyle, for example, existed on the page a long time before Michael Kitchen was cast but only when that decision had been made did the real work begin. There was always a tension between the two of us. For example, Michael insisted almost from the start that Foyle would never ask questions, which made life difficult for me and seemed, to say the least, unusual for a detective. And yet it wasn't such a stupid idea. We found other, more original ways to get to the information that the plot demanded. Foyle had a way of insinuating himself, getting suspects to say more than they intended. In this way, year after year, the character developed.

Anyway, I talked to the students about this and many other things and I'm not sure how much they benefited from the session. I enjoyed it very much, though. There's nothing a writer likes more than talking about writing.

I had been invited by an associate director. I'll call her Liz as she's asked not to be identified. I telephoned her from the café. Fortunately, she happened to be at RADA that afternoon and agreed to see me for an hour at three o'clock. Liz is a smart, rather intense woman, a few years older than me. She had trained to be an actor herself but had ended up writing and directing. She had gone back into teaching following a bruising encounter with the press. This had involved a play about British Sikhs which she had directed. Though well intentioned, it had led to riots, with two local councillors (she told me they had neither read nor seen the work) whipping the crowds into a fury. The artistic director had grovelled. The play had been cancelled. Nobody had come to Liz's defence. Even now, many years later, she prefers to remain anonymous.

RADA's main building on Gower Street is an odd place. The entrance, with its two statues of comedy and tragedy sculpted by Alan Durst in the 1920s, is both imposing and barely noticeable. The narrow door leads into a building that seems far too small for the three theatres, offices, rehearsal rooms, craft shops and so on that it contains. I remembered it as being a maze of white corridors and staircases, with swing doors everywhere, so that on my first visit I felt a little like a laboratory rat. This time, I met Liz in the rather chic new café on the ground floor.

'I remember Damian Cowper very well,' she told me. We'd both sat down with cappuccinos, surrounded by black-and-white photographs of the current third year. There were a few other students at the tables around us, chatting or reading scripts. She kept her voice low. 'I always had a feeling he'd do well. He was a cocky little sod, though.'

'I didn't realise you were teaching here then,' I said.

'It was 1997. I'd just joined. Damian would have been in his second year.'

'You didn't like him.'

'I wouldn't say that. I tried to keep my feelings about all the students under wraps. The trouble with this place is that everyone is super-sensitive and you can all too easily get accused of favouritism. I'm just telling you the facts. He was very ambitious. He'd have stabbed his own mother if it would help him to get cast.' She considered what she'd just said. 'That's not very appropriate, is it, given the circum-stances. But you know what I mean.'

'Did you see his Hamlet?'

'Yes. And he was absolutely wonderful. I almost hate to admit it. He only got the part because the boy who was cast got glandular fever. We had a bit of an epidemic that year and for a while the whole place was like London during the Great Plague. Of course, he'd wanted the lead from the very start. He did it for his Tree, which was his way of showing off. Actually, you know, you were right – what you said a moment ago. I didn't like him. He had a way of manipulating people which I thought was a little creepy and then there was that business in Deal.'

'What about it?' I was suddenly interested. Was there a link between the car accident and the drama school which Hawthorne didn't know about and which we had both missed?

'Well, it's just that he used it in one of the acting classes. We were exploring what we called public solitude and the students had to bring in an object that mattered to them in some way and talk about it in front of their classmates.' She paused. 'He brought in a plastic toy, a London bus. He also played us a recording of a song, a nursery rhyme: "The wheels on the bus go round and round". You must know it? He told us it had been played at the funeral of the little boy who had been killed in the accident, when his mother had been driving the car.'

'What exactly was creepy?' I asked.

'I actually had a bit of a set-to with him afterwards. He was very emotional about it. He said the song had torn him to shreds, that he couldn't get it out of his head – all that sort of stuff. But the truth is, I didn't feel he was really connected to what had happened. I felt he was using it, almost like a prop. His monologue was too self-centred. In a way, that was the object of the exercise but in this case an eight-year-old boy had died. Damian's mother might not have been entirely responsible but she had killed him. I didn't think it was appropriate to use it in class and I told him so.'

'What can you tell me about Amanda Leigh?' I asked.

'I remember her less well. She was very talented but quiet. She and Damian went out for a while and they were very close. I'm afraid she didn't have very much of a career after she left. A couple of musicals but nothing much else.' She sighed. 'That's the way it happens sometimes. You can never really predict which way it's going to go.'

'And then she disappeared.'

'It was in the newspapers and we even had the police asking questions here although her disappearance must have been four or five years after she'd left. There was some talk that she'd gone to meet a fan . . . you know, a stalker, although later on the police changed their minds and said it was probably someone she was dating. She'd dressed up smartly and her flatmates said she was in a good mood when she left. She was sharing a place somewhere in south London.'

'Streatham.'

'That's right. Anyway, she went out and she was never seen again. Maybe there would have been more fuss about it if she'd been more famous or if anyone had made the connection between her and Damian Cowper. He was already making quite a name for himself. But I suppose lots of people go missing in London and she was just another of them.'

'You said you had a picture.'

'Yes. You're lucky because there are far fewer photographs from that time. These days, of course, everyone has phones. But we kept this because of the *Hamlet*.' She had brought a large canvas bag with her and lifted it onto the table. 'I found it in the office.'

She took out a framed black-and-white photograph which she laid between the coffee cups and I found myself looking through a window into 1999. There were four young actors, posing with almost exaggerated seriousness for the camera on a bare stage. I recognised Damian Cowper immediately. He hadn't changed very much in twelve years. Back then he had been slimmer and prettier . . . cocky was exactly the word that sprang to mind. He was looking straight into the lens, his eyes challenging you to ignore him. He was dressed in black jeans and a black open-necked shirt, holding a white

Japanese mask. Grace Lovell, who had played Ophelia, and the boy who had played Laertes were standing on either side of him. They both had fans, spread out over their heads.

'That's Amanda.' Liz pointed to a girl with long hair, tied back, standing just behind them. She was playing a male part and was wearing the same clothes as Damian. I have to say that her photograph disappointed me. I'm not sure what I'd been expecting but she looked quite ordinary ... pretty, freckled, hair tied back in a ponytail. She was standing on the very edge of the group, her head turned towards a man who was approaching from the side.

'Who's that?' I asked.

The man had barely entered the frame and I couldn't make out his face. He was black, wearing glasses, holding a bunch of flowers, noticeably older than the others.

'I've no idea,' Liz said. 'He's probably one of the parents. The photograph was taken after the first performance and the GBS was packed.'

'Did you ever ... ?'

I was about to ask her something about Amanda's relationship with Damian but it was just then that I saw something and stopped, mid-sentence. I was looking at one of the people in the photograph and quite suddenly I knew who it was. There could be no doubt of it and with a rush of excitement I realised that I had discovered something that might be important and that, just for once, I was one step ahead of Hawthorne. I knew something he didn't! He had deliberately taunted me when we left Grace Lovell's home and all along he had treated me with an indifference that sometimes edged close to contempt. Well, how amusing it would be if I was able to tell him what he'd missed when he got back from Canterbury. I couldn't help smiling. It would be a delicious payback for all those hours following him around London, watching silently from the sidelines.

'Liz, you've been brilliant,' I said. 'I don't suppose I can borrow this?' I was referring to the photograph.

'I'm sorry. It can't leave the building. But you can take a picture of it if you like.'

'That's great.' My iPhone had been on the table, recording our conversation. I picked it up and took a shot of the image. I stood up. 'Thanks a lot.'

Outside RADA, I made three telephone calls. First, I arranged a meeting. Then I called my assistant, who was waiting for me at my office. I told her I wouldn't be coming back this afternoon. Finally, I left a message for my wife, saying I might be a bit late for dinner.

In fact, I wouldn't have dinner at all.

Twenty-two
Behind the Mask

From Gower Street, I took the tube back out to west London and walked down to a square, red-brick building on the Fulham Palace Road just five minutes from Hammersmith roundabout. It's no longer there, by the way. It was knocked down when they constructed a brand-new office block – Elsinore House. By a weird coincidence, HarperCollins are based there. They publish the American editions of my books.

The building that I visited that day was deliberately dis-creet, with frosted-glass windows and no signage at all. When I rang the front doorbell, I was greeted by an angry buzz and a click as the lock was electronically released from somewhere inside. A CCTV camera watched as I entered an empty reception area with bare walls and a tiled floor. It reminded me of a clinic or some obscure department of a hospital, though perhaps one that had recently closed down. At first I thought I was alone but then a voice called out to me and I went into an office just round the corner where the funeral director, Robert Cornwallis, was making two cups of coffee. The office was as unremarkable as the rest of the building, with a desk and a collection of very utilitarian chairs – padded without being remotely comfortable. A coffee machine stood on a trestle table to one side. There was a calendar on the wall.

This was the facility that Cornwallis had mentioned when we were at his home. His clients came to South Kensington for consultations but the actual bodies were brought here. Somewhere close by there was a chapel, 'a place of bereavement' Irene Laws had called it. Certainly, this wasn't it – for the room I had entered offered no solace at all. I listened out for other people. It had never occurred to me that we might be alone but it was late afternoon by now and perhaps everyone had gone home. I had actually telephoned Cornwallis in his office but he had insisted on meeting me here.

He greeted me by name and as I came in and sat down he seemed warmer and more relaxed than the last two occasions I had seen him. He was wearing a suit but had taken off the tie and undone the top two buttons of his shirt.

'I had no idea who you were,' he said, passing me one of the cups of coffee. I'd given him my name over the phone. 'You're a writer! I have to say, I'm quite surprised. When you came to my office – and my house – I had assumed you were working with the police.'

'I am, in a way,' I replied.

'No. I mean, I thought you were a detective. Where is Mr Hawthorne?'

I drank some of the coffee. He had added sugar without asking me. 'He's out of London at the moment.'

'And he sent you?'

'No. To be honest, he doesn't know I'm seeing you.'

Cornwallis considered this. He looked puzzled. 'On the telephone, you said you were working on a book.'

'Yes.'

'Isn't that a little unorthodox? I thought a police enquiry, a murder enquiry, would be conducted in private. Will I be appearing in this book of yours?'

'I think you might,' I said.

'I'm not sure that I want to. This whole business with Diana Cowper and her son has been extremely upsetting and I really don't want the company dragged into it. As a matter of fact, I'm sure you'll find quite a few of the parties involved may have objections.'

'I suppose I'll have to get their permission. And if anyone really does object, I can always change their name.' I might have added that there was nothing to stop me writing about real people if they were in the public domain, but I didn't want to antagonise him. 'Would you prefer it if I changed yours?' I asked.

'I'm afraid I'd insist on it.'

'I could call you Dan Roberts.'

He looked at me curiously. A smile spread across his face. 'That's a name I haven't used for years.'

'I know.'

He took out a packet of cigarettes. I didn't know that he smoked although now I thought about it there had been an ashtray of some sort in his office. He lit a cigarette and shook out the match with an angry wave of the hand. 'You mentioned on the telephone that you were calling from RADA.'

'That's right,' I said. 'I was there this afternoon. I was seeing . . .' I told him the name of the associate director. He didn't seem to recognise it. 'You never told me that you went to RADA,' I added. I'd drunk half of the coffee. I set the mug down.

'I'm sure I did.'

'No. I was there on both occasions when Hawthorne spoke to you. Not only were you at RADA but you were there at the same time as Damian Cowper. You acted with him.'

I was sure he would deny it but he didn't blink. 'I never talk about RADA any more. It's not a part of my life that I remember with any great fondness and from what you yourself told me, I didn't think it was relevant. When you came to see me in my South Kensington office you made it quite clear that your investigation – or, I should say, Mr Hawthorne's investigation – was directed towards the car accident that had taken place in Deal.'

'There may still be a connection,' I said. 'Were you there when Damian talked about it? Apparently he used it as the basis of one of his acting classes.'

'As a matter of fact, I was. It was a long time ago, of course, and I'd forgotten all about it until you brought it up.' He came round the side of the desk and perched on the edge, hovering over me. There was a harsh neon light in the room and it reflected in his glasses. 'He brought in a little red bus and he played the music. He talked about what had happened and the impression it had made on him.' Robert Cornwallis reflected for a moment. 'Do you know, he was actually quite proud of the fact that immediately after she had run over two children, killing one of them as it turned out, his mother's thoughts were entirely focused on him and his career. The two of them were really quite remarkable, wouldn't you agree?'

'You acted with him,' I said. 'You were in *Hamlet*.'

'The Noh production. Based on Japanese classical theatre. All masks and fans and shared experience. Ridiculous, really. We were just children with big ideas about ourselves but at the time it mattered more than you can possibly imagine.'

'Everyone says you were brilliant,' I said.

He shrugged. 'There was a time when I wanted to be an actor.'

'But you became an undertaker.'

'We discussed this when you were at my house. It was the family business. My father, my grandfather . . . remember?' He seemed to have an idea. 'There's something I'd like to show you. You may find it interesting.'

'What is it?'

'Not here. Next door . . .'

He stood up, expecting me to follow. And that was what I meant to do. But when I tried to get to my feet, I discovered that I couldn't.

Actually that's not even the half of it. What I'm describing was without question the single most terrifying moment of my life. I couldn't move. My brain was sending a signal to my legs – 'get up' – but my legs weren't listening. My

341

arms had become foreign objects, attached to me but not connected. I was aware of my head, perched like a football, on a body that had turned into a useless pile of muscle and bone and somewhere inside my heart was hammering away in panic as if it could somehow break free. I will never fully be able to describe the bowel-emptying fear I felt at that moment. I knew that I had been drugged and that I was in terrible danger.

'Are you all right?' Cornwallis asked, his face full of concern.

'What have you done?' Even my voice didn't sound like me. My mouth was having to work twice as hard to form the words.

'Stand up . . .'

'I can't!'

And then he smiled. It was a horrible smile.

Moving very slowly, he came over to me. I flinched as he took out a handkerchief and forced it into my mouth, effectively gagging me. It hadn't even occurred to me until then that I really ought to have screamed, not that it would have made any difference. I knew now that he had made sure we were on our own.

'I'm just going to get something. I won't be a minute,' he said.

He walked out of the room, leaving the door open. I sat there, exploring my new sensations – or rather, my lack of them. I couldn't feel anything – except fear. I tried to slow my breathing. My heart was still pounding. The handkerchief was pressing against the back of my throat, half suffocating me. I was actually too terrified to work out what should have been obvious to me: that I had blithely walked into a place of death – and that my own death was almost certain to be the result.

Cornwallis came back pushing a wheelchair. Perhaps he used it for corpses although it was more likely that he kept it for the elderly relatives who came to pay their last respects to the departed. He was whistling quietly to himself and there was a curious, empty quality to his face. He was no longer wearing his tinted glasses and I looked at his twinkling eyes, his neat little beard, his thinning hair, with the knowledge that they were nothing more than a mask and that they had concealed something quite monstrous which was now showing through. He knew I couldn't move. He must have put something in my coffee and I, fool that I was, had drunk it. Already I was screaming at myself. This was the man who had strangled Diana Cowper and had sliced up her son. But why? And why hadn't I worked it out – hadn't it been obvious? – before I came here?

He leaned down and for a moment I thought he was going to kiss me. I recoiled in disgust but he simply picked me up and dumped me in the wheelchair. I weigh about eighty-five kilograms and the effort made him pause for breath. Then he brushed himself off, straightened my legs and, still whistling, wheeled me out of the office.

We went past an open door with a chapel on the other side. I glimpsed candles, wood panels, an altar that might be equipped with a cross, a menorah or whatever religious icon was appropriate. At the end of the corridor there was an industrial lift, large enough to hold a coffin. He pushed me in and stabbed at a button. As the doors closed, I felt my entire life being shut off behind me. There was a jolt and we began our descent.

The lift opened directly into a large, low-ceilinged work-room with more neon lights, evenly spaced. Everything I saw filled me with fresh horror, intensified by the fact that I was completely helpless. At the far end there were six silver cabinets, refrigerated compartments arranged in two sets of three, each one large enough to hold a human body. A whole side of the room was given over to what looked like a basic surgery with a metal gurney, shelves containing darkly coloured bottles and vials, a table with an array of scalpels, needles and knives. He parked me so that I was facing them, with my back to the lift. The walls were white-washed brick. The floor was covered in grey sheet vinyl. There was a bucket in one corner, and a mop.

'I really wish you hadn't come here,' Cornwallis said. He still had that very reasonable, mannered way of speaking which he had cultivated over the years and which suited the role he had taken. Because I knew now that it was just a role. With every second that passed, the real Robert Cornwallis was revealing himself to me.

'I've got nothing against you and I don't want to hurt you but you made the decision to come here and poke your nose into my fucking business.' His voice had risen as he completed the sentence so that by the time he reached the swear-word it was a high-pitched scream. He recovered himself a little. 'Why did you have to ask about RADA?' he went on. 'Why did you have to go digging around in the past? You come here asking me these stupid questions and I have to tell you and then I have to deal with you – which I really don't want to do.'

I tried to speak but the handkerchief prevented me. He pulled it out of my mouth. As soon as it came free, I found my voice. 'I told my wife I was coming here,' I said. 'And my assistant. If you do anything to me, they'll know.'

'If they ever find you,' Cornwallis replied. His voice was matter-of-fact. I was about to speak again but he held up a hand. 'I don't care. I don't want to hear anything more from you. It doesn't really make any difference to me any more. But I do just want to explain.'

He touched his fingertips to the side of his head, staring into the mid-distance as he gathered his thoughts. And I just sat there, silently screaming. *I am a writer. This can't happen to me. I didn't ask for any of it.*

'Do you have any idea what my life has been like?' Cornwallis said at last. 'Do you think I enjoy my job? What do you think it's like, sitting day after day after day listening to miserable people going on about their miserable dead mothers and fathers and grannies and grandpas, arranging funerals and cremations and coffins and headstones while the sun is shining and everyone else is getting on with their lives? People look at me and they see this boring man in a suit who never smiles and who says all the right things – 'my condolences, oh I'm so sorry, please let me offer you a tissue' – when inside I actually want to punch them in the face because that's not me and it's not who I ever wanted to be.

345

'Cornwallis and Sons. That's what I was born into. My father was an undertaker. My grandfather was an undertaker. His father was an undertaker. My uncles and aunts were undertakers. When I was a boy, everybody I knew was dressed in black. I was taken out to see the horses pulling the hearse along the street. That was a treat for me. I'd watch my father eating his dinner and I'd think to myself that he'd spent the whole day with dead people and that those hands of his, the same hands that had embraced me, had touched dead flesh. Death had followed him into the room. The whole family was infected by it. Death was our life! And the worst of it was that one day I would be exactly the same because that was what they had planned for me. There was never any question about it. Because we were Cornwallis and Sons – and I was the son.

'They used to tease me about it at school. Everyone knew the name, Cornwallis. They'd pass the shop on the way to get the bus and it wasn't as if it was Jones or Smith or something forgettable. They called me "funeral boy" . . . "dead boy". They asked me if my dad got off on corpses . . . if I did. They wanted to know what dead people looked like with no clothes on. Did they get hard-ons? Did their nails still grow? Half the teachers thought I was creepy – not because of who I was but because of what my family did. Other kids talked about university, about careers. They had dreams. They had a future. Not me. My future was, quite literally, dead.

'Except – and this is the funny thing – I did have a dream. It's strange how things happen, isn't it? One year, they gave me a part in the school play. It wasn't a big part. I was Hortensio in *The Taming of the Shrew*. But the thing is, I loved it. I loved Shakespeare. The richness of the language, the way he created a whole world. I felt so excited standing there in costume, with the lights on me. Maybe it was just that I had discovered the joy of being someone else. I was fifteen years old when I realised that I wanted to be an actor and from that moment the thought consumed me. I wouldn't just be an actor. I would be a famous actor. I wouldn't be Robert Cornwallis. I'd be someone else. It was what I had been born for.

'My parents weren't happy when I told them I wanted to audition for RADA – but do you know what? They let me go ahead because they didn't think I had a hope in hell of getting in. Secretly, they were laughing at me but they decided that if they let me get it out of my system I'd forget about it and slip back into the family tradition. I applied for RADA and without telling them I applied for Webber Douglas and the Central School of Drama and the Bristol Old Vic too and I'd have applied for a dozen more until I got in. But I didn't need to. Because the fact of the matter was that I was good. I was really good. I came alive when I was acting. I breezed into RADA. I knew, the moment I auditioned, they were never going to turn me down.'

I said something. It came out as an inarticulate noise because by now the drug had gone to work on my vocal cords and it was difficult to speak. I think I was going to plead with him to let me go but it was a waste of time anyway. Cornwallis frowned, went over to the table and picked up one of the scalpels. As I stared at him, he walked over to me. I saw the light of the neon shimmering in the silver blade. Then, without hesitating, he plunged it into me.

I stared in complete amazement at the handle jutting out of my chest. The strange thing is that it didn't hurt very much. Nor was there a lot of blood. I just couldn't believe he'd done it.

'I told you I didn't want to hear from you!' Cornwallis explained, his voice once again rising into a whine. 'There's nothing you can say to me that I want to hear. So shut up! Do you understand? Shut up!'

He composed himself, then continued as if nothing had happened.

'From the first day I entered RADA, I was accepted for what I was and what I had to offer. I didn't use the name Robert Cornwallis and I never talked about my family. I called myself Dan Roberts . . . no-one cared about things like that. It was going to be my stage name anyway. And I wasn't "funeral boy" any more. I was Anthony Hopkins. I was Kenneth Branagh. I was Derek Jacobi. I was Ian Holm. All those names were up there on the boards and I was going to be one of them, just like them. Every time I went into the building I had this sense that I had found myself. I'm telling you now, those were the happiest three years of my life. They were the only happy three years of my life!

'Damian Cowper was there too. You were right about that – and don't get me wrong. I liked him. To begin with, I admired him. But that was because I didn't know him. I thought he was my friend – my best friend – and I didn't see him for the cold, ambitious, manipulative swine that he was.'

I glanced down at the scalpel, still jutting obscenely out of me. There was a pool of red spreading around it, no bigger than the palm of my hand. The wound was throbbing now. I felt sick.

'It all came to a head in the third year. Everything was more competitive by then. We all pretended to be each other's friends. We all pretended to support each other. But let me tell you, when it came to the showcases and the final play, that's when the gloves came off. There wasn't a single person in that building who wouldn't have pushed their best friend off the fire escape if they thought it would help them get an agent. And of course, everyone was sucking up to the staff. Damian was good at that. He'd smile and he'd say the right things and all the time he had his eye on the main prize and in the end, guess what he did?'

Cornwallis paused but I was too afraid to speak. He stared at me, then snatched up a second scalpel and, even as I cried out, stabbed it into me, this time into my shoulder, leaving it there. 'Guess what he did!' he screamed.

'He cheated you!' I somehow managed to force out the words. I didn't know what I was saying. I just had to say something.

'He did more than that. When I was cast as Hamlet, he was furious. He thought he was entitled to the part. He'd already performed it as part of his Tree. He wanted everyone to see how good he was. But it was my turn. The part was mine. That last production was my opportunity to show the world what I could do and he and that bitch girlfriend of his tricked me. They did it together. They deliberately made me sick so that I couldn't come to rehearsals and they had to recast.'

I didn't understand quite what he was talking about but right then nor did I care. I was sitting there like a bull in the ring with two scalpels sticking out of me, both hurting more and more. I was certain I was going to be killed. He seemed to be waiting for me to speak. Fearful that my silence would only enrage him more, I muttered: 'Amanda Leigh . . .'

'Amanda Leigh. That's the one. He used her to get at me but I caught up with her in the end and made her pay.' He giggled to himself. It was the most convincing portrayal of a lunatic I'd ever seen. 'I made her suffer and then she disappeared. Do you know where she is? I can tell you if you like – but if you want to find her, you'll need to dig up seven graves.'

'You killed Damian,' I rasped. It took every effort to form the words. My heart felt as if it was going to explode.

'Yes.' He brought his hands together and bowed his head as if he was praying and even then I got the sense that there was something mannered about what he was doing. This was a performance for an audience of one. 'People said I was great in the run-up to *Hamlet*,' he continued. 'I should have *been* Hamlet. But I couldn't do that because I was ill, so I ended up as Laertes and I was great as Laertes too. But the problem is, Laertes only has half a dozen scenes. He spends most of the play off-stage. I had about sixty lines. That's all. And at the end of it I didn't get the agent I wanted and when I left RADA I didn't get the career I wanted either. I tried. I kept myself in shape. I went to acting classes. I went to auditions. But it never clicked.

'There was a season playing Feste in *Twelfth Night* at the Bristol Old Vic and I thought that was going to be the beginning of everything. But after that, nothing happened for me. I came so close! I had three call-backs for *The Pirates of the Caribbean* before they gave the part to someone else. There were TV shows, new plays . . . and I was always thinking it was going to happen for me but for some reason it never did and all the time I was getting older and the money was running out and as the months became years I had to accept that there was something broken inside me and that something had been broken by Amanda and by Damian. When you're an actor, unemployment is like cancer. The longer you have it, the less chance there is of finding a cure. And all the time my fucking family was watching from the sidelines, waiting for me to fail, to come back into the fold. They were almost willing it to happen.

'Well, one thing after another: my agent decides to drop me. I'm drinking too much. I wake up in a filthy room with no money in my pocket and I realise I'm not having any sort of life. And finally the penny drops. I'm not Dan Roberts any more. I'm Robert Cornwallis. I put on a dark suit and I join my cousin Irene in South Kensington – and that's it. Game over.'

He paused and I flinched, wondering if he was going to pick up another scalpel. The first two were burning into me. But he was too absorbed in his own story to hurt me any more.

351

'I was actually very good at the job. I suppose you could say it was in my blood. I hated every single minute of it but then is there such a thing as a cheerful undertaker? The fact that I was miserable probably made me more suited to the role. In the words of the song, I lived the life I was given. I met Barbara at her uncle's funeral – isn't that romantic? – and we got married! I never really loved her. It was just something I had to do. We had three sons and I've tried to be a good father but the truth is they're foreign objects to me. I never wanted them. I never wanted any of it.' He half smiled. 'It amused me when Andrew said he wanted to be an actor. Where do you think he got that from? I'll never let it happen, of course. I'd do anything to protect him from that particular circle of hell.

'Hell pretty much describes my life for the last twelve years. I managed to catch up with Amanda in the end. One day, when I couldn't bear it any more, I tracked her down and invited her out to dinner. She was the first one I killed and doing that gave me a real sense of gratification, I'll admit it. You probably think I'm crazy but you don't understand what she did to me, she and Damian. He was the one I really wanted to deal with: Damian Cowper, who was winning awards and getting more and more famous and making films in America. But I knew it was just a dream, that he was out of my reach. How could I get anywhere near him?

'So you can imagine how I felt when, one day, his mother walked into the funeral parlour. *Come into the parlour, said the spider to the fly!* I recognised her at once. She had come to RADA quite a few times and she'd been there for *Hamlet*.

352

She'd even complimented me on my performance. And here she was, sitting in front of me, arranging her own funeral! She didn't recognise me but then why should she have? I've changed a lot in the time since I left drama school. I've lost my hair and then there is the beard and the glasses. And at the end of the day who looks at an undertaker anyway? We're a type. People who deal with the dead live in the shadows and nobody really wants to acknowledge that we're there. So she chatted to me and chose her willow coffin and her music and her prayers and she didn't notice that I was sitting there quite stunned.

'You see, I'd been struck by the most remarkable thought: if I killed her, Damian would come to her funeral and then I would be able to kill him! That was what came to me in the space of about one minute. And that's exactly what I did. She had given me her address and I went round to her house and I strangled her. And then, a couple of weeks later, I stabbed Damian to death in his fancy flat. I enjoyed doing that more than you can possibly imagine. I'd been careful to avoid him at the funeral. I let Irene have all the personal contact. But you should have seen his face when I told him who I was! He knew I was going to kill him even before I took out the knife. And he knew why. I just wish I could have made it last longer. I'd have liked him to suffer more.'

I waited for him to continue. There was so much he hadn't explained and while he was talking he wasn't attacking me. But he'd stumbled to a halt and I think we both knew at the same moment that he had nothing more to say. There was still no movement in my legs and arms. I wondered what drug I had been given. But if I was paralysed, I wasn't numb. The pain in my chest and arm was radiating outwards and there was a lot of blood on my shirt.

'What are you going to do with me?' I just about managed to articulate the words.

He looked at me, dully.

'I've got nothing to do with this,' I said. 'I'm just a writer. I only got involved because Hawthorne asked me to write about him. If you kill me, he'll know it was you. I think he knows already.' I was having to work to make myself understood but it seemed to me that the more I spoke to him, the greater my chances of surviving. 'I have a wife and two sons,' I said. 'I understand why you killed Damian Cowper. He was a shit – I thought so too. But killing me is different. I'm nothing to do with this.'

'Of course I'm going to kill you!'

My heart sank deep into my bowels as Cornwallis snatched a third scalpel off the table. This one was going to be the murder weapon. He was a little wild now, his face livid, his eyes unfocused.

'You really think I'm going to tell you all this and leave you alive? It's your fault!' He sliced the air with the scalpel, emphasising the point. 'Nobody else knows about RADA . . .'

'I told lots of people!'

'I don't believe you. And it doesn't matter anyway. You should have stuck with your stupid children's books. You shouldn't have interfered.'

He advanced towards me, measuring his steps.

'I'm really sorry . . .' he said. 'But you brought this on yourself.'

In that last moment, he had the soulful look of the professional undertaker greeting a new customer. The scalpel was in his hand, slanting upwards. He ran his eyes over me, wondering where to strike.

And then a door which I hadn't even noticed burst open and a figure moved into the room, on the very edge of my field of vision. I managed to turn my head. It was Hawthorne. He was holding his raincoat in front of him, almost like a shield. I didn't have a clue how he had got there but I couldn't have been happier to see him.

'Put that down,' I heard him say. 'It's over.'

Cornwallis was standing in front of me, no more than a couple of metres away. He looked from Hawthorne back to me and I wondered what he was going to do. I also saw the moment when he made up his mind. He didn't put the scalpel down. Instead, he lifted it to his own throat, then drew it across in a single, decisive, horizontal slash.

The blood exploded out of him. It gushed over his hand, curtained down his chest, pooled around his feet. He remained standing with a look on his face that still gives me nightmares to this day. I would say he was gleeful, triumphant. Then he collapsed, his entire body twitching spastically as more blood spread around him.

I didn't see any more. Hawthorne had grabbed hold of the wheelchair and spun me away. At the same time, I heard the comforting wail of sirens as police cars approached, somewhere high above.

'What are you doing here? Jesus Christ!'

Hawthorne crouched beside me, staring wide-eyed at the two scalpels, wondering why I wasn't getting to my feet. And I can honestly say that Watson had never looked up to Sherlock Holmes nor Hastings admired Poirot more than I loved Hawthorne right then and my last thought before I passed out was how lucky I was to have him on my side.

Twenty-three
Visiting Hours

In retrospect, it's a pity that I decided to write all this in the first person as it will have been obvious all along that I wasn't going to die. It's a literary convention that the first-person narrator can't be killed although it's true that one of my favourite films, *Sunset Boulevard*, breaks all the rules with its opening shot and there are one or two novels, *The Lovely Bones* for example, that do the same. I wish there had been some way to disguise the fact that I would make it through to this chapter and wake up in the A&E Unit of Charing Cross Hospital, just a short way down the Fulham Palace Road, but I'm afraid I couldn't think of one. So much for suspense!

I'm a little embarrassed that I had managed to pass out a second time during the course of a single investigation but the doctor assured me it was more to do with the drug I had been given than my own faint-heartedness. This turned out to be Rohypnol, the date-rape drug no less. We would never discover where Cornwallis had managed to get it from – although his wife, Barbara, was a pharmacist so perhaps he had got it through her. I never found out what happened to her and her children, by the way. It can't have been much fun discovering that she had been married to a psychopath.

I was kept in overnight for observation but generally I wasn't in such bad shape. My two scalpel wounds hurt a lot but needed just two stitches each. I'd been badly scared. It would take between eight and twelve hours for the effects of the drug to wear off.

I had visitors. My wife came first, interrupting a busy production schedule to make her way up to the second floor where I had now been transferred. She wasn't too pleased to see me. 'What on earth have you been doing?' she demanded. 'You could have been killed.'

'I know,' I said.

'And you're not really going to write about it, are you? You'll look ridiculous! Why did you even go into the building? If you knew he was a killer . . .'

'I didn't know it was empty. And I didn't think he was the killer. I just thought he might know more than he was saying.'

It was true. I had recognised Robert Cornwallis in the photograph that Liz had shown me but the trouble was, in the back of my mind, I'd already decided that if it wasn't Alan Godwin, then Grace's father, Martin Lovell, must have been responsible for the murders. He'd been in the photograph too, the man with the flowers on the edge of the frame. He had a good reason to want Damian Cowper dead.

He would have done anything to protect his daughter and help her restart her career. I'd been so sure I was right that I hadn't thought it through and had almost got myself killed.

'Why did you never tell me you were writing this book?' my wife asked. 'You don't normally keep things from me.'

'I know. I'm sorry.' I felt wretched. 'I knew you'd think it was a bad idea.'

'I don't like the idea of you putting yourself in danger. And look where it's got you: intensive care!'

'It was only four stitches.'

'You were very lucky.' Just then her mobile phone rang. She glanced at the screen and got up. 'I brought you this,' she said.

She'd brought a book and laid it on the bed. It was *The Meaning of Treason* by Rebecca West, the book I was reading for *Foyle's War*. 'ITV are waiting to hear about the new series,' she reminded me.

'I'll write it next,' I promised.

'Not if you're dead, you won't.'

My two sons sent nice texts but they didn't come to the hospital. It was the same when I'd had my motorbike accident in Greece the year before. They were quite squeamish about seeing me horizontal.

Hilda Starke looked in though. I hadn't seen or heard from my agent since our lunch and she was in a hurry, on her way to a BAFTA screening. She came bustling into my room, perched on a chair and examined me briefly. 'How are you?' she asked.

'I'm all right. They're really only keeping me in for observation.'

She looked doubtful.

'I was drugged,' I explained.

'This man, Robert Cornwallis, attacked you?'

'Yes. And then he committed suicide.'

She nodded. 'Well, I have to admit that will make a terrific end for the book. I've got news on that front, by the way. Good news and bad news. Orion don't want it. I told them the idea and they just weren't interested. At the same time, they want you to stick to the three-book contract so it may be a while before you can write it.'

'What's the good news?' I asked.

'HarperCollins have already confirmed American rights. And I've spoken to a terrific editor, Selina Walker, and she likes your work enough that she's prepared to wait too. She's coming back to me with a deal.'

I could see the books piling up in front of me. Sometimes, when I'm sitting at my desk I feel as if there's a dump truck behind me. I hear the whirr of its engine and it suddenly off-loads its contents . . . millions and millions of words. They keep cascading down and I wonder how many more words there can possibly be. But I'm powerless to stop them. Words, I suppose, are my life.

'I've also been in contact with the police,' Hilda went on. 'Obviously, some of this is going to get into the newspapers but we're trying to keep you out of it. First of all they're embarrassed that you were involved in the first place but, more importantly, we don't want people to know the story before you write it.' She stood up, ready to leave. 'And by the way,' she went on, almost as an afterthought, 'I've spoken to Mr Hawthorne. The title is "Hawthorne Investigates" and we're splitting the profits fifty-fifty.'

'Wait a minute!' I was stunned. 'That's not the title and I thought you said you were never going to agree to that deal.'

She looked at me curiously. 'That was what you agreed,' she reminded me. 'And it was the only deal he was prepared to accept.' She was nervous about something and I found myself wondering if there was something Hawthorne knew about her and if he had used it in the negotiations. 'Anyway let's talk about this when we hear back from Selina.' She paused. 'Is there anything you need?'

'No. I'll be home tomorrow.'

'I'll call you then.' She was gone before I could say another word.

My last guest arrived later that evening, long after visiting hours were over. I heard a nurse trying to stop him and the snap of his reply: 'It's all right. I'm a police officer.' Then Hawthorne appeared at the foot of my bed. He was holding a crumpled brown paper bag.

'Hello, Tony,' he said.

'Hello, Hawthorne.' It was odd, but I was very glad to see him. More than that I felt a warmth towards him that had no basis in logic or reason. Right then, there was nobody I wanted to see more.

He sat down on the chair that Hilda had vacated. 'How are you feeling?' he asked.

'I'm much better.'

'I brought you these.' He handed me the bag. I opened it. It contained a large bunch of grapes.

'Thank you very much.'

'It was either that or Lucozade. I thought you'd prefer grapes.'

'That's very kind of you.' I set them aside. I'd been given a private room, perhaps because I was involved in a police enquiry. The lights were low. There were just the two of us, the chair, the bed. 'About Hammersmith,' I said. 'I was very glad you turned up. Robert Cornwallis was going to kill me.'

'He was a total loony. You shouldn't have gone in there on your own, mate. You should have called me first.'

'Did you know he was the killer?'

Hawthorne nodded. 'I was about to arrest him. But I had to sort out that business with Nigel Weston first.'

'How is he?'

'A bit pissed off that his house burned down. Otherwise he's fine.'

I sighed. 'I don't really understand any of it,' I said. 'When did you first know it was Cornwallis?'

'You up for this now?'

'I'm not going to get any sleep unless you tell me. Wait a minute!' I reached for my iPhone. The movement tweaked the wounds in my chest and my shoulder, making me wince. But I had to record him. I turned it on. 'Start from the beginning,' I said. 'Don't leave anything out.'

Hawthorne nodded. 'All right.'

And this was what he said.

'Right from the start, I told you we had a sticker. What

Meadows and the rest of them couldn't get their head round was this. A woman walks into an undertaker's to arrange her funeral and six hours later she's dead. That was the bottom line. If she hadn't gone to the undertaker's, there'd have been nothing very strange about her murder. It might have been that burglar Meadows was going on about. But we had two unusual events and the trouble was, we couldn't work out the connection.

'But actually, it became pretty clear to me why Diana Cowper had gone to Cornwallis and Sons. It's what I told you on the train. You've got to think of her state of mind. This is a woman who spends her whole life on her own. She misses her husband so much that she still visits the memorial garden where they used to live. She can't trust anyone. Raymond Clunes has just ripped her off. Her beloved son has pissed off and gone to America. She's got so few friends that after she was killed it took two whole days for anyone to notice she was dead and even then it was only the cleaner. It struck me from the start that she must have been pretty bloody miserable. And that's why she was thinking of doing herself in . . .'

I took a sharp breath. 'Committing suicide?'

'Exactly. You saw what was in her bathroom. Three packets of temazepam. More than enough to kill her.'

'We saw her doctor!' I said. 'She couldn't sleep.'

'That's what she told him. But she wasn't taking the pills, she was stockpiling them. She'd more or less decided that she'd had enough and then her cat went missing. My guess is that it was Mr Tibbs that pushed her over the edge. She'd already been visited by Alan Godwin and he'd threatened her and, reading the letter he'd sent her, she must have decided that he'd killed the cat. *I know the things that are dear to you.* Mr Tibbs disappearing was the final straw: that was when she decided to do it. But being the sort of woman she was, all neat and methodical, she wanted everything to be arranged, including her own funeral. So, on the same day, she resigns from the board of the Globe Theatre and goes to Cornwallis and Sons.'

He made it sound so obvious. 'That's why she knew she was going to die,' I said. 'Because she was about to commit suicide!'

'Exactly.'

'She didn't leave a note.'

'In a way, she did. You saw her funeral choices. First of all there's "Eleanor Rigby". *All the lonely people, where do they all come from?* That's a cry for help if ever I heard one. And then there's that poet, Sylvia Plath, and the composer, Jeremiah Clarke. I don't think it's a coincidence that they both topped themselves, do you?'

'And the psalm?'

'Psalm 34. *Many are the afflictions of the righteous: but the Lord delivereth him out of them all.* It's a psalm for suicides. You should have talked to a vicar.'

'I suppose you did.'

'Of course.'

'And what was the first thing Diana Cowper saw when she went to the undertaker's?' I asked. 'You said it was important.'

'That's right. It was the marble book in the window. And that had a quote too.'

When sorrows come, they come not single spies, but in battalions. I knew it off by heart.

'It comes from *Hamlet*. I don't know a lot about Shakespeare – I would have thought that was more up your street – but the funny thing is, he's been everywhere in this case. Diana Cowper had Shakespeare quotes on her fridge and there were all those theatre programmes on her stairs. There was another quote on that fountain we saw in Deal.'

'*To sleep, perchance to dream*. That was *Hamlet* too.'

'Exactly. It's *Hamlet* that's on her mind when she goes into the funeral parlour – because of what she'd seen in the window – and that was going to play a part later. But what happened first was that Robert Cornwallis recognised her. Obviously she's got a famous name but my guess is that she boasts about Damian. And Cornwallis goes mental. Actually, he's been mental all along.

'You know already that Cornwallis was at RADA with Damian Cowper.' Hawthorne had settled back in the chair, enjoying this. 'You remember that ashtray we saw in his office? It was awarded to Robert Daniel Cornwallis, Undertaker of the Year. He took his second name and his first name and he put them backwards and he became Dan Roberts.'

'He told me. He didn't want anyone to know his family were all undertakers.'

'The funny thing is that Grace Lovell thought that Amanda Leigh was the one with the false name. It seems these drama types didn't care too much what the kids called themselves. Cut forward a few years and it was suddenly quite useful for Cornwallis. He didn't want us to know that he'd tried and failed to become an actor. He didn't want us to make the link with RADA.'

But I had, I thought. I had made the connection even if I'd missed its full significance. How different everything would have been if I'd simply picked up the phone and called Hawthorne!

'When we were at his house, he was careful not to tell us what he'd done in his twenties,' Hawthorne continued. 'He said he sowed a few wild oats but you only have to do the maths! He's in his mid-thirties. He said that he'd been in the funeral business for about ten years. So there were at least five years before he started when he was doing something else. And while we were there, his son, Andrew, announced that he wanted to be an actor. That was what Barbara Cornwallis told us: *Acting runs in his blood*. She meant that he took after his dad. But when Andrew came downstairs and started talking about himself, his father jumped right in: *Let's not talk about that right now*. Andrew knew that his dad had once been to drama school and Cornwallis was scared he'd give it away.'

'That's what this was all about,' I said. It was all falling into place. 'A production of *Hamlet*! It was meant to be Robert Cornwallis's – I mean, Dan Roberts's – moment in the sun. He'd got the lead part in the end-of-year show and all the main agents were coming. But then Damian stole it from him.'

'Did he tell you how?'

'No.' I thought back. 'Damian Cowper was going out with Amanda Leigh. But Grace told us that they split up and that just before rehearsals began she saw Amanda in a clinch with Dan.' Suddenly it all made sense. 'It wasn't true!' I exclaimed. 'Damian put her up to it!' I remembered something else. 'My friend, Liz, said there was a bad case of glandular fever doing the rounds . . .'

'Glandular fever is also known as the kissing disease,' Hawthorne added. 'Amanda deliberately passed the virus on to Dan. Dan was forced out of the play. Damian got the main part and the rest is history. Except that Robert Cornwallis never forgave them. Four years later, he caught up with Amanda Leigh and killed her.'

'He chopped her up and put a piece of her in each one of his next seven funerals.' I remembered what Cornwallis had told me.

Hawthorne nodded. 'If you want to get rid of a body, I suppose being an undertaker is certainly a help.'

'I'm surprised his wife never noticed that anything was wrong.'

'Barbara Cornwallis had the wrong end of the stick,' Hawthorne said. 'She told us that he'd seen everything Damian had done. He'd watched the DVDs over and over again. She thought he was a fan. She didn't realise that he was actually obsessing about him. All he ever thought about was his failed acting career. He'd only ever had one success and he even named his kids after it.'

'Toby, Sebastian and Andrew. They're all characters in *Twelfth Night*.' Why hadn't I seen it before?

'It was the one play he performed in after he left drama school. The poor sod probably dreamed of killing Damian Cowper every day of his life. He blamed him for everything that had gone wrong.'

'And then Diana Cowper walked into his office.'

'Exactly. Cornwallis couldn't reach Damian. He was in America. He was famous. He'd always have an entourage. But at a funeral – that would be the perfect opportunity to do what he wanted, what he'd been dreaming of for years. That's why he killed the mother. Simply to get Damian in his reach.'

'He told me that.'

Hawthorne grinned unexpectedly. 'It had to be somebody on the inside, putting that music player into the coffin. Think about it. They had to know what type of coffin it was, that it was the sort that could be opened in a couple of seconds. They had to know exactly the moment they could reach it and Cornwallis was the one giving the instructions. He could have been alone with it at any time. He knew how much the nursery rhyme would mean to Damian; he'd heard all about it in acting class. He must have been skulking in the cemetery, watching the whole thing. The idea was to get Damian back to the flat and murder him there – and it worked perfectly. You know, when I called Cornwallis after the funeral, he was probably waiting on the terrace. And when Damian arrived on his own, that was it. Psycho time!' Hawthorne slashed at the air with an invisible knife.

'How did he get there so quickly?' I asked. He couldn't have left the funeral that long before Damian.

'He had a motorbike. Didn't you see it parked in his garage? And of course he was wearing leathers, which would have protected him from the blood splatter. After he killed Damian, he took off the leathers and either dumped them or took them home. He was clever, that one. When we saw him that afternoon, his wife asked him why he was still wearing his suit. It was because he knew we were coming and he wanted to show us that it was clean, that it wasn't covered in blood. He went to the school play. He went home. He had tea. And all that on the same day he'd chopped up his best mate.'

I lay there, thinking about what Hawthorne had said. It all made sense and yet at the same time there was something missing. 'And Deal had nothing to do with it?' I asked.

'Not really.'

'So who attacked Nigel Weston? Why did you say that was my fault?'

'Because it was.' Hawthorne took out a packet of cigarettes, remembered he was in a hospital and put them away again. 'When we interviewed Robert Cornwallis that first time, you asked him if Diana Cowper had said anything about Timothy Godwin.'

'You were angry with me.'

'It was a rookie error, mate. What you did was, you told him that we were interested in the accident that had happened in Deal. And so he decided to use it to misdirect us. It was also what gave him the idea of "The wheels on the bus go round and round". He knew it would upset Damian but at the same time it would send us in the wrong direction. And setting fire to Weston's place was genius. Weston was the judge who'd let Diana walk free, so he became a target too. But it was like I told you all along: it wasn't the tenth anniversary of the accident. It was nine years and eleven months. If Alan Godwin or his wife had really wanted to pay Diana Cowper back for what she'd done, you'd have thought they'd choose the right day.'

'But what about the text that Diana Cowper sent?'

Hawthorne nodded slowly. 'Let's go back to the first murder,' he said. 'It's unplanned . . . a bit spur of the moment. Cornwallis has Mrs Cowper in his office. He knows where she lives. It's possible that she's mentioned she's alone – I'm sure he got as much information out of her as he could. But he needs an excuse to see her, at her house, later. You remember I asked if she was ever left on her own? I was trying to find out her exact movements at the undertaker's and it turns out that she used the loo. My guess is that she left her handbag behind in Cornwallis's office and that was when he nicked it.'

'What?'

'Her credit card. It was on the sideboard in her living room and I wondered at the time what it was doing there. We also know that Cornwallis telephoned her just after two, when she was at the Globe Theatre. I asked him about that and he gave us some bullshit about needing to know the plot number of where her husband was buried. Why would he think for a minute that she would have that information? Why didn't he just ring the Chapel Office and get it from them? I knew he was lying to us. What he did was to ring her, all sweetness and light, and tell her that he'd found her

credit card and that he would drop it in later that evening:
"Don't worry, Mrs Cowper. No trouble at all."

'So later on, he turns up at her house and although it's
getting dark and she's on her own, of course she lets him in.
"Here's the credit card!" He puts it down but stays for a chat.
And that's when the penny drops. Diana Cowper remembers
the quote from *Hamlet* that she saw in the window. There
are the programmes on the stairs and the fridge magnets and
maybe they help. Suddenly she recognises Robert Cornwallis
and remembers where she has seen him before. It was a long
time ago and they probably only exchanged a few words.
He's changed a lot. He's an undertaker in a dark suit. But
she knows that he's Dan Roberts and maybe there's something about his manner that's a little bit creepy and she's
afraid. She knows that he's come to do her harm.

'What does she do? If she raises the alarm, he'll attack
her. Perhaps she can see that he's a complete nutcase. So she
smiles at him and offers him a drink. "Yes, please. I'd like a
glass of water." She goes into the kitchen – and that's when
Cornwallis unties the cord from the curtain that he's going
to use to strangle her. At the same time, as quickly as she
can, Diana sends her son a text.'

At last, one second before he said it, I realised. 'The phone
auto-corrected!' I said.

'That's right, mate. *I have seen the boy who was Laertes and
I'm afraid*. She couldn't remember his real name but she wanted
her son to know who it was in her living room. She was text-
ing quickly – she was nervous. She didn't even have time to
add the final full stop.

'And she didn't see that the text had auto-corrected and it came out: *I have seen the boy who was lacerated*. I thought it was a bit odd. Surely Mrs Cowper wouldn't have referred to Jeremy Godwin as the boy who was lacerated, even if she was in a hurry. The boy who was injured, maybe. The boy who was hurt – that's only four letters. It was just bad luck that we saw brain lacerations in the newspaper report and leapt to the wrong conclusion.'

I wondered if that was true. Hawthorne was paid by the day. The wider the investigation, the more places he visited, the more he earned. It may be stretching it but it was in his interest to examine every possibility.

He went on. 'After she'd sent the text, she went back into the living room, taking the water with her. She was probably going to ask Cornwallis to get out of her house. I can imagine she was a bit braver, now that Damian knew what was going on. But Cornwallis was too quick. The moment she put the water down, he slipped the cord over her neck and strangled her. Then he went round the house, taking a few things, making it look like a burglary. Then he left.'

Hospitals are strange places. When I had first arrived at Charing Cross, the entire place had been bright, busy, chaotic. But quite suddenly, after visiting hours, everything seemed to have stopped as if someone had thrown a switch. The lighting had dimmed. The corridors were silent. There was a stillness that was almost uncomfortable. I was tired. My stitches were hurting and although I could at least move my limbs, I didn't want to. It was possible I was still in shock.

Hawthorne could see it was time to leave.

'How long are they keeping you here?' he asked.

'I'll go home tomorrow.'

He nodded. 'You're lucky I got there in time.'

'How did you know to get to the mortuary?'

'I rang your assistant to check in with you. She told me where you'd gone. I couldn't believe it when I heard that. I was worried about you.'

'Thank you.'

'Well, who's going to write the book if it isn't you?' He suddenly looked sheepish. It was something I'd not seen before and it gave me a glimpse of the child he had been, the one who was still lurking inside the man he had become. 'Look, mate, I've been meaning to say . . . I lied to you.'

'When?'

'In Canterbury. You were having a go at me and I was pissed off with you – but I didn't speak to any other writers about this book. You were the only one I approached.'

There was a long silence. I didn't know what to say.

'Thank you,' I muttered, in the end.

He stood up. 'I heard from that agent of yours,' he continued, briskly. 'I liked her. It looks like we're going to have to wait a bit to get published but she says she can get us a good advance.' He smiled. 'At least, the way it worked out, you've got something to write about. I think it's going to be good.'

He left and I lay there thinking about what he had just said. 'It's going to be good.' He was right. For perhaps the very first time, there was a chance it might be.

Twenty-four
River Court

I went back home. I started work.

I could see that my working method was going to be very different from what I was used to. Normally, when I have an idea for a book, it will sit in my head for at least a year before I start writing. If it's a murder mystery, the starting point will be the murder itself. Someone kills somebody else for a reason. That's the core of the matter. I will create those characters and then gradually build the world around them, drawing links between the various suspects, giving them a history, working out their relationships. I'll think about them when I'm out walking, lying in bed, sitting in the bath – and I won't begin writing until the story has a recognisable shape. I'm often asked if I start writing a book without knowing the end. For me, it would be like building a bridge without knowing what it's got to reach.

This time everything had been given to me and it was more a question of configuration than actual creation and I wasn't entirely happy with some of the material. In all honesty, I wouldn't have chosen to write about a spoiled Hollywood actor because I've known too many of them and occasionally I've even worked with them. But unfortunately it was Damian Cowper who had been killed and I was stuck with him, along with his mother, his partner and the various associates who had turned up at the funeral. It was also worrying that I'd met them all so briefly. Raymond Clunes, Bruno Wang, Dr Buttimore and the others had played only a very peripheral part in the story, and since Hawthorne had done all the talking I'd been unable to find out very much about them. Should I add more characters of my own? As things had turned out, everything that had happened in Deal had been, at least to an extent, irrelevant. I wondered if it was fair to leave it in.

The question I had to ask myself was – how closely should I stick to the facts? I knew I was going to have to change some names so why couldn't I do the same with events? Although I hate using card systems, I scribbled down a heading for every interview and every incident and laid them out on my desk, starting with Diana Cowper's arrival at the funeral parlour and continuing with my involvement, my visit to her house and so on. I had more than enough for ninety thousand words. In fact, there were scenes – hours of my life – that I could drop altogether. Andrea Kluvánek droning on about her childhood and a particularly dull afternoon spent with Raymond Clunes's accountant were two examples.

Looking through my notes and iPhone recordings, I was relieved to see that I hadn't been completely obtuse. When

I first met Robert Cornwallis I had jotted down that 'he could have been playing a part' – which was exactly what he had been doing. I had also questioned whether he enjoyed being an undertaker, which turned out to be the heart of the whole matter. All in all, I hadn't done too badly. I'd noticed the motorbike parked outside his house, the motorbike helmet in the hall, the fridge magnets, the glass of water, the key holder . . . in fact, I would have said that at least seventy-five per cent of the most important clues were written down in my notebook. It was just that I hadn't quite realised their significance.

Over the next couple of days, I wrote the first two chapters. I was trying to find the 'voice' of the book. If I was really going to appear in it, I had to be sure that I wasn't too obtrusive, that I didn't get in the way. But even in that very tentative first draft (and there would eventually be five more) I saw that I had a much bigger problem. It was Hawthorne. It wasn't too difficult to capture the way he looked and spoke. My feelings towards him were also fairly straightforward. The trouble was, how much did I know about him?

- He was separated from his wife – who lived in Gants Hill.
- He had an eleven-year-old son.
- He was a brilliant, instinctive detective but he was unpopular.
- He didn't drink.
- He had been fired from the murder squad for pushing a known paedophile down a flight of stairs.

- He was homophobic. (I'm not, incidentally, making any connection between homosexuality and paedophilia, but both these points seemed noteworthy.)
- He was a member of a reading group.
- He had a good knowledge of WW2 fighter planes.
- He lived in an expensive block of flats on the River Thames.

It wasn't enough. Whenever we had been together, we had barely talked about anything except the business at hand. We had never had a drink together. We hadn't so much as shared a proper meal – breakfast in a Harrow-on-the-Hill café didn't count. The only time he had ever shown me any kindness was when he'd visited me in hospital. Without knowing where – and how – he lived, how could I write about him? A home is the first and most obvious reflection of our personality but he still hadn't invited me in.

I thought of telephoning Hawthorne but then I had a better idea. Meadows had given me his address, River Court, on the south side of the river, and one afternoon – about a week after I came out of hospital – I abandoned the scattered index cards, the crumpled balls of paper and the Post-it notes on my desk and set off down there. It was a pleasant day and although the stitches were pulling underneath my shirt, I enjoyed walking in the warm spring air. I followed the Farringdon Road all the way down to Blackfriars Bridge and saw the block of flats on the other side of the river in front of me . . . as I had seen it a hundred times on my way to the National Theatre or the Old Vic. It was extraordinary to think that Hawthorne lived here. My first thought was exactly the same one I'd had when Meadows first told me. How could he possibly afford it?

Despite its amazing position – nestling close to the bridge opposite Unilever House and St Paul's – River Court is far from being a beautiful development. It was built in the 1970s, I would say by a group of colour-blind architects who drew their inspiration from the simplest mathematical forms, quite possibly matchboxes. It's twelve floors high with narrow windows and a collection of balconies that feels haphazard. Some flats have them, some don't: it's just a matter of luck. In a city where spectacular glass towers are shooting up almost daily, it feels painfully old-fashioned. And yet perhaps because it's so ludicrous, because it sits there so doggedly determined to sit out the twenty-first century (the pub next door is actually called Doggett's), there is something attractive about it. And it has wonderful views.

The entrance was around the back, on the road leading down to the Oxo Tower and the National Theatre. Meadows had given me the name of the building but not the number of the flat. I saw a porter standing beside an open door and walked up to him. I'd had the presence of mind to bring an envelope with me and took it out of my pocket.

'I have a letter for Daniel Hawthorne,' I said. 'Number twenty-five. He's expecting it but I've rung the doorbell and I'm not getting any answer.'

The porter was an elderly man, enjoying a cigarette in the sun. 'Hawthorne?' He rubbed his chin. 'He's up in the penthouse. You want the other door.'

The penthouse? The fact that he lived in the building was surprising enough but this was more so. I waved the envelope and went to the door but I didn't ring the bell. I didn't want to give Hawthorne an excuse not to let me in. Instead, I waited about twenty minutes until finally one of the residents came out. At that moment, I stepped forward, holding a bunch of keys as if I'd been about to let myself in. The resident didn't give me a second glance.

I took the lift up to the top floor. There were three doors to choose from but some intuition made me go for the one with the river view. I rang it. There was a long silence but then, just as I was cursing the fact that Hawthorne must be out, the door opened and there he was, staring at me with a look of bemusement on his face, wearing the same suit he always wore but without the jacket and with his shirtsleeves rolled up. He had grey paint on his fingers.

Hawthorne 'at home'.

'Tony!' he exclaimed. 'How did you find me?'

'I have my methods,' I said, grandiosely.

'You've seen Meadows. He gave you the address.' He gazed at me thoughtfully. 'You didn't ring the bell.'

'I thought I'd surprise you.'

'I'd like to invite you in, mate. But I'm just going out.'

'That's all right,' I said. 'I won't stay long.' It was a stand-off; Hawthorne blocking the door, me refusing to go away. 'I want to talk to you about the book,' I added.

It took him another few moments to make up his mind but then, accepting the inevitable, he stepped back, fully opening the door. 'Come in!' he said, as if he had been pleased to see me all along.

So here was part of the mystery of ex-Detective Inspector Daniel Hawthorne revealed. His flat was very large, at least two thousand square feet. The main rooms had been knocked together into a single space with wide doorways separating a kitchen and a study from the main living area. It did indeed look out over the river but the ceilings were too low and the windows too narrow for a real 'wow' factor. Everything was beige, the same colour as the exterior, and modern. The carpets were brand new. The room was almost completely without character. There wasn't a single picture on the walls. He had almost no furniture: just a sofa, a table with two chairs and a number of shelves. There were not one but two computers on the desk in the study, along with some serious-looking hardware connected by a tangle of wires.

I noticed books, scattered on the table. *The Outsider* by Albert Camus was on the top. Next to the books was a pile of magazines, at least fifty of them. *Airfix Model World. Model Engineer. Marine Modelling International.* The titles, in bold letters, grabbed my attention, reminding me of the antiques shop in Deal. So his interest wasn't historical. He made models. Looking around, I saw there were literally dozens of them, planes, trains, boats, tanks, jeeps, all of them military, sitting on shelves, positioned on the carpet, hanging from wires, half assembled on the table. He had been putting together a battle tank when I'd rung the bell and that was presumably why it had taken him so long to answer.

He saw me examining them. 'It's a hobby,' he said. 'Model-making.'

'That's right.' Hawthorne's jacket had been on the back of one of the chairs where he'd been working. He put it on.

I looked at the tank, spread out on the table, some of the pieces so tiny that you would need tweezers to pick them up. I remembered being given Airfix kits when I was a child. I'd always start with the best of intentions but it would go wrong all too quickly. The pieces would stick to me, not to each other. I'd have a spider's web of glue between my fingers. I never left anything long enough to dry and if I did manage to finish what I was building, which happened all too rarely, it would be lopsided, hopelessly unfit for service. Painting was even worse. I'd line up all those tiny pots of paint but I'd use too much. The paint would run. It would smudge. When I woke up the next morning, I would guiltily bundle the whole thing into the bin.

Hawthorne's work was a world apart. Every model in the room had been put together immaculately, with extraordinary care and patience. They had been beautifully painted. I had no doubt at all that the various markings — the jungle camouflage, the flags, the stripes on the wings — were completely accurate. He must have spent hundreds of hours making them. He had the computers but there was no television in the room. I suspected it was pretty much all he did.

'What is this?' I asked. I was still examining the tank.

'It's a Chieftain Mark 10. British built. It went into service with NATO in the sixties.'

'It looks complicated.'

'The masking's a bit tricky. It means you can't fit the sub-assemblies until you've done the painting and the turret baskets are devils. But the rest of it's easy enough. It's nicely engineered. The company knows what it's doing. It's beautifully moulded.'

The only time I had ever heard him talk like this was when he was describing the Focke-Wulf plane in Deal.

'How long have you been doing this?' I asked.

I saw him hesitate. Even now, he didn't want to give anything away. Then he relented. 'I've been doing it for a while,' he said. 'It was a hobby when I was a kid.'

'Did you have brothers or sisters?'

'I had a sort of half-brother.' A pause. 'He's an estate agent.'

So that explained the flat.

'I was crap at making models,' I said.

'It's just a question of patience, Tony. You've got to make sure you take your time.'

There was a brief silence but for the first time I felt it wasn't an awkward one. I was almost comfortable with him.

'So this is where you live,' I said.

'For the moment. It's only temporary.'

'You're like a caretaker?'

'The owners are in Singapore. They've never been in the place. But they like to keep it occupied.'

'So your half-brother put you in here.'

'That's right.' There was a packet of cigarettes on the table and he snatched it up but I noticed there was no smell of tobacco in the room. He must smoke outside. 'You said you wanted to talk about the book.'

'I think I may have a title,' I said.

'What's wrong with "Hawthorne Investigates"?'

'We've already had that discussion.'

'What then?'

'I was going through my notes this morning and I came upon something you said to me when we first met in Clerkenwell, when you asked me to write about you. I was saying that people read detective stories because they were interested in the characters and you disagreed. *The word is murder. That's what matters.* That's what you said.'

'And . . . ?'

'"The Word Is Murder". I thought that would make a good title. After all, I'm a writer, you're a detective. That's what it's all about.'

He thought for a minute, then shrugged. 'It'll do, I suppose.'

'You don't sound convinced.'

'It's just a bit poncey. It's not something I'd read on the beach.'

'Do you ever go to the beach?'

He didn't answer.

I nodded at the pile of books. 'How are you getting on with *The Outsider*?'

'I finished it. I quite liked it in the end. Albert Camus . . . he knew how to write.'

The two of us stood facing each other and I began to wonder if I hadn't made a mistake coming here. It had given me what I'd needed. I'd learned something about Hawthorne. But at the same time I had an uneasy feeling that I'd broken faith, going to Meadows behind his back, coming here without permission.

'Maybe we could have dinner next week,' I said. 'I might have a couple of chapters to show you by then.'

He nodded. 'Maybe.'

'I'll see you, then.'

And that might have been it. I might simply have walked out, slightly regretful that I had come here at all. But as I turned, I noticed a framed photograph on a shelf. It showed a fair-haired woman with glasses dangling around her neck. She had her hand resting on the shoulder of a young boy. I knew at once that this was Hawthorne's wife and son and my first thought was how unfair he had been to me. When we were in Diana Cowper's house, I had seen a photograph of her dead husband and he had snapped at me. *If they were divorced, she wouldn't keep his picture.* But he was divorced and he had done just that.

I was about to say as much when something else occurred to me. I knew this woman. I had seen her before.

And then I remembered.

'You bastard!' I said. 'You fucking bastard.'

'What?'

'Is this your wife?'

'Yes.'

'I've met her.'

385

'I don't think so.'

'She was at Hay-on-Wye, at the literary festival, two days after you came to see me. She laid into me. She said my books were unreal and irrelevant. She was the reason why . . .' I stopped myself. 'You put her up to it!'

'I don't know what you're talking about.'

He was looking at me with innocent, even child-like eyes but I wasn't having any of it. I couldn't believe I'd allowed myself to be manipulated so easily. Did he really think I was so stupid? I was furious. 'Don't lie to me.' I almost shouted the words. 'You sent her. You knew exactly what you were doing.'

'Tony . . .'

'That's not my name. I'm Anthony. Nobody ever calls me Tony. And you can forget the whole thing. It was a bad idea and it nearly got me killed. I should never have listened to you in the first place. I'm not going to do it.'

I stormed out of the room. I didn't bother with the lift. I took the stairs twelve floors back down to the ground floor and out into the fresh air. I didn't stop walking until I was halfway across Blackfriars Bridge.

I took out my mobile phone.

I was going to ring my agent. I was going to tell her that the deal was off. I still had two books to write for Orion. There was the new series of *Foyle's War*. I had plenty enough to be getting on with.

And yet . . .

If I walked away, Hawthorne would just go to another writer and what would be the result of that? I'd end up as a minor character, nothing more than a sidekick in someone else's book, which would actually be considerably worse than being a real character in one of my own. They would be able to do anything they liked. They could make me look like a complete idiot if they wanted.

On the other hand, if I wrote the book, I would have control. Hawthorne had admitted that he had come to me and only me. It was *my* story. Hilda had done the deal and, now that I thought about it, I'd already done half the work.

I was still holding my phone.

My thumb was hovering over the speed dial.

By the time I reached the other side of the river, I knew exactly what I was going to do.

Acknowledgements

A great many people helped me with this book.

I am very grateful to Edward Kemp, the Director of RADA, for inviting me into the academy to watch him rehearse. Lucy Skilbeck, the Director of Actor Training, provided me with further background material and also introduced me to Zoe Waites, who gave me a brilliant account of her time there – she was roughly contemporary with Damian Cowper. Charlie Archer, a recent graduate, also described his auditions and gave me further insights and the theatre director Lindsay Posner provided me with notes from his still-celebrated production of *Hamlet*.

In order to understand Robert Cornwallis, I spent time with Andrew Leverton, whose own funeral service is nothing like the one described in these pages. Colin Sutton is a former detective who, like Hawthorne, has worked with many television companies. I have to say that he was far more helpful with background detail than Hawthorne himself. My brother, Philip Horowitz, gave me a legal briefing on Diana Cowper's traffic accident and the case that followed.

I have a brilliant new editor in Selina Walker at Penguin

Random House and both Hawthorne and I were delighted that she accepted the book. We are also grateful to our very diligent copy-editor, Caroline Pretty, and to Jonathan Lloyd at Curtis Brown, who gave us invaluable advice when Hilda Starke was unavailable.

As always I must thank my wife, Jill Green, and my two sons, Nick and Cass, who not only read the book and helped me with it in its early stages but didn't object too much when they found themselves drawn into it.

About the Author

ANTHONY HOROWITZ is the author of *New York Times* best-sellers *Magpie Murders* and *Moriarty*, and the internationally bestselling *House of Silk*, as well as the *New York Times* best-selling Alex Rider series for young adults. As a television screenwriter he created *Midsomer Murders* and the BAFTA—winning *Foyle's War* on PBS. He lives in London.